To: Ma

Thanks for the long hours
and your wonderful suppas,
I love you!
Sincerely,
Shirley

The Lost Jewels of Grayhorse

The Lost Jewels of Grayhorse

A Legacy Lost and Found

Shirley M. Sebree, Ed.D. (Kele)

VANTAGE PRESS
New York

Although many of the names, characters, and places in this book are based on actual historical people and locales, this is a work of fiction. Any similarity between the names and characters in this book and any real persons, living or dead, is purely coincidental.

Frontispiece illustration by Renee Wayton. Used with permission.

Published by Vantage Press, Inc.
419 Park Ave. South, New York, NY 10016

Manufactured in the United States of America
ISBN: 0-533-15095-7

Library of Congress Catalog Card No.: 2004098679

0 9 8 7 6 5 4 3 2 1

This book is dedicated to
My loving and supportive husband, James;
My precious nephews, Anthony "Tony" and John;
My dear brother, Robert Lewis;
The precious jewels, lost AND now found;
And to the memory of
My precious great-grandparents, Grayhorse and Mother Ellen

Contents

Preface

The storyline in *The Lost Jewels of Grayhorse: A Legacy Lost and Found* is based on the actual history of the Grayhorse family. The Grayhorse family resided for more than six generations in Caldwell, Lyon and Trigg Counties in the river basin of Western Kentucky. The story is filled with adventure and romance spiced with traditional struggles and practices that the family endured. It evolves around conflicts and successes of four generations that survived social and political challenges of the time. The story is embellished with fictional events to enhance and enrich its movement through the lineage of Grayhorse, Cherokee and patriarch great-grandfather of what evolved to be the "Gray" family.

Native American history reflected in the story is limited to the history and social practices of the Cherokee Indians. It is further limited to the family practices and culture of the Cherokee, Grayhorse as passed through his family and assimilated with the African American and Caucasian cultures of his wife, Ellen. The family legacy passes through the Grayhorse lineage to his favorite son, Roaring Bull (Stonewall), to Roaring Bull's son, Rising Sun (Sully), to Rising Sun's son, Thundering Eagle (Robert Lewis). The family history is limited to the descendants and events that come through the lineage of Grayhorse's grandson, Rising Sun (Sully).

The story is told by Rising Sun's daughter, Cheyenne (Shirley). She unveils the family saga through its history, traditions, romance, and family conflicts as revealed to her by her family elders, her patriarch uncle, Clyde and her matrix aunt, Helen. A genealogical history, compiled in three volumes by her cousin, Harvey Gray, Jr. added much insight to the research. Much data were also collected from other family documents and records (birth and marriage certificates, records of family gatherings, and birth lineage) preserved in the Gray family. It is from our great-grandfather, Grayhorse, that the family name "Gray" evolved. Grayhorse then is the family hero around whom the story is focused.

In *The Lost Jewels of Grayhorse,* the story is formulated around the number "four." The number "four" is a number of power in the Grayhorse culture. Important decisions, events, and situations evolve from this number. The power of the Four Winds that emanate from the four compass points dictates the movements, successes and failures of the life cycle for an individual or for the happenings in a family. These Four Winds come from the East, West, North and South. The East Wind brings success and good times. The West Wind brings turbulent times. The North Wind brings cold desolate times. The South Wind brings peace and goodwill. This concept is so important to the Native American culture that different tribes assign colors of distinction to these directions. For the Cherokee, the East color is red, the West it is blue (sometimes purple), the North is black and the South is white.

The format of the book is divided into four major sections. In each section, the action takes place and evolves around the direction of its particular wind. The climax and the resolution of the story line, the successes and failures of the events are dictated by the directions of these important winds. The timeline is restricted to four generations represented by four seasons. The family legacy is revealed in four visions by the Spirit of the White Buffalo. The legacy must pass through the male gender to the fourth son of each generation. If there is no fourth son in a particular generation, then it must pass to the fourth child.

The purpose of this adventure is to trace the lineage of the seedling jewels of Rising Sun's son, Thundering Eagle to the great-grandfather, Grayhorse. It is also to perpetuate the lineage of Grayhorse and to help rebuild and repopulate the Cherokee nation. Most important, is to have this document serve as a connector that can be utilized to reconnect and bond the lost family seedling jewels. These jewels have been isolated and unidentified. Consequently, they have also been eliminated or left out of the family lineage and family history. It is my hope that this labor of love will identify and complete the lineage cycle of Grayhorse.

The wisdom of Grayhorse is important. It has been respected by the family for generations. Even after his death, his spirit continues to appear in dreams and vision to the sons who have been selected and entrusted as keepers of the family legacy. When the legacy is broken, the jewels are lost and the family disconnected, the spirit of Grayhorse does not rest. His spirit cannot be at peace until the legacy is rebuilt, the jewels found, and the family reunited. At the beginning of each section of the book, the wisdom of Grayhorse is revealed through the gift of Cheyenne.

The Lost Jewels of Grayhorse reveals the strength of the "Gray" family. It underlines the family's struggles to survive. It is a strength that has been protected through the bonding of the lost jewels as they watched over each other through tests of survival and family rejections. In spite of these omissions and brokenness to the Gray family, a flickering fire spirit and a passion of love has prevailed. This spirit leads them back to the family and helps them find ways to remain together and survive as a unit united, connected, and unbroken.

The climax of the story resolves with a prevailing passion and a pure joy that is shared by the twelve seedling jewels of Thundering Eagle and their matrix and only paternal aunt, Cheyenne. When the seedlings are found, they take their rightful places in the Gray family. The legacy is finally placed in the rightful protective custody of the fourth son of Thundering Eagle, named Rising Eagle. His responsibility is to restore and maintain the legacy. Unlike his great-grandfather, Stonewall, he earns and maintains the respect of his sibling jewels and their offspring.

The second jewel, of the third season, Silver Cloud, is challenged to continue to demonstrate, nurture and perpetuate the strength, dignity and pride of the Grayhorse women. She is to epitomize not only the spirit of Grayhorse but also the beauty, grace, dignity, charm, and aggressiveness of their great-great-grandmother, Ellen, and their matrix aunt, Cheyenne. The first son, Leaping Deer, of the first season, is entrusted with the spirit character of wisdom and fidelity. He is to become a mentor of wisdom and knowledge for the future offspring. He must plant seeds to enlighten their minds with wisdom and knowledge. He is to enlighten them on the protection of their bodies and souls with values of fidelity that are lasting and pure. The life walk of this first son and the life walk of the fourth son of the second season are to become models for the Gray youth to follow. Beginning with Sully (Rising Sun), the names of the seedling jewels have been changed to character names in the story that represent the culture of Grayhorse. It is my hope that this change will help to soften any hurt or bitterness caused by the lost legacy. It also is my hope that it will assist in mending any brokenness among the connectors of the family lineage.

It is my wish that every jewel will be able to identify himself as presented through these characterizations. It is my wish that this love journey will serve as a historical record to help keep the Gray family alive.

Acknowledgments

THANKS . . .

To my dear husband, James, for supporting my zeal to relive the trauma of my past; for sharing the strength that I needed to search for the data of which much was hidden in the archives of time; for providing the emotional and mental space that kept me focused to the task as well as the quiet time that provided an enhancement for the work to be completed; for the financial support that the project demanded; for scheduling rest times, both near and far, whenever I needed a break; and for loving me unconditionally. I love you, James! It is your unwavering love and support that has kept our life together unbroken.

To my precious nephews, Tony and John, and my dear niece, Linda, for all of the joy that you bring into my life. For continuously encouraging me to tell our story. For providing data to support my research. To Tony, thanks for being a perfect courier, transporting precious data to and from my pre-editorial reader.

To my patriarch uncle, Clyde, and my matrix aunt, Helen, for passing on to me the fire spirit of Grayhorse and the dignity and poise of Mother Ellen. Thanks Grayhorse and Mother Ellen for the inspiration to seek and walk proud. To my dear aunt Clara Mae (age 92), for remembering connectors for bonding and tiny details.

To the beautiful twelve seedling jewels represented in the story by the twelve turquoise gems. Thanks for allowing me to love you so much and thanks for loving me back.

To my brother, Robert Lewis, I love you dearly. With a pure spirit, I know that you walk with me as I retell our story, supporting me as you did when we were children.

To the pre-editorial readers, thanks for the long hours. To my niece, Trinesia Gray; my husband, James Sebree; my lasting friend Helen Easterly; and my spiritual colleagues, Barrington Nauts, and his wife Marcia.

Thanks to Renee Wayton for sketching my perspective of Grayhorse and to my dear friend Mattie Bacon for the tedious hours of typing.

Finally, to the driving spirit of my mother, Myrtle Rice, that continues to drive and point me toward life goals and new beginnings. Thanks Mom for always being present in my spirit.

Introduction

Grayhorse is the Native American ancestor of the Gray family. During his stay at Big Spring Bottom in Quarry Town, he dropped the word "horse" from his name to protect his identity. He was then known as J. Gray. The legacy of Grayhorse was revealed through a vision by the Spirit of the White Buffalo. The first call of the legacy was to love, respect, and build a relationship with the Great Spirit. The second call was to perpetuate the lineage of Grayhorse and the Cherokee nation through the seedling descendants of Rising Sun (Sully). These descendants were the offspring (children and grandchildren) of Rising Sun through the lineage of his son Thundering Eagle (Robert Lewis). Thundering Eagle's offspring represent the lost jewels of the lineage.

The keeper of the legacy was to be entrusted via the male gender to the fourth son. The third call of the legacy was to nurture the character spirits that represented the family values and moral philosophy for the good life. The keeper of the legacy was committed to nurture, protect, and rebuild broken connectors and to strengthen relationships in the Grayhorse lineage. When Grayhorse passed the entrustment of the legacy and the precious jewels that he had collected to Roaring Bull (Stonewall), the sixth and favorite son, the turbulence for a lost legacy began. This misgiving of passing the legacy to an undeserving son was honored by Roaring Bull who passed it to his sixth son, Rising Sun (Sully). Sully passed it to his first son, Thundering Eagle (Robert Lewis). Sully rejected the responsibility of entrustment of the legacy and divided the responsibility among his three children. The legacy as well as the family unit became broken and disarrayed.

The brokenness of the legacy caused the children of Rising Sun and the seedlings of Thundering Eagle to become disconnected from the family unit and displaced in the family lineage. Sully passed the role of planting the seedlings to Thundering Eagle, the first son. Cheyenne, the fourth child, is to protect and nurture the seedling jewels and to maintain the legacy. This responsibility was given to Cheyenne, the fourth child, because

Rising Sun did not have a fourth son. Broken Arrow (James "Rook"), the second son, was to watch over the family relationships and connectors. Cheyenne misunderstood her role to the legacy. She believed that because she was female, it was her responsibility to spread the seedlings and to perpetuate the linage. She believed that they were to be conceived and born from her womb. The Spirit of the White Buffalo clearly revealed that this responsibility must pass through the male gender.

When Cheyenne's seedling was planted, she became very ill. The fetus became ill inside her and was born dead. Cheyenne wept in pain for many seasons. She became depressed, despondent and turned away from her family. She lost her yearning for the seedlings and the family legacy. The legacy was broken and lost. This brokenness led to a separation between Cheyenne and her brothers. The love relationship that Cheyenne and Thundering Eagle shared as children was lost by this separation. Cheyenne and Broken Arrow were not raised together as children; their sibling relationship did not blossom until adulthood. Broken Arrow loved Cheyenne and searched for her. Even during his illness, he drew Cheyenne near him and sought to build a strong sibling relationship and the family legacy. Cheyenne and Rising Sun grew up together as children but had now been separated for more than fifty years. Cheyenne came to realize that she might never see her brother again, nor would she ever be able to resume a relationship that she had cherished and loved dearly.

During those lost years, Thundering Eagle had been sowing seedlings. The first seed was planted in Quarry Town. Leaping Deer, his first son, was born in Quarry Town and was very dear to his aunt Cheyenne. He was taken away from the Gray family as an infant to be raised by another family. Meanwhile, Thundering Eagle planted eleven additional seedlings in Ohio. These twelve offspring represent the twelve seedling jewels that had been protected by the vision and legacy of Grayhorse for four generations. Rising Sun became very ill in Kentucky. He was found by his offspring and brought to Ohio by his children. A place where Cheyenne had lived for over thirty years not knowing that the seedlings had been planted and grew up around her.

Cheyenne had nurtured loneliness and a longing for family that had not been filled. When her brother, Broken Arrow died, the spirit of Grayhorse visited Cheyenne and the daughter of Broken Arrow, Whispering Wind (Juanita). The message was that her brother Rising Sun was alive and was now very near her. Most important, the message was that the twelve seedlings had been planted and the legacy and the family could be rebuilt and saved. The twelve seedling jewels were identified and it was discovered that seven of the jewels lived either in Water City, Ohio or very near by. The message was clear that the character spirits and the precious jewels, planted by Thundering Eagle, were waiting to be received into the family lineage.

A family meeting was arranged by Whispering Wind, Moon Rae, (Thundering Eagle's first daughter), and Cheyenne to retrieve and unite the jewels with their matrix aunt, Cheyenne. It was also a glorious opportunity for Cheyenne to reunite with her brother Rising Sun, whom she had not seen for more than fifty years. This meeting evolved into a restructuring of the family. Cheyenne was in awe. It overwhelmed her with joy to be reunited with her family and to identify these precious jewels. It was a rebirth of memories and sibling love to be reunited with her brother.

Cheyenne now understands her role for the legacy and the vision of Grayhorse. She has been called to nurture, love and protect the precious jewels. She welcomes this responsibility with much passion and love. She has also been called to maintain and protect the family legacy with the fire spirit of Grayhorse, to perpetuate the wisdom and spirit of Grayhorse, and to mirror the pride, dignity and elegance of Mother Ellen. She feels responsible to function as a family anchor for the twelve jewels. She wishes to assist with the nurturing and care of Thundering Eagle who now resides in a nursing facility in Water City.

The legacy has been retrieved, the spirit of Grayhorse has been reborn and entrusted to the precious jewel of Thundering Eagle ((his fourth son, Rising Eagle), where it rightfully belongs. The spirit of Grayhorse is now free to be at rest. It will no longer have to roam. It will forever be protected and be at peace by the jewels of Thundering Eagle and Cheyenne, the descending lineage of Rising Sun (Sully). The offspring of the twelve precious seedling jewels now number more than 45.

Characters

Grayhorse—Cherokee Ancestor, Great-Grandfather of the Gray Family

Ellen—Daughter of a Runaway Slave, Great-Grandmother of the Gray
    Family

Stonewall Jackson Gray—Grandfather of Gray Family, Father of Sully
(Roaring Bull)Third son of Grayhorse and Ellen

Ida—Wife of Stonewall, Mother of Sully, Grandmother of the Gray
    Family
Sully (Rising Sun)—Sixth son of Stonewall and Ida, Father of Robert
    Lewis, Shirley, and James
Sully's Offspring—Robert Lewis (Thundering Eagle), Shirley Mae
    (Cheyenne)
    James "Rook" (Broken Arrow)
    Roseline and Douglas McArthur (Deceased as infants)
Whispering Wind (Juanita)—Daughter of James (Broken Arrow)

Twelve Jewels of Thundering Eagle

First Season:Leaping Deer—John (First Son)
Second Season:Moon Rae—(Robin) (First Daughter)
        Rising Star—Manuel
        Painted Pony—Ulysses
        Rising Eagle—Anthony "Tony" (Fourth Son)
        Echo Calls—Tammy
Third Season—Cherokee Star—Caroline
        Silver Cloud—Linda
        Running Bear—Robert
        Clear Water—Andre
        Prancing Bear—Marquette
Fourth Season:Bright Shadow—Tycie

Spirit Seedlings of Character

Passion and Love
    Labor and Toil

Wisdom and Fidelity
    Beauty and Aesthetics

        Searching (Wandering and Creative Spirit)
        Solitude (Quiet Spirit)

Aggressiveness (Fire Spirit)
Persistence
Reverence to God (Great Spirit)
Elegance
Dignity
Proclamation
A saga that was
Echoes
A story that is
Revealing the Past
Confounding the Present
Reclaiming the Future

The Legacy

The family legacy of Grayhorse was revealed to him in a vision on a foggy morning, following a mysterious sunset, in a damp, dark painted cave at Big Spring Bottom located on the northeast side of Cedar Bluff Quarry in Quarry Town. The vision was revealed following twelve days of fasting by Grayhorse in search of new beginnings. A few weeks earlier, he had been disbanded from an original band of Cherokee who were camping along the river bank of the Cumberland River in Kuttawa, Kentucky. Grayhorse and his partner pony, Misty, had traveled far to reach this place of solitude. He had been awakened from a deep sleep by a voice calling his name. When he opened his eyes he saw standing before him an image of a white buffalo. The spirit spoke to Grayhorse softly and announced the following message:

"Grayhorse, you and your seedlings must love, respect and give reverence to the Great Spirit. You can only live in peace with the rest of the universe when you are guided by the Great Spirit. The last seeds that were spread by you have been devoured. You must plant new seedlings over a period of four seasons. Your mission is to rebuild the broken and lost links that connect the character spirits to the original band of Grayhorse. Like seedlings of the earth, this must be done by spreading connectors that will retrieve the true seedling spirits of character for you and your offspring. Through these seedlings, your relationship with the Great Spirit can be renewed. Each seedling must nurture a character spirit to be reborn."

"The legacy must be practiced and relived until it is no longer just an artifact of beauty but an untold natural beauty relived in each of their spirits. The legacy is to pass through four generations (seasons) through the male gender. It must follow the birth lineage of the fourth son of each generation until it resolves to the number sixteen. You are to seal this commitment by fasting sixteen days. Follow four periods of fasting. Fast for four days beginning the first day after the first full moon of the following four periods of light and four periods of darkness. You must keep the spirits of character alive in each seedling. The seedling(s) must seek to be connected to each other in the full moon of the following four periods of light and four periods of darkness. The Grayhorse band will then be rebonded and the family will be strong. These seedlings will be known as the seedling jewels of Grayhorse."

"This rebuilding can never take place as long as the spirit of Grayhorse does not rest. It cannot be rebuilt as long as there is a missing link or a brokenness among the seedlings."

"If there is a disconnection and the legacy is lost, it must be retrieved through the female gender of the third wind as long as she is the fourth child. It must then be passed to the fourth seedling of the fourth wind. The heart of the true legacy is to mend the brokenness in the family unit and replenish the earth with the seedlings of Grayhorse."

"In each season there is to be a keeper of the legacy. By numerical birth order, the keepers are to be of the male gender, the fourth son. The seedling carriers and the rebirth of the legacy is to be retrieved and reborn through the lineage of Sully's son, Thundering Eagle. The female retriever of the third wind is Sully's daughter, Cheyenne. The connecting messenger will appear as Whispering Wind, the daughter of Broken Arrow."

Grayhorse listened and buried this message deep inside his heart and soul. He chanted the following words of wisdom. The chanting takes hold of a steady drum beat in the distance. It is then picked up by the rushing water beating against the pebbles in a nearby stream. At the shallow end of the stream near the mouth of the Big Spring cave, Grayhorse chants the following:

"Things that are good and have quality take time.
It takes many seasons to form a diamond, a ruby, an emerald, a pearl.
A spinner spins thread by thread; a potter spins turn by turn.
A painter paints strokes by stroke; a butterfly slowly changes
from a caterpillar to a butterfly.
Be patient as you wait, take time and remember.
A rose never yields to force to bloom, it always takes time.
So will the jewels of Grayhorse need time to complete their cycle of life.
The life cycle nor the spirit cycle cannot be forced, they need time.
They need time, patience, wisdom, passion and love.
They will master the will to survive and conquer.
When the spirit of Grayhorse completes its cycle,
the legacy will be reborn."

The Lost Jewels of Grayhorse

PART I

East Wind
The Spirit of Grayhorse

(Grayhorse, a descendent of the Cherokee Nation, the grandfather of Rising Sun, the great-grandfather of Thundering Eagle, Broken Arrow, and Cheyenne.)

"The Essence of Time . . ."
Gift of Cheyenne

Time is like a nugget of gold;
    Issued to man in proportions.
        Treasure its wealth; Hold on to its worth,
            Use it wisely, Do not waste, Do not haste.
Take your time on life's journey;
    Never rush it away.
        Be always conscious of time left over;
            And make good use of it each day.
Promptness is time's inside master;
    It regulates man's inner self and stabilizes his mind.
        Tardiness is the generator of one's broken word;
            Interrupting the rhythm of mind and soul.
It tempers man's character and deflates his being;
                So
Practice promptness in your spirit;
    Be timely in your movement;
        Be dependable when you give your word.
        Be wise and respectful with the time that you have.

When it is lost, it cannot be found, When it is spent it cannot be
    replaced.
Be careful with time that belongs to others, you cannot give back that
    which you take.
Value the time in your life, Hear these words forever retold.
Time is an Essence, Time is a nugget of Gold.
                —The Wisdom of Grayhorse

1

The Sacred Journey

He had waited until morning so that the sun could burn away the fog, provide light and warm the air for the long ride. The damp misty rain continued as they rode into town. The weather grew worse as the journey grew longer. The journey began with scattered clouds and a brilliant sunrise. Both he and Misty had been on the trail before. Misty, his gray-spotted horse and trusted companion had been with him since she was a pony. Now she was growing old and Grayhorse took every precaution to take good care of her. Grayhorse would never dream of leaving her behind.

As they moved soft-footed along the foothills of the Blue Ridge Mountains, Grayhorse was careful to stay out of sight so that they would not be noticed. The last time Grayhorse visited Quarry Town in Caldwell County, Kentucky, he had been escorted out of town by the town leaders and warned not to return. He was led to the mouth of the Cumberland River in Eddyville, Kentucky and pointed toward a trail that led due south. Grayhorse had found companionship in Quarry Town and he had returned each year during crop season to be near her. The trail was long and winding and this time there were plenty of pot holes and puddles that had not been filled for quite some time, maybe not since the last trading. Grayhorse was certain that this was the trail that the slave traders had used and that it would lead him straight in to Quarry Town. If he stayed close to the shoreline of the Tennessee River, it would connect with the Cumberland a few miles up ahead and lead to Eddyville, which was only twelve miles west of Quarry Town. This would be the final trip for Misty if he could only get Ellen to leave with him.

As they reached the summit around Jellico, a chill blew in with the wind and was followed by a thick fog that created a darkness that appeared to be darker than midnight. When they reached the area around Cape Girado, the three rivers Cumberland, Tennessee and Ohio came to a point

5

but refused to mix. This was a familiar landmark for travelers, providing needed orientation of locality.

Grayhorse and his family had used it each time that they had made this journey. Here they would relinquish the Tennessee shoreline and follow the shoreline of the muddy Cumberland that would lead them straight into Kentucky. This trail would take them to Paducah, across Lyon County into Grand River Valley, Gilbertsville, Eddyville, Kuttawa, and finally into Quarry Town (known today as Princeton, Kentucky) in Caldwell County.

Big Spring Bottom was located on the east side of Quarry Town. It could be reached if they followed the Varment Trace Road to Main Street. Big Spring was nestled somewhat to the right of Gathering Place at Court House Square. Grayhorse wanted to avoid the Square and come in the back way. After a rest break at the river bend, Grayhorse shared a piece of beef jerky with Misty. Once again, they hit the trail, hoping to reach Quarry Town by dusk.

As they approached the city, the sun was just beginning to make its descent behind the western hills when it exploded into a burst of colors made up of orange, yellow and red with a reflection of purple from the storm clouds in the distance. His favorite dwelling place at Big Spring Bottom was well in view. No one called it Princeton any more, not since the black residents had taken over the entire area of Big Spring Bottom and the black men were driving trucks and bursting stone at Cedar Bluff Quarry. The quarry was a lifeline for the entire town. People depended on the quarry for work and livelihood. It was not Princeton to them anymore; everyone knew that it had to be called Quarry Town.

This was Grayhorse's final journey to Quarry Town alone. This would be different. He had not seen Ellen since she was a young maiden, age fourteen. She was now eighteen years old and this time he came to take her away; he was not going to take "no" for an answer. It mattered not that he was a descendant of the Cherokee Nation and that Ellen was the mulatto daughter of Venus, a runaway slave girl who had been impregnated by Master Jones. It didn't matter that Grayhorse had been previously warned that he was not to mingle with the blacks, not to bother Ellen and not to return to Quarry Town.

The rhythm of his heart beat stronger and faster. He loved Ellen and he had to make her understand.

Grayhorse was born in 1837. He had met Ellen when he was four years old. It was his first journey and his mother had joined with his father heading to Oklahoma along the Trail of Tears. The family traveled through Caldwell County following the trail which led across Master Jones' farm, sleeping secretly in Master Jones' barn. Little Ellen and the maid slipped food to him and his family and gave them extra food for travel. He had played with Ellen during those four days and she stayed in his childhood memory as a best friend. Ten years had passed before he saw Ellen again. Grayhorse now age sixteen had returned on a second journey with a group of Cherokee en route to the Cherokee reservation in Eastern Tennessee. They would meet at the bend of the river and talk for long periods of time. Finally one day, he touched Ellen's chin and she allowed him to hold her hand. Before he went away, she gave him his first kiss with passion without saying the words goodbye, but silently hoping that one day, Grayhorse would return. Although he had asked Ellen to wait for him and be his wife, she refused to give him an answer. Grayhorse was then forced to leave the town because of an uprising which he was believed to have organized among the crop workers. This time, Ellen would say "yes" and he would take her away.

As he reached the outer edge of Quarry Town, Grayhorse paused to read the faded marker on Varment Trace Road just beyond the main street of town. This marker indicated the trail that the Cherokee Nation travelers had followed on the Trail of Tears. The trail wound along Varment Trace Road, pass the "Gathering Place" at Court House Square, and across Master Jones' farm land. As Grayhorse viewed the surroundings, the trail pointed to the place where his family had camped and slept in Master Jones' barn for two nights on his first journey. The land was fertile and full of wild game. Grayhorse's plan was to farm and hunt in the area until Ellen settled her pondering over his proposal and gave her approval to be his wife.

The reflection of the sun against the western sky reminded Grayhorse of his childhood and youth. He remembered innocent childhood days spent in North Carolina, and days of his youth when he grew up on the reservation in Eastern Tennessee and Oklahoma. He thought of the dangers and struggles for survival that his family went through while on the Trail of Tears. Now this final foot journey from Eastern Tennessee to Big Spring Bottom in Kentucky would be the beginning of a different adventure in his life. This time, it would include Ellen and life would be different.

The trail that he and Misty had followed to reach Big Spring had taken them across uncharted land. Misty was coming down with a cold and was growing tired and a bit weary from traveling the long distance and the weight of the heavy load that he was carrying. Four knapsacks were loaded and strapped along Misty's side. Some items were strapped near the front of her body so that they would be easily located when needed. Items such as Grayhorse's dream maker, hand carved reed wood flute, feathered eagle wing wands, and water drum were needed often at dusk and early dawn each day. These were his tools to communicate with the Great Spirit. The eagle wands and wooden mask used for the eagle dance were well protected. Misty moved the cargo as if she knew that these items were not to be damaged. She always walked carefully over rough trails so that they would not slip and become damaged. They were each special to Grayhorse and Misty.

Silent Stones

Grayhorse wore a necklace of divination stones, strung on a string of animal sinew, around his neck. He had used this necklace along with chants and prayers to locate lost objects, and this evening he had planned to use it to try to locate Ellen. Grayhorse stretched out under a wide-branched huckleberry tree and glanced again at his precious necklace. He wanted to give the stones to Ellen and thought if he strung them she might wear them as a special totem to remember their sacred bonding and the precious seedling offspring of Ellen and Grayhorse. He counted and polished each precious stone with his fingers and the tail of his shirt. There were three brilliant silver nuggets which he had found in a North Carolina creek bed; and twelve beautiful lovely turquoises that he had found on the reservation in Oklahoma—a total of fifteen precious stones. Grayhorse always carried these precious jewels in a deer skin pouch, kept close to his heart in a pocket inside his deer skin vest. He needed to watch them closely and keep them protected. They represented the offspring of his future. These offspring would be his contribution to help perpetuate the growth of the Cherokee nation. These twelve nuggets of turquoise and three silver, a total of fifteen precious seedling jewels, would also carry forward the character spirits of the family legacy. These character spirits would have to be protected by the spirit of Grayhorse.

Soon after sunrise, Grayhorse and his trusted companion, Misty were going to Master Jones' farm to look for work. If Master Jones refused to give him work, he would have to live off the land as he had done before, at least until Ellen made up her mind to join him. First, he would need to rise

8

well before the sun and repeat his vows to the Great Spirit. Second, he needed to stake out a permanent dwelling place for himself and Misty.

Dwelling Place

When the sun arose, Grayhorse and Misty were well on their way to Master Jones' farm. Today would be a different day. Not only was he going to stake a dwelling place but he was also going to find Ellen. He and Misty needed to settle on the dwelling place before nightfall. He needed a place to cook, sleep, and pay his vows and respect to the Great Spirit. For most of his life, Grayhorse began each new day with this routine.

Poetic images were kept sacred for the Grayhorse family. These images were depicted through song pictures and the rhythms of visions and dreams through musical chants and dance. Grayhorse drew pictures that reminded him of ideas, visions, and dreams that gave tribal connections to the earth. Yesterday, he selected a birch tree near the bend of the creek. He wanted to carve petroglyphs of family history and experiences which would give meaning to his visions and dreams. The tree that he selected was steady and tall with soft inner bark, just right for carving. The tree was located only a few steps from the underground entrance to a nearby cave. He would have to carry water for him and for Misty but they both needed the exercise. As the leaves of the birch tree waved in the whistling wind, Grayhorse thought that the tree would make a wonderful addition to the family as a family marker.

Grayhorse stood quietly and whispered to Misty, "How wonderful this spot will be when me and Ellen are married. I will carve song pictures for the birth of each child. It will be like a totem tree. This birch tree will become a keeper and protector of the Grayhorse family history. Birth scrolls of petroglyphs, pictographs, pictomyths, family happenings, and sacred songs that only the members of the Grayhorse family will understand. It will be taught and protected by the Grayhorse family birch tree." One thing remained certain: for the Grayhorse culture, a young man needed to learn his father's songs. Grayhorse had kept them all in his heart and rehearsed them while doing his morning and evening vows.

As Grayhorse looked up high near the top of the stately birch tree an image of the totem spirit of Whispering Wind appeared in its branches. She whistled a familiar tune that Grayhorse remembered from his youth. She caught the spirit of the wind as it gently blew and the leaves fluttered an applause of approval. The silver lining on the flip side of each leaf glistened in the morning dew while the sun rays set off a colorful mist of gray. It created a reflection of worth for the jewel seedlings of Grayhorse.

Every Native American boy carved his own reed wood flute and created his own personal song as a rite of passage into manhood. Grayhorse had rehearsed his song from youth. He wanted to play it for Ellen. It would become their personal mating song. Maybe the Great Spirit would bless this mating song for the bonding of their relationship? Or maybe he would grant the musical gift of power to the fourth son. If not, then maybe the first son, or the sixth son, but with the gift of Ellen, why not to a dozen sons?

Grayhorse walked down to the Big Spring when he realized that his thoughts of Ellen had once again caused his mind to wander. He climbed upon Misty and they rode down to the creek bed. He unloaded his water drum, made from a keg of sassafras wood with a groundhog skin for the drum head, and began to play a soft and steady but driving syncopated rhythm. He needed the drum to arouse the attention of the Great Spirit. He needed the water stream to catch the sound vibrating from the drum across the earth, and carry it along the water current until it reached the Great Spirit. Grayhorse was consistent in his chanting. One thing he had learned from Misty was that he could chant his songs and rhythms in a quiet soft tone and the spirit gods would hear him. Like Misty, the gods seemed to respond most and best to soft, small emotions.

Today, his prayers were for Ellen and the dwelling place. He spoke directly, asking the gods to help him find, and anchor him in his new dwelling place. The cave at Big Spring and Cedar Bluff was large, dark and long. Like Mammoth Cave, there were passageways winding and steep. There were three main entrances to the underground. The entrance at Big Spring was wide enough and tall enough for Misty to come inside. So was the North Quarry entrance. The entrance and passage way at Cedar Bluff wound their way across the center of Quarry Town and opened again above ground at the North point of the city. A large pond rested just beyond the ascending hills that nestled the entrance at North Point.

As Grayhorse walked along the river path to his favorite spot, he began to offer his daily chants and morning prayers to the Great Spirit. He rehearsed his mating tune on the flute. The Kentucky cardinals and young blue jays picked up the tune and cheerfully imprinted a descant that carried across the river, over the tree tops, and rested on the ebb of a soft breeze until—wishfully—it reached Ellen. Time had no beginning and no end. Before Grayhorse realized it, the entire morning had floated away on the air

10

of a song. Two days passed and there was still no sight or sign of Ellen. Surely, she had heard their song today. Surely, in her heart she knew that he had returned. Surely the Great Spirit would send him to her soon. . . .

Grayhorse thought of three lasting truths in the Grayhorse legacy that he must share with Ellen. Ellen also had beliefs and truths in her heart that she would need to share with him. He knew and respected that Ellen was strong-willed and followed her own mind. He wondered if she would understand and accept these truths that had been passed on to him by his father. These were truths to be followed by a strong son for a good life. First, the actions of an individual are based on one's own decisions but the actions of a family are based on the consensus of the family elders. Second, sharing is essential. The well-being of each family member must be taken into account. Charity and generosity are permanent principles that all members of a family must abide by. The third truth concerned Grayhorse more. Would Ellen accept his principle of man's relationship with nature? Man is a part of nature. He is a part of the Mother Earth, woodlands, and the natural world. These truths cannot be owned or exploited but they must be protected. The legacy also strongly states that it is a family's responsibility to reproduce, plant, and nurture seedling offspring to perpetuate the growth and continued strength of the Cherokee Nation. For this family it must begin through the lineage and bonds of Grayhorse and then be carried forward by the seedling offspring from his bowels.

As Grayhorse reached the spot where Misty was waiting, he took one more look at the cave entrance. This time he had to decide to accept the direction of the Great Spirit or move on. He observed Misty in her comfort zone, grazing under the birch tree and offered one final chant to the Great Spirit, a chant of gratitude for directing him back to Big Spring Bottom, for the birch tree, and for Ellen. The chant ended with these words in the Cherokee language. . . .

And this shall be my dwelling place both now and for future generations. Even after the spirits of Grayhorse and Ellen have ceased to wander.

With this thought, he carved his first petroglyph on the old birch tree. The message read, "The Grayhorse Clan." Below the title, he sketched the Cherokee symbol for wisdom and whispered aloud, "O Great Spirit, Grant Us Wisdom." Grayhorse then stooped to collect his flute and water drum, whistled for Misty to follow, and made his way into the cave entrance at Cedar Bluff.

11

2

The Search for Ellen

Weeks had passed since Grayhorse returned to Big Spring and there was no sight or sound of Ellen. When Ellen's mother, Venus, left the Jones farm, she carried Ellen's young sister with her. Ellen stood under the willow tree and watched her mother and sister being taken away. They had been sold to the slave traders and were being transferred to another farm owned by the Matthew family. There were only a few slave masters in the area. Venus had begged to stay at the farm because of her daughter Ellen, but her request was refused. Ellen believed that her mother had been selected to be traded so that she could not talk about sexual encounters between Master Jones and the slave women on his farm. Ellen was left behind with her father, Master Jones, because she looked like him and her younger sister looked like her mother Venus. Before Venus left, she warned Ellen to stay away from the cellar and away from close places with Master Jones. Venus told her daughter to always latch her bedroom door and be mindful of Master Jones' glances and inappropriate touches.

When Venus left, Master Jones sat on his horse at the summit of the hill and watched from afar. He was making sure that Venus and her younger daughter were off his property and that Ellen was left behind. Master Jones had also heard from a farm hand that Venus and another family were planning a breakaway once they cleared his property and had reached the trail. Master Jones promised that he would not tell anyone as long as she left Ellen behind. He even allowed Venus to fill her knapsack with food and water, enough to last at least three days. Venus stayed at the rear of the group until they reached the trail. Once they were settled on their journey, Venus broke away by way of the Varment Trace Road and never looked back. Ellen's sister was too afraid to join her and remained with the group. She wept silently, as Venus left with two other Negro families and an Indian who knew the trail. One family was to have gone to the Matthew's farm along with Venus and the other family was to have gone to the

Pendleton farm. Their breakaway created a stir all around Quarry Town. Later the news came that a group of runaway slaves fitting this description had crossed over the state line into Ohio by way of the Ohio River in Cincinnati. For many days Ellen stood under the willow tree and wept long and hard. She needed her mother.

It was only a few days after Venus left that Master Jones began to make advances and take advantage of his daughter Ellen. He became over-protective of her and made passionate glances toward her when no one was around or he thought no one was watching. He did not want Ellen to talk to anyone or be around anyone at the farm except him. More than once, he had entered her room at late evening or early morning and awakened her from her sleep to satisfy his sexual pleasure. He had touched her in the same way that he had touched her mother Venus. These times of touching and periods of intimacy with her father made Ellen very fearful and very angry. She was so worried that he would impregnate her with his child. Although the term incest was not in her vocabulary, Ellen felt dirty, just knowing that this was happening to her and that it was being done by her father.

She no longer wanted to be near her father. Neither did she want to live at the big house. More than once now, she thought of hurting him. One evening, he pushed his way into her room, shoved her into a corner, ripped her clothes, abused her inner spirit, and met his pleasure. Ellen thought of using a razor blade for protection or even putting rat poison in his coffee. It didn't matter that he was her father. Ellen became so afraid, angry, and depressed over her father's behavior and the loss of her mother and sister that she refused to eat her meals and withdrew from everyone around her. The slaves at the quarters had watched her behavior. They had seen it happen before and they were aware that Master Jones was being his old self and abusing the slave women again. But this time it was his own daughter.

One rainy morning, after breakfast, Master Jones approached Ellen in the kitchen, wrestled her on top of the kitchen table and met his pleasure while Ellen resisted him and wept silently. But this time, Ellen fought back with all the strength inside her. He slapped her ferociously across her face, cursed at her and called she and her mother and younger sister half-breed Niggers and farm whores. Master Jones was so angry and enraged, he stamped out the back door, cursing under his breath, looking straight ahead, walking toward the barn. In a misty rain, Ellen packed all that she could carry and moved most of her belongings to a little shanty house at Big Spring Bottom. It was the place where the Negro crop workers had

13

stayed before they were sent away following the last crop season. The quarters were small and seemed to retain a queer odor that was left behind from the workers stay. It wasn't much but it was much better than staying with Master Jones at the big house, so Ellen cleaned it out and called it home, especially since Venus and her sister were no longer there.

Master Jones would not likely come to the shanty house in Big Spring. The residents of that area were mostly Negroes and Indian crop workers and he would not want to be identified hanging around Big Spring, where everyone looked out for each other and Ellen felt that she would be safer there than at the big house at the Jones farm. One evening around dusk, Willie, the farm hand, came to Big Spring looking for Ellen. When he located her, he informed her that her father was seriously ill and needed her to come home. Even though Ellen was disconnected from her father, she still had affection for him in her heart and did not wish to see him die alone without family near by. Reluctantly, Ellen packed a few belongings and climbed into the wagon with Willie. As they approached the farm, Ellen could tell that something strange had happened. People with sad faces were standing around in the yard weeping quietly. As the wagon pulled into the gate, they were met by the house attendant, Martha Sue, who had run out to meet them and to tell them that Master Jones had died while Willie was away.

Following three days of house wake and mourning, the funeral was held at Eddy Creek Church. Master Jones' body was laid to rest beside his first wife, Ruth Ann, at Caldwell County Cemetery located at the end of Green Street. It was only a few days later that Ellen gathered her belongings and moved back into the big house to help run the Jones farm. Master Jones had left all of his possessions to Ellen: the farm, the big house, his financial assets and even the slave workers who had remained on the farm. Ellen thought of her mother and her younger sister and quickly released all of the slave residents, both Negro and Indian workers that Master Jones had held on to. Only two chose to remain on the farm with Ellen. Willie stayed to help out on the farm and take care of the farm animals. Martha Sue stayed to run the big house. Both of them were there when Ellen was born and they loved her dearly. Ellen also respected them as surrogate parents because they had taken care of her all of her life.

The last time that Grayhorse had seen Ellen, she was staying at the shanty house. He was on his way to Tennessee, but he stayed a few days longer to help repair the roof, steps, and secure the front door. He was hoping that she was still there were he had last seen her. He had asked around and no one in Big Spring seemed to know of her whereabouts. He walked down to the shanty house just hoping that there might be some clue of where she might have gone. He turned the corner and reached the path that led him closer to the shanty house; He looked around, but there was no trace of Ellen. The place looked as if no one had been there for quite a long time. The windows were boarded from the inside and weeds had grown tall around the porch and the doorstep. As Grayhorse walked closer, he noticed that the front door was ajar. On a table in the corner was a picture of Ellen on a horse with Master Jones standing beside her. Grayhorse picked up the picture and gazed at it for a long while. Passion for Ellen began to fill his heart and tears came to his eyes. Grayhorse placed the picture inside his vest pocket next to his heart. All the way back to the cave he thought of nothing but Ellen. *Some days the Great Spirit just provides special blessings,* he thought.

Grayhorse wondered if Ellen was back at the farm or if she had left the area. Perhaps she had met up with an accident or maybe even passed away? This was a thought that Grayhorse did not want to ponder on or even have come into his mind. He decided to go to the Jones farm at sunrise and ask Master Jones for work. Even though Master Jones had forbidden him to see Ellen, he would take courage and ask him if he knew where she was, although, he already expected Master Jones would refuse to answer his questions.

At early sunrise, Grayhorse saddled Misty and together they faced the west wind, headed up Main Street, around the courthouse square and hit the Eddyville Trail that led to the Jones farm. The trail was bumpy and narrow. As usual, Misty took her time. At the pace they were traveling, it would take nearly two hours to reach their destination. Misty was growing old and Grayhorse no longer pushed her to exert more energy and go faster as he used to do when she and he was younger. As Misty made a left turn to enter the farm gate, Willie gave them a greeting and walked out to meet them.

"I need to see Master Jones," said Grayhorse. Willie shook his head in refusal and looked down at the ground as if he did not understand.

Grayhorse repeated louder, "I need to see Master Jones."

Willie replied, "Master Jones is not here anymore. We had to put him away. He died and we buried him a few months ago."

Grayhorse responded, "I am looking for work. I need to speak to someone in charge of the farm hands."

There is no one here," answered Willie. "If you want work, you have to see Miss Ellie, but she's not hiring nobody these days. There's no more work around here."

Grayhorse asked, "Ellie—Miss Ellie? Did you say Miss Ellie?"

"Yes," said Willie. "She's in the garden at the back of the house. There's not much to do around here since Master Jones died and Miss Ellie took over. She let everybody go away. I do the heavy work. There ain't nothing for an Indian like yourself to do around here. All the Indians left at the end of the crop season Anyway, where did you come from and how do you know Miss Ellie?"

"Thanks anyway," answered Grayhorse. "I need to see Miss Ellen."

As Grayhorse made his way toward the garden, he could see Ellen's profile shadow against the ground, pointing toward the cistern, holding a water bucket. She was drawing water for the garden plants. Grayhorse paused to look at her and his heart began to beat faster. His heart fluttered as he continued to walk towards her. He smiled inside himself and thought, *What's wrong with my heart, it jut skipped a beat. It's only Ellen, after all. I came to get her and the rhythm of her heart must have also warned her that I am here and that I came to take her back.* Soft footed, he walked closer to her without her noticing his presence and softly whispered her name out loud.

"Ellen, dear Ellen, is this you?"

Ellen turned to see who called her name. She sat her bucket down and, smiling; she walked toward Grayhorse with open arms. As she dropped the bucket, it tilted and water ran out in a steady stream as she spoke.

"Grayhorse, are you back again? I have longed for you, Grayhorse! When those angry men led you to the county line and warned you not to return to Quarry Town, I was so angry and so afraid. I knew in my heart that I would never see you again."

"It's me, Ellen, it's really me. I came to get you, Ellen, I came to take you away. I want you to come with me so that we can be together from now on. Ellen, I want you to be my wife. Me, you and Misty need to be a family."

Ellen laughed, "Misty? That old horse? Why she is older than these hills."

"I want you to come with me this time, Ellen," pleaded Grayhorse. "I came to take you to be my wife."

"Now, just you listen," said Ellen strongly. "You and me have got some talking to do. I can't just up and leave this place. Anyway, we think and live like oil and water, you and me. There is just no way that the two of us are going to mix for a lifetime. I've got my ways and you've got yours.

You're wasting your time, Grayhorse. It's just not meant to be. Me and you forever? What a story!"

Walking toward Ellen, Grayhorse continued to plead with her. "Please Ellen, just listen to me. I've been searching for you for days now. I found your picture at the shanty house in Big Spring and it led me to you. When I saw Master Jones standing beside you in that picture, I knew then that you had to have moved back to the big house. When Willie met me at the gate and told me that Master Jones had passed away, I knew that there was a chance for me and you to be together. I need you, Ellen, I've got to have you by my side."

Ellen was listening to every word that Grayhorse had to say even though she had turned her back and walked a few steps away. "Come on inside, Grayhorse, I'll make you some coffee and you can sit a while."

Grayhorse picked up the bucket, refilled it with water and caught up with Ellen as she reached the back step at the big house. Entering the kitchen he thought, *Inside the big house? Well, here I am inside. Things are sure changing in Quarry Town.*

Grayhorse followed Ellen to the kitchen table. Ellen took the bucket of water and moved smoothly around the kitchen, finding her way to put on the coffee pot, a chore that Martha Sue had always done. Ellen placed a plate of shortbread on the table with plates and coffee cups and invited Grayhorse to help himself.

"I will, Ellen," he said. "But first I must listen and obey my heart."

He reached out to Ellen and locked her in his arms, embracing her in the same spirit of that first kiss that they had shared in autumn at the bend of the Cumberland River. Ellen leaned passionately forward pressing her head lightly against his chest. Both of their minds reached back to those pleasant moments together during those early meeting days at the river.

Grayhorse whispered softly to Ellen that he loved her and they were intimately lost in a lasting kiss. Grayhorse had found Ellen—and for Ellen, Grayhorse was back home where he belonged and the time had come to do what had to be done.

Misty grazed outside the window near the willow tree while she waited for Grayhorse. The sun had dropped behind the western skies and dusk had turned to darkness. Ellen lit a candle and placed it on the kitchen table. They talked together until past midnight.

'It's time," said Ellen. "It's time for us to do what we must do." She dimmed the oil lamp and blew out the candle. Misty neighed her approval and walked gently toward the barn.

3

Secret Vows

Courtship to Proposal

Morning broke and Martha Sue was just making her way down the stairs to the kitchen when she smelled fresh brewed coffee and heard the rattle of pans on the kitchen stove. "Is that you, Miss Ellie?" she called. "I must have slept late."

"It's me, Martha Sue," said Ellen. "No, you didn't sleep late, I rose early. I rose before dawn, just thinkin' about Grayhorse. Me and him talked in the kitchen until after midnight," Ellen continued.

"From the looks of this morning's guest, either he didn't go back to Big Spring or he arose mighty early."

Both Ellen and Martha Sue looked out the kitchen window to find Misty looking back at them.

"Poor Misty! Did Grayhorse leave you grazing here all night? I wish she could talk," said Ellen. "There's so much I need to know about Grayhorse that only Misty can tell."

"Grayhorse is in the barn," answered Willie, who had been standing in the kitchen doorway listening to Martha Sue and Ellen's conversation. "I checked on the horses in the barn and Grayhorse had slept in the loft, he was already awake," Willie continued. "Are you going out to the barn, Miss Ellie?"

"Yes," Miss Ellen responded. "Grayhorse and me have things to talk about."

"Are you going to leave the farm, Ellie, now that Grayhorse is back?"

"Don't worry, Willie, we'll work it out somehow, and it doesn't matter who goes and who stays, you and Martha Sue will always have a welcome place to call home right here at the Jones' big house. Did you hear me, Willie? You will stay right here with the rest of us."

"Thanks, Miss Ellie," said Willie, nodding his head in approval. "I'll get the bucket and give Misty a drink. "She must be pretty thirsty by now."

Willie left by the side entrance to the sun porch, whistling for Misty. The horse followed him to the cistern.

Just as Grayhorse turned to adjust his pillow of straw, he noticed Ellen entering the barn.

"Good morning, Ellen," said Grayhorse. "Are you going to be making yourself busy around the barn today?"

"Howdy, Grayhorse," Ellen responded. "My chores are not at the barn, I have plenty of work to do at the big house and in my garden." She handed Grayhorse some sweetbread and coffee that she had brought from the kitchen! "Why did you sleep in the barn last night Grayhorse? Why didn't you go back to Big Spring?"

"Well, Ellen," replied Grayhorse, "I've been thinkin' about what you said about not leavin' the farm, and what you had to say about me and you being like oil and water. You know, Ellen, in the Cherokee way, a man is responsible for his own behavior but the behavior of a family is left to the decision of the council elders. Well, Ellen, in this case, I'm taking responsibility for my behavior. I know that I am not welcome in Quarry Town. I'm not even supposed to be here, but my heart stops here with you, Ellen. My heart says that I have to be here with you. This decision is about family. If you and me agree that we can be family, then the council elders will accept our proposal and we can be together, Ellen! You can be my wife, and we can make a family.

"Since you will not leave with me, Ellen, then I am taking responsibility for my behavior and I am staying in Big Spring, right here in Quarry Town. I'll sleep here in the barn or at the cave in Big Spring until your heart yields to me, then we can be one. Do you understand me, Ellen? I'm not leavin' you again, I want you with me."

Ellen wept quietly as Grayhorse spoke and walked quickly out the door to the garden. As she left, she heard Grayhorse playing their song on the flute pipe. The music touched Ellen's heart and she knew that one day, before too long, her heart would yield to Grayhorse's request. This time, Grayhorse found a spot near a stately oak tree, using his water drum and his flute; he offered his vows to the Great Spirit. After surveying the beautiful branches and the perfect umbrella shape of that stately old oak tree, he whistled for Misty and made his way down the path toward Big Spring. He needed the time to think and to exercise so he walked along beside the trotting horse.

19

Ellen Searches for Grayhorse

Three days passed and Grayhorse did not see or hear from Ellen. On the fourth day, Grayhorse picked up his fishing gear and made his way along the path to his well-remembered favorite fishing hole on the banks of the Cumberland river. He remembered to carry his bow and arrow with the facetted point for fishing and plenty of flint. He stopped about four miles from Gilbertsville, on the Cumberland side, which was known as the Land Between the Lakes. Schools of fish had been running in that area and Grayhorse wanted to stake his spot early before the fish left the area or too many other Quarry Town fishermen came down for the same reason. Grayhorse anchored his pole and pointed his flint arrow just waiting for a hit. He missed a few hits in a row because his thoughts were for Ellen and not about fishing.

Just as a big strike hit his line, he looked up and saw a cloud of dust along the path that led to Big Spring. In the midst of the dust cloud, he could see two people in a wagon. As the wagon rounded the curve, it turned to follow the path down to the river bank. The wagon came straight down to his favorite spot and as it drew closer, Grayhorse could tell that the passengers were Ellen and Willie.

When Ellen spotted Grayhorse, she had Willie stop the wagon while she disembarked and walked hastily toward Grayhorse. In her stern but quiet voice, she called out, "Grayhorse, Grayhorse! Just you listen to me. Marrying you ain't so hard to do; it's living with you and watching you follow some of the strange things that you believe that bothers me."

"I've been thinkin', if you would be willing not to interfere with how I pay my vows to my God, then I can do the same for you. If you can learn to stomach my cooking trilogy of leafy greens, rice, and sweet potatoes, then I can learn to stomach your cooking trilogy of maize, beans and squash."

"What about my meat vittles, Ellen? I don't mean birds, rabbits and squirrels. I'm talkin' about raccoon, bear, opossum and maybe sometimes a little beaver. What about my outdoor cookin' pot?"

"Oh Grayhorse," said Ellen, "you can keep your cookin' pot. You can stash it away just for vittle meat somewhere outside the barn."

"Oh, Ellen, I knew that you would listen to me! Come closer, Ellen, come close to me, we can be together for a lifetime."

Willie had turned the wagon around and now Misty turned her back so that Ellen and Grayhorse could have their privacy. Ellen walked into

20

Grayhorse's open arms and together they were exactly where they belonged, yielding to the rhythm of each other's heart, longing to be one.

Willie whistled for Misty and walked toward the river bank to wait for Ellen.

"You can go home, Willie," Ellen called out. "I'm stayin'. I'll ride home with Grayhorse.

Grayhorse baited another arrow while Ellen slid down the embankment and sat on the ground next to Grayhorse. Ellen even shared the trilogy lunch that Grayhorse had brought along, which consisted of the Cherokee trilogy and a large chunk of groundhog meat. Ellen ate the vegetables but she left all of the groundhog meat for Grayhorse. As the midday sun stood over them, Ellen and Grayhorse packed the fishing gear to begin their journey back to the farm. Grayhorse had a small catch of perch that needed to be iced and put away at Big Spring. Ellen climbed onto Misty's back and Grayhorse walked along beside her to lighten the load for Misty. He carried the perch in a pail of fresh river water, thinking that they would make a tasty supper after he returned from the farm. A light gentle breeze blew across their faces as they made their way. The only thing on the minds of both Ellen and Grayhorse was that love was in the air and it was now in their hearts.

"You know, Grayhorse," said Ellen, "love really is the essence of man's soul."

Grayhorse Shares Legacy with Ellen

Grayhorse took a few minutes to clean his catch of perch, iced them down, and he and Misty made their way back to the farm for supper. Martha Sue had made a steaming pot of rice, pot roast with potatoes and carrots (the Cherokee trilogy special) for Grayhorse, a special upside-down cake with a pineapple bottom and plenty of lemonade. Grayhorse took his time and ate well. He broke the Cherokee tradition of eating only enough to curb hunger. More than once, he filled his plate over again and each time he ate all of the food on his plate. When supper was over, Ellen and Grayhorse found their way to the front porch and sat together arm in arm in the freshly painted swing. Grayhorse reached for Ellen's hand and whispered softly in her ear. Ellen cleared her mind so that she could listen intently to everything he had to say. Sometimes Grayhorse had spoken of strange beliefs and this time, Ellen had be certain that she had heard every word correctly.

Grayhorse reached inside his vest and took out the deerskin pouch with the precious jewels that he had collected.

"Ellen," he said, "I want you to look at these jewels. There is a total of fifteen gems in this pouch that I have collected from silent springs along the way on my last two journeys to Quarry Town. There are three silver and twelve turquoise nuggets. For two journeys I dreamed of giving you these beautiful gems as a keepsake for you and me. Last night in my bed, I was visited by the Spirit of the White Buffalo, a totem spirit, who came to me from the East Wind, entering my life from the East compass point. He counsels my spirit and directs my decisions for important happenings in my life that I am to follow. Whenever he visits me in a vision or a dream, evil fate does not trail my path if I follow his guidance and his directions. Last night he warned me not to release these jewels until he gave me directions. Eventually, the jewels will belong to a seedling heir from my lineage who will protect and maintain them. When time speaks well for us, the White Buffalo will reveal my family lineage, identify who we are as a family, and our purpose on this earth.

"These jewels are to represent the seedling offspring that will come through your loins and mine. These offspring are to nurture the spirit and character of Grayhorse. The legacy is to be carried through four generations that follow me. It is to be passed through the male gender by way of the fourth son of each generation. When there is no fourth son, then it is to revert to the fourth child. I have been blessed by the Great Spirit and given the responsibility to protect the jewels and maintain the legacy until my spirit seeks rest. My spirit will never be at rest if the legacy is lost or my family becomes disconnected. When we make family, the Spirit of the White Buffalo will return. We will know then how the jewels and the legacy are to be passed." As he spoke to Ellen, he clenched the jewel pouch tightly and lovingly in his hand and hers.

Grayhorse then looked deeper into his vest pocket and pulled out a beautiful round turquoise locket attached to a leather necklace. The locket was inscribed on the back with a Cherokee petroglyph that stood for love. The locket had been passed to him by his mother to be given to his bride and then passed to the first-born daughter. Grayhorse had carefully drilled a hole in the top and laced it on a string of deer sinew. "This is for you, Ellen, I've been saving it until I could meet your approval."

He placed it in Ellen's hand next to her heart and closed her hand tightly over the jewel.

"This is a symbol of our coming together and our new beginning."

Ellen wept quietly and struggled to fasten the gift around her neck.

Grayhorse reached gently to assist her, tying the sinew extra tight with a second knot so that the locket would be secure and would not slip off. Grayhorse reached over to embrace her while she rested her head on his shoulder. The swing seemed to propel itself as they each sat quietly.

"I love you, Ellen," said Grayhorse, interrupting the silence.

"Oh, Grayhorse," Ellen continued, "you are the strangest man!"

As Ellen wiped away her tears, she spoke out loud with strong assurance. "We need to talk about our life together, we need to agree on when and how we can do a ceremony. I've been thinkin' about maybe we can have two ceremonies; one in the Cherokee way, and a quiet ceremony in the African way. This way, both of our traditions and cultures can be followed." "I spoke with Rev. Fox some time ago about coming to the big house to talk about my way. You can plan your way. Remember, Grayhorse, you really are not allowed to be here in Quarry Town, so we will need to keep both ceremonies quiet. We must use a place and select a time when we will not be seen and no one will know that the wedding is taking place except those who will attend."

The moonlight illuminated the moment as Misty stuck her head around the corner of the house and neighed her approval. Grayhorse kissed Ellen goodnight and made his way down the steps to lead Misty back to Big Spring.

Ellen called out to Martha Sue and knocked on Willie's bedroom door so that she could share her good news. Martha and Willie would need to prepare for both ceremonies. The three plotters sat together at the kitchen table and talked until near dawn about this special celebration for Ellen and Grayhorse. In her elegant dignified way, Ellen told them her story never minding if she appeared to be in love. Ellen was deep in love with Grayhorse and it showed. She was a proud lady and now she would be even prouder to be the wife of Grayhorse. Mrs. Ellen Jones-Grayhorse! The sound of it was different, precious and exciting.

With These Vows

For several days, Grayhorse pondered over how he would plan the Cherokee wedding ceremony and the celebration for himself and Ellen. Everyone who knew about the Cherokee traditions lived down in Tennessee on the reservation, and Grayhorse needed to seek permission and advice from the council of elders, take the Cherokee oath, and go through the marriage ritual. He and Ellen would need to make a trip to the reservation. But first, he had to get approval from Ellen's family to marry her.

In Grayhorse's culture, marriages were arranged by the older women of the clan but the couple made the ultimate decision. If a man was attracted to a girl from a different clan, he did not speak to her directly; he would turn to a maternal aunt and ask for help. Grayhorse understood that he had already taken a step out of sequence by asking Ellen first but his heartbeat spoke louder and he followed his inner spirit by doing so. He had to pray now that this misstep would not cause an omen to befall upon their marriage. He held on to the faith in his heart and believed that Ellen's aunt would say, "Yes" to his request to approve their marriage. Then a series of discussions would have to follow the visit for approval. Neither the male nor the female's father needed to be considered for their views but they could be informed as an act of courtesy.

Grayhorse made arrangements to visit Ellen's Aunt Star Hope, her mother Venus's sister. Aunt Star Hope was a slave worker and resided on the Matthew farm near Trigg County. The meeting was arranged to take place after sundown so that Grayhorse would not be recognized. There were crop workers in the area and Grayhorse had planned to dress as one of them to disguise himself. Ellen had agreed to visit her Aunt Star Hope before Grayhorse made the journey so that she would be expecting him and would not get into trouble with Master Matthew. Aunt Star Hope arranged to meet Grayhorse at the fork road near Cadiz, the county seat of Trigg County.

Grayhorse met Aunt Star Hope at early evening, after sundown, the following day. After convincing her of his deep love for Ellen, she wished them well and gave them her blessings for marriage. Star had not seen Ellen since the day that she and her sister Venus were separated and sold to different slave masters and taken away to separate farms. Star had heard that her sister Venus had slipped across the line in Ohio. She loved Ellen dearly and she had promised Venus that she would look out for Ellen; and then she was also taken away. Master Jones had not allowed Ellen to have any contact with her mother's relatives, or with slave workers outside his farm. Grayhorse promised Aunt Star that she no longer would need to worry about Ellen, that he would take care of her for the rest of her life and together they would stay away from any trouble around Quarry Town.

Now that Grayhorse's request had been approved, he needed to inform Ellen of her aunt's consent. Ellen would have to signal her acceptance or rejection in the Cherokee way. Ellen and Grayhorse agreed to a little Cherokee ceremony at a prearranged time. Ellen was to set a bowl of food on her front step. Grayhorse would come by and request to eat the food. If Ellen agreed it meant that she had given her acceptance to his proposal. If he ate the food and she did not agree, it meant that she had not given her consent to marry him. In the Cherokee society, this was a final means of allowing Ellen to say "No" without directly rejecting Grayhorse and sparing his feelings. If, on the other hand, her answer was "Yes." Grayhorse would be allowed to eat the food. Since Ellen's answer was "Yes," Grayhorse was now ready to seek the approval of the council elders and make preparations for the ceremony.

Grayhorse set aside the next month of crop season to travel to Eastern Tennessee to visit the reservation. He wanted Ellen to be accepted by his relatives and the Cherokee council of elders. Willie hitched fresh horses to the wagon, which he had loaded with plenty of food and fresh water. Ellen carried along an extra blanket and her favorite yellow wool shawl to cover her shoulders and shelter her from the brisk autumn wind that had begun to set in for the new season.

When they reached the reservation, Grayhorse met privately with the council elders to ask for their blessings and approval. He needed to prove his manhood by building a longhouse for himself and his new bride. He also needed to go on a hunt with the other men to kill an animal for food for the village. Since his plans were not to reside at the reservation, the requirement to build a longhouse was suspended by the elders. The couple was allowed to share space in the family longhouse even though they were not yet married. In early morning, Grayhorse accompanied the men on a hunt. He carried along his bow and arrow with plenty of flint for the hunt. Some arrows had straight points for small game and some had blunt arrows for birds. Grayhorse carried his head spear for large game. The men returned from the hunt with a large buck and a medium-sized black bear. Grayhorse was given credit for killing the buck. He butchered the animal and gave some to Ellen. The larger portion he gave to the elders to be shared with the other people of the village. This act of victory, killing a large animal, symbolized Grayhorse's power and willingness to support his bride. An act to accept the feast signaled an approval of his proposal by the elders.

Ellen in turn, accompanied by the ladies of the clan, gathered ears of corn, beans, squash, and berries and then made fresh fry bread from maize to prove her womanly accomplishments. This exchange of gifts was in fact the wedding ceremony but only for a trial marriage. The couple was now free to leave the reservation. If they remained together for four seasons, the marriage would be considered a firm union. If not, their ties to each other would be automatically dissolved. In either instance, when Grayhorse built the longhouse or whatever dwelling they chose together, it would belong to the woman.

Grayhorse was not interested in taking on the responsibility of other wives. He loved Ellen and she alone had taken his heart. Monogamy, though often practiced in the Cherokee society was not considered to be a moral imperative for men. A man could take a second or third wife if he desired—and if he could afford to take care of her. He would of course, need to obtain his first wife's consent. Grayhorse understood and accepted Ellen's position to never give this kind of consent. In the Cherokee society, there was usually no problem with consent if the second or third wife was the sister of the first wife. The first wife acclaimed the status of priority spouse and a second wife would mean a helper for domestic and agricultural chores. If the second wife was unrelated to the first wife, the second wife would have her own dwelling.

Once wed, the wife was expected to remain faithful. Sometimes women were punished for acts of adultery by having their ears cut off. If a woman became a widow, she observed a period of mourning for four years before she could remarry unless she married a man from the same lineage as her husband.

Cherokee Ceremony

Born in 1837, Grayhorse had already reached his nineteenth birthday and was considered to be an adult in the Cherokee society. Ellen, nearly two years younger, would soon be 18 years of age. Grayhorse had requested an official ceremony from the council of elders. He wanted to be married in the official Cherokee way. Members of the clan had begun to make gifts for the bride-to-be. The ladies were busy sewing wampum belts for both Ellen and Grayhorse to wear to the ceremony. The belts were white with blue beads arranged in pictographic design from the Cherokee language. The pictograph message expressed wishes for love, good health and a long life. The elders ordered Grayhorse and Ellen to come to the longhouse for counsel concerning their life together. The session was filled with ritual, chants, dance and much counseling. Grayhorse wore his large eagle wing wands so that he could participate in the chants and dances. Following the long ritual, the council gave its approval for the marriage.

At high noon the following day, the official ceremony began. Grayhorse wore his copper earrings and a feathered cape. Ellen wore a white deerskin skirt with a sky blue top fringed at the bottom. They each wore the wampum belts that they had been given by the clan with soleless buckskin moccasins. The ceremony began with a circle dance to the sun done by the ladies, followed by a hunting dance done by the men. The movements depicted a buffalo hunt. Each man carried a large spear in his hand. Chants of gratitude were offered to the Great Spirit. Following the chants, Grayhorse and Ellen were ushered to the center of the room. The elders sang chants, offered prayers with a laying on of hands for Grayhorse and Ellen. They placed their hands on their heads as they chanted and shared a drink with the elders from a common cup. All during the ceremony, Grayhorse clenched tightly in his hand the pouch with the precious jewels. In his heart, he prayed to the Great Spirit to bless the seedling offspring of his lineage represented by these jewels. Ellen noticed his actions and placed her hand on top of his to join in the blessing. She clenched his hand tightly as if to protect the jewels. They prayed silently that the council elders and the Great Spirit would anoint these seedling jewels with blessings that would pass on to four generations.

The ceremony ended with the smoking of the calumet pipe. The elders began the procedure and then passed the pipe around the circle to the right until it reached Grayhorse. One leader brought the pipe to Grayhorse. Grayhorse participated in the ritual by inhaling a puff of smoke from the calumet. (Ellen was not required to participate in that part of the ceremony.) The ritual of partaking of the smoke from the calumet sealed the marriage vows that Grayhorse and Ellen had made to each other in the session with the council and during the ceremony. The ceremony then moved to a different longhouse reserved for clan activity. The room was set to accommodate a large crowd of people; and a large feast had been prepared. The entire village had been invited to come. The meal consisted of venison that Grayhorse had slaughtered; bear roast, the Cherokee trilogy: berries, grape dumplings and fry bread.

Grayhorse and Ellen slept easily after all of the activities had settled. They had been well received by the clan and most importantly; they had received approval from the council elders. At sunrise, Grayhorse and Ellen loaded the wagon and started their three-day journey back to the farm. The short trail was bumpy and not as well maintained as the trail that they took going down to Tennessee but it was beautiful with lots of scenery. The leaves were beginning to turn beautiful colors, and they took plenty of rest stops along the way just to observe the artwork that nature had created. They talked about what their life together would be like and how that life would change once they made family. They visualized the young seedlings riding along beside them and filling the back of the wagon.

Silent Vows

Their next step was to prepare a marriage ceremony to be celebrated Ellen's way. It would take place inside the cave at Big Spring. Rev. Fox of Quarry Town would be in charge of the ceremony. They set the date only three weeks away. There was much work to be done and Ellen's initial step was to extend invitations to all of the people that would be in attendance. It would be a sacred ceremony of secret vows and those invited to attend were being asked to come in secret and tell no one about the event. None of the plans, including the invitations, were to be discussed. The ceremony would be held at the cave at Big Spring because having it at the big house would arouse too much attraction to Grayhorse.

The ceremony was to begin at 10:00 P.M. and end at midnight. No horses or wagons were to be parked anywhere near the cave entrances. People were told to park in Quarry Town and walk to the cave entrance. Martha Sue and Willie were in charge of notifying those who were being asked to attend.

Martha Sue worked day and night preparing food for the feast that was to follow the ceremony. Candlelight and oil lamps would brighten the darkness in the cave. Slave hands from the Matthew and Pendleton farms had been asked to perform African chants and ritual dances. Ellen purchased a new broom at the hardware store in Quarry Town. She certainly wanted to jump the broomstick with Grayhorse in keeping with the traditional African marriage custom. Rev. Fox was asked to arrive at the cave by 9:30 P.M. so that despite his habitual tardiness the ceremony could begin promptly at 10:00 P.M. In the character spirit of Grayhorse, being on time or being late was a character trait. It was a true temperament of a person's character. Grayhorse would surely speak out loud about Rev. Fox's tardiness if this should happen. To avoid that problem, Willie was told by Ellen to pick up Rev. Fox in the wagon not later than 9:15 P.M. This would avoid any embarrassment and the ceremony could begin on time.

Martha Sue and Willie had the wedding feast prepared and delivered to the cave at early evening. The feast consisted of smoked salmon, wild roasted turkey, wild stewed rabbit with thick gravy, Ellen's trilogy of leafy greens, sweet potatoes and rice, ambrosia, sweet potato pies, sweet breads, homemade custard with a little light liquor and grape wine from Master Jones' cellar with homemade lemonade, a traditional beverage. Martha Sue and Willie made several trips to help Grayhorse clean the place and put things in order. This occasion was special for Miss Ellie. It was Miss Ellie's wedding; and Martha Sue and Willie intended to do everything in their power to see that everything was in perfect order. It had to be a perfect occasion for Miss Ellie. The place looked so innocently beautiful with candles and lots of wild autumn flowers spread around. The women from the reservation were bringing straw mats for the guests to sit on unless they desired to bring their own decorative pillows.

Aunt Star Hope had been asked to lead the processional, in lieu of the absence of Ellen's mother, and the bride had selected Martha Sue to be her matron of honor while Willie would be serving as Grayhorse's best man. Ellen would be wearing a special ivory dress trimmed in dainty lace sewn for her by Aunt Star Hope, matching a top that the industrious aunt had made for Grayhorse (without the lace).

Grayhorse was not to see his bride until it was time for the ceremony. Ellen stayed well hidden and quietly entered the cave by the entrance at the north point of Quarry Town. All of the guest entered the cave soft-footed, using both entrances. Just as the ceremony was about to begin, Grayhorse was surprised to see four elders from the reservation entering, along with a wagonload of his relatives, who were carrying gifts for both Grayhorse and Ellen. They also brought a bear roast that they had saved from a special hunt to be shared with the guests which, when partaken of, would symbolize the sharing of inner strength for the new couple.

Fifteen minutes later than expected Willie arrived with Rev. Fox who carried a large bible under his arm. He was dressed in his favorite black suit with tails, the one that he always wore for such occasions, and he wore small-rimmed spectacles resting gently on his nose so that he could read the fine print in the dim light of the cave. Grayhorse wore his copper earrings, wampum belt with blue beads and a deerskin breechcloth over his western pants.

Rev. Fox started the ceremony promptly at 10:00 P.M., a great relief for Ellen who certainly did not want to see Grayhorse on his soapbox making a speech about character and timeliness. The processional began at the

29

north entrance of the cave. Grayhorse and Willie stood in the center of the room along with Rev. Fox. Once again, Grayhorse was waiting for his bride—but this time, he knew where to find her.

Aunt Star Hope led the processional followed by Martha Sue. Then came beautiful, elegant Ellen, who walked from the entrance to the center of the room. Her hand-sewn ivory dress flowed gently in the flickering candlelight., and she wore her turquoise earrings and the necklace Grayhorse had given her when he proposed. A soft breeze from the east blew gently through the cave and accented the room with the essence of perfume from the lovely wild flowers that had been placed around the room. Even though no one could see, all were assured that the moon stood still long enough to pierce the cave roof top and punctuate the evening with a romantic air that only moonlight can afford. Ellen had remembered to wear her lovely turquoise earrings and the lovely necklace that Grayhorse had given to her when he proposed. She was also wishing in her heart that Grayhorse had remembered to bring the pouch with the precious jewels because the seedling offspring were also to be a part of this special new beginning.

Slave workers from the Matthew and Pendleton farms sang an African melody of gratitude for the good life, which the men followed with a dance in tribute of good health. Rev. Fox questioned the bride and groom on their commitment to each other. As Grayhorse answered the questions, he held tightly to Ellen's hand. In his other hand, he clenched tightly the deerskin pouch with the precious jewels that he was protecting, symbolic of the seedling jewels of his future which would perpetuate the lifeline and lineage of his family. He silently prayed to the Great Spirit to bless these jewels and the seedlings. Ellen smiled at him, held his hand tightly in hers and then joined Grayhorse by offering the same petition to her Great Spirit. For a quiet moment, silently, they took their sacred vows.

Aunt Star Hope made remarks based on the wisdom of the African culture, that included a challenge for the good life for Grayhorse and Ellen. A song of good spirit was led as a chant, everyone who knew it joined in. Grayhorse was told by Rev. Fox to publicly kiss his new bride. Then the couple jumped the broomstick together. Rev. Fox pronounced them husband and wife. It was then time for the feast and fellowship to begin. At midnight Willie began to dim the oil lamps and blow out the candles. The guests congratulated the couple and quietly began to leave the cave, making their way out of Big Spring and across Quarry Town to reach their homes before daybreak.

Ellen and Grayhorse were now officially married in both Ellen's and Grayhorse's cultures. When Willie asked Ellen when he should be dropping her off she responded happily, "Tonight I'm staying at the cave with Grayhorse, not at the big house, and not in the barn, but right here at the cave in Big Spring. This is my second dwelling and this is where I belong." As Willie and Martha Sue turned to leave they looked back at Ellen and Grayhorse with a smile on their faces. Grayhorse grinned back and snuggled his shoulders as if to agree with Ellen. When everyone left the cave, Grayhorse snuffed out all the candles except for one small flame left flickering in the darkness. Together the newlyweds embraced in the quiet darkness of the cave. They talked long of their future together, and then slept snugly in each other's arms. The sound of crickets and cave noises added to the ambience of that special moment. Misty neighed and stood watch near the front entrance while they slept. Once again the Great Spirit had blessed Grayhorse and answered his prayers. They were now together as a family: Grayhorse, Ellen, and Misty.

4

Solemnity of a Name

Ellen Jones Grayhorse, thought Grayhorse. *She is no longer just Ellen Jones but Ellen Jones Grayhorse.* Rev. Fox had insisted he write his full name on the certificate of marriage issued by the Caldwell County office of records. Grayhorse responded that "Grayhorse" was his given birth name; In the Native American culture, a child is not given a name as a surname. A child is given a name according to some animal, person, or event that will provide an influence and some guidance for his life cycle. The name "Grayhorse" had significant meaning for him but not for Ellen or his off-spring. To satisfy Rev. Fox's request, Grayhorse told him that his first name was "J." Since Grayhorse could not write his name in English, Rev. Fox indicated that he could simply sign an "X" on the dotted line. Ellen then signed his name as J. Grayhorse.

Ellen asked Grayhorse how he happened to select "J" as his first name. Grayhorse then shared with her that he had a friend in Virginia whose name was John Thornton Jackson, known as Stonewall Jackson. Stonewall had developed a strong relationship with the Native Americans and African slaves of the area who needed assistance to leave the state or to work through some of the pressures of slavery. Sometimes he wrote his name as Stonewall J. Grayhorse, but he was not sure if the "J" stood for John or Jackson. Because of his respect for his relationship with Stonewall, Grayhorse had also used the letter "J" to represent either Jack or Jackson. From that day forward, Grayhorse was known as J. Grayhorse. Ellen then dropped the name "Jones" and began to use her legal name, Ellen Grayhorse.

Grayhorse Moves to the Farm

While Grayhorse waited for Willie to arrive with the wagon, he took a final walk through the cave to be certain that he had packed all of his belongings. He was going to be moving into the big house at the Jones farm, which now belonged to Ellen. He would be sleeping in Master Jones' master bedroom with Ellen. Misty, of course, would be taking up residence in the barn, where a special stall had been prepared with plenty of hay and water and a few extra apples and sugar cubes to delight the horse. Somehow he knew that Ellen would want to change the name of the farm to the Grayhorse farm. Grayhorse realized that this action would have to wait until he had been accepted back into Quarry Town. He smiled anyway and on the inside, he chuckled out loud.

Grayhorse carefully packed his eagle wing wands and tied them securely to Misty's side. Misty was used to carrying them carefully on long journeys. His vittles pot and his mother's cooking bowls he packed to be loaded in the wagon. He carefully covered his water drum and reed flute pipe so that he could carry them himself. He checked the inside pocket of his vest to be sure that all of the precious jewels were still in place and well protected. Grayhorse opened the pouch and carefully spread the jewels on the floor of the cave. The three silver nuggets were shining and brilliant. The twelve turquoise gems were awesomely beautiful. Grayhorse put the jewels back in the pouch, clenched it tightly and uttered a quiet prayer to the Great Spirit to protect the seedlings of his lineage.

Grayhorse checked the position of the sun. Where was Willie? Being on time was a strong character trait for Grayhorse. One could set their timepiece by his given word. He often would arrive early or appear right on the minute of his arrival time. Ellen was expecting them to be at the farm by noon, and he did not want to keep her waiting. Just when Grayhorse was beginning to wonder if something unexpected had happened at the farm, he heard footsteps at the north point cave entrance. Willie had backed the wagon into the cave so that the neighbors would not be able to see any loading activity. Willie reported that his tardiness had been caused by a large crowd around the Court House Square on Main Street. They had gathered for a special meeting concerning some land dispute along Varment Trace Road and Willie had been forced to follow a back road trail, which took him longer to reach the cave.

Willie loaded the wagon while Grayhorse hitched Misty on to the back. Before climbing aboard the wagon, Grayhorse walked over to the family birch tree. He observed the petroglyphs that he had carved when he found Ellen and when they were married. Just yesterday, he had carved a fresh petroglyph to mark the beginning of their new life together as a family. Today, he was moving to the farm and nothing was going to be the same again. Deep inside, he wanted to move the tree to the farm but it was large and firmly anchored and there was no way to move it without damaging its life span. He and Ellen would need to select a new tree at the farm and the petroglyphs would have to be recarved.

As they left the cave, they carefully covered the loaded wagon with burlap and blankets and moved quietly to make sure that no one saw them leave. They made their way around the Court Square on Main Street and headed down the old Eddyville trail. Half way down the trail, a heavy mist of rain began to fall. The Eddyville trail sometimes became difficult to travel when the rain was heavy. Willie was sure that they would reach the farm before any water damage could be done, but the trail was getting pretty muddy and the pot-holes rather frequent. On the way, Grayhorse and Willie talked about their new relationship and what life would be like at the farm. Willie assured Grayhorse that he would be comfortable at the farm and well protected from any enemies. He stated that he would appreciate a good hand to help out with the farm chores, animals and agriculture.

When they entered the foot gate of the farm, Ellen who was watching from the front window, walked out to the front porch and greeted Grayhorse with a tender embrace. As Willie disembarked from the wagon, Ellen helped unload Grayhorse's belongings, indicating where everything belonged as she passed them along. Martha Sue had prepared a steamy chicken soup for lunch. Grayhorse and Ellen finished unloading the wagon and sat down for soup at the kitchen table while Willie went straight to the barn to put Misty and the other horses in their new quarters. Grayhorse, however, interrupted his lunch and carefully entrapped the precious eagle wing wands from Misty's side. He carried them upstairs and placed them on a special shelf that Ellen had cleared for him in Master Jones' closet. This spot would be the special place for all of Grayhorse's spiritual artifacts used for his worship rituals to the Great Spirit. Grayhorse returned to the kitchen, apologized to Ellen for the interruption, and finished at least two large bowls of Martha Sue's chicken soup without stopping. He was now ready for a quiet talk with Ellen.

Willie rushed to the kitchen for his lunch, as the rain poured heavily and beat against the roof for hours. It flooded the entrance gate to the farm and low places along the Eddyville trail, chasing the farm animals into the barn. Grayhorse and Ellen made their way upstairs to finish putting his belongings away. They walked to the bedroom window, arm in arm and watched the rain fall steadily against the ground. The rain smelled fresh and clean. It appeared to cause the grass and the flowers to glisten and to even wash away unclean thoughts from the past and launched them into new beginnings. The rain was their friend, creating moments of free spirit that neither wanted to go away. Ellen and Grayhorse decided that for now, the packing could wait for its own time but the movement belonged to their hearts.

The Pride and Dignity of Ellen

Six months later, Ellen sat quietly in her rocking chair with the door closed. She had not been comfortable with her bedroom door open since the intrusion of her privacy by her father, Master Jones. He had done the same thing to her mother, Venus. He had impregnated her twice. Both Ellen and her younger sister were conceived this way, against their mother's will. Master Jones had forced this behavior on her mother and later, he had forced it on his daughter Ellen. Her father's abusive behavior had turned this slave house into a ghost house of memories.

She could have given Grayhorse the bedroom across the hall but now that she was Grayhorse's wife, Grayhorse would not understand or accept this separation. Ellen arose early to take her bath while Grayhorse was outside by the oak tree paying his vows to the Great Spirit. When he returned, Ellen had already finished getting dressed. This early rising had become a routine for Ellen. Her freshly starched petticoats gave body and style to her dainty blue gingham dress. Ellen had covered it with a freshly ironed white-bibbed apron. She wore her hair wrapped in a bun on top of her head and walked proudly with her shoulders back. Her eyes always seemed to be focused, signaling that she knew where she was headed and was secure in what she wanted to do. When she spoke, her soft, quiet tonality demanded others to listen. To the women of Quarry Town, she was Miss Ellie. Her presence filled the room with dignity, poise, and elegance. She was a lady with pride.

Ellen wondered if that would change, especially with the women of Quarry Town. Now that she would be known as Ellen Grayhorse, she was actually proud to drop the name Jones. Since her father had invaded her privacy, the name Jones was disgraceful to her. Fulfilling his sexual pleasure had scarred her for life as a young child and as a young woman. Day by day she had fought to maintain her dignity. Now her marriage to Grayhorse was offering her a new beginning. She would work to bring closure to those past memories. She would try to be patient with Grayhorse and hoped that he would also be patient with her.

Ellen had not shared any of Grayhorse's spiritual practices with anyone at the farm including Martha Sue and Willie, as she was afraid that the family and the neighbors would not understand his behavior and would begin to label him as eccentric. She had discussed this with Grayhorse and he had promised to keep his spiritual practices private and out of sight of the neighbors so that Ellen would not have to explain. In no way did Ellen wish to push her hurtful memories on Grayhorse. Whenever he would enter their bedroom, she would shamefully turn her back and attempt to hide her privacy from him. She had yet to undress in his presence, carefully moving her body away from Grayhorse's sight. Grayhorse noticed her discomfort and would always knock before entering the bedroom, even if the door was open. Today, Grayhorse decided that he no longer needed to knock on his own bedroom door. He simply opened the door and walked in. When Ellen turned around, he was standing next to her as she undressed for bed. She scolded Grayhorse and declared that his entrance was an intrusion of her privacy. Grayhorse held her by the shoulders and spoke softly into her ear, assuring her that she had no reason to be embarrassed or fearful of him entering their private quarters or of him observing her body. Twice they had taken sacred vows. They were no longer two people but one.

"I will always love and respect you, Ellen. What is between us is mutual respect and forever. I assure you that I will always love and protect you. Any other males in your presence must do the same. This is our private quarters, it is for you and me—and no one else belongs in these quarters when you have your private moments. We belong together and I will always be here for you. Trust me, Ellen, no one else will ever be able to harm you again."

Ellen needed to hear these words from Grayhorse. She felt security and another level of comfort as Grayhorse spoke to her.

"You are my wife, Mrs. Ellen Grayhorse, you must never again be afraid. We must never hide our feelings from each other. You are a proud, strong woman, Ellen; a woman of strong character, integrity, dignity, and worth. We no longer have two hearts but one. Together, we can make family."

Grayhorse then held Ellen close to him, kissed her gently, and wiped her silent tears away. Dressed in her yellow flannel gown and her ruffled sleeping bonnet, Ellen snuggled close to Grayhorse as he blew out the candles. Immediately, they heard a neigh, Misty had been watching every action as she peeped through the bedroom window. When the last candle went out, she made her way to her sleeping stall in the barn because she was also a part of this new family.

Choosing a Petroglyph Tree

"When morning breaks," said Grayhorse, "we need to take a walk together and survey the trees on the farm. It is time to select a new petroglyph tree for our remembrances. It will replace the petroglyph birch tree that we left at Big Spring, where I had started a petroglyph record of our family history using Cherokee symbols."

Ellen responded, "I know just the tree! It stands in exactly the right place to welcome our new beginnings."

The following day after breakfast, Ellen and Grayhorse strolled across the farmland in search of a suitable tree. Their first stop was under the branches of a stately old weeping willow tree anchored in the front yard. It was a tree with much character. Its slender branches hung long and low, almost touching the ground. But they both agreed that because the trunk of the tree was hidden under the branches, the petroglyph carvings would never be noticed. This would take away from the real meaning to have a tree. Not far from the garden spot stood a tender young birch tree. Its bark was soft and just right for carving. They glanced at the tree and decided that it was too young to carry such an important load like a family history. Ellen then pointed to an oak tree down near the front gate. It was the solid and stately tree that she had thought of earlier. It had witnessed many happenings at the farm and seemed to be waiting to be carved. It had been a favorite tree for the family and had hosted many family events like picnics and other family gatherings. Friends and neighbors alike were always attracted to its branches. It had grown tall and would continue to grow as the Grayhorse family grew. It would proudly carry the family history year after year.

When Grayhorse saw the tree, he was pleased and responded joyfully. "This is the tree and this is the spot the Great Spirit has directed us to! This tree will shelter our household, grow with our family and teach us to withstand the storms and tests of life."

Ellen and Grayhorse stood arm in arm under the oak tree while Grayhorse thanked the Great Spirit once again for granting them a blessing and for giving them wisdom and direction to follow his leadership. For the next several days, Grayhorse spent time carving Cherokee petroglyphs on the trunk of the old oak tree. He began by recarving the ones that he had left behind on the birch tree at Big Spring Bottom. The first petroglyph labeled the tree and identified the family as the Grayhorse family. Already, the tree had provided a home for squirrels and nesting branches for birds. Plenty of acorns had fallen underneath its branches. Together Ellen and Grayhorse gave the tree a name. They named it 'Charity' because of its sharing spirit with the other creatures of nature.

Family and Rearing

A year had passed since the wedding day at the cave. Grayhorse had reached his twenty-first birthday and Ellen was now nineteen years of age. It was a misty morning. Ellen had been up most of the night with a sick stomach. She had not been able to hold food for several days. She felt bloated and her clothes were no longer comfortable to wear. It was time for her to go into Quarry Town for a visit to Dr. Hatten's office. Willie drove Ellen in the wagon and Grayhorse went along for support, riding in the back of the wagon. Dr. Hatten had Ellen in his office only a few minutes when he diagnosed her first pregnancy. Ellen and Grayhorse had conceived their first child.

When her pregnancy was three months old, Ellen began to show that she was with child. Quarry Town was a small community and news traveled like lightning. It was a hot news flash for the women of Quarry Town. Miss Ellie was with child! As only a few people knew that Grayhorse and Ellen were married and that Grayhorse lived at the farm, the rumor among most of the townspeople was that Ellen was with child by one of the farm hands who stayed in Big Spring for the crop season.

They named their first child Robert; he was born in 1857. Three years later, 1860, a daughter, Belle, was born. Four years later, Harvey James was born in 1864 and in 1866, the third son, Stonewall Jackson was born, and named after Grayhorse's army general friend in Virginia, John Thornton Jackson, known in history as Stonewall Jackson. Two years later, 1868, Matt was born. Three years later, 1871, Dave was born and four years later, 1875, John was born. In 1876, another daughter, Minnie, was born. Two years later, 1885, Otis was born, then in 1887, Harmon and a year later, the youngest son, Otha, in 1888. Over a period of thirty-one years, Ellen and Grayhorse had twelve children, ten sons and two daughters. Ellen was fifty-one years old when she gave birth to her youngest son and Grayhorse was fifty-three.

Grayhorse had hopes that these twelve children were a fulfillment for the twelve precious turquoise gems that he had protected in his deerskin pouch for many years. He had hoped that they would represent a fulfillment from the Great Spirit to increase the Cherokee nation through his lineage. For so long he had prayed and waited for a message from the Spirit of the White Buffalo. All of the visions that he received led him to believe that this was only a first step, just a beginning for the fulfillment of the family legacy. The true interpretation would be revealed by the Four Winds and would be spread over four seasons represented by four generations. Grayhorse shared this vision with Ellen and together they realized that the birth of their ten sons and two daughters only marked a beginning of the fulfillment of his future lineage. Again, Grayhorse counted the jewels, paid his vows to the Great Spirit for the making of their family and carefully replaced the jewels in the deerskin pouch. Prayerfully, he then tucked the pouch away inside the pocket of his deerskin vest.

The 'Gray' Name

Following the birth of the fourth son, Matty, it was no longer a secret for the people of Quarry Town that Grayhorse was married to Ellen, living at the big house on the former Jones farm and that together they had five children. It only took a short while for the news to circulate and perpetuate a warning from the town leaders that Grayhorse was still not welcome in Quarry Town. He and his family continuously received threatening letters and warnings from the Nightriders, Klansmen and city law officers to leave town. Native Americans were not to be in the area when it was not crop season. When they were there, they were not to be around the women, have relationships, and be befriended by the white residents, particularly the white women. They were also warned to stay away from the Negro settlements for fear that together both groups would become proactive against the whites as their life styles would create social friction and they would not get along together. Grayhorse ignored all of the threats and warnings. He continued to live with his family at the farm and was careful to stay away from people that he did not trust. Because Grayhorse continued to ignore these threatening messages, the law officers watched him closely and harassed him with constant verbal warnings.

When he was last in Quarry Town, Grayhorse had organized the crop workers into proactive activities to protest against living and working conditions on the farm where they stayed. He was ushered to the county line by the law officers and told not to ever return to Quarry Town. This time was different, he was there for a different reason. He came for Ellen and he had vowed to stay away from trouble.

Ellen did not want any trouble at the farm for Grayhorse or the family. Nightriders frequently set fires and whipped Negro and Indian slaves who were illegal to the area or that they were unhappy with. Recently, Grayhorse had received another harsh warning to leave Quarry Town immediately. In the late evening, Ellen accompanied Grayhorse to the barn and cut his beautiful long, shiny black coarse hair. Grayhorse hid his Native American ritual artifacts in the hayloft in the barn. He put away his Native American clothes and sent Willie to Quarry Town to the dry goods store on Main Street to buy some western clothes for him to wear. He then took a final step that all but broke his spirit. He gave up his birth name. He dropped the word 'horse' from his name and became J. Gray.

The petroglyph on the oak tree was changed to read THE GRAY FAMILY. Ellen and all of the children took the last name "Gray."

The wind and weather had tanned and toughened Grayhorse's skin so that his appearance was closer to Negro than Native American. From that day forward, he lived under the disguise of a Negro. He kept his hair cut short. Quietly, he and Ellen tutored their children in the culture and practices of the Grayhorse ancestors. Petroglyphs were carved on the oak tree to mark this important change in their lives. The birth year for each child was also added to the petroglyph history.

Child Rearing

All of the children were reared with strong family values and high morals. Ellen carefully trained her daughters, Belle and Minnie. She taught them politeness, poise and the dignity of womanhood. Meanwhile, Grayhorse trained his sons in the mastery of being good fathers and loving husbands. They were taught to respect their mother, their elders and their sisters. Even to mold the children's behavior into the proper merger of African and Cherokee cultures and traditions, Ellen and Grayhorse refused to raise their voices to reprimand them. Neither did they lavish them with continuous praise, or promise material rewards. They were taught not to be wasteful with natural resources and were trained to use only what they needed for survival, the rest should be left for others to use. Educational learning and honest labor were strongly emphasized.

All of the children were reared to develop a good relationship with the spirit world. When the children reached puberty, they were required to go through a pre puberty fast that lasted from one to ten days depending on the child's endurance. This was a traditional practice that was common to both cultures. They were required to abstain from certain food and drink and to meditate and fix their mind on spiritual things. It did not matter if their relationship was with Grayhorse's god, the Great Spirit or with Ellen's God, Jehovah. This ritual was performed in the hope that the child would receive a guardian spirit (totem) often visualized in the form of an animal, angel, person, or some natural phenomena. The guardian spirit would provide wisdom, knowledge, guidance and power to influence the course that the child's life cycle would follow. Grayhorse's totem spirit was the Spirit of the White Buffalo.

Ellen took charge of teaching the children religious and moral values and taking them to church in Big Spring Bottom. She carefully watched over them to be sure that they were exposed to sound economic, religious and political practices. They were trained to be thrifty with their money and to save their pennies. The boys were known in Quarry Town and in Big Spring as good, respectable sons and hard workers, while Belle and Minnie were recognized as being courteous, poised and well mannered. These lessons had been learned from all of the members of the household and the respected elders of the town.

Willie and Grayhorse taught the boys to be skilled hunters and avid farmers. They learned to set traps for the animal hunts and to use spears for spear fishing. Minnie and Belle followed their mother and learned to pick berries and herbs. Martha Sue taught them to sew and how to make jellies and preserves. Making apple butter, maple syrup and churning butter was a chore reserved not only for the girls but also for the boys.

Tobacco and corn were the main cash crops for family survival. At harvest time, Willie, Grayhorse and the boys would load the wagon and carry the crops to Hopkinsville, Kentucky (Christian County) to the Chisolm Tobacco Warehouse to be sold. Hogs and cows were also sold at the Christian County slaughterhouse. This trip was an all day journey. Grayhorse always stopped by the general store on the way home to buy horehound candy and licorice for the boys. That was their wages for a long day's work.

41

One thing was for certain; every Sunday, Ellen dressed in her petticoats and feathered hat and the boys in their starched shirts and knicker bottom pants, attended church at Big Spring Bottom. This church was the mother church for what is now known as Shepherd Street Baptist Church in Princeton. Willie would drive the wagon and the boys would all sit in the back. Belle and Minnie always sat up front close to their mother. Taking the family to church was a regular job for Misty, whose old age was slowing her down. To shelter her from the hot sun, wind and rain, Grayhorse made her a hat with flowers. He always attached a bell to her harness and put an extra blanket in the back of the wagon to cover her painful limbs while she waited for the family. This was a family affair and Misty was a part of the family.

While the family was away at church, Grayhorse would take his water drum and flute pipe and go down to the oak tree to pay vows to the Great Spirit. He always offered chants of thanksgiving, dance and music. Each Sunday, he asked the Great Spirit to anoint the life cycle of his twelve seedling jewels. He also continued to seek blessings for all of the offspring that would come through his lineage. Grayhorse still wanted these jewels to symbolically represent his twelve children but the Spirit of the White Buffalo would not confirm his wish. Grayhorse continued to wait for the Spirit of the White Buffalo to give him direction for his life cycle.

Not long after noon, when the family would return from church. Martha Sue always welcomed them home with the smell of fresh baked pies and a large Sunday dinner. The first ritual was for the children to go immediately upstairs and remove their Sunday clothes so that they would be fresh for the next Sunday. The dinner hour was always changed from late evening to mid-afternoon. No work chores were done on Sunday. After the dinner hour the family would sit around the fire or on the front porch, if the weather was warm, for family talk and sharing. The children never joined in adult conversation. They always found their place somewhere in the yard for child's play or learning.

5

Visions from the Spirit of the White Buffalo

Grayhorse loved those woods surrounding his new home. Before he moved to the farm, he often wandered away from the main trail to follow the hidden path. He remembered scenery and beautiful natural settings that his father had pointed out to him when his family came through the area on its way to the reservation in Tennessee. Many times he had slipped away to think and to just remember these experiences now that he lived so close to them at the farm. There was one special place in particular that he seemed to be drawn to whenever he needed to communicate with the Great Spirit. Once before, his guardian spirit (totem spirit), the Spirit of the White Buffalo, had appeared to him as he sat near the waterfall to meditate.

Grayhorse had felt anxious and somewhat depressed for the last several days. He had experienced problems with a shortness of breath and increased breathing problems. Consultations with Dr. Hattan had been occurring more frequently. Ellen and the rest of his family had pleaded with him to accept these annoyances as symptoms of emphysema and a heart irregularity. His asthma attacks were handled by ordering him to stop smoking the calumet and to stay away from Big Spring and the quarry, because the dampness and the dust seemed to help trigger these attacks. Grayhorse had fasted for four days and pleaded to the Great Spirit for guidance and direction. He was hoping that today would be a different day when the Spirit of the White Buffalo would appear to him again.

Grayhorse arose early so that he could reach the waterfall by sunrise. When he arrived, accompanying the beautiful waterfall was a perfect rainbow that completely encircled the falls and touched the earth from point to point. He sat on the ground looking up for a moment just to absorb the beauty of this spectacular moment in nature. Suddenly there appeared in the mist of the cascading rushing water of the falls a profile of the White Buffalo. The image captured Grayhorse's attention. Quickly, the White Buffalo began to speak to the searching man about the meaning of the Four

Winds. Grayhorse sat very still and quiet. He carefully listened as the White Buffalo spoke with much wisdom and gave precise directions about the course that Grayhorse's life would take. Grayhorse realized that he needed to pay close attention and follow directly every step that was laid out in these directions.

The Spirit explained to Grayhorse that the Four Winds represented four directions in the Native American universe: East, West, North and South with Mother Earth below and Father Sky above. The Four Winds emanated from the four points on the compass and dictated the direction that one's life cycle would follow. The Spirit of the White Buffalo was revealing this message to confirm for Grayhorse that he had listened well and had taken the correct turn in his life by marrying Ellen, moving to the farm and making family. He also confirmed that Quarry Town, though sometimes unpredictable, was where he needed to be in spite of the opposition against him by the town leaders who wanted him to leave. He needed to remain in Quarry Town in order to fulfill his obligations in the legacy and to perpetuate the growth and reproduction of the Cherokee nation.

The Cherokee nation had been geographically dispersed by the government according to the Four Winds. The Northern Native Americans were descendants of the Mighty Five Nation Iroquois League; the Native Americans of the Southwest were descendants of the Five Civilized Tribes. These were the groups that escaped the Trail of Tears and occupied land where the ancient Mississippians built earthen pyramids and temple mounds. In North Carolina, the Eastern Band of Cherokees were headquartered at the foot hills of the Great Smoky Mountains in Eastern Tennessee. Grayhorse was aware from his travels and his father's instructions that these descendants influenced and imprinted the early years of his life cycle. In Oklahoma, once known as Indian Territory, some thirty indigenous and exile tribes, including Cherokee, were now living shoulder to shoulder at Native American crossroads.

The closer Grayhorse listened, the more he understood that he was not misinterpreting the vision by following his dream to return to Tennessee to live on the reservation. He was confident that he was being guided by the Great Spirit. This visit from the White Buffalo helped him to understand that the heavy heart and depressed feelings that he was carrying were really a result of his discomfort at having to move from the farm and snuff out his traditions of social and religious practices.

The Spirit of the White Buffalo then spoke to Grayhorse concerning his health. His weakness and shortness of breath had become a major concern for his family. In spite of his asthma, emphysema and heart problems, Grayhorse continued to consistently smoke the calumet and drink firewater even when he was not involved with his ritual practices. He was consuming regular portions of wine and homemade liquor from Master Jones special collection in the cellar. Grayhorse rationalized this increase in consumption by declaring that it lessened his arthritic knee pain and settled his nerves. He complained frequently that the knee pain had slowed his ability to walk or do heavy work around the farm. Most of the farm labor had been turned over to Willie with the help of Grayhorse's sons. Whenever he had to go someplace, Willie always drove the wagon and stayed with him while Grayhorse leaned heavily on his walking cane and trusty companion. Grayhorse sought instructions from the White Buffalo for a mixture of medicinal herbs that he could use to improve his breathing and relieve some of the pain in his knees.

Grayhorse was directed by the totem spirit to select a son to mentor in the practice and traditions of the family legacy that Grayhorse was to receive. This selected son would nurture, protect and maintain the truths, values and spirits of character of the legacy. He would perpetuate the bonds and connectors for the family relationships and thus would strengthen the rebirth of the Cherokee nation. The spiritual characters of wisdom and fidelity should remain with the first son but the protection and perpetuation of the family legacy must be passed to the fourth son. The rainbow then dissipated and Grayhorse was left alone with the cool, clear, cascading water of the waterfall.

Grayhorse pondered why this spot had been selected by the Great Spirit for the delivery of such an important message. Then he remembered the wisdom and instruction of his father that water is a conductor of sound and communication. The waterfall provided a perfect setting to communicate with the Great Spirit. Rainbows are symbolic covenant reminders. They reminded Grayhorse that the promises from the Great Spirit are eternal, real and will come to pass.

On the way home, Grayhorse wondered if he would be able to make Ellen understand that Stonewall, the third son and not Robert, the first son, would be the one to receive the anointing for the birthright to receive the family legacy. Matt, the fourth son, would never be able to carry the weight of such an assignment to protect the legacy and look after the jewels. Somehow he knew that the Great Spirit would confirm this truth. The transaction would not take place until the White Buffalo had conveyed a message to grant this approval. He wanted to remind her that Robert would be blessed with wisdom and must follow the moral value of fidelity. Along the way, Grayhorse stopped to gather medicinal herbs to be made into a stew or tea for his physical ailments. For now, he just wanted to breathe clean air and a sigh of relief in knowing that he was following the wisdom of the totem spirit. For once in his life, he was in the right place. Eventually he knew that the legacy would be entrusted to the right son, if not in his season, then in the second, third or fourth season to follow. Even if the legacy became lost or misplaced, under the protection of the Great Spirit, it would someday and somehow find its way into the protected trust of the fourth and properly selected son.

Legacy Revealed: Power of the Number Four

Ellen's favorite son was Robert, her first born. In the African culture, Robert would be the first heir to the family possessions. It would become his responsibility to lead and hold the family together. He would be responsible to take charge of all important matters when needed. In the Cherokee society, the number four was more powerful. The number four was applied in all situations and to every decision of importance. Stonewall was not the fourth son but he was Grayhorse's choice to receive the family anointing. In regards to Stonewall receiving this honor, the Spirit of the White Buffalo had not revealed this message from the Great Spirit to Grayhorse. The only message received was that this honor had to pass through the male gender to the fourth son. This decree had been firmly declared by the totem spirit. Grayhorse was a little nervous about having to carry out this responsibility of selection but he had been assured by the White Buffalo that he would guide him well until he had fully mastered his responsibility.

Ellen questioned Grayhorse regarding clan relationships and matrilineal inheritance for sons and their relationships to their fathers in Cherokee culture. Ellen knew that Grayhorse's opinion would overrule her wishes concerning her first son.

"We have ten sons," said Ellen. "How can you favor only one son?"

Grayhorse's response was that in the Cherokee society, the number four was always considered to explain the why, when, what or how of any events that took place or any decisions that had to be made. Much consideration was always given to the Four Winds, the four compass points, the four seasons, and the fourth son. In this particular case, the fourth son did not have the strength, wisdom or interest to carry the weight of this responsibility.

Belonging to a Cherokee clan was a matter of blood ties, of kinship. Members of a clan were all related to one another matrilineally; that is, they were all descendants from a common ancestress through the female line. In keeping with this matrilineal nature of clan membership, the son of a married couple was considered to be the mother's progeny and was only casually related to the father. In large measure, the mother's role was taken over by the mother's brother, usually the oldest, if she had more than one brother. It was the uncle who taught the boy the communal games, hunting, fishing and other skills. The boy's father performed these duties for the male children of his sister. Since Ellen did not have a brother and Grayhorse did not have a sister, Martha Sue and Willie fulfilled these surrogate roles. Grayhorse continued to hold firm to the passing of the legacy to Stonewall, his favorite son. Choosing Stonewall would also pave the way for the birthing of seedling offspring through the fourth son of the fourth generation.

The Fourth Son

On Grayhorse's next adventure to search for his totem spirit, he decided to take Stonewall along so that the young boy could be enlightened about the beliefs and traditions of his people. Stonewall was made to understand if the White Buffalo should appear, he was not to speak or interfere with conversation or invade his presence or space. They loaded their boat onto the back of the wagon and made their way down to the Tennessee River in Gilbertsville, Kentucky. It was a slow ride along the Eddyville Road but it gave Grayhorse and Stonewall time to be together as father and son. Grayhorse remembered his father's instruction about choosing a calm setting near the water to reach the intimate presence of the Great Spirit.

Universe: Three Worlds

Since the catch was slow and fishing was not really their reason for being there, Grayhorse took the opportunity to teach Stonewall about what the Cherokee believe about the universe. They believed that the universe was made up of three different worlds: the Upper World, the Lower World, and the World that we live in. The world, a round island resting on the surface of water, was suspended from the sky by four cords attached to the island at four cardinal points of the compass. Lines suspended to connect opposite points of the compass from North to South and from East to West, intersected the world into four wedge-shaped segments. Each segment of the world was identified by its own color. According to Cherokee belief, the East was associated with the color red because it was the direction of the sun, the greatest deity of all. Red was also the color of sacred fire, directly connected with the sun, blood, and life. Red also represented the color of success.

The West was the moon segment, it provided no warmth and was not life giving as was the sun, so its color was black, which also stood for death and the region for the souls of the dead. North was the direction of cold and its color was blue (sometimes purple). It represented trouble and defeat. South was the direction of warmth, its color was white. It was associated with happiness and peace.

Above their home in this World, Native Americans believed was the vault of the sky, which they envisioned as an inverted bowl. Twice each day at twilight and dawn, the bowl rose and fell to allow the sun and the moon to pass underneath and shine on THIS WORLD. The greatest deity, the sun, had a representative on THIS EARTH. This representative was Sacred Fire depicting the highest degree of purity. They believed that the sun had gender identification, female. Sacred Fire was thought of as an old woman, and they fed it a portion of each meal. To profane a Sacred Fire by spitting in it or dousing it with water was to court a swift retribution, usually by being afflicted with a disease. The Sacred Fire was usually set and kept burning throughout the year in the main building for community activities. From it, all of the household cooking and eating fires were ignited. When it was ceremoniously extinguished, it was an annual ritual to mark both the culmination of the old year and the inception of the New Year.

Second Vision of the White Buffalo

The chill in the air was changing so Grayhorse paddled the canoe over to the riverbank to unload his fishing gear and head back to the farm. Suddenly, with a flash, a strange phenomenal took place. A blaze of fire appeared on the shore illuminating the entire area. It was approximately twelve feet from where Grayhorse was about to unload his boat. In the midst of the fire stood a profile of the Spirit of the White Buffalo. Stonewall was fearful and returned to the boat.

The Spirit spoke to Grayhorse "Do not be afraid, Grayhorse, I have only come to bring you a message concerning your family legacy and the precious jewels that you carry." Grayhorse stood very still and faced his totem spirit. He listened closely to hear and understand what the message would be.

The White Buffalo questioned Grayhorse concerning the protection of the precious jewels. Grayhorse was directed to place the jewels on the ground. He retrieved the deerskin pouch from the inside pocket of his vest, carefully opened it, and placed each jewel on the ground. He was then directed to separate the silver nuggets from the turquoise gems. The silver nuggets represented seedling offspring of the third season (generation). The twelve turquoise jewels represented seedling offspring of the fourth season. The time had come for Grayhorse to entrust the keeping and protection of the jewels into the care of the special son. Only he or the fourth son should have possession of the jewels until they were to be passed to the heir of the next generation.

After the rise and fall of four quarters of light and darkness the jewels were to be released to the selected son. In preparation to receive the anointing, the fourth son was to engage in four periods of fasting, one fasting period per quarter. Grayhorse was to also engage in one four day period of fasting in preparation to release the jewels, anoint the son and pass the legacy. During the periods of fasting there were to also be periods of meditation at dawn and dusk. They were to see guidance and direction from the Great Spirit for their life cycle. When the jewels were transferred, they were to be placed in a safe, protective, secret place until further directions were given by the totem spirit. Then as suddenly as the Spirit of the White Buffalo appeared it vanished.

Stonewall stayed in the boat, astonished and afraid. He asked his father many questions about what would happen to him and if he would also receive the guidance of a totem spirit. He worried about what would happen to him if he received the legacy not being the fourth son. Grayhorse explained to him that it would be the decision of the Great Spirit. Grayhorse told Stonewall that if he lived his life close enough and should build a relationship strong enough with the Great Spirit, and if he would meditate for guidance and direction, the Great Spirit would listen to him and provide the guidance that he would need, maybe even give him a totem spirit.

This was all so new and awesome for Stonewall. When they returned to the farm, Stonewall wanted to share these experiences with his brothers Dave and Arthur, but then he thought and was reminded that no one was to know. Stonewall kept these secrets in his mind and heart and discussed them only with his father. Ellen noticed a change in Stonewall's behavior. She also noticed a secrecy about Grayhorse. She wanted to ask some questions but she respected Grayhorse's traditions and practices and chose not to interfere.

The Third Vision of the White Buffalo

For some unknown reason Grayhorse felt different today. There was a yearning inside of him that continued to pull at his heart to return to Big Spring Bottom. His steps had grown slower so he called Willie early to take him to Big Spring in the wagon. Willie agreed that they should enter the cave at the north entrance because only a few people lived in that area and it was not likely that they would be noticed. No one knew that they had left the farm. They left a little past sunrise and reached the cave around midmorning. Willie was instructed to wait at the entrance while Grayhorse went further along the shadow path. There was a familiar place not far from the entrance where Grayhorse used to go to pay vows to the Great Spirit. As he drew closer to the place he could hear water dripping against the rocks. This hidden waterway was the mother source of the beautiful spring at Big Spring Bottom. The residents used the spring for fresh water. A larger drip a little farther ahead had cut a path to the outside and emptied into what was called North Quarry Spring. Quarry Spring was a favorite swimming hole for the youth of Quarry Town.

Grayhorse took his water drum and flute pipe and began to chant rhythms and play his favorite tune for his worship ritual to the Great Spirit. He reached inside his vest for the deerskin pouch that was carefully protecting the precious jewels and clenched them tightly in his hand. Grayhorse had been there only a short time when he was distracted by a swift cool wind that blew across his face from the east side of the cave. Grayhorse looked up at the ceiling of the cave near the east wall and observed the Spirit of the White Buffalo near the ceiling. The image was just above the area where the water was seeping through the wall. This time the image was closer and clearer than it had ever been before. The totem spirit got Grayhorse's attention by calling his name sternly. Grayhorse was startled because the totem spirit had never appeared in this manner before or with this kind of forceful behavior, or with such a stern voice. It was almost as if the spirit was angry or displeased.

The White Buffalo called out to Grayhorse, "Grayhorse? Listen to the voice that brings wisdom for your family legacy!" The legacy consisted of three calls:

1. The first call was love and respect. The family members were decreed to build a relationship with the Great Spirit. Man is to live in harmony with all of nature including the Great Spirit.
2. The second call was that the family of your people (Cherokee) was to be perpetuated through the lineage of Grayhorse through the second, third and fourth generations. This legacy is to be fulfilled through the seedlings of Stonewall, Sully, and Sully's first born. It is to be continued by the seedlings of the fourth generation from Sully's first born. This message was a confirmation for Grayhorse that Stonewall was being confirmed by the Great Spirit to receive the anointing for the entrustment and protection of the family legacy and the precious jewels. In order for the lineage to continue through Sully it had to come also through Stonewall even through he was not the fourth son. It is to begin with the twelve seedlings of the second season, the seedling offspring of Stonewall. Then it is to be carried by the seedling offspring of Sully in the third season. Then the twelve seedling offspring of Sully's first born will bear the entrustment at which time the legacy will fall upon its rightful heir, the fourth son.
3. The third call was that four character spirits upon which the moral strength of the family must be anchored must be sustained and passed along and also entrusted to the seedling jewels of the fourth season. These character spirits are:
   Wisdom / Knowledge
   Passion / Love
   Integrity / Fidelity
   Dignity / Pride

The legacy will be lost if the seedling jewels are not protected and nurtured. The spirit of Grayhorse will not rest or be at peace if the legacy is lost or the family is disconnected. When family relationships are broken, the family will scatter and the spirit of Grayhorse will vanish. Individuals are responsible for their own behavior but the behavior of the family is the responsibility of the elders. Family behavior is determined by the decision and behavior of the family elders.

Grayhorse then asked the Spirit of the White Buffalo if the lost legacy could be retrieved and if the disconnected family could be reunited so that the seedling jewels could be saved. The White Buffalo responded, "Even after your spirit has taken flight it will not be at rest or at peace as long as there is dissension, brokenness, or disconnection in the family. The legacy will have to be retrieved and entrusted into the hands of one of the protective jewels in the family. The twelve jewels of the lost generation must be found and given a rightful place in the family history and the family lineage. Remember, the legacy must be carried through the male gender and entrusted to the fourth son. If there is no fourth son then it must be carried by the fourth child."

Grayhorse now understood the approval for Stonewall because Stonewall was the fourth child.

Just as Grayhorse started to ask another question the totem spirit disappeared. Grayhorse turned to walk away when Stonewall's voice called out to him. He had entered the cave by the Big Spring entrance and from a distance he had quietly watched the encounter between his father and the Spirit of the White Buffalo.

"Where are you? Grayhorse?" asked Stonewall. "Everyone at the farm has been worried about you! No one knew that you and Willie were coming here today. Neither you nor Willie have been seen or heard from since sunrise. Mother Ellen is worried sick about your breathing and heart problems, not to mention your arthritis, many things could happen to you!"

"There's no need to worry," answered Grayhorse. "The Great Spirit takes care of me. Anyway, I need not say to you whether I am here or there, I'm the father, remember? I only need to make a clear reason to Ellen. I'm your father, Stonewall, I'm the daddy."

With that answer, Grayhorse joined Willie in the wagon at the north cave entrance. Stonewall crawled into the back of the wagon to hitch a ride around and down the hill from the Big Spring entrance. He needed to retrieve his horse, Sonny and make his way back to the farm.

On the way home, there was not much conversation in the wagon. Willie didn't ask questions and Grayhorse sat quietly, trying to put together all of the pieces of today's experiences that the White Buffalo had revealed to him.

As they reached the front gate, Ellen was waiting for them under the branches of the willow tree. She had been standing there for a long while, waiting for any sight of Willie and Grayhorse. When she saw them, she walked up to her bedroom, no questions asked. She had wanted to send her oldest son, Robert, to look for his father but somehow she knew that his disappearance would have some meaning for the family legacy and some relationship to the Spirit of the White Buffalo. When Stonewall, Grayhorse's favorite son and the fourth child, had volunteered to search for his father, Ellen readily agreed.

The Fourth Vision of the White Buffalo

Rain had set in for the evening and continued unceasingly during the night. Heavy thunder and frequent lightning had startled the horses. Only a few months ago, Misty had died following a severe lightning storm. No one was sure if she was scared to death by the lightning, or if she was just old and worn out from her other illness causing her heart to stop. In any case, things just got to be too much for the old warrior. She was found one morning lying very still inside her stall. Old age, arthritis in her hip and legs, and a change of temperament in her personality along with a sudden case of pneumonia caused her to change into an unhappy animal. Misty even lost patience with Grayhorse during her last days. She and Grayhorse had been family since she was a young foal. Her death had affected Grayhorse so much that he himself had become selfish, stubborn, unhappy, short-tempered and hard to get along with.

As the rain poured heavily, Ellen watched Grayhorse from the bedroom window. This was something that she had learned to do now that he was growing older and had sometimes wandered out the front gate into the woods, sometimes staying away for a long time. One morning, for instance, he and Willie rode into Big Spring unannounced to Ellen or anyone else in the family. Grayhorse was dripping wet, yet he played his water drum and flute pipe loud and long. He danced a ritualistic dance while he paid his vows to the Great Spirit. His voice was strong as he chanted louder than ever in the rain. Then he began to play beautifully on his pipe.

Ellen listened carefully. He was not playing the tune that he usually played for worship. Instead, he was playing his and Ellen's special song. This was a melody that he learned to play as a child when he first made his flute. It made Ellen very happy to hear their song, yet it saddened her heart to think that it also carried a hidden message for Grayhorse. His steps had grown slower and his body was much weaker. His health was more fragile.

53

Grayhorse's days were getting shorter. Ellen realized that it would not be too many more of those days before Grayhorse would be on his spirit journey.

Suddenly, Grayhorse stopped playing, as if someone had pushed a button or as if something startled him. He was staring up at the sky with both arms lifted high and he immediately turned to face the East, the direction of the rising sun, announcing a new day. The rain continued to pour. Almost instantly, a rainbow appeared, encircling the oak tree, reaching above its tallest branches and touching the earth from point to point. Grayhorse understood from previous visions that the appearance of a rainbow symbolized the fulfillment of a promise from the Great Spirit. Grayhorse thought immediately of the precious jewels. He lifted them from the secure deerskin pouch that he had tucked away in the inside pocket of his vest, clenched them in his hands and again lifted his arms upward to the sky. He asked the Great Spirit for protection and a good life for each of the seedlings of his lineage. Then he counted them to be certain that they were all still there, three silver nuggets and twelve turquoise gems.

As he lifted his arms, in the midst of a mist of heavy rain, he could see a shadow nestled inside the arch of the rainbow. It was the Spirit of the White Buffalo, whose voice was soft with passion as he spoke to Grayhorse concerning his health and passing the legacy while he still had ample use of his mental faculties. Again, Grayhorse was instructed to pass the legacy to the fourth child, Stonewall, instead of to the fourth son, Matty. He was also instructed to pass the jewels along with the legacy. Grayhorse was warned not to delay the passing of the jewels and the legacy so that they would not fall into the hands of someone who had not been sensitive to the meaning of the legacy and would not properly protect the jewels.

"It is not good to wait much longer," said the White Buffalo. "Your only reason not to release the jewels and legacy would be a selfish one. That reason would be because you have enjoyed the power of overseeing the jewels and wish them to remain in your care. You would also like to remain in your protective role. Do not become selfish, but trust your son. It is the choice of the Great Spirit."

As the spirit vanished, the rain stopped. Ellen's voice called out from the kitchen, asking her daughter, Minnie, to tell Grayhorse to help administer a curative potion to the bedridden Martha Sue, who had been ill for at least three weeks and was thought by Dr. Hatten to have had a severe stroke. In his words, "Death had set in." She carried a deep cough with a strange rhythm in her breathing. Ellen had been giving Martha Sue frequent doses of a mixture of herbs that Grayhorse had gathered while on his walk in the woods. It was supposed to help her breathing but recently, nothing seemed to bring her any relief. Before Grayhorse could gather his belongings from under the oak tree and get upstairs to her room, Martha Sue had closed her eyes and quietly slipped away.

It took three days to prepare Martha Sue for burial. After three days, her body was returned to the big house by the mortician and she laid at stake for wake for a two-day period of mourning. She was then carried to the church at Big Spring for a funeral. A slave family from the Pendleton farm wanted to bury her in their way with other family members who had been traded into slavery at the Pendleton farm.

Everyone in the family at the big house attended Martha Sue's funeral and burial. When they returned to the farm, Willie took the horses to the barn, Ellen went to her bedroom, and Grayhorse sat heavily in the rocking chair in the bedroom, watching Ellen change out of her funeral clothes. He remembered the days of discomfort when he would be present in the room while Ellen undressed. He sighed and thought of how comfortable she was now with him present. He then jolted his memory and thought of what he had to do next. He had already met with Stonewall. Stonewall needed to begin his days of fasting and Grayhorse had to release the jewels and pass the legacy. While thinking of how he would go about this responsibility and just when he would begin, he fell asleep in the rocking chair.

The hour was growing late; Ellen shook him and insisted that he go to bed. He arose, talked under his breath about how he would approach Stonewall while he dressed for bed in a long flannel nightshirt and a nightcap. "Good night, Ellen," whispered Grayhorse. He snuggled next to her under the covers. Ellen answered not a word, she was fast asleep.

6

Keeper of Legacy

Now that both Willie and Grayhorse had grown old, six of the sons had taken wives and moved into Quarry Town. Arthur had married but continued to live on the farm. Stonewall, Otha and Harmon were also still living at the farm. Minnie and Belle had both married but spent most of their time at the big house to assist Mother Ellen with chores. Things had changed in Quarry Town and the Gray family had dispersed and settled into an area identified as "The Hill" where most of the Negro families resided. Most of the men worked on surrounding farms. The ladies either stayed home to take care of the children or worked as nannies or domestic workers for the white families.

I remember my Gray relatives so well. When I, Cheyenne, grew up in Quarry Town, I knew that these sons of Grayhorse and Mother Ellen and my Aunt Minnie were my grandfather Stonewall's brothers and sister. There were so many "Gray" offspring and we all were strongly bonded as a family. Everyone in Quarry Town just referred to us as "The Grays." It was not yet clear to me as a child growing up in this small town just how special we really were. The Grays were not rich and famous or well educated but they certainly were considered by the community to be well bred, respectable, intelligent, courteous, hard working people. Even in school or community activities as a child, if the Gray children were involved they almost always left an imprint at the top as winners or pace setters in leadership. This became a family value and a trademark of the Gray family that was expected.

The Gray men were of stately stature with beautiful hair and well-defined features. They were good husbands and reared their children in the fear of God with fine moral values. Like Mother Ellen, Minnie was an elegant lady, always well groomed and well dressed. She was recognized for her beautiful signature wide-brimmed hats that she always wore; she was looked upon as elegant and dignified, full of pride, and was a leading lady at the Quarry Town Baptist Church that later became known as the Shepherd Street Baptist Church. I remember so well the family bonding with my uncles Dave, Arthur, Otis and Otha, men of strong character and much wisdom.

The offspring of Grayhorse and Mother Ellen were:

Children of Grayhorse and Mother Ellen	Spouse
Robert Gray (1857)	Alice
Belle Gray (1860)	John Walls
Harvey James Gray (1864)	Allie
Stonewall Jackson Gray (1866)	Ida Hollowell
(Our grandfather—Roaring Bull)	(Our grandmother)
Matty Gray (1868)	McGoodwin (daughter)
Dave Gray (1871)	Sarah
John Gray (1875)	Jane Lemon
Minnie Gray (1876)	Will Hollowell
(Married into our grandmother Ida's family, the Hollowells)	
Arthur Gray (1883)	Daisey
Otis Gray (1885)	Katie
Harmon Gray (1887)	(Not Married)
Otha Gray (1888)	(Not Married)

Identifying the Fourth Son

Now that Grayhorse seldom left his room, Ellen realized that his illness was bothering him more. Ellen had carried in her heart that Grayhorse had all this time actually miscalculated the lineage of their fourth son. But Stonewall, Grayhorse's favorite and the fourth child, was not the fourth son. By birth lineage, Matty was still the fourth son. Matty had not been groomed to receive the legacy and it was doubtful that he could be trusted to protect the precious jewels. He had not followed the mentoring of Grayhorse and he had not learned the practices and traditions of the Cherokee people. Ellen's choice continued to be Robert, their first-born son but since the legacy followed the teachings of the Cherokee society, the choice was not hers to make. She understood and supported Grayhorse's strong will to follow the power of the number four.

Ellen entered the bedroom to discuss this dilemma with Grayhorse. She was afraid that some evil omen might befall their family if they failed to follow precisely the directions that had been revealed in the visions by the Spirit of the White Buffalo. When mention was made that the blessing should be bestowed upon Matty, the fourth son, Grayhorse became outraged. He accused Ellen of being prejudiced against Stonewall, initially in favor of their first son, Robert, and now Matty, further accusing Ellen of creating broken relationships in the family; and he firmly declared that he had in no way misunderstood the meaning of the vision. He reaffirmed that protection of the jewels and the legacy were both ordered and selected at birth to be passed to Stonewall and unless Grayhorse was directed by his totem spirit to follow a different message Stonewall would receive the blessing.

Ellen left the room disturbed and angry with Grayhorse because of his stubbornness. She was very worried that both the visions and their messages were being misunderstood. Would this mean that such a beautiful family legacy and the precious future seedlings offspring would be lost and become disconnected? After all, these precious jewels were her seedlings also and she had a maternal right as a grandmother to see that they were protected, in spite of Grayhorse and his stubbornness.

This confrontation with Ellen also upset Grayhorse. His temperature and blood pressure became elevated. He stayed in bed, not speaking to anyone for the next several days. It was time to begin preparations to transfer the legacy. Grayhorse began his preparation by fasting and refusing solid food. He accepted only intakes of liquid. Grayhorse had already completed two quarter periods of fasting and was now in the final fasting period for the third quarter. It never left his mind that Stonewall was to receive the blessing. If not, surely there would be another visit from the White Buffalo to reveal this to him before it was too late. Nothing had changed and three quarters had passed.

Before Grayhorse completed his final period of fasting, he became very ill. Grayhorse sent a message for Stonewall to come to his bedside. Before Stonewall could be located, Ellen also sent a message to Matty to come and visit his father. Matty was not interested in the legacy and had not grown close to his father. Matty was now more aware of the miscalculation of the fourth son. Stonewall's visit to Grayhorse was delayed because he had not received his father's message. Meanwhile, Matty came and sat beside his father's bedside for seven days. Grayhorse spoke not one word to Matty concerning the transfer or protection of the jewels and the legacy. Matty sought diligently to keep his father comfortable and meditated on his behalf.

When Matty left to return to his home in Quarry Town, Grayhorse again sent for Stonewall to come to his bedside. This time, Willie went to Trigg County to search for Stonewall. When Willie found him, he delivered his father's request. Stonewall joined Willie in the wagon and they returned with haste to the farm. Ellen was disturbed to learn that Grayhorse had not mentioned to Matty that this legacy entrustment belonged to him and was actually being passed to his brother Stonewall. The legacy had to be in place in order to reach its final fulfillment and pass through the lineage of Sully's first-born son.

Stonewall Receives the Jewels

Stonewall entered his father's bedroom and discovered Grayhorse lying very still with his eyes closed. He called out to his father, using his Cherokee name. "Grayhorse, can you hear me? It's Stonewall, your son, I am answering your call to come to you."

Slowly, Grayhorse opened his eyes. "Stonewall, is it you, my son? What took you so long to get here?" his voice was weakening.

"It is me, Father," Stonewall replied. "Willie found me and we came as quickly as we could."

"But I sent for you days ago," answered Grayhorse.

"But I only received your message today, no one told me or came for me days ago."

Grayhorse did not respond to Stonewall. In his heart he knew why Stonewall had been delayed. The message had been given to Ellen, and she had sent for Matty to come visit his father instead of Stonewall. It was Ellen's move to have Grayhorse bestow the blessing on Matty rather than Stonewall.

"It is time for you to take charge of the precious jewels that represent the future offspring of my lineage," said Grayhorse. "Look between the bed spring and the feather bed mattress that I am resting on. There you will find the deerskin pouch with three silver nuggets and twelve turquoise stones."

Stonewall followed his father's directions. He felt for the pouch and found it nestled near the center of the bed between the bedspring and the mattress, just as his father had said.

"Count them," ordered Grayhorse. "Be certain that they are all there.

See that not a single stone has been damaged. Are they all there? Are they all well protected?"

Stonewall answered, "Yes, Father," to each question. Stonewall had emptied the jewels on the bed and they had fallen near Grayhorse's hand.

Grayhorse picked up two or three of the jewels and clenched them tightly in his hand. Then he allowed them to fall gently through his fingers onto the bed. He caressed each stone lovingly and ordered Stonewall to put them all back into the pouch. Then firmly he gave the pouch to Stonewall. Stonewall gripped his father's hand tightly with both of his.

Grayhorse then directed Stonewall to come closer to him. Grayhorse hung the deerskin pouch firmly and securely around Stonewall's neck. "These jewels are precious to our family legacy," he said to Stonewall. "They represent our future seedling offspring. The silver nuggets represent offspring that will come through my lineage in the third season. The twelve turquoise jewels represent seedling offspring in the second season and the fourth season that will come through your lineage. Protect them, keep them near you, close to your heart. Do not release them to anyone, anywhere. They must become a part of who you are, blood of your blood and flesh of your flesh. When the time is right for them to be entrusted to the offspring of another season the Great Spirit will send you a message. Either by your own totem spirit or by some other force from the Great Spirit."

Then Grayhorse closed his eyes and fell asleep quietly. Stonewall sat silently by his father's bedside for a while longer. He then walked over and slightly opened a window to allow some air to freshen the room, closed the door and walked quietly down the stairs.

Stonewall sat quietly in the swing on the front porch. He placed the pouch hanging around his neck inside his shirt. This, he thought, will be a dwelling place for the precious jewels. He remembered that his father had collected them from streams along the trails as he made his way to and from Big Spring on at least three separate journeys. For every jewel that he collected, it was as if the Great Spirit had directed him to that special place. Each stone had a different shape, color and fossil imprint. This implied to Stonewall that every single offspring represented by one of these jewels would also be very special and very different. Before leaving his father's bedroom, Stonewall had held his father's hand and said a prayer asking for protection of the jewels and for the precious offspring that were to follow. As he arose to leave the front porch, he quietly murmured a prayer. Grayhorse had made no mention to Stonewall that he was not the fourth son.

When Stonewall left the porch, Ellen had made her way around from the garden and was waiting for him under the branches of the willow tree, so that they could share what had taken place between her son and his father. He gave his mother a loving hug and arm in arm they returned to the house by the back door. They went to the kitchen table where Belle had put on a pot of coffee and water for tea. As his mother tightly held on to his arm, Stonewall made a solemn promise to himself that the jewels belonged around his neck and that he would never remove them again. They would remain next to his heart both day and night, even when he slept. He hung the pouch around his neck and tucked it inside his shirt so that he would not have to discuss or explain to anyone where the pouch came from or what was inside.

Stonewall Receives the Legacy

When Stonewall completed the final quarter of fasting, Grayhorse again requested that he come to his bedside. Minnie had lit a scented candle to freshen the aroma in the room. This time Stonewall came with haste because he realized the importance of the legacy to the family and knew that his father's days were growing short. It seemed as if Grayhorse's spirit journey was being delayed until Stonewall had completed his days of preparation to receive the entrustment. Grayhorse was propped up in bed with pillows behind his back, waiting for Stonewall to arrive. When Stonewall entered the room, he went straight to his father, sat on the side of the bed, and reached for his father's hand. Grayhorse reached out to check to see if Stonewall was wearing the pouch that had been placed around his neck.

"Son, are you ready now to receive the entrustment for our family legacy?"

"I am, Father," answered Stonewall.

In a weak voice, Grayhorse took his time and spoke slowly, outlining the legacy as it had been given to him in four separate visions by the Spirit of the White Buffalo. As Grayhorse spoke, an image of the White Buffalo appeared on the East Wall of the bedroom. The spirit did not speak to Grayhorse as he once more explained the legacy for Stonewall, step by step. Since the totem spirit was in their presence, Grayhorse was certain that it would speak in disapproval if Stonewall were not to receive the blessing. When Grayhorse finished, the image of the White Buffalo disappeared. Grayhorse then asked to be turned on his right side, facing the East window, closed his eyes, and slept for the rest of the day.

When Stonewall left the room, he made his way down to the oak tree. He carved two petroglyphs on the trunk of the tree commemorating the day that he was entrusted with the jewels and the day that he actually received the entrustment for the family legacy. When Stonewall finished the carvings, he knelt under the branches of the tree, facing the East, direction of the sunrise, and offered thanks and praise to the Great Spirit for the blessings that he had received. Stonewall also prayed that his father would have a quiet spirit journey. Stonewall had noticed that his father was sleeping more; his breathing was more difficult and it had been over four weeks since he had been out of bed. His appetite was poor and he was surviving mostly on liquids. Stonewall was saddened and concerned about his father.

As Stonewall arose to return to the big house, he noticed Mother Ellen watching from the window and his brothers Otha and Harmon, following him. Could it be that they were watching him because of his strange behavior? Stonewall let his brothers know that he was aware of their presence by ordering them to help with chores that needed to be done for the animals. Minnie went to the bedroom to carry her father a bowl of soup. She found him in a deep sleep so she quietly left the room, closed the door behind her and carried the bowl of soup back to the kitchen.

Stonewall's Blessing

There was still a final step to be taken to complete the transition of the legacy. Grayhorse needed to anoint his son with a blessing to seal the process. When Stonewall went in to be with his father, Mother Ellen, Minnie, and Belle, Harmon, Otha, Robert, Dave and Arthur went also. Grayhorse spoke quietly and announced to his family that this blessing was being bestowed on Stonewall and that he had already received the jewels and the transfer of the family legacy. As Grayhorse gave the blessing, he referred to Stonewall by his Cherokee name, Roaring Bull. Grayhorse explained that his totem spirit, the Spirit of the White Buffalo, had appeared during the fourth vision and that this blessing had been approved, that Stonewall had been selected by the Great Spirit, and neither he nor Mother Ellen would intervene into the spiritual process for the purpose of changing it.

Ellen passed Grayhorse his water drum. He called Roaring Bull closer to his bedside. He placed his right hand on Roaring Bull's forehead and his left hand over Roaring Bull's heart. Grayhorse chanted a lengthy prayer for the protection of the jewels, the legacy and the guidance of Roaring Bull. Then Grayhorse shared a bowl of stew prepared from a mixture of medicinal herbs that Minnie had gathered and prepared following her father's directions. He sipped a hearty portion. The rest he gave to Stonewall and ordered him to drink it all. Grayhorse closed the ritual with a melodic chant accompanied by a melody on his flute pipe. In spite of his poor breathing, he played as if the Great Spirit lengthened his breath control. The melody came through clear and perfect. Suddenly, a cool breeze passed over both he and Roaring Bull.

Grayhorse recognized that this was the Spirit of the White Buffalo. A prism of colors encircled the light from a burning candle on the table by the window. It reflected as the rainbow had appeared that day over the waterfall. This action was a confirmation for Grayhorse that the action that he had taken had been received and approved by the Great Spirit. Grayhorse announced to the family that he was tired and wanted them to leave the room. One by one they left quietly. Belle was the last one to leave, adjusting her father's pillows before she left the room.

Mother Ellen waited for Stonewall as they left the room. She paused to let him understand that her love for him was strong and unwavering and that she would support him in his endeavors to maintain the legacy and protect the jewels. Stonewall did not answer but quickly hugged his mother, turned and walked away from her. He walked to the barn, whistled for his horse, Sonny, and took a ride down the trail to the riverbank where he could be alone. He had often come along with his father to visit this spot when he wanted to think, be alone or to meditate. Stonewall wanted to think about his new responsibilities and how he would have to change his life in order to meet this challenge. Following not far behind were his brothers, Harmon and Otha. When they observed that Stonewall was meditating, they left and returned to the farm. Time passed quickly and Stonewall stayed longer than he had planned. All of nature seemed to engulf him. He felt close to the Great Spirit. He departed from that place knowing that he was not being led by the Great Spirit and hoping that someday he would have his own totem spirit. This was an answer to the prayers that his father had offered on his behalf.

7

Grayhorse's Spirit Journey

Ellen woke up in the middle of the night, got out of bed and walked across the hall to the second bedroom where Grayhorse had been staying since he had become very ill. It had become a routine for her to check up on him about every hour for the last several days. The family was keeping close watch and someone was staying in his room around the clock since Dr. Hatten made his last visit. Dr. Hatten had announced to the family that death stages had set in and death could come at any time. Ellen wanted to take care of him in the Cherokee way as he approached his spirit journey.

Their sons Robert and Roaring Bull had made a fast trip to the reservation in Tennessee to request assistance from the council elders in preparation for this funeral ceremony and burial. Roaring Bull dressed in some of his father's Cherokee clothes to make the journey. The loud wailing chants that could be heard coming from Grayhorse's bedroom came from one of the Cherokee council elders, Rising Deer. He had accompanied the sons back to the farm. He was wailing loudly in the Cherokee way to announce the crossing over of Grayhorse's spirit.

Ellen entered the room quickly, hoping for a few minutes alone with Grayhorse. Her sons asked her to wait until the elder had completed his ritual so that the communicating spirit would not be interrupted. The other children and Willie were quickly informed. Soon everyone had gathered at the farm. When the elder finished his chant Grayhorse breathed his final breath. Weeping quietly Ellen walked over to her husband's bedside and closed his eyelids, kissed him on his cheek and said goodbye.

Burial

Arrangements for a Cherokee burial were already in progress. The sons and neighbors from the adjoining farms had gathered down by the old oak tree with shovels and picks to dig a grave for his body to be laid to rest. In keeping with the Cherokee tradition, the burial had to take place before sundown. He died at early morning so only a few hours remained to prepare the ceremony and perform the burial rites. The spirit journey was a four-day journey.

Following directions from the council elder the sons washed and dressed the body in his finest Cherokee clothes and ornaments including his deerskin vest, turquoise armband, and copper earrings and wampum belt. His deerskin moccasins were placed in the grave next to him along with his wooden bowls and eating utensils, water drum, flute pipe, dream maker, bow and arrow and calumet. Grayhorse's body was placed in a fetal position and wrapped in a light, soft, cheesecloth and then wrapped again with light tree bark. His head was placed facing the West because that was the direction of the spirit journey.

The Cherokee elder, Rising Deer, included much music and dance in the funeral ceremony. Native Americans never undertook a ceremony without the involvement of music. Scarcely anything depicts the Native American more elegantly than his dancing. The dance that was rendered manifested all that he was, his attitude toward life, his faith, his experiences and his joy. Before covering the body, Rising Deer administered the ceremony underneath the old oak tree. The family gathered sorrowfully around to mourn the death of their father. Rising Deer performed the Dance of the Ghost, which some may associate with the appearance of the Northern Lights. It was a ritual dance believed to assist the deceased in crossing over the great gap between this World and the Next World. The grave was then covered with thin bark and rush mats. Tearfully, Roaring Bull stepped forward and began to carve a petroglyph on the oak tree to mark the crossing over of his father's spirit.

Feast of the Dead

Friends from Big Spring Bottom and neighbors from Quarry Town, where the children lived, brought much food to prepare a mega feast. In the Cherokee society this feast was known as "The Feast of the Dead." In Ellen's African culture, it was referred to as the "Funeral Meal." In the Cherokee society the host village would have resurrected the bodies of those persons who had died since the last feast and reinterred them and other remains. Ellen had requested that this procedure be suspended and that the celebration be only for Grayhorse. A common grace was offered and the large buffet meal was served to family and friends. During the celebration, everyone participating in the meal, also participated in the dancing, games of skill and music. These activities served as qualifying condolences to the family. Visitors also brought gifts of food and finance to the family. These gifts were to assist the family with funeral expense.

Mourning

When the guests dispersed and went home Ellen and the children sat at the kitchen table with Rising Deer and discussed the period of mourning that was to follow Grayhorse's burial. Rising Deer began by reminding Ellen that the mourning period for her was to last at least four years. If she chose to remarry, she would have to wait that long to be accepted in the Cherokee society. He then instructed them in the following Cherokee practices:

1. Some believe that souls remain in the world after death (perhaps living in a spiritual form) and assisted friends in times of danger and disorder. In order for the spirit of Grayhorse to reach peace and be at rest, the legacy and the precious jewels entrusted to the custodial care of his son must be maintained. The perpetuation of his lineage must be continued. His spirit would not rest if the legacy is lost or if family relationships are disconnected or broken. His spirit will continue to appear and bring messages via his totem, the Spirit of the White Buffalo.
2. Others believe that the souls of brave woodsmen and warriors go to the campground of eternal bliss and carnal pleasure, while dissolute spirits continue to wander in darkness, exposed to ravages of wolves, bears and other flesh-eaters.
3. From spring (maple syrup camp time) to winter (deer hunt time)—from childhood to old age, the world is filled with spirits that control the world, provide live games for hunters and affect the healers.

4. Religious thoughts were focused on placating these super naturals so that family members could satisfy their elementary economic needs and enjoy death and a long life.

Remember that symbolism was a major part of Grayhorse's life and spirit. To Native Americans symbolism is more than an emblem. It conveys meaning, its color, shape and design reflect the life of an individual of the Cherokee clan. It has a hidden meaning. Native American Symbolism extended into every aspect of Grayhorse's life. Myths, legends, artifacts and actions reveal these meanings. The elder told the family "Maintain and nurture your petroglyph tree, it retains your family history, the hidden messages of your family and reflects your world."

The elder then left the house by way of the kitchen. He mounted his horse at the front gate, paid his respects to Grayhorse, resting under the oak tree, then headed up the trail leading to Trigg and Christian Counties. He wanted to cover a long distance of the journey back to the reservation before sundown. As the family left to return to their homes in Quarry Town, Ellen made her way down to the old oak tree to spend a few minutes alone with Grayhorse. . . . The girls stayed at the farm longer than Ellen had anticipated. They wanted to help Mother Ellen get settled. Harmon, Otha and Roaring Bull continued to live at the farm.

Only a few weeks had passed when Willie walked down to the kitchen to speak with Ellen. He was carrying a suitcase in each hand, dressed in his Sunday clothes. Ellen set her coffee cup on the table and stood up to see where Willie was headed. Surprisingly, Willie announced to Ellen that his family from St. Louis was waiting for him at the front gate. They had come to take him away to spend his last days with them. He had grown old and farm labor had become more difficult for him to handle. Arthritis had settled in his knees and hampered his ability to work or even walk as well as he used to. It bothered him to even take care of the animals.

His sister's children had come for him and Willie was ready to go. Ellen said, "Willie, you will always be a real part of this family. This place will always be your home. I understand your longing to be with your family. I yearn for my mother and my sister, Adeline. So, go while you have the chance to go."

With these words, Ellen gave Willie a big hug, held him by the shoulders, looked into his eyes and said goodbye, saddened when she thought of how much he would be missed at the big house.

"Thank you, Miss Ellie, Thank you. I hope to come back this way some day. If so, you can just know that I will be by to see you."

Without looking back, Willie then turned and walked straight through the front gate but not without first pausing by the oak tree to pay his final respect to the spirit of Grayhorse. Ellen remembered how Martha Sue and Willie had taken care of her when she was a child and how they protected her when her mother left the farm. They had always been there for her during hard times. With tears in her eyes, Ellen slowly made her way back to the kitchen.

It was time for Dave and his wife Sarah to return to their home in Quarry Town. It was obvious to them that Mother Ellen was very lonely since the loss of Grayhorse. Dave could not bear to leave her this way. After a consultation with Ellen it was decided that she would come to Quarry Town to live with him and Sarah.

Reluctantly, Ellen agreed to move in with them. She packed her clothes, left the farm, and only returned when she wanted to visit the grave of Grayhorse. She turned the farm and all of its possessions over to her children. One snowy morning in midwinter, Ellen was seated in her favorite rocking chair. Sarah went to call her down for breakfast and found her just sitting there with her eyes closed, her hands folded and a smile on her face. She too had taken her spirit journey and her spirit had crossed over the great gap. It was only fitting and right that she be buried under the old oak tree at the farm, next to Grayhorse. Once again, Mother Ellen and Grayhorse were together. Roaring Bull carved one more petroglyph on the trunk of the old tree. This time it marked the crossing over of Mother Ellen. Mother Ellen, elegant, proud, and a woman of dignity. Mother Ellen was truly the mother of the "GRAY" family.

Voice of Cheyenne

Since I was not blessed to be born when my great-grandparents Grayhorse and Mother Ellen lived, I am saddened when I ponder over all of the rich experiences that I could have learned from them and all of the love that Mother Ellen would have showered on me. I am in awe to realize that my life was represented by one of the precious silver nuggets that Grayhorse carried in his protective pouch and for which he prayed to the Great Spirit. It is so special to me having grown up knowing my grandfa-

68

ther Stonewall's siblings and my dear uncles Otis, Otha, Arthur, Robert, and Dave. Aunt Minnie was so special to me and I love her even more now that I know the real story of her parents and my great-grandparents, how much they were in love, how they conquered their struggles, and molded the legacy for a family that would last for an eternity.

May Their Spirits Forever Be at Rest,

Cheyenne

PART II

West Wind

The Spirit of Grayhorse

Turbulent Winds, Smothering Fire

"Infinity of a Promise"
Gift of Cheyenne

Promises are everlasting, timeless, enduring, eternal.
> They elevate your thinking. They illuminate your mind and stroke the soul.

> They create hope and faith for new beginnings.
> Promises are binding and forever.

Promises are like rainbows, colorful, encircling the heart.
> They carry harmonic overtones, never fading, stretching the soul.
> They are contracts, agreements, securing the mind.
> They are not confined, fleeting or ephemeral.
> They are pure, warm and real.
> Promises are constant and forever.

Take your vows and your oaths with confidence and sincerity.
> Make your word your guidepost, dependable, and trustworthy.
> Keep your word steadfast and steady so that it symbolizes your character.
> When you send out your word, keep it pure, unbounded, and clean.
> Plight your word with honor . . . it symbolizes you.

Promises assign you a name; they identify what you stand for.
> Broken promises break relationships with family, comrades, neighbors, companions,
> > And foes.
Avoid making false promises; promises that fail.
> Broken promises are like purple rain clouds, creating sadness, fear, anger,
> > Mistrust, and hurt.

Promise only that which you can guarantee.

SO

Cover your promises with infinity, truth, and lots of rainbows;
Season them with sunbeams;
Make them eternal and forever.

THEN

Cover your immeasurable blessings that float through windows of joy;
Laughter never ending

WHEN

Promises are real and forever.
(The Wisdom of Grayhorse)

8

Words Untold

Brother's Fury

Roaring Bull was beginning to understand why his brothers, Harmon and Otha, had been following and watching him so closely. They had also been watching their brother, Matty, whenever he came to the farm. Matty had been staying at the farm for at least two weeks. His behavior did not seem to be the same. His conversations carried a strange overtone and his behavior seemed unusual. He had avoided any close contact with Roaring Bull. He would divert most of his conversations to Arthur or Harmon. He always wanted to talk about how things were going at the farm and what had taken place to protect the family legacy. He had even mentioned to Robert and to Dave that maybe it would be better to sell the family farm and divide the assets equally among the Grayhorse children.

Otha had also noticed that during Matty's stay this time, he had not paused, even once, under the oak tree to pay respect to his father, Grayhorse, and Mother Ellen's spirit. Overtones of bitterness peppered Matty's speech and vengeance was revealed in his eyes. Whenever Roaring Bull would enter the room where Matty was or come into Matty's presence at any time, without speaking a word, Matty would leave the room in haste. Harmon and Otha were certain that fury was burning within the hearts of their two brothers and that it would not be much longer before an outrage of fire spirit would break loose. They were certain that these bitter feelings were being fueled by jealousy over the birthright of the precious jewels and the entrustment of the family legacy bestowed by Grayhorse upon his sixth son when it should have been bestowed upon Matty, the fourth son.

Mother Ellen had anticipated this silent battle from the very beginning. It was a dilemma that Grayhorse thought had been settled under the guidance of the Great Spirit. Grayhorse became belligerent whenever the matter was brought up and refused to even discuss it with Matty. Matty had never shared his feelings with anyone, not even Mother Ellen. The time had come for these words to be spoken, for his feelings to be revealed, and for him to confront his brother, Roaring Bull.

In Matty's mind, Roaring Bull had stolen his birthright. It was a possession to which Matty was rightfully entitled by birth. In the Cherokee society, he was the rightful heir to a heritage that was to have been passed to him by his parents. This privilege was attached to a rank that was sealed and protected by the lineage of his birth. It was to pass to the heir that followed by generations, from parents or predecessors to child. Not only did Matty feel that he was being robbed of his birthright but so were the future seedlings of his lineage. How could his father, Grayhorse, not comply with what was socially legal in his culture? How could Mother Ellen keep silent and not challenge Grayhorse to do what was right in his behalf? How could they keep from him what was rightfully his? Matty's hurt and disappointment had now turned to anger, bitterness, resentment, jealousy, and vindictiveness. He wanted Roaring Bull to leave the farm. He also wanted him disowned by the family and to no longer be entrusted with the family legacy and the protective care of the precious jewels.

Matty arose before sunrise and made his way to the barn. He had heard from Otha that Roaring Bull would be leaving early to visit their sister, Minnie, in Trigg County. No one was in the kitchen, so he picked up a carving knife from the kitchen counter drawer, tucked it in his front pocket and walked quickly across the yard. When he entered the barn, he noticed a pitchfork in the corner by the door. Matty took the fork and climbed up the few steps of the loft ladder to reach the hayloft. He nestled himself in the hay and waited quietly for Roaring Bull to enter the barn. Matty was so engrossed in his plot that he did not notice Harmon and Otha as they followed him into the barn using the back entrance. They waited quietly behind the animal stalls to see just what Matty had in his mind to do.

Roaring Bull descended the stairs with a new burst of energy. Following a good night's sleep, he had packed his bags early for the day's journey. He was anxious to spend a few days in Ceruleum (Trigg County) with his sister Minnie and her husband, Will. He had looked forward to the visit for a few weeks. Minnie was his favorite sibling, she had not been feeling well, and he had promised her that he would come soon for a visit. In the spirit of his father, Grayhorse, a promise made was always a promise to be kept.

Roaring Bull greatly missed his father. Some days he would take a walk into the woods and reminiscence about their days together as father and son. Almost daily, he paid reverence to his father's spirit by visiting his grave site underneath the family oak tree. Since his father's death, he had used his Cherokee birth name more frequently than his given name, Stonewall Jackson Gray. He had put aside many of the stereotyped feelings that had tested his father's courage. He was trying hard to retain the practices and traditions of the Cherokee culture that his father had followed. He now dressed in Native American clothing and held fast to the use of traditional artifacts for ritual ceremonies. Before coming downstairs, Roaring Bull made certain that the deerskin pouch with the precious jewels was securely placed around his neck, next to his heart as his father had asked him to always do. He took the time to pay his morning vows to the Great Spirit on behalf of the future seedlings, a practice that had been passed on to him by his father. Roaring Bull reached for a second piece of Sarah's sweet bread, baked the day before, to go along with his morning coffee. As he picked up his bags to leave, Dave questioned him as to how long he would be away from the farm. Roaring Bull simply responded, "Until Minnie will not need me anymore."

Without looking back, Roaring Bull walked straight to the barn. He had to saddle Sonny and strap his load to her sides. When he entered the barn, he whistled for Sonny. Sonny turned to acknowledge him and neighed as if to say "Good Morning." Roaring Bull patted Sonny on the head and worked quickly. He wanted to be on the trail by midmorning.

As Roaring Bull turned to mount Sonny, Matty took careful aim and hurled the pitchfork toward him. He did not want to injure Sonny. His plan was to take Sonny and ride away quickly into Quarry Town or to take the back trail across the state line into Tennessee. Roaring Bull heard a rustling in the hayloft and turned to investigate the noise. Instantly, the flying fork reached its target and pierced Roaring Bull deeply in his left side. Blood spattered in all directions. Roaring Bull fell to the ground and cried out in agony, as the prongs of the fork seemed to reach all the way through his body.

Harmon and Otha quickly left their secret hiding place and ran over to assist Roaring Bull. Otha yelled, "Watch your back, Roaring Bull. Watch out, he's gone plum mad!"

Matty then descended from the hayloft by jumping down to the floor of the barn with drawn knife in his left hand, ready to strike. He tackled Roaring Bull unexpectedly from behind. He cut the sinew string of the deerskin pouch and snatched it from around Roaring Bull's neck. Matty dropped the pouch onto the barn floor. Roaring Bull kicked the pouch with his foot out of Matty's reach. Roaring Bull was growing weak from the loss of blood but he continued to wrestle with Matty using all of his remaining strength. Finally Roaring Bull was able to arm-wrestle the knife out of Matty's hand. Harmon picked up the knife and held on to it, threatening to use it on Matty if he didn't let go.

As they rolled around on the floor of the barn, Matty reached out and grabbed the pouch with the jewels. Angrily, he held them up to Roaring Bull and declared, "These are mine, you thief, these belong to me! Your blessed birthright was given in vain. You will never get your hands on these again. They rightfully belong to me."

In pain, Roaring Bull tackled Matty by his legs and Matty fell to the floor. Harmon and Otha tried desperately to separate them but to no avail. They were simply tossed to and fro around the barn. Roaring Bull finally broke away from Matty and reached for a hammer that was hanging on the wall. He staggered forward and approached Matty from behind. Using all of the strength that he had left, he hit Matty on the head with the hammer.

Matty fell forward down to the floor of the barn. Harmon and Otha ran to him.

"This is awful," said Harmon. "What shall we do? Now you have killed him, Roaring Bull, you have killed Matty!"

"You could have stopped before you killed him," said Otha.

"God help us!" cried Harmon.

"What would father and Mother Ellen say if they could see us?"

"They do see us," said Roaring Bull. "Their spirits are never that far away. How do you think I was able to save these jewels?"

"It was either him or me," said Roaring Bull. "I took an oath to protect these jewels and our legacy even unto my death, maybe one day both of you will understand. Go to the big house for help," ordered Roaring Bull. "I will contact you when I reach my place of dwelling."

Roaring Bull then reached for the pouch with the jewels and snatched it out of Matty's hand. He placed the pouch inside his shirt pocket, mounted Sonny, and swiftly rode away from the farm. As he rode away, Harmon and Otha heard him say, "I took a solemn oath to protect these jewels and the seedlings. A promise is a promise, a promise is a promise forever. My word will forever be my badge of honor."

Harmon and Otha ran to the big house for help. Dave and Arthur quickly made their way to the barn. Dave felt for Matty's pulse and announced, "It is weak but he does have a pulse, he's still alive."

Quickly, they worked to revive Matty. After almost an hour, Matty began to come around and they carried him to the big house where they cleaned his wounds and put him to bed. Sarah gave him a cup of warm chicken soup and Dave placed an ice pack on his head to take care of the swelling that resulted from the blow on his head with the hammer.

Matty, Dave, Arthur, Harmon, and Otha called a family meeting in the kitchen. They had a heart to heart discussion about their father's intentions when he passed the birthright. They argued that if the issue had not been settled before their father's death, then it was absolutely wrong to settle it now. To continue to pursue the issue would only spread the bitterness to future generations and the family legacy would then be lost. Their father's spirit was continuing to roam and would not rest as long as the family was in dissension.

Matty did not agree. He felt isolated from the family bonding. He did promise not to instigate any further confrontations concerning the matter at the farm. The discussion concluded with the agreement that it certainly was a family matter and it was well understood that whatever happened in the family was to remain in the family and away from foreign ears. The fact that Matty was left half dead in the barn and that Roaring Bull had left the farm seriously injured and nearly hemorrhaging to death was information belonging only to the family. Both incidents were considered "a word in the family."

Roaring Bull Leaves Quarry Town

Roaring Bull was bleeding steadily from the wound in his side. He followed a side trail that led to a pond on the trail side a few miles outside Quarry Town. He searched in his saddle bag for a cloth that he could use to stop the bleeding and a bottle of peroxide to clean the wound. He then bandaged it and rested underneath a tree, with his head on a stone. Finally, he continued his journey to Ceruleum. When he reached the house, Minnie was waiting for him. The hour was growing late and she was beginning to worry about him. She had received word from the big house that he and Matty had a terrible fight and that Matty had been left for dead. She knew that Matty had been revived and that Roaring Bull was badly injured.

Roaring Bull was so late arriving, Minnie had asked her husband, Will, to go on the trail to search for him. She heard Chum, the family dog, barking and hoped that her brother had arrived. She walked to the front porch and there was Sonny moving slower than usual. Roaring Bull was leaning to the side as if he could not travel much farther. Will went out to meet him and help him off his horse. When Roaring Bull proceeded to share with them what had taken place,

Minnie immediately told him that Matty was not dead. She looked at Roaring Bull's injury and decided to re-bandage it. Roaring Bull told her how he almost lost his life and how he almost lost the precious jewels to Matty. They agreed that Roaring Bull must stay away from Quarry Town. Minnie invited him to stay with her and Will at least until Matty seemed to be settled down. Roaring Bull really did not want to move to Trigg County but he did not want Minnie to worry about him so he agreed to stay. He knew that this would probably be best for the protective care of the family legacy and the precious jewels.

Appearance of the White Buffalo

Roaring Bull gazed out the sitting room window and noticed that there was a fish pond just across the field on the west side of the house. He decided to take a walk across the way to check it out for fishing. The sun was beginning to set and a fresh array of colors in brilliant orange and red created an awesome beauty that only nature could have brought about. Roaring Bull sat down by the water and began to think about the vision trips that he had taken with his father. Suddenly, a burst of color in bright yellow appeared and penetrated the beautiful sunset. In the midst of the glow, an image of the White Buffalo appeared. Its voice carried the tonality of Grayhorse. The spirit called out the name of Roaring Bull soft and clear. The voice was followed by a very chilled brisk wind with a strength that bent the branches of the surrounding trees and rustled the leaves with a sound of anger. It was Grayhorse's totem spirit, the spirit of Grayhorse had returned.

Roaring Bull was afraid. He arose and stepped back a few steps to maintain his balance. The spirit spoke sternly but gently. "I am not pleased that you and your brother were in battle," said the spirit. "The birthright that was entrusted to you cannot be given away or taken from you. You remain the protector of the family legacy and the precious jewels. You must keep the jewels close to you and always carry them near your heart so that they are not vulnerable to be lost or taken from you. My spirit will remain with you for as long as you nurture the legacy. Dissension between you and your brothers must cease. When family relationships are destroyed, this destruction is passed on to your offspring of the next generation. My spirit is not at rest. You must approach the Great Spirit for forgiveness and for guidance."

As the spirit spoke, Roaring Bull ceased to be afraid. This time, it was the spirit of his father, Grayhorse. Roaring Bull trusted the spirit to guide him through this dilemma. Roaring Bull walked closer to the water, raised his arms, faced the west, and prayed aloud to the Great Spirit, the god of his father. He prayed for guidance and protection and he gave thanks for the safe return of the precious jewels.

Quietly, he made his way back to the house where Minnie had set the table for supper. "Is that you, Roaring Bull?" asked Will. "I expected you earlier; come in and have some supper, it's about to get cold."

Roaring Bull pulled a chair up to the table and they began to talk about old times, childhood days, his horse, Sonny, and the journey along the Trigg County trail. But inside his mind was a vision of Matty, lying on the floor of the barn, unable to move. The secret had not gone away and Roaring Bull knew that it would not go away soon, not until he could make things right with his brother. It was an evil, bitter battle between them that neither had created. Only the Great Spirit and the spirit of Grayhorse could make a difference. Matty was not ready to accept that difference.

9

Burning Fire

Twin Forks

The flood water was beginning to crest along the Wet Fork of Little River. Most of the families had begun to clean and pitch away what had been completely destroyed by the angry water. Little River ran along the county dividing line of Caldwell and Trigg Counties. The east side of the river was known as Dry Fork and the west side was known as Wet Fork. The people who lived along the river basin referred to them as Twin Forks of Little River. The season had been peppered with heavy torrential rains. Water covered everything as far as the eye could see. Crop fields were flooded and many homes had been damaged beyond repair. Will's Aunt Lucy, her sister Minerva, and Minerva's two daughters, Addie and Ida, lived about a quarter of a mile up the river on the wet side. Lucy and Minerva had lived at Dry Fork for several years but only two years ago, they moved into a dwelling on the west side to be near their father, Noah Hollowell.

Only families that lived along the Wet Fork had been bothered by the flood. Families that lived along the Dry Fork were able to go about their regular routines but the neighborly thing to do was to help those families who needed help. Will and Roaring Bull had walked most of the way to the Hollowell farm to help out. They rode in the wagon to the bend of the river. The water had spilled out of its banks in that area also. They untied one of the canoes that had been left tied to a tree for those who might need one to reach the other side. Will had family living on both sides of the river. They stood on the summit of a steep hill to survey the damage. Water was everywhere. Most of the houses in its path were already surrounded by the water. Roaring Bull asked Will, "How in the name of goodness did you and your family ever reach this place? How did they ever come to leave Virginia and North Carolina to settle in a place like this?"

Will shook his head and responded, "Well, Roaring Bull, if you have about five days to listen, maybe I can tell you the story." Roaring Bull perched himself on a rock while Will leaned against a tree and started to explain to Roaring Bull just who these Hollowells really were.

"When the Hollowells settled into this area they arrived in two groups. They were one of the original families to settle in the area of south-western Kentucky. Miles Hollowell, a Quaker from Virginia; his wife, Ann Southwick; eight children; his sister and brother-in-law, Stephen Peele; and a large family of slaves moved into Kentucky by wagon train. The Hollowells owned their own land. They settled on Muddy Fork of Little River, just south of the present county line that separates Trigg and Caldwell Counties.

"Miles and his sons, Irwin and Noah, bought land on the Dry Fork of Eddy Creek and became successful farmers. Around 1829, Irwin married Mary Ann Parker, the daughter of Robert G. Parker. Irwin and Robert were very close partners and a lot of interchanging took place between them: money, land, and slaves. Together they owned approximately 40,000 acres of land in the Dry Fork area of Eddy Creek, located between Caldwell and Lyon Counties. They even donated money and the land for the establishment of Eddy Creek Baptist Church, which continues to flourish today.

"Noah never married but he fathered several mulatto children with slave girls. Irwin and his son became the legal guardians for these children as they inherited both land and money from the Hollowells. Noah had two lovely granddaughters, Alva and Alvie. Their father was Noah's son, William. Alvie married the eminent John Dotson who is remembered for rebuilding Dotson High School in Quarry Town (presently named Princeton, Kentucky). The school was previously built of wood. John rebuilt it with brick. It was originally built for the black children of the community. The school was then named Dotson School in recognition of John Dotson.

"Irwin had four sons. One son was Dr. Issac Parker, Lucy and Minerva's father. Their mother was a slave girl. Dr. Parker was born in 1831 in Caldwell County. My mother, Minerva, was married to John Hollowell and together they had five children. My sisters, Ida and Addie are still living at home. Ida is young and quiet. My mother Minerva watches over her closely. She does not intend for anyone to ever take advantage of her daughters the way that they did her. The original Hollowells were immigrants from Ashly St. Ledger in Northhampton, England. They are the family of my great-great-great grandfather, John. John and his grandson, Thomas, moved to America in 1673. They settled in Norfork, Virginia.

Even though Noah lived at Eddy Creek in Caldwell County. He finally moved to Trigg County to work on the farm with his father, Miles."

As Will and Roaring Bull surveyed the flood plain, Roaring Bull noticed that there was still plenty of land in the area for him to build a dwelling place. He had seriously thought of building a home for himself and never returning to the Gray farm because of the conflict that he had with his brother, Matty. Soon it would be time to burn off the land to sow plant beds for the burley and dark tobacco crops. Since the Hollowells were such successful farmers, Roaring Bull was certain that he could find work with them. He was willing to accept anything. He would work the crops (tobacco, corn, or wheat) or tend the hog, sheep, or dairy farms.

The Hollowell women were beautiful. They had perfect features, lovely hair, and excellent complexions. Lucy and Minerva lived only a short distance from Minnie and Will. Lucy had been down to the house several times for visits or for busy talk, trivial domestic trading, or borrowing. Mostly, her visits were to catch a glimpse of Roaring Bull and maybe have an opportunity to talk with him. Earlier that week, she had come down to bring a steamy fresh baked pear cobbler for their dinner. When Roaring Bull saw her coming, he simply smiled at her and left the room without saying one word. Minnie never encouraged Lucy to stay very long, as she did not want to encourage her feistiness around her brother, Roaring Bull.

Will and Roaring Bull descended the summit, untied the canoe, climbed in and rowed back across the river. Will mentioned to Roaring Bull that his Aunt Lucy's visits really were covering a hidden motive. Her true intent was to capture a boyfriend, which she had never really had. The pickings in that area were pretty slim and she intended to catch her a mate well before someone else wooed his heart away or even she began to lose interest. Roaring Bull listened to Will intently, smiled, and responded, "Well, maybe one day her real heart throb will come along. Maybe then she can enter a real Sadie Hawkins race."

When they reached the yard, Minnie announced that the next day, Lucy, Minerva, and Minerva's daughters, Addie and Ida, were moving in with them until Minerva's husband, John, could get their house repaired and cleaned up from the flood damage. Early the next morning, Minerva and Lucy loaded the canoe with their personal belongings and supplies and headed to Dry Fork for their stay with Minnie and Will. Will met them at Muddy Fork with the wagon so that they would not have to walk and carry their heavy load all the way. By now, the house was getting pretty full.

Minnie and Will had 18 children of their own. Five were still at home with them: Marshall, Que Bee, Johnnie Bee, Carrie Lee, and Robbie. Ida and Addie shared a room with Carrie Lee and Johnnie Bee. Lucy and Minerva took the space in the attic where Roaring Bull had been sleeping. Roaring Bull realized that space was tight and decided to sleep in the basement. He did not want to allow Lucy any additional space for her personal chase. The basement space was small and rather cramped so Roaring Bull gathered his belongings and set up sleeping quarters in the hayloft in the barn. The space was open and small, the head board was hard, the pillows were scratchy, the noise was constant, and the smell was almost unbearable. Roaring Bull was thankful to have even the hayloft for a home. He thought of Mother Ellen's often spoken words, "A home can always be a home, no matter how humble."

Lucy's Play for Roaring Bull

One morning, Roaring Bull decided to sleep later than usual. It was the first time that he had lowered his guard to be cautious around Lucy since she had come to stay there. Lucy went looking for Roaring Bull and found him sleeping in the hayloft. Lucy had told Minnie that she was going to the barn to help with the milking. She had also asked Minnie not to tell Minerva where she went. Minnie made no response. Minnie knew very well that this would be the day when Lucy would try to trick her brother, Roaring Bull into her web. Lucy had planned her way and she was prepared to reel in her big catch. Lucy stopped on the back porch and picked up two milk pails and headed towards the barn. Quickly she climbed the loft ladder and stretched her body alongside Roaring Bull as he slept. She removed the hat that he was using to cover his eyes to keep the light out and used it to cover her own eyes. As Lucy twisted and turned, restlessly, in the uncomfortable hay, she aroused Roaring Bull. When he awoke, to his surprise, there she was lying beside him. Lucy lay very still, pretending to be fast asleep.

Meanwhile, Ida and Addie came into the barn, carrying milk pails. They each sat on a stool and proceeded with the milking. Roaring Bull noticed that Ida's skin was a luscious cocoa brown and velvet-soft. She had perfect facial lines and curly black hair. She was awesomely beautiful. This was the first time that he had ever taken a good look at Ida. She was fourteen years old and already her body had begun to naturally curve, an-

85

nouncing its debut into the adult world. Roaring Bull sighed and wished to be able to stop his world at age twenty-seven and wait for her. He was thirteen years older than Ida. Her soft spoken voice and her quiet spirit had stopped his heart and stolen it away. He knew that her mother, Minerva, would never approve of his love for her, even if he politely met all of the requirements of her mother's demands. He wanted to reach out and take Ida in his arms and whisper in her ear how much he wanted her and how much he loved her. He wanted her to understand that he loved her but he did not want to frighten her away, so he quietly watched her from afar without letting her know that he was even there.

Suddenly, a breeze blew through the barn and the hay began to move and bother Lucy's nose. She sneezed out loud several times and Ida and Addie turned and looked up. To their surprise, they saw their Aunt Lucy lying in the hay side by side with Roaring Bull.

Addie called out, "Why, Aunt Lucy? Is that you?"

Lucy responded, "What are you girls doing out here in the barn? Now get along out of here and I had better not hear one word about this from either of you."

Ida and Addie left the barn, turned over the milk pails on their way out, and giggled all the way back to the house. Lucy worried that they would tell Minerva what they had seen. She feared that they might also tell Minnie and Will; then both she and Roaring Bull would be in trouble.

By then, Roaring Bull was sitting straight up looking strangely at Lucy. He snatched his hat away from her and asked, "What the dickens are you doing here?"

Lucy didn't answer but giggled and snuggled near him. Roaring Bull jumped down to the barn floor from the hayloft and repeated, "I said, what the devil's eye do you think you are doing here?"

"Roaring Bull," she responded, "You know exactly why I am here. Don't you dare play games with me."

Roaring Bull stamped out of the barn door, angry and baffled over what game Lucy would play next. He whispered under his breath as he left, "That woman's the devil's angel in disguise. Lord of mercy, please keep her away from me!"

Embarrassed, Lucy climbed down the loft ladder, picked up the milk pails and finished the milking. If anyone should have asked, this would have been her reason for being in the barn.

Roaring Bull's Passion for Ida

Roaring Bull was troubled over how often he would find himself watching Ida as she moved around the house and the yard doing her daily chores.

One day he walked along behind her as she made her way down the hill to the cistern to fill her water buckets. It was a day to do the family laundry and the girls always needed to carry enough water to the house. Once before, Roaring Bull was watching when Ida used some of the extra water to wash her hair. The sun glowing against her wet hair gave an appearance of innocence that caused Roaring Bull's heart to throb and beat rapidly. Ida held her head low and allowed her hair to fall gently forward. She massaged it vigorously and allowed it to curl naturally. Roaring Bull wanted to go to her, hold her close, and run his fingers through her damp hair. That was the day when he noticed that Ida was also watching him. With her head bowed and her beautiful eyes raised, Ida noticed him leaning against a tree. She smiled at him but then rushed away. Roaring Bull took a short cut and walked very fast in order to catch up with Ida before she reached Muddy Fork.

Today was a different day. He felt that Ida was ready to talk to him. He waited for her to fill her water buckets and then he moved closer to the cistern. He moved quietly but stayed in plain view so that he would not frighten her. He approached her by asking if she liked staying at the house with Minnie and Will. She smiled without uttering a word and nodded her head in the affirmative. Roaring Bull could not resist her much longer. He passionately said to her, "You are such a lovely young woman, Ida! Would you please sit with me for a while? It is so beautiful here at the top of the hill and the breeze is calming today. We can sit and talk."

Ida responded, "What will we talk about?"

"Just how lovely it is here and things that you like and things about me and you."

Ida smiled at him but began to back away. Roaring Bull reached out to her and took her hand. He held her hand snug in his and placed his left hand on top of hers.

"Ida, just allow me to tell you how lovely you are. I have been watching you, Ida. I know, I know I am falling in love with you."

Ida snatched her hand away and turned her back to him.

"Don't turn away Ida, please don't turn away. Just take your time Ida, take your time. I am going to wait for you, Ida, I will wait a lifetime if I need to. Oh, if I could only make time stand still while I wait for you, Ida. While we are waiting, Ida, just know for certain that I love you.

"Ida, I am not asking for anything in return. Just listen to your heart and maybe you can grow to love me too."

Ida looked at him with intrigued eyes as if she wanted to speak. Roaring Bull put his fingers across her lips and said to her, "Don't talk now Ida, don't talk at all. This may be all too hard for you. You don't have to speak a word. I can read your heart and soul. Just know that I love you and I'll watch out for you. No one is ever going to hurt you here. Your Aunt Lucy is just trying to start trouble because you happened to see us lying beside each other in the hayloft."

Ida quickly turned her back and began to walk away.

"Don't go, Ida, please listen to me! I didn't even know that she was there, I was asleep and she plotted a trick to snare me into her web. Don't you ever trust your Aunt Lucy again, Ida, not for one minute."

Ida continued to walk ahead down the hill. Roaring Bull picked up her water buckets and carried them for Ida.

Lucy had followed Roaring Bull all of the way and had watched and listened to his pleading conversation with Ida. This confrontation caused a fire of fury inside Lucy; now she not only would have to win Roaring Bull's heart but she also needed to discredit Ida with the rest of the family. As she waited in hiding behind a tree, she planned in anger how she would reveal every word that she had heard and every action that she saw to her sister Minerva. She also thought of approaching Ida with a warning that she must never be seen alone with Roaring Bull again.

At midmorning when Roaring Bull went to the house, Lucy had baked his favorite hickory nut custard pie and had it cooling on the table.

"Good morning, Roaring Bull," said Lucy, as she thought, *Is it not a fact that a man's love can always be won through his stomach?*

"Wouldn't you like a cup of fresh coffee and some sweetbread?" she asked. "Anyway, how about a little morning chat together while you sit down a while?"

"Oh, maybe I will take a little coffee," Roaring Bull responded.

"She is much too young for you, Roaring Bull," Lucy began her conversation. "She is only fourteen years old, can you imagine that? She's just a child! You are twenty-seven years old, a grown man. Why can't you just leave her be and let her enjoy her childhood and youthful years? She will never be able to catch up with your old antiquated ways. I will not stand by and watch you ruin her life. Trust me," Lucy scolded. "I am telling Minerva and Will and your sister Minnie about this."

"You would do that, wouldn't you, Lucy? You would do that to hurt us both, wouldn't you?"

"There is nothing in your heart for me and you?" asked Lucy. "Nothing? Please tell me if there is even a little spark, because my love for you can survive on just a little love from you."

"Not even the smallest thimbleful," Roaring Bull responded.

"Roaring Bull, why are you turning away from me? I felt more than a thimble full of love from you the night when you made love with me in the hayloft in that barn. You do remember, don't you?"

"What are you talking about Lucy? What in the dickens are you talking about?" asked Roaring Bull.

"I'm talking about that night when you made real love with me. It only takes one night, Roaring Bull. One night only. I stole your heart away that night and you know it. Did you also know that you left me with child? I'm carrying your child, Roaring Bull! Now do what any decent man would do. You are a member of the Gray family and I know that you know to take on your responsibilities. When is the wedding? You set the date and make it soon," she ordered.

"Wedding?" yelled Roaring Bull. "Who else have you slept with in the hay loft? My conscience is clean, my mind is clear. You are not carrying my child so don't try that game. Lucy, you are not pulling that game on me," declared Roaring Bull.

"Are you waiting for young Ida to grow up like you said?" angrily asked Lucy. "Admit it—I love you and now you have to love me. That is the way that it is and that is the way that it was meant to be."

"Woman!" Roaring Bull yelled. "You are losing your mind. You are simply going crazy. All of your working mental parts have been taken away."

Roaring Bull stamped out the kitchen door looking for Will. He paused and noticed Ida walking toward the woods. Just overhead he heard a clap of thunder. The sky opened up and the rain came in a heavy downpour, leaving both he and Ida dripping wet.

Ida ran as fast as she could to seek shelter under the branches of an oak tree. She could feel Roaring Bull's presence as he followed her. She smiled inside, knowing that at any moment he would catch up with her and this would be the time when she would admit and confess her love for him also.

Roaring Bull walked faster and began to call out to her, "Ida, wait for me! I need to talk to you." she waited for him and he took her by the shoulders and passionately kissed her in the rain. She rested secure in his arms and they both fell into uncontrolled laughter, dripping wet, and heart free because of their love for each other. They sat on the wet ground and watched the busy squirrels scurry around their feet under the tree looking for acorns. Neither of them could hold back any longer; they talked about their love for each other and Ida emptied her heart to Roaring Bull. Roaring Bull was so overjoyed when Ida expressed her willingness to wait for him for as long as it would take, even if he had to marry Lucy.

When Roaring Bull asked her again if she was certain of her love for him, Ida responded with a kiss and replied, "I do love you, Roaring Bull, more than you will ever know, and I will love you forever."

She raised her beautiful eyes and they touched his heart affirming the words that she had spoken. He kissed Ida with long passion and pledged his love to her forever. He told Ida that his plans were to go away but that he would return soon and when he did return, he would be coming back for her.

Roaring Bull arose and headed toward Dry Fork in search of Will. It was imperative that he talk to Will about his love for his sister, Ida, and how Lucy was trying to trick him into marrying her by claiming that she was carrying his child. As Ida got up to leave, she saw Lucy's profile just ahead of her as she returned to the house. Again, Lucy had followed them and watched their exchange of love for each other. Lucy was angry, she had run very fast to beat Ida to the house so that she could share with Minerva all that she had seen and heard.

When Lucy told Minerva, Minerva was furious. She encouraged Lucy to marry Roaring Bull to save the family image. She also promised that she would never permit Ida to marry Roaring Bull.

Roaring Bull found Will working in the field with his horse and plant setter as it was the time of year to set tobacco plants. Roaring Bull beckoned to Will to meet him half way across the field. Will listened carefully as Roaring Bull told his story. Will assured him that he had heard Lucy and Minerva talking the evening before and he knew that Lucy was spinning a web to catch Roaring Bull. On the other hand, Will was going to protect his sister, Ida. He was going to be certain that as a child, she would not be caught in the middle of this ugly plot. He did not know how much Roaring Bull was really involved in complicity, but he told Roaring Bull that he had no choice but to stay away from Ida and not be caught alone with her again.

Finally, he told Roaring Bull that he had no option except to marry Lucy because she was carrying his child.

When Minnie heard the complete story, she agreed with Will and also talked about it with Roaring Bull, reminding him that the people of Trigg, Caldwell, and Lyon Counties would not deem it to be proper for a young woman to be with child without a husband. Roaring Bull was a "Gray" and was entrusted to protect the legacy of the Gray family. The spirit of Grayhorse and Mother Ellen would dictate that he do the right thing. The right thing would be to give the child a legal name, protect the character of the girl with child, and bring no hurt to the family name, as the entire Gray family would have to bear the consequences of disrespect if he demoralized the family name and the family image.

Roaring Bull again tried to explain to Minnie that he was being framed. Minnie responded that she had watched Lucy and was aware of what she was doing but that Ida was also an issue. "You have no choice but to choose to do the right thing, and do it before the entire world knows what has taken place."

Both Minnie and Will encouraged Roaring Bull to rush a wedding date, which he agreed to do. The wedding would be within the next three weeks, as he wanted the wedding to be over before Lucy began to show her pregnancy.

They were married on a beautiful Sunday afternoon at the home of Minnie and Will. The smell of honeysuckle filled the air and Minnie made sure that a beautiful bouquet of the flowers graced every room. A wonderful feast was prepared and there was plenty of fiddle music and stamping dances from both the African and Native American cultures. Just as the guests were beginning to go nonstop with the dancing, the sky opened up and the rain began to pour down, turning the festive day wet and soggy. Roaring Bull reverted back to his Cherokee culture and assumed that this was an omen for an unstable beginning for their marriage.

Ida did not attend the wedding but watched the celebration from her bedroom window, weeping silently. Roaring Bull could feel her presence and knew that she was there. In his spirit and in his heart, it was Ida that he should have been marrying. She remembered that Roaring Bull had promised to return for her and to take her away with him. She knew in her heart that some day the time would come when they would be able to rekindle their feelings for each other in spite of her Aunt Lucy. How could Lucy ever have peace in taking away what was rightfully hers? Loneliness and anger began to fester inside of Ida.

As each day passed, Roaring Bull longed more and more in his heart for Ida. He needed to find a way to bring this nightmare to an end. He watched the storm clouds on the horizon and realized that very soon now a fury would be upon him. The West Wind had begun to blow, bringing with it pestilence, ill will, and the work of evil spirits. Roaring Bull thought of the legacy that he was nurturing and protecting. He realized that since his coming to Trigg County, he had distanced himself from the Gray legacy. It had been some time since he had paid vows to the Great Spirit. He had removed the deerskin pouch from around his neck and placed it in safe keeping among his personal belongings. Many days had passed and he had not even paused to count or check the stones. Minnie reminded him of what would happen to the family if he lost the jewels or rejected the legacy. Already, the family was becoming disconnected; a bitter West Wind was blowing. It was strong and turbulent, and peace and good will in the family were whirling out of control.

10

Promises Broken

Roaring Bull Neglects the Legacy

Now that Roaring Bull and Lucy were living in Trigg County with Minnie and Will, he had no intention of returning to Caldwell County. Since Roaring Bull was no longer living at the Gray farm Dave and Sarah had moved back to help run the place. Roaring Bull had concluded that his responsibilities to maintain the family legacy had ended now that he was away. In his mind, it was time for the responsibilities to be passed on to a succeeding heir. Surely, a vision from the Spirit of the White Buffalo would soon dictate the path to be followed. He had returned to practicing Cherokee rituals and paying his daily vows to the Great Spirit in hopes that an answer would be given soon. He realized that this relationship had to be kept alive. It was his only means of communication for guidance and direction for both his life cycle and strength for his family.

Much trouble had followed his path since the West Wind had taken control of his life cycle. He felt a disconnection from his brother Matty since their fight in the barn over the entrustment of the legacy and he was beginning to sense a strong disconnect from the Great Spirit. His father, Grayhorse, had been directed to remain in Quarry Town or near by. Could this mean the same for him? Roaring Bull was beginning to wonder if maybe his father had listened and misinterpreted the meaning of the legacy by anointing him with the entrustment. Why not Matty, Dave, or Otis? What about Robert, the first son? The Great Spirit did not make errors. Roaring Bull realized that he had taken a sacred oath. Promises are not made to be broken; promises are eternal and forever.

Dr. Hatten Reveals Lucy's Secret

Lucy and Roaring Bull were struggling to maintain the secrecy of their marriage vows. Most of their days were filled with tension, dissension, arguments, and much silence. They seldom spent time together or talked to each other. Roaring Bull became concerned that no signs of Lucy's pregnancy had surfaced. He had not been able to even talk her into a visit to the doctor's office for a checkup. Six months had passed and her pregnancy had not been medically confirmed. She had not gained one pound and continued to eat like a bird. She was still comfortably wearing her regular clothes and no changes in her physical appearance were apparent. Roaring Bull was unhappy and now he was quite certain that Lucy had faked a false pregnancy. There were absolutely no signs of illness, fatigue, or increased weight.

Roaring Bull contacted Dr. Hatten's younger son in Quarry Town for an office visit for Lucy. He had taken over his father's office practice and Roaring Bull wanted him to have a good look at Lucy. He told Lucy that he had to visit the doctor's office concerning his asthma and irregular breathing, as his shortness of breath was triggering more frequent asthma attacks. Roaring Bull insisted that he needed Lucy to ride along with him in the wagon just in case he became ill, then she could drive the wagon back home. He hitched two companion mules, Cole and Nellie to the wagon when they were ready to leave.

Lucy came out to board the wagon wearing a freshly starched bonnet and a covered apron. Her floral gathered skirt and matching shawl accented the color of her hair, her shawl covered her shoulders and hung down long to cover her stomach. Without any hesitation or assistance from Roaring Bull, she hastily climbed into the wagon. Roaring Bull was also concerned that Lucy had drawn inside herself and seldom spoke to him. All the way across the county line there was almost no conversation between them. They reached the doctor's office well past noon. Most of the morning patients had been served and Doctor Hatten was waiting for them when they arrived. Dr. Hatten called Roaring Bull into his office. Immediately Roaring Bull stated, "I brought Lucy along today. She is carrying our first baby. I want you to check her over to be sure everything is alright with her. She has not been sick one day; I see little or no signs of a child. Tell us the truth, Doctor. I am worried about both Lucy and the child."

Roaring Bull's request caught Lucy by surprise. She stood up and responded with anger, "Well, I do declare, I am just fine! I will be the one to say when I need a doctor. You go with him to the examining table, Roaring Bull, this visit is for you," she ordered. Roaring Bull denied on her request. "Oh no, Lucy—this one is for you."

Dr. Hatten insisted that Lucy go into the examining room ahead of him. "Here, Lucy, I will be right with you," he stated. As she stepped inside. Roaring Bull heard her screaming and weeping through the wall. It was only a short time until Dr. Hatten asked Roaring Bull to join them in his office. Roaring Bull stepped inside. Slowly and calmly Dr. Hatten began to break the news that exposed Lucy's big secret. "Roaring Bull, you and Lucy are not having a baby. Lucy is not six months pregnant. She has never been pregnant. There are no signs of pregnancy or any sexual relationship of any kind, ever. To be direct about this matter, Lucy is still a virgin."

Roaring Bull walked to the window and wrung his hands in anger. How could he have been so stupid? Why could he not have read into Lucy's motive and lies from the very beginning? All of this time it was just a deceiving trick to trap him into marriage and keep him away from his real love, Ida.

Lucy continued to weep out loud with no consultation from Roaring Bull. Dr. Hatten walked out of the room and closed the door behind him, leaving them alone. Roaring Bull walked over to Lucy and stood her up by the shoulders, speaking softly as he said, "How could you, Lucy? How could you tell such a lie? I had never slept with you and you knew it! You will pay for this lie. You have nurtured and fed this lie for six months. How long did you think that you could hide yourself?"

"I am so sorry," sobbed Lucy. "Please forgive me, Roaring Bull. I will make it up to you, I promise! I love you, Roaring Bull; and I simply cannot bear the thought of you being with someone else. Forgive me, please!" she pleaded.

"Let's go to the wagon, Lucy. You had better start praying that you haven't just driven me straight into her arms and even deeper into her heart. I have no promise to make; it all depends on the West Wind. The plan for Ida and me will now be dictated by the West Wind."

Lucy left the room and walked quickly to her side of the wagon, waiting for Roaring Bull to help her. Instead, Roaring Bull walked briskly behind her and went straight to the driver's side of the wagon, climbed aboard, and left Lucy standing on the ground.

"Let's go, Lucy," he announced. He gave a crack of the whip, the mules caught the message for a brisk take-off, and journeyed home much faster than they came. This time, the entire journey was made in complete silence. Roaring Bull spoke softly to the mule team while Lucy sobbed all the way home. Roaring Bull was thinking all the way home about how he would break the news to Ida. He knew that he wanted to and he knew that he had to, but more than this, he knew that he would. Maybe, this was the first step in his return to Ida.

Roaring Bull Hides the Jewels

All the way home, Roaring Bull thought of nothing but his dilemma and the responsibilities of the vows that he had made, not just to his family but also to the spirit of Grayhorse. He walked into their bedroom without uttering one word to Minnie or Will. He opened the center drawer of the chest-of-drawers and removed the deerskin pouch with the precious jewels that he had placed there for safe keeping. After he emptied the jewels on the chest of drawers, counted them, he let them fall again gently through his fingers. The jewels were well polished and all in place. There were three lovely silver nuggets and twelve awesome pieces of turquoise. Roaring Bull no longer wanted to keep them in the house. He felt that some evil force was beginning to overshadow every act of good, not just for him but for the entire family. And he did not trust Lucy. He surely did not want her to get her hands on the jewels or come near them in any way. He placed the pouch around his neck and tucked it inside his shirt next to his heart. He did not want to explain their significance to anyone, nor did he want anyone to ask him any questions concerning them, especially Lucy.

Roaring Bull remembered that there was an oak tree located in the woods about a mile and a half from the house on the West Fork side. He had observed that the tree had a large hole on one side where the squirrels had built nest for the winter. He walked in the direction of the river in search of the tree. Near Muddy Fork, approximately six feet from the river bank, he located the tree. Its branches hung steady, secure, and low. Its leaves seemed to beckon him announcing a secure place to store the jewels at least until he could receive guidance from the Spirit of the White Buffalo for their protection.

Roaring Bull reached down to pick up a branch that had fallen to the ground. Using the branch he cleared away all of the debris that the squirrels had carried into the hole. He removed the pouch from his neck and clenched it tight in his right hand. Then he paused and paid vows to the

96

Great Spirit. He chanted a prayer that he had learned from his father. Roaring Bull reached inside the hole to determine its approximate depth, which he estimated to be about a half foot deep. He nestled the pouch into a bunch of dry leaves and tucked it in the hole as far back as he could reach without them falling down farther into the hole. Then he stuffed leaves in front of the pouch and covered it with a mixture of sand and silt from the river bank. He then planted a stake at the base of the tree to easily identify its location when he returned. With the job completed, he rested on the ground and breathed a sigh of relief. At least, the jewels were no longer in the house. And out of the way of Lucy. Here they would be protected because only he and the Great Spirit knew where they were. He was keeping his promise; the jewels would be protected.

Every day, Roaring Bull, his brother-in-law, Will, and Minerva's husband, John Hollowell worked diligently building a dwelling place for him and Lucy. The place was located on the Wet Fork side of the river approximately two miles in each direction from Minerva and John's place and across the Dry Fork side from Minnie and Will. Roaring Bull and Lucy had continued to live with Minnie and Will until their place was completed, hopefully before the winter weather set in. The rainy season had not been kind to them and the work had slowed down for several weeks. It was also crop season and the men had to stop to work the harvest and carry the crops to Christian County to be sold. Their trips to the tobacco warehouse, the granary, and the stockyard to sell the hogs and cows were long and tedious. But the Hollowells were family, so everyone did their share of the work to get the job done. In spite of interruptions, it seemed certain that Roaring Bull and Lucy would be in their new dwelling place in time to share their first Thanksgiving dinner with the family.

Lucy had worked hard preparing Thanksgiving dinner. She had tried to prepare all of Roaring Bull's favorite foods such as ham, roast turkey, sweet potato pies, ambrosia, leafy greens, and homemade Parker House dinner rolls. All of the family was invited to come to the dinner. Dave and Sarah came and brought along Otis, Arthur, and Otha. Robert came and brought his wife but Matty ignored the invitation. Minnie and Belle came early to help prepare the meal. Minerva also came to help; but Ida stayed home. Everyone was invited to bring their favorite dish to add to the meal.

Lucy shared with Minnie and Belle about how sorry she was for tricking their brother into marrying her, but that she had good welcome news to share with them at the dinner table. After grace had been said, she began by admitting her guilt and remorse to the family and asked to be forgiven, adding that her life goal would now be to make Roaring Bull and their future seedlings happy.

"Somehow," she declared, "I will make all of this up to Roaring Bull. A good wind is blowing our way. We have a steady new dwelling place and I am carrying our first child. I have visited with Dr. Hatten and he has confirmed it to be so. I am three months with child; did you hear that, Roaring Bull? We are having our first child." Roaring Bull shook his head, arose, and left the room.

Will, John, and Dave followed Roaring Bull out the kitchen door. They found him out by the back fence with his head in his hands. Will spoke. "Roaring Bull, were you listening to Lucy? You are going to be a father and this time it is real."

"I don't know if I even have the strength to believe her," said Roaring Bull.

"Oh, you can believe her," said Dave. "John and Minerva brought her to the Gray farm and me and Sarah took her to Dr. Hatten's office to be examined. It only took him a minute to confirm that Lucy was with child."

"Come on, Roaring Bull," said Will, "it is your turn to be a man. Just tell her that you will try to forgive her and love this child. You have no choice," said Dave. "You are a Gray and the keeper of the legacy for the Gray family. You must do what a good, honest Gray man would do. Now raise your head and be a Gray man of distinction! In the spirit of Grayhorse, you have no other option."

Together, they made their way back to the gathering. Roaring Bull sat quiet for the rest of the day; he watched Lucy's every move but he never promised to love her.

Roaring Bull took good care of Lucy and tried to stay close to her during her pregnancy. Lucy made every effort to make him feel comfortable when he was around her. When she reached full term, Lucy gave birth to a baby boy. They named him Harmon Gray. Roaring Bull loved him dearly. He was the pride of his father's heart. A year later, Nina was born. This was a more complicated pregnancy for Lucy. Two years later, their third child, Hattie, was born. Lucy was then warned by the doctor that it would not be safe for her health to have more children. Lucy had developed a spinal condition from a tick virus that she contracted from a tick carried by the family dog, Rex.

With each birth, Ida resented her Aunt Lucy more and more. The children were fulfilling a void for Roaring Bull that Ida felt should have been hers to fill. Roaring Bull continued to carry love in his heart for Ida. His love for Ida was a promise unbroken and somehow and some way, their day would come.

11

Thundering Spirit

Minerva's Passion for Lucy

As each day passed, Lucy's struggle with her illness became more challenging. The virus had settled in her spine and damaged a couple of vertebrae causing her movements to become more restricted. Minerva had John bring the wheelchair down from the attic for Lucy to use, as she complaining more and more that the pain had become unbearable. Dr. Hatten had given his diagnosis that the illness had reached a critical state and not much more could be done to relieve the severe pain. He recommended to Minerva to keep Lucy's body wrapped in a warm blanket and see that she took her medicine regularly and on time.

Lucy sat in that wheelchair day in and day out with a blanket over her legs and a heavy shawl around her shoulders. Minerva always checked to see that she had a comfortable pillow behind her back for support. Another concern was helping Roaring Bull take care of the three children. With Lucy virtually incapacitated the children had begun to accept Minerva as their surrogate mother. Minerva would often come and stay over for several days at a time. Whenever she would come to stay over, she always brought her daughters, Ida and Addie, along. Both of the girls had passed their teen years and were approaching early adulthood. Since Ida had approached early adulthood she had become even more beautiful.

Roaring Bull did what he had to do to keep Lucy comfortable. Now that Lucy had lost most of her appetite, he always tried to be with her at meal times—at least for the breakfast and dinner meals. Ida made a concerted effort to stay away from her Aunt Lucy's room and to avoid any contact with Roaring Bull. She restricted herself to the kitchen to assist with the meals, the laundry, and the cleaning chores for the downstairs area. Ida loved to work outside so she spent much time tending the garden plot on the east side of the house. She often thought that her only reason for being there was to appease her mother's request concerning family values and family support in times of need such as for illness and death. Roaring Bull watched Ida closely. He knew her work routine and began to schedule his work chores so that he would be near Ida. Ida had felt him watching her on several occasions. When he would do this, she would always turn away, or busy herself until Roaring Bull would leave.

Every time that they would come to stay over, Minerva would give Ida a warning about Roaring Bull. Ida had been told several times not to be caught near him and that there was to be no touching and no secret talks. Minerva promised Roaring Bull that she would personally see to it that he would be made to leave the Hollowell land if either he or Ida made even one move to cause any heartaches for Lucy, especially now that she was carrying this illness. Ida promised her mother over and over that she would not be a problem. Ida moved around the premises in fear because she was afraid that Roaring Bull would not remain faithful to this request and she could always feel his presence. Ida felt that she was always being watched by Minerva, Roaring Bull, or some other secret spy member of the family, like Addie or Will. Roaring Bull gave Minerva no response except a stern stare, a forced smile, and a brisk turn away.

Minerva loved her sister with much passion. She often looked at Lucy and remembered their childhood years together. Lucy seldom spoke; but she would weep frequently and silently especially whenever Minerva or Roaring Bull would come in the room to take care of her. Minerva had considered moving Lucy to her place to make things easier for her and the children, but she knew that it would break Lucy's heart to be moved away from Roaring Bull.

Each day the illness captured more and more of Lucy's physical balance and mobility. It had begun to tighten the muscles in her neck and draw her head back. This made it very difficult for Lucy to swallow so the doctor inserted a feeding tube in her stomach. Her son, Harmon, did not understand the seriousness of her illness and seldom stopped by her room because he could not handle seeing his mother in this condition. Minerva would bathe her, put on her fresh clothes, and comb her hair daily. Lucy looked forward to that special time. She always asked for body powder. She liked to smell fresh and clean for Roaring Bull when he stopped in.

Roaring Bull Reaffirms His Love for Ida

It was a day that Ida had looked forward to. She had thought it through and finally made up her mind. She had nurtured a broken heart throughout Roaring Bull's marriage to Lucy. Now that he and Lucy had molded their family and anchored their vows, his allegiance belonged to his family. They had three children and a new home so why shouldn't she move on with her life? She had waited long enough and nothing was going to change the existing situation. Now they hardly saw each other and when they did, the tension was so thick that one could cut it with a knife.

James, the youngest son in the Crumbaugh family from Kuttawa, Lyon County, had shown more than a casual interest in Ida. He made several trips to the house to visit her during the last few months. Ida was impressed with his good manners and his gentlemanly character. A few Sundays before, he waited for her after church, held her hand, and walked her home along the long path. Last Sunday, he had come to the house with his horse and wagon to drive her to church. She loved how he helped her down from the wagon and pulled out her chair when she was ready to sit. Ida really liked James. She liked his company and missed him when he would return to Kuttawa. Minerva was quite pleased that James and Ida were keeping company together. Ida overheard Minerva say to Addie, "Now that is the kind of young man that you need to look for. He will be good to Ida and he is from a nice family. I know them all very well. Thank you, Lord, for sending him by this way for Ida."

Ida knew from these words that young James had already won her mother's heart and an affirmative answer when the time would come for him to ask for her hand. Anyway, there was only a space of two years between their ages. Not so for Roaring Bull, who was now well in his forties. Ida had made a promise to James that she would talk to Roaring Bull when she had an opportunity. *It's over,* she thought. *I will just not stall around with the subject. He will have to know out right. I am not waiting any longer. The wait time has passed; and it is over for me and Roaring Bull.*

Roaring Bull could tell by the way that Ida was moving around the garden spot that she wanted to talk to him. This time she made no effort to run away, or to drop her head in shame. Instead, she was watching and waiting for him when he came around the east side of the house with his rake and shovel in his hand. "Roaring Bull," she called out, "I need to talk to you and I need to do it right away."

Surprised to hear her call out to him, Roaring Bull stopped dead in his tracks and quickly walked toward her. Ida began to walk away, leading the way along the back path that led to the thick trees of the wooded area. Roaring Bull followed along the back fence, close behind. Ida wondered if her sister, Addie, or Will might be watching or maybe even Minerva. No one else appeared to be around.

Eyes do not lie. Minerva had placed Lucy's wheelchair near her bedroom window so that she could see the seasonal scenery. What Lucy saw was cold and much too much for her to behold. She watched Roaring Bull as he caught up with Ida, took her in his arms, stroked her beautiful curly hair, and kissed her with much passion. She saw Ida yield to his passion down by the Fork of Little River. She observed Ida as she melted in his arms and they yielded to each other's passion. Ida was fulfilling a feeling for Roaring Bull that Lucy had never been able to fill even when she conceived her children. It was a yearning in him that only Ida could fill. Lucy wanted desperately to push herself away from the window but she did not have the strength in her arms and legs to do so. So she wept silently and waited, realizing that time itself cannot douse out a fire spirit that has been kindled by a love as true and pure as theirs. It was true love burning with passion like a thundering fire. Even though Roaring Bull had married Lucy, given her three children, and remained with her in marriage, the wait for Ida had only kindled the fire in his heart to burn brighter and grow deeper and purer.

Before Ida could even begin to tell him all of the things that she had promised James that she would say, Roaring Bull had recaptured her love and rekindled the fire spirit that she carried in her heart for him. Softly, he whispered in her ear, "Not a word, Ida, please do not talk now. It is not over for us, it will never be over for us. I know about James and that only makes my love deeper for you. Just wait for me. Please wait just a little while longer and I promise that I will be there for you. Nothing has changed, Ida. You were my first love and that kind of love does not wash away. Ida, I love you now more than I ever have. Tell me that you will continue to wait for me.

"Look at me, Ida. Look into my eyes and tell me that you no longer are in love with me and that you want me to go away. If you can do that, I will simply walk away. I will vanish out of your life with no return. Can you do that, Ida? Answer me now, Ida. Go ahead and tell me that there is no longer any love for me in your heart. Can you say it and mean it, Ida? Can you tell me? Tell me now, Ida, while I wait for you."

Ida began to weep and melted deeper into his arms.

103

"You don't have to speak, Ida, your heart has already spoken and I know that you love me." Lucy, broken-hearted, continued to watch everything that took place, sitting in her wheelchair by the window.

Ida and Roaring Bull found their favorite tree and sat down together on the cold damp ground. Ida confided to Roaring Bull that James was creeping into her life and how difficult the situation was becoming. She was forced to stand by and watch Roaring Bull's children grow up and to see Aunt Lucy ill and hurting because she loved Roaring Bull so much. Roaring Bull explained to Ida how difficult it was for him to have to wait to hold her in his arms or to even talk to her. He could hardly bear to be in her presence. Roaring Bull felt that it was all so unfair to both him and Ida. "But together," he declared, "we are strong, together we are one! I am who I am because we are. We can make it Ida, of this one thing you can be certain."

"But what about James?" Ida asked. "Are you suggesting that I tell him to just go away? Are you asking me to tell him to leave? Are you asking mc to turn my back and just pretend that he is no longer there?"

"Almost," responded Roaring Bull. "Ida, that's just the way that it is. A man always knows when a woman loves someone else. Pure love will always surface to the top. If James is the man that you think he is, he will recognize our love for each other and walk away. He will understand and let's hope that it will happen before too many hearts are broken and it's too late for each of us."

Roaring Bull stood Ida up close to him and kissed her on the forehead passionately, then walked her back to the house.

"No more hiding, Ida," he said, "we belong together. Lucy already knows about us and other people will have to know too. If our love is rejected in the hearts and minds of others then that will just have to be their problem because it's time for others to also know that we love each other. You are a woman now and Minerva really has no further say over you. Even Minerva cannot slaughter true love so we will just have to let our love surface where it may."

Minerva had come into the room to put Lucy to bed. She walked over to the window and found Lucy out of control, weeping silently. Minerva looked out the window and observed Ida and Roaring Bull walking back to the house, arm in arm. Minerva said to Lucy, "You have been watching them haven't you?"

Lucy looked up at her with pleading eyes and nodded her head. Minerva became very angry with fire in her spirit. She worked with haste to put Lucy to bed and then quickly went down the stairs to confront Ida and Roaring Bull.

"Save your breath," announced Roaring Bull to Minerva. "It is no use any more! We love each other and that is how it will be. I will take good care of my children and love them forever but I also love Ida. My heart belongs to Ida and to no one else. And that's the way that it will be! There is no one else for me, Minerva, so stay out of our lives and don't bother to look back."

Ida spoke softly to her mother. "Mama, I am sending James away and I am asking him not to come back again. I have to listen to my heart. I have waited so long for me and Roaring Bull to be together, and I am not willing to wait any longer. I love him, Mama; and I will love him forever. I am not hurting Aunt Lucy. Her heart has already released him. Their love has no substance. Roaring Bull has never been in love with her. Back away, Mama! It's me and Roaring Bull's decision. We are forever!"

Minerva turned her back and walked away. "You will pay, you two!" she screamed. "As sure as there is a light of day, the two of you will surely pay, just you wait and see! Ida! she called out in a stern voice, "You are not my daughter! I refuse to own you any more as my child! Pack your belongings and leave, Ida! Just go your own way and don't you bother to ever come back! I won't stop you this time. Did you hear me, Ida? I want you to leave now!"

Under her breath Minerva spoke to herself. "What has happened to my child? I never raised her to be disrespectful to her elders."

"Roaring Bull," Minerva continued, "you are an evil creature and you will pay for all of this hurt that you have brought to Lucy and to this family. I refuse to leave Lucy here with you alone. I am staying here to take care of my sister because I know that you do not care about her. I hope that one day before long you will just rot; I want you to rot in such a way that you will smell the stink from your own self. You are not fit to live, Roaring Bull; you are not fit to be with people. You are not fit to be put under the dirt that would be used to cover you when you die!"

She slammed the kitchen door and briskly walked away.

Ida said to Roaring Bull, "Poor Mama—maybe one day she will love us both the same but right now she is carrying a nail in her heart. I will wait for you Roaring Bull. I have to wait for you because promises are forever. A promise made is a promise to be kept forever."

Minerva Confronts Roaring Bull

Minerva set her mind to follow through with her threat to run Roaring Bull off Hollowell land. She took a trip to visit Irwin Hollowell concerning the dissension in the family with Roaring Bull. She knew that Irwin had allowed Lucy and Roaring Bull to not only build on Hollowell land that was rightfully Lucy's but also on additional land that was not hers and Roaring Bull was claiming to be his without her knowledge. She was also concerned that Lucy's name was not written on the deed for their home or the deed for the additional land. Her primary request was that Roaring Bull would no longer be allowed to live on the land. One thing she was certain of, Irwin had no space in his heart for Native Americans. She shared with Irwin about Roaring Bull's continued practices of Cherokee rituals and traditions. Like Quarry Town, Native Americans were not welcome in Trigg County as permanent residents. They were only allowed to live on the farms during crop season. They were not welcome to mix and live in the village areas of the cities.

More than ever before, Roaring Bull was making a special effort to maintain the traditional practices of his Cherokee heritage. He had become very comfortable with these practices, which had been passed on to him by his father, Grayhorse. He needed to do this to maintain his relationship with the Great Spirit and to remain in contact with the Spirit of the White Buffalo. He wore traditional Native American clothing and artifacts and preferred to answer to his Native American name.

When Irwin heard these things, he was very angry that he had allowed these details to pass him by. He had thought that the name Roaring Bull was a nickname for Stonewall but not necessarily a meaningful given name from his Native American culture. Irwin felt bitter and deceived. He blamed Lucy as well as Roaring Bull for using deceit to appropriate his land. Irwin promised Minerva to see to it that Roaring Bull would lose his rights to any Hollowell possession. He assured Minerva that she would not need to worry about Lucy, as he would help her to see that Lucy was taken care of and that Roaring Bull received the penalty that was due him for his unjust treatment of Lucy. Irwin was also concerned that Roaring Bull, being a member of the Gray family had been abusing the good name and character of his granddaughter, Ida.

Roaring Bull hitched the mule team, Cole and Nellie, to the wagon and went straight to Minerva's house to see what had happened to Ida.

When he pulled up in front of the house Ida was on her way out the front door with a suitcase in each hand. Her sister, Addie, followed along behind her with a bag of food for her journey. Addie passed the bag of food to Ida, hugged her tenderly, and wept silently as Ida walked away. Ida wore a fresh bonnet, a bright colored shawl, and comfortable shoes. She was prepared to walk the twelve mile distance if she had to.

Roaring Bull climbed down from the wagon and loaded Ida's suitcases in the back. As he helped her climb aboard, he asked, "Where are you headin', Ida?"

"I'm going to Quarry Town; and I am not coming back to this place, not ever. I'm going to my brother, Robert and Lizzie's place. I didn't ask them if I could come and stay with them but I will when I get there. I know that it will be all right with them. Their sons, Ralph, Richard, and Winfred already share space but I will be willing to stay in the attic if I need to." Roaring Bull cracked the whip for his little mule team and they trotted along at due mule speed.

Minerva had one more stop to make before nightfall. She needed to speak to Will concerning the outburst of love between his sister, Ida, and his brother-in-law, Roaring Bull. She knew that it would not pay to talk to Minnie because she had already established a protective wall around her brother, Roaring Bull, to shelter him from the vindictive Hollowell poison. Minerva wanted Will to speak with Roaring Bull and encourage him to turn the house and the care of the children over to her. She also wanted Will to ask Roaring Bull to leave the place. Minerva wanted Will to agree to convince Roaring Bull to let her take the children and Lucy to her place, at least while he was still there. Minerva tried with all of her might to make Will realize just how ill Lucy really was. Roaring Bull had already expressed his determination in harsh words to not leave the place. Minerva thought if Will would agree to help take care of Lucy and if he and Minnie would take care of Harmon, then she would take the girls and maybe Roaring Bull would have no further reason to stay. Since Roaring Bull's ownership extended only to his share of the house and the extended land that Irwin had allowed him and Lucy to have, then maybe, just maybe with the right amount of applied pressure, he would want to give up his share. After all, what good is a home if a home is really not a home?

Will disagreed with all Minerva's suggestions. He and her husband, John, had helped Roaring Bull build the house and he knew just how much the little place meant to both him and Lucy. Besides the children, it was the one thing that they had together. Will felt that a marriage vow is a promise eternal. When a man and a woman take a marriage vow that says, what is yours is also mine and what is mine is yours, that means that all of your possessions belong to each of us. For Lucy and Roaring Bull that meant not only the house but also the allotted land. That was the legal interpretation of the law.

Will loved Harmon as his own son and there was no way that he was going to stand by and see him not being taken care of. Harmon would always have a home with Will and Minnie. Lucy had been like a second mother to him, Addie, and Ida; and there was no way that he and Minnie would not always be around to care for them. He and Minnie were aware of the struggle in Lucy and Roaring Bull's marriage, but they also knew how much he and Ida loved each other. Will already had talked to both Ida and to Roaring Bull about their love affair. They had both pledged to wait for each other no matter how long it would take, and Ida had promised not to do anything to hasten this process as long as her Aunt Lucy was alive. However, Roaring Bull had made no pledge to do the same. Will had watched the two of them embrace in the woods down by the river bank and even once at the house. He had observed how they looked at each other. He thought, *Why drive another arrow into their hearts by demanding that they not see each other or that they not be together? If Minerva wanted to help care for the children, then that's a good thing. If she felt obliged to care for her sister, Lucy, then that is her right. But she had no right to interfere and place herself in the middle of their marriage affairs—and neither did he and Minnie.*

So, Will's surprise answer to Minerva was "No, count me out," he said. "Just play your little game all by yourself."

Roaring Bull of course was Minnie's brother and Will had no intention of asking him to leave Hollowell land. He would always have a welcome place with him and Minnie, both in their hearts and in their home. Now Minerva knew that she would not be able to count Will in on her little scheme, but she did trust Irwin to keep his word. She wondered when and how Irwin's promises would begin to take place. Minerva knew that she really should not begin to play with her sister's life. She felt strongly, that she owed it to Lucy to move with haste to slow up the pace of this triangular but unconsummated love affair. The only recourse left for her to follow was to confront Roaring Bull. She could not bear the thought of looking him in the eye. She really was not happy about having to read his lying lips, or watching his devilish eyes as he denied his true involvement with Ida or his love for her. She expected him to defend his position of ownership for the house and land and to either politely or with arrogance invite her out of their home and out of their lives. To lessen the blow of this face-to-face encounter, she wrote him a long letter explaining all of her concerns. She invited him to meet her at the bend of the river near Muddy Fork. Minerva envisioned that when their conversation reached an impasse, he would soften and adhere to her request.

Minerva dressed in her riding clothes and rode to Muddy Fork on her favorite horse, Cocoa. She began her conversation by asking Roaring Bull what he intended to do about Lucy now that her condition was growing worse and her body was getting weaker. Roaring Bull responded that he had observed the same. He very strongly expressed that he no longer wanted Minerva to come to the house, not even to care for Lucy. Even though Minnie was not well, she was still willing to come and bathe Lucy daily and to see that she received her meals. His sister, Belle, would be there on weekends; and he and the children were getting by the best that they could.

"When push comes to shove, Minerva, we will make it, even without you."

"What about my daughter, Ida?" Minerva asked. "She is a young woman now but I simply will not stand by and watch you ruin her life. I am really not too concerned about your so-called love affair. Ida deserves a chance to be with somebody her own age. Please, give her a chance to love someone else who loves her. You are from a different generation. You are more than a decade older than she! Release the ties that you have on her heart and let her go."

"You let her go, Minerva! You chased her away. She will never come back where you are. She is a woman, Minerva, let her live her own life. You poisoned Lucy's mind about me from the very beginning, now you are busy working on Ida. You are an evil woman, Minerva. Satan has your heart strings. You are not concerned about Ida. You are concerned about the Hollowells and the Hollowell land. It is also about me—right, Minerva? It is all about me. I should have known that nothing good would come from your heart."

"You are not a Hollowell, Roaring Bull; you are a Gray. I know about your Cherokee background and your father, Grayhorse. I know about your Native American practices and beliefs. I have sat with Lucy while we watched you worship with those strange artifacts. It is not normal and I don't intend for you to pass those strange things on to these children. I have heard all of the stories about your father and how he was a real Cherokee

109

Indian. It is that Indian blood in you, Roaring Bull. You are not normal. You are still doing strange things. Lucy told me all about those things and I have watched you doing ceremonies. It's strange. Who are you anyway? Who are you, Roaring Bull? Are you some Cherokee Indian or are you Stonewall Jackson Gray?

"I spoke with Irwin Hollowell about your house on Hollowell land. Now he also knows who you are, a half-breed Cherokee. And do you know what? Indians are not allowed to own land around here. We know that Lucy's name is not anywhere on that deed and you know that the land is not rightfully yours. Well you can start packing, Roaring Bull, you are on your way off this land. Nobody, I mean *nobody* plays these games with the Hollowells."

"Over my dead stiff body, Minerva! Did you hear me? I'll leave when they carry me away, feet first and my body cold, and it won't be because of you. Go back where you came from, Minerva. I don't expect to see you or ever hear about any of this again. You are right about one thing, Minerva, I am half Cherokee in my blood but I am whole Cherokee in my heart. What about you Minerva? Who are you, really? Do you have an ancestral pass? Do you really know what it is like to be half African and half Caucasian? Would that be mulatto, Minerva? Do you honestly know who you are?"

"Oh, yes," answered Minerva. "I know exactly who I am. By the way, Roaring Bull, what about that deerskin pouch that you carry around? Where did it come from? Where is it now? What about those jewels, and who do they belong to? Did they come from the Cherokee, too? Why are they such a secret? Why haven't you shared the jewel secret with Lucy? Don't worry, Lucy knows everything. Are you keeping them for Ida? Well, I know exactly where they are. I saw you place them in that hole in the tree at Muddy Fork. Do you know what else? I am telling all of these secrets to Will and Minnie so don't you worry about who gets the land because you will be leaving anyway. Just you wait and see. By the way, don't you even think about moving those jewels because you won't be taking them off the land. They are no longer yours to keep. This is Hollowell land and now those jewels belong to Lucy and the children."

With those words, Minerva straddled her horse, Cocoa, slapped his hips with the whip, and rode away in haste with her hair blowing in the wind. Roaring Bull stood wiping his eyes from the dust that blew in his eyes from the mini dust storm kicked up by Cocoa as she left at a thorough-bred pace.

Roaring Bull whistled for his horse, Sonny. He walked him down to the river bank to give him a drink of water before they started their journey. Sonny always seemed to understand him whenever he needed to talk to someone.

"It is just another test, Sonny," Roaring Bull began, "A test for you and me. We've been tested before, old boy. It's a test from the West Wind. When the West Wind blows and turbulence sets in a storm will surely come. When the storm passes over, these dark clouds will be replaced with beautiful rainbows. Rainbows are symbols of covenant promises from the Great Spirit. Promises that do not fade away but are forever. You know what, Sonny? Let's you and me just wait for the rainbows. The jewels will be safe if we follow the wisdom of the White Buffalo. It worked for my father and it will work for us."

Roaring Bull Visits Ida

Roaring Bull rode straight to Quarry Town to visit Will and Ida's brother, Robert, and his wife Lizzie. Lizzie was the sister of Horatio and Homer Osborne. Ida loved staying with them and Lizzie loved her as her own daughter. She welcomed Ida to live at their house until she could get her own place. Ida loved being there and had become even closer since Horatio had proposed to her sister, Addie. They were to be married during the coming spring.

When Roaring Bull came around the corner at Green and Cave Streets, he saw Ida sitting in the porch swing with her crochet basket. She had promised Lizzie that she would have dollies completed for the living room by the end of the week.

Roaring Bull drove the wagon up to the gate and Sonny stopped without even being given a command.

The busy talk around Quarry Town was that Roaring Bull was keeping company with Ida while still living with his wife, Lucy, in Trigg County. Neither Ida nor Roaring Bull put forth any effort to hide their relationship. It was no longer a secret that they loved each other, and everyone knew and expected that it would only be a matter of time until they would be together as husband and wife.

Roaring Bull was in dispute with the Hollowells; and neither was that a secret in Quarry Town. But Roaring Bull was a Gray, loved and respected by the people of Quarry Town. So this family feud was not in good favor with the townspeople. Whenever anyone mentioned Lucy to Roaring Bull it was usually to inquire about her well being. Often it would be mentioned in the same tone as to ask, "Is she still living? How much longer must you and that poor Ida have to wait to be married?"

When Roaring Bull disembarked from the wagon, he began to tell Ida his story before he greeted her or even before he reached the front porch. Ida put her crochet basket down and arose to greet him. She listened intently to everything that he had to say. Roaring Bull told her all about his fiery confrontation with her mother, Minerva. He reiterated how Minerva had threatened him if he did not cease his relationship with Ida and pledge not to see her again. He talked about Minerva's visit to see Irwin Hollowell and her request to have him ejected from Hollowell land. He told Ida that Minerva had requested him to rescind his property rights for their home and to give Lucy full ownership. Minerva had even gone a step further to poison the minds and to sway the opinion of Ida's brother Will and his wife Minnie by spreading rumors that he no longer loved Lucy and was neglecting her care and his devotion for her at a time when she was not able to fight back. Minerva believed that her only real motive for spreading all of this evil was her love for her sister, Lucy, and her sincere motherly duty to save her daughter, Ida from the snares of a selfish and evil old man, Roaring Bull.

When Ida heard these reports, she was fiercely angry with her mother. She vowed to never go near her again, to stay away from Hollowell land in Trigg County, and to write her mother a fiery letter revealing her disappointment and mistrust. Roaring Bull tried to explain to Ida that it was never his intent to turn her against her mother but that he feared what might happen to her if she did not know the details and true motives of the story. He pleaded with Ida not to repay vengeance with vengeance by turning against her mother. At the same time, he warned her to remain vigilant while they waited for their opportunity to be together.

Ida promised Roaring Bull that she would follow his suggestions and not speak to her mother or her sister, Addie, concerning the issue as long as she did not have to come in contact with Minerva. Addie either visited or heard from her sister at least once a week. Minerva was not certain just whom Ida was living with in Quarry Town. She thought that she might be living with someone in the Gray family. Roaring Bull did not want to stay away from Ida too long because he did not trust Minerva. He had grown even more concerned since Minerva told him that she knew where he had stored the jewels and had threatened to take them away. His plans were to remove them from the tree hole now that someone knew where they were.

He and Sonny would stop on the way home today and take them back. He would have to find a new place for them where they would be safe. Roaring Bull said goodbye to Ida, gave her his usual embrace, boarded the wagon, and started to make his way back home. He had to reach the tree where the jewels were stored well before sundown.

Visit from the Spirit of the White Buffalo

Sometimes the journey across the Caldwell/Trigg County line seemed farther away. One thing was for certain, Roaring Bull had to follow the path that led to Muddy Fork in order to retrieve the jewels. He needed to stop at the mouth of the river to rest Sonny and give him fresh water from the creek that emptied into the river.

Roaring Bull unhitched Sonny to give him a break and then took off his shoes and socks to rest his feet. Just overhead, he heard a strange crackling sound moving through the branches of the trees. Amazed, he looked up and observed a female image in flight moving along the shore line of the river. The image was accompanied by a brisk wind and a piercing light that blinded his vision. He knew right away that this image had to be the image of Whispering Wind. His father had mentioned that she had visited him sometimes preceding the appearance of the Spirit of the White Buffalo. Maybe the Great Spirit had assigned her to be his totem spirit. Sonny neighed out of fear and quickly backed away from the river's edge.

With no fear, Roaring Bull called out, "What in the name of the Great Spirit do you want to say to me? Who are you? Why are you here?"

Without speaking, the image dissipated into the water and the form changed into the Spirit of the White Buffalo. Roaring Bull recognized the image and settled down to receive its message. It had been quite a while since he had experienced a vision. He had begun to wonder if the Great Spirit had removed his protective shelter from him. When the Spirit spoke, the intonation mirrored the voice of Grayhorse. The image identified itself as the spirit of Grayhorse. It addressed Roaring Bull by his Cherokee name. It said, "Roaring Bull, my son, I have come to bring comfort to your spirit. You have made a terrible mistake. You have neglected the legacy and placed the precious jewels in danger of being lost forever.

"Before today's sundown and before the turbulence of the West Wind, you must retrieve the jewels so that they are again in your custodial care. After sundown, they will no longer be in place and you will never see

113

them again! You must return to Quarry Town, the place where the Gray legacy was born. You must return to the founding of its people. Renew the covenant promises that you made when you took the oath of entrustment and became the mentoring spirit for future seedlings to follow. Your family history is going to be lost. It is becoming disassembled and your family relationships are becoming broken and disconnected. Your brother has already given up the desire to challenge you for ownership of the legacy and the jewels. He is ready now to work with you as a cooperative spirit. There is a tempest raging inside of you because you have tried to transfer the legacy and the jewels from the Gray roots and anchor them into the roots of another family, the Hollowells. Bonding the legacy with another family means that you are altering the family values, morals, traditions and devotions. RETURN TO YOUR COMMITMENT.

"My spirit will not be at peace until these conditions are met. Your life cycle will not follow a peaceful path as long as you rebuff my spirit and move against the currents of the West Wind."

With these words, there was a sharp flash of lightning, a heavy downpour, followed by the appearance of a brilliant rainbow. A very calm spirit came over Roaring Bull. He felt very tired as the spirit vanished as quickly as it had appeared. Sonny was so afraid that Roaring Bull had to calm him down. Roaring Bull gently rubbed his neck and whispered comforting words in his ear. As he hitched Sonny back to the wagon, darkened clouds appeared overhead. They steadily made their way towards Muddy Fork, riding with haste against the brisk wind. The wind became so strong that it took all of Sonny's strength to pull the wagon against the current. Roaring Bull feared that if the wind did not settle soon they would have to find shelter.

As they moved closer to the tree, he could tell from a distance that someone had been there and that they had tampered with the hole. It did not appear to have been the work of a squirrel, woodpecker, or some other animal. The stake that he had planted at the base of the tree had been taken down, dismantled, and thrown in two separate directions. The mud that sealed the hole had been chipped away by someone using a sharp metal object, and the object was resting on the ground nearby. He thanked the Great Spirit for guiding him to camouflage the pouch by covering it with leaves and by shoving it as far back into the hole as he could reach. Several of the leaves in the front were in disarray. Nervously, he felt among the leaves for the pouch. He stretched to reach as far back as he could reach. Surprisingly, he caught hold of the string of the pouch. There it was, he had it once

114

again in his own hands! He gently pulled it toward him and prayed that all of the jewels were accounted for and in good condition.

Someone had been there. The pouch had been removed and returned to the hole. The person who did it had placed it back among the leaves as if it had not been disturbed. *Could this have been the work of Minerva? Had she sent John or some other culprit to do her evil work?* One thing he knew for certain, if the jewels were still in the pouch, he had no choice but to carry them with him. Without opening the pouch, he sat on the ground next to Sonny and offered a chant of thanksgiving to the Great Spirit. Nervously, he opened the pouch, turned it upside down, and slowly and stately, the jewels gently slid onto the ground. A piece of torn yellow lined paper fell to the ground among the jewels. Printed in uneven letters was the message, "IF NOT THIS TIME, THEN THE NEXT TIME FOR SURE."

Roaring Bull sighed a deep sigh of relief and counted the stones to assure that they were all accounted for. He counted three silver nuggets and twelve beautiful brilliant blue turquoise gems. He gently polished them with the corner of his shirt and returned them to the pouch. Roaring Bull knew that this had to be a follow-through for the threat that the jewels would not leave Hollowell land. Carefully, he retied the sinew string on the pouch and placed it carefully around his neck where it belonged. He tucked it inside the left side of his shirt next to his heart and made a solemn promise to himself, "Never again!"

He remained vigilant all the way home, afraid that he might be followed or confronted by the intruder. He thought, *Minerva would need to use a ladder or have someone assist her to do this. She is not tall enough to reach the hole without some assistance. If someone had climbed the tree and perched on a branch, they would be too far away from the hole to get the task done. Whoever used the sharp object to chisel the mud seal away from the hole seemed to still be too short to reach all the way back into the hole. What about the message? How did it get into the pouch? Maybe John was helping Minerva. Could it have been one of the original Hollowells or one of his my own brothers seeking retribution for the legacy? There is always the possibility that it may have been a passer-by just seeking to find what he could find.* Roaring Bull had a feeling that he was being followed. He felt much discomfort as he rode along. He rode along the trail with a watchful eye and was even more vigilant around his in-laws.

Minerva and Will were waiting for him when he reached the house. They were anxious for him to come home so that they could share urgent news about Lucy. He crumpled the message on the yellow paper that he had taken from the hole and slung it on the kitchen table. Minnie picked up the paper and read it. "Does someone want the jewels?"

"Yes," responded Roaring Bull, "and someone also wants my blood." Will made no verbal response but shook his head and looked at Minnie as if to agree with Roaring Bull's assessment. Minnie walked over to him and placed her hand on his shoulder. "Let me keep the jewels," she asked. "I heard our father's request of you when you received the entrustment. I will keep them safe! Trust me, Roaring Bull, I am your sister. No one will ever know except you and me.

Roaring Bull responded with anger, "Not on your life! They were entrusted to me and I will protect them any way I can. A promise is a promise," he declared. "They will not be lost and they will never be taken away."

"Then you must be more protective of them." Minnie scolded. "Be careful, Roaring Bull, be mighty careful! Keep rotating your eyes and keep a guard dog watching over your back. Why don't you go back to Quarry Town? There is much bad blood here between you and the Hollowells. Find your way home where you belong."

"No one is going to chase me away," declared Roaring Bull. "I may return to Quarry Town one day but when I do, it will be on my own terms."

With those words and without even asking about Lucy, he stamped out of the kitchen on his way up to the attic and fell face forward across his cot.

Lucy's Final Agony

Minnie and Will followed him upstairs. They had waited most of the day for his return, but they could not wait much longer to talk to him about Lucy. Her condition had taken a turn for the worse early that morning just after he left for Quarry Town. Her voice and her spirit had weakened. Lucy had talked with Minnie and Will about having them assist Roaring Bull with the children after she passed away. Lucy had been calling for Roaring Bull most of the day. After they talked to Roaring Bull about her condition, he rushed down the stairs to her bedroom in his bare feet.

Her eyes were closed when he entered her bedroom. He called out to her softly, "Lucy, Lucy dear, I'm home. I'm home to be with you." She opened her eyes slightly and spoke with a soft voice.

"Roaring Bull, my time is passing quickly and my life is fading away.

116

I want you to take good care of our children. Let Minnie and Will help you take care of anything about the children that you do not understand. I have to release you, Roaring Bull. I am letting you go now. Go ahead and be with Ida. I have watched you in each other's arms too many times. It no longer breaks my heart to say this or to think of the two of you together. I know how close you have grown to Ida. I have to release you so that my spirit will be at peace for my spirit journey. I do not want to leave this world with a wandering spirit. So, go to her, treat her well, and the two of you be happy. I have felt tears flowing from her heart. I know that she loves you. She is my niece and this is the last thing that I can do for her. In the spirit of peace, I am letting her go.

"Roaring Bull, I know about this war between you and Minerva. Minerva is my sister but this battle over the land is between me and you. I am releasing my share to you and the children. I have talked to Minerva and asked her to withdraw the axe. I love you, Roaring Bull, that has never changed. I realize that I have not been able to be a good wife to you. But do carry this to your grave, I love you.

"Now may the peace of your Great Spirit and the wisdom of your father, Grayhorse, always follow you. May the West Wind always be at your back and never in front of you. There is a strength in you that I have always admired. It is the force that drew me to you." Lucy reached out to take his hand, turned her head to the side and observed tears flowing down his cheeks. She threw him a kiss and drew her last breath.

Roaring Bull gasped for air, wiped his teary eyes and reached down and closed Lucy's eyes. He walked over to the window where she always waited for him, only to behold the piercing arrows to her broken heart. He wept aloud and said to her even though she could no longer hear him, "I did love you Lucy. You will always remain in my heart. You gave me three wonderful children."

Now he needed to talk to the children. He needed to explain to them about death and what it all meant now that their mother was gone.

Minnie and Will stayed close by to help Roaring Bull through those trying days. His sister, Belle, came right away to be with the children. There was not a mortician in Trigg County that black families could use, but Babbage Funeral Home was located only a few miles away in Hopkinsville, Kentucky. Belle contacted them to come and take care of the body. The girls wanted their mother to be buried in a white dress so Belle got busy and sewed one for each of the girls to wear also.

Following the traditional three days of mourning, an all night

117

wake/watch was held at the house. All of the mirrors in the house were covered with sheets so that unwanted images would not reflect in the mirrors. The body was embalmed, dressed, and returned to the house around midday. The funeral was held the next day at Shiloh Baptist Church in Trigg County. The cemetery was located on the church grounds. Lucy was buried near the back fence facing the East and the Shiloh School, which was also located on the church grounds. Minerva preferred that her sister be buried at Hollowell cemetery in Caldwell County, the land which had been donated by Dr. Isaac Parker Hollowell and had always been for burying all of the Hollowell family. But Roaring Bull was in charge and he wanted nothing more to do with the Hollowells, not even in death.

Neither Ida nor Addie attended their Aunt Lucy's funeral but both of them came to the cemetery and watched the interment from across the back road with tears in their eyes. After leaving Addie and Horatio's house, they traveled the back path to the cemetery so that they would not be noticed. They stayed away from the family and made themselves invisible as, sobbing, they watched the proceedings.

After the funeral, Belle followed Roaring Bull and the children home to help them get settled in. As days passed, the children really missed their mother. The girls wept a lot and told their Aunt Belle and their father that they no longer wanted to live in Trigg County. Roaring Bull agreed that the girls could be with their Aunt Belle, but Harmon chose to remain with his father. Nina stayed with Belle for only a short time before her uncle, Harvey James and his wife Allie, took her to live with them. They trained her well in the ethics and social graces of womanhood. She was beautifully poised, very well groomed, and demonstrated well-bred qualities of courtesy and respect.

Harmon missed his sisters. He had helped his father load their belongings in the wagon and felt that the family was becoming disconnected when his sisters left. He wanted to visit them often. His father continued to remind him that it would not be much longer until they would be joining his sisters in Quarry Town. It only took a few weeks until Roaring Bull decided that the time had come for he and his son to leave. There were so many forces that were drawing him back to Quarry Town: his children, the legacy, Ida, and his yearning to be with his real family, the Grays. Without much hesitation, Roaring Bull made preparations to return to the Gray farm. His decision was accented by a command from the Great Spirit, which had directed him in a vision at Little River shores to return to Quarry Town. Right now, Roaring Bull's life cycle seemed to be spinning in a cir-

118

cle. He no longer felt that he was in control of his destiny. It was as if he was being carried by a turbulent wind. He pondered over how these life movements were taking place. His life was following the forceful currents of the West Wind.

Trigg County Restrains

Roaring Bull had one more move to make before he left Trigg County. He had returned to the house two days earlier to collect any belongings that he and Harmon might have overlooked. Around supper time, he took a trip to Wet Fork to have a talk with Irwin Hollowell concerning the house and the land. He explained to Irwin that he was in no way interested in owning any Hollowell land and that he did not want his children to own any Hollowell land, not even if it had been inherited from their mother, Lucy. In a fit of anger, Roaring Bull held their house-and-land mortgage up high in the air equal to Irwin's nose and lit it with a match, allowing it to burn down to one corner. Then he threw it on the ground and stamped the fire out with his foot. Not another word was spoken between them. Roaring Bull rode away and called out with a loud voice, "This is how I feel about you and your land."

As he rode along the path raising dust clouds behind him, the road curved and wound around to the back side of the house where he and Lucy had lived. He stopped the wagon at the top of the hill to survey the place then drove the wagon around to the front of the house, disembarked, walked around to the back of the house. He reached under the back porch, struck a match, and threw it on the porch to ignite the gasoline.

The fire caught instantly. Roaring Bull walked around to the front of the house, climbed aboard the wagon, and rode away without looking back. As he rode away, he could smell the fumes from the gasoline and the charred wood from the burning fire. When he rounded the curve up ahead, he could see a dark plume of smoke in the sky encircling the area from the burning inferno. He reached inside his shirt for the pouch with the precious jewels and clenched it tight in the palm of his hand, thanking the Great Spirit for returning the jewels to him and hoping that he had turned the final page to bring closure to this turbulent cycle in his life. He wanted to end all feuds and close the book on his relationship with the Hollowells.

Seek Wisdom

It dwells in the portals of the Universe;
Created and mastered by God.
Entrusted to elders and children;
To enlighten our path as we trod.

SO

Collect its portions and value it deeply.
It forms our paths, enriches our presence,
And
Directs our future each day.

SO

Seek wisdom and carry it with you
As you travel along life's way.

From
Gift of Cheyenne

12

Shadows of a Crescent Moon

Moonlight Slips Away

It was a wintry morning in 1899. Ida had began to worry that they would not be able to travel the treacherous twenty-mile trail from Caldwell to Christian County. The talk around Quarry Town was that Roaring Bull had changed his mind about marrying Ida. Roaring Bull was handsome and tall and the single women of Quarry Town had begun to show an interest in the fact that he might no longer be spoken for. One element that was holding back the Quarry Town women was Roaring Bull's continued practice of Cherokee rituals and his frequent display of a trusted dreammaker that was attached to the back of his wagon. The wedding date had been set twice and each time the ceremony had been canceled a few days before the scheduled date.

In his mind, Roaring Bull was still feuding with the Hollowells—and Ida was a Hollowell. Neither of them wanted a wedding where the towns-people would be invited to attend. How could they possibly invite the Grays and not invite the Hollowells? Ida was certain of her love for Roaring Bull but she could feel a shadow from the past beginning to hover over their marriage even before it took place. Roaring Bull had set his foot down so that her mother would not be a welcome guest.

He had contacted Judge Fred Metcalf in Hopkinsville and made arrangements to meet in his office at 7:00 P.M., Judge Metcalf had asked Rosie, his secretary, to work late so that she could be a witness for the ceremony. The prospective newlyweds needed three witnesses. Ida's sister, Addie, and Harmon agreed to go along and serve as the other two witnesses. Ida knew that if they left in the afternoon they would be traveling after sunset and the journey would be dark and cold, and she was wondering what was keeping Roaring Bull so long since he also wanted to leave early. He had worked on the wagon most of the morning. The wagon was a hand-me-down from the Gray farm that his father had used and it had become rickety and unbalanced. Roaring Bull was not making much progress with the repairs, so he talked to Horatio about using their wagon. At least the wheels on their wagon were balanced and strong and the spokes were new.

Horatio soaked the wheels in water so that the spokes would expand to steady the ride. He had also added a plank across the back of the wagon to make a second seat so that Harmon and Addie would not have to ride on the wagon floor. Roaring Bull brought over two horses from the Gray farm. He had selected Big Red a retired draft horse, to be teamed with Sonny, his trusted favorite, who was much older, slower, and seldom pulled the wagon anymore.

When Ida saw the horse team, she thought, *Oh my stars, why in the dickens would he use Sonny in weather such as this?* She knew that their journey would be much slower now that Sonny would be helping to pull the load; but she also knew that Roaring Bull loved Sonny so much and there was just no way that he and Ida would undertake an important event such as this and Sonny not be there as part of the family.

The snow was almost ankle deep and Ida was determined that nothing was going to stop the wedding this time, not even the snow, the cold, and certainly not Minerva.

Ida gathered a bundle of blankets in her arms for each of them. She put on extra clothing, boots, gloves, and a wind-proof hat to help weather the storm. Twice, she had checked her purse to be sure that she had picked up all of the papers that she needed to carry along for Judge Metcalf.

Roaring Bull looked as handsome as ever. Ida could not help but notice that he was dressed in his best clothes and was wearing his father's jacket with a blanket draped around his shoulders. She had hoped that he would not wear his Native American clothes or perform any Cherokee rituals in the judge's presence, as she did not want to do anything that would cause the judge to question if he could legally perform the ceremony. The law in Christian County was the same as it was in the adjoining counties. Native Americans were not considered to be legal residents and the practice of their traditional rituals was not acceptable. They had no legal right to be married in a regular court. The women of the area were encouraged not to associate with them. Ida had asked Roaring Bull to use his birth name, Stonewall Jackson Gray. He rebutted her request on the grounds that he needed to retain his relationship with the Great Spirit in order to properly carry out his commitment to the family legacy. Without further consideration, he helped the ladies climb into the wagon, cracked the whip, commanded the horse team, and kept quiet afterward.

Addie and Ida chatted most of the way. When Ida questioned Roaring Bull about his unusual silence, he responded that he was watching the road and paying attention to the weather. He stated that he wanted to keep the horses calm so that they could handle the difficult journey. Harmon asked if he could trade places with Ida and ride up front with his father. Ida agreed because to ride with Addie would provide some much-needed quality time for herself and her sister that they had not been able to share for several months. As soon as Roaring Bull found a smooth spot, he pulled over to the side and stopped the wagon to allow them to trade places. Ida simply climbed over the back of the seat to join Addie while Harmon jumped down and ran around the back of the wagon to climb up front with his father. The rest of the way, Harmon pointed out little animals enjoying the new snow, figures in the clouds, and unusual snowflakes. He also shared childhood stories and memories with Roaring Bull. The trade also provided for Harmon some quality time with his father. Roaring Bull was thinking about how his life would change in just a few hours. He and Ida had waited almost a decade for this day. He wanted to be as happy as Ida that their day had come. *Why wasn't he?* He reached inside his pocket. Yes, he had remembered. The jewels were pressing against his chest and their protection was pressing against his heart. He knew Ida would understand his devotion to the legacy and the protection of the jewels.

Roaring Bull really needed to rest the horse team since they were both old generals but the snow was not letting up and the weather was not getting better. The wind had shifted and was beginning to blow stronger from the West. The women were getting chilled and the hour was growing shorter so he needed to keep traveling in order to be on time for the appointment with the judge. It was necessary to do this ceremony in the judge's chambers after work hours because according to the law, Judge Metcalf was not supposed to marry Native Americans. It was not to take place between Native Americans and white women, between each other, and definitely not between Native Americans and black people. No one was to know about their visit to the office except the judge and his secretary, who had been trusted not to tell anyone about anything that had taken place that evening. A crescent moon appeared in the sky overhead encircled by a brilliant ring of light that brightened their path as they drove into town. Harmon pointed out a dim light that shone through a small window in Judge Metcalf's office, which was located on the second floor in the east corner of the building. Addie reminded everyone that they only had five minutes to reach the office if they wanted to be on time. Addie and Harmon moved quickly and walked ahead so that the judge would be aware that they had arrived. Roaring Bull waited for Ida and helped her down from the wagon. For some reason, she was moving slower than usual. He took her hand and spoke to her softly.

"Ida, this is our beginning. I always intended for this night to come. My vow to you is to do whatever will make your life easy and to keep you happy. I love you, Ida. We have waited a long time for this time. I am going to begin this change with your request. I must honor my relationship with the Great Spirit, I am committed to protect the jewels, and I have to keep my oath to the family legacy. I am giving up my Cherokee name for you Ida, just for you. Beginning this night, I am going to use my birth name, Stonewall Jackson Gray, the name given to me by my father. I have always wondered why I needed two names, tonight it is very clear to me. The people of Quarry Town know me as Stonewall. I do not want anything to hinder the legality of our marriage. Can you accept me as I am, Ida? I am Stonewall but deep in my heart and in my blood, I am Cherokee. As my father was, so am I. I am because he was."

They hurried up the stairs and reached the office just as the clock in the hallway chimed 7:00. Judge Metcalf was rushing around the table in the room as if he wanted to send them on their way before anyone noticed that he was in his office after hours. Rosie had already filled out the papers and signed her name as a witness. Ida looked in her purse and handed the judge the birth records for both herself and Roaring Bull. She also had documents from Dr. Hatten, verifying that they were both in good health. The doctor had checked on Roaring Bull's report that he had asthma and a slow heartbeat. When Ida gave the papers to the judge, without looking at them, he laid them aside on a nearby table. The judge was in such a rush that he had each of the witnesses sign on the proper line before the couple took their vows. Ida thought this was so that if something happened to interrupt the procedure, the papers would already be signed. Ida wanted to say her vows when the hand on the clock was moving up. She looked at the clock, which read 7:18 P.M. Without checking the clock, the judge read words of commitment from a small black book and they were each asked to repeat after him. By 7:25 P.M. he announced to them that they were man and wife according to the power invested in him as a judge in Christian County, in the state of Kentucky. Without saying words of congratulation or even goodbye, Judge Metcalf rushed everyone out of his office and sent them on their way. Before the wedding party could board the wagon, both he and Rosie had turned out the light and on their way out, passed them by on the front porch and drove away in the judge's wagon.

As he left the judge's office, Roaring Bull had paused to pick up their personal documents that the judge had placed on the small table. Roaring Bull was a little irritated that the judge had very bluntly ordered him not to use his Cherokee name but to be sure to write his name as Stonewall Jackson Gray. The judge stated that "this will keep both you and me out of trouble with the law." For Roaring Bull, it was just one more way for a white judge to intimidate blacks and Native Americans. The authorities seemed to always find a way to play around with one's name. In Stonewall's heart, an arrow fell; these words were an outburst of insensitive nonsense, a fountain of mean-spirited fear that came from the heart of one he had trusted. On the way home, Stonewall chuckled over how terrified the judge was about their being there. Ida did not join in the chuckles. For her, it was a serious moment and she did not expect the judge to make it any different. Ida and Addie had found humor in the way the judge was so attentive to Rosie as she boarded the wagon. The implied truth about their relationship had already reached the Hopkinsville townspeople.

The judge's horse team seemed to already know the way to their destination as they trotted away from the office. They made an immediate left turn without being given a command and headed away from the home trail. As the evening began to grow late, the breeze was chilly. There was a crescent moon above and Rosie and the judge had every intention of taking advantage of this romantic opportunity. Mrs. Metcalf had been bedridden for several years and Rosie's husband, Sewell, always worked late hours at the livery stable on old Guthrie Road, so there was no rush for either of them to get home but they were later than usual because of the after-hours wedding ceremony. They did not want Miss Willie Mae to cancel their space at Cambridge Boarding House and assign their regular rooms to someone else. To make up the time lost at the office they did not take the regular trail but they cut through Second Street until they reached Walnut Street and then crossed over to Durrett Avenue which was a shorter route where fewer people were likely to notice them.

When they reached the boarding house, the snow had picked up and they were each covered with soft white pellets. Miss Willie Mae was expecting them and led them to their usual place. It was midweek, Wednesday, and they always came on that day. The judge ordered the usual meal for room service and he and Rosie settled in for their usual uninterrupted affection. The snow continued to fall quietly; the judge closed the drapes, lowered the light in the oil lamp, and snuggled under the covers with Rosie. Rosie was his longtime sweetheart whom he loved dearly. To miss this evening with Rosie would have been a little more than he was ready to sacrifice. It was the Judge's weekly break away from the stress and confinement that he sometimes saw as a burden since his wife had been ill. It was a golden reason for the fast exit from his office after the wedding.

The judge rested his head on Rosie's shoulder and spoke quietly in her ear, "Glory be, sweet thing! I thought they would never leave."

When the wedding party reached the Caldwell County line, Stonewall turned at the dairy and went through Big Spring to drop off Addie. Then they traveled to the Gray farm where he, Ida, and Harmon would spend their first night together as a family. Dave and Sarah had left a light on in the kitchen. Stonewall stopped near the front porch to help Ida get down from the wagon.

Sarah had made boiled custard and left a freshly baked fruit cake on the counter for their arrival. It was representation of their wedding cake and a special gift from Sarah. The family did not allow the use of liquor or liquor flavorings. Stonewall poured himself a healthy glass of boiled custard and cut a king-sized portion of Sarah's fruit cake. Ida got herself an extra fork and shared his late night treat instead of having her usual cup of tea. Stonewall walked Ida up the stairs and introduced her to the bedroom of her new place of abode. Jokingly he teased her by stating, "I would have kept our family tradition and carried my new bride up the stairs but that large slice of fruit cake with custard would have all but broke my back."

They had planned to remain at the farm until Stonewall could make arrangements to live at a small place that he was fixing up in Shiloh. Meanwhile Ida was comfortable living with the Grays and being around Sarah. Dave and Sarah had opened their arms and heart to make her feel welcome and she already felt like she was an integral part of the family. Ida's new bedroom was squeaky clean and cozy warm so it was only a few minutes until she said goodnight and was fast asleep. Peacefully, she nestled into her fluffy new featherbed that Stonewall had moved over from the guest room just for his new bride. Stonewall lowered the light on the oil lamp, slipped into his flannel night shirt, and slid into bed beside her. It was a time long awaited. Years plus days had passed and finally he was with his Ida. Ida was so tired that she knew nothing of his thoughts and dreams but he took her in his arms anyway, held her close to him, and longed for new beginnings. When the door cracked, it was Rex, with his snowy paws, looking for his usual resting place on the floor at the foot of the bed. It was on the right side, next to Stonewall, the dog had no intention of giving it up for Ida. It mattered not to him that she was a new bride.

Family Expands in Shiloh

A year later, on a fresh new morning in 1899, the family moved into their own little place on a farm in Shiloh. The weather was a carbon copy of their adventurous journey to Christian County for their wedding. Their house was off Hollowell land and far enough away from Quarry Town to quiet the town gossip, yet close enough to the Gray farm for Stonewall to remain in contact with the spirit of Grayhorse. Before beginning the journey, Stonewall made a trip to the petroglyph tree to pay respect to his father and mother's spirit. He had checked the jewels at early rising, polished and counted them before paying his vows. He even carved a new petroglyph on the tree to mark these new beginnings with Ida. Ida was carrying their first child so all of the packing and lifting of their belongings was done by Stonewall and Harmon and his brothers at the farm. Ida had just reached her twentieth birthday and Stonewall was now forty-four years old.

Their new place was special to Ida, their first real endeavor of ownership together. The house was roomy with plenty of kitchen and bedroom space. There was a food pantry and the cistern to draw water was located just next to the back steps. It was located less than a mile from the Shiloh church where all of the Grays came to worship. The Black Hollowells had also found their place among the Shiloh worshippers.

Included on the church grounds was an adjacent cemetery and a one room school for grades one through eight with one classroom teacher to take care of instruction for all of the grades. The teacher was also responsible for cleaning the building and for making a fire in the pot bellied stove each day when the weather was cold. The church was organized and administered by the black residents of the area and the school was under the administration of the church. The cemetery was also tended by the people of the church on land donated by the Hollowells. When someone was to be buried there, the church people would dig a grave, inter the body, and cover the grave. Cemeteries in these counties were usually identified by family name or were under the direction of an area church congregation. Most of the Grays and Hollowells were buried at Shiloh cemetery. Later some were buried in Caldwell County at McGoodwin and Tinsley cemeteries. Black residents and Native Americans had not gained the right to bury at Cedar Hill cemetery, the main burial place in Quarry Town, a practice that continues for many black residents even today.

Ida was happy and loved their new dwelling place. She enjoyed rising early and tending her special garden spot. It was a perfect beginning and a blessed place for them to begin their new family. Ida's fetus had almost reached full term and Belle had come over to help her out and stay for awhile since this would be Ida's first experience with childbirth. Belle brought her niece Hattie with her, but Hattie had very little tolerance or love for Ida because of what had happened to her mother, Lucy. However, she loved being near her brother, Harmon, and her father. Hattie made every effort to be respectful to Ida. She tried to avoid any family dissension. She kept busy and stayed out from under Ida's feet.

As time passed, Ida and Stonewall birthed thirteen children, not including the three children that he fathered with Lucy. All of the children attended either Shiloh or Goose Creek School. There was always some strained tension between the Caldwell County Grays and the Trigg County Hollowells. The birth lineage for Ida and Stonewall's children and their spouses is as follows:

(Stonewall and his first wife, Lucy Hollowell birthed three children before he married Ida Hollowell. They were: Harmon, Nina, and Hattie Gray.)

Children of Stonewall and Ida

Children	Spouse
Helen (1900) Our Matrix Aunt	John
Frank (1902)	No Wife
Walter Jack (1903)	Dixie
Proctor (1904)	Lillian Clute
Capatolia (1906)	Grandville King
Sully (1908) (Our Father)	No Wife
Mary Dee (1909)	Frank Ephram
Adeline (1910) (Namesake for Mother Ellen's Sister)	Butch Johnson
Ulyssee (1911)	Willie Belle Harper
Clyde (1913) (Our Patriarch Uncle)	Clara Mae Hollowell
Lincoln (1914)	No Wife
Matthew (Matt) (1917)	No Wife
Harvey (1919)	Susie Eison

Over a period of nineteen years, Ida and Stonewall's thirteen children were born. Ida birthed her last child at age thirty-nine and Stonewall was sixty-three years old.

Lesson Unlearned

Stonewall had fathered sixteen offspring and hoped that they were the fulfillment of the seedling offspring requirement set forth in the legacy and represented by the precious jewels. He waited, fasted, and prayed to the Great Spirit. He had interpreted in his own mind that the three silver nuggets represented the three children that he had fathered with Lucy. Not once did he stop to realize that he was a sixth son and that the seedling jewels were not to come from the lineage or from his generation. They had to come through the lineage of the as yet unborn Sully, a generation to follow. Stonewall's role was only to serve as a custodian for the protection of the jewels.

Once again, the covenant for the family legacy had been broken. He had forsaken the rooted base for the legacy. Stonewall was now in Shiloh and just beyond Trigg County. Even though he was still living in Caldwell County, he was too far away. His offspring had been planted and rooted too far away from the values and morals of the Gray family. Again, he was moving under a threatening cloud from the West Wind. Did he need a new vision from the spirit of the White Buffalo? Would he be able to adjust the tilt and correct these mistakes with his own strength? How would he ever be able to make Ida understand that after nineteen years and at age sixty-three, he needed to return to Quarry Town?

As days passed and Stonewall pondered over his dilemma, he spent much time around the waterways of Grand River Basin. Each time that he had encountered a vision from the Great Spirit, he had been near the water. His sons loved to go along with him whenever he went fishing or went on a vision trip. This time, he allowed Clyde, Proctor, and Sully to come. He collected his camping and fishing gear and set out to follow the markings along the path that led to that portion of the Trail of Tears that ran through Lyon and Caldwell Counties. It was the same trail that his father had followed when he settled in the area. It led up from the Tennessee line to Kuttawa, Eddyville, and Grand River in Lyon County. Little River wound its way around through Calloway County and emptied into the mouth of the Cumberland around this area. Stonewall was searching for a place where he could reconnect with his father's spirit. He had prayed much to the Great Spirit and this time when his totem spirit appeared to him, he was prepared to ask some questions. He desperately wanted to relinquish his responsibilities to watch over the legacy and the jewels. As he grew older, he had grown tired of carrying all of the stress that rested on his shoulders in order to keep his commitment.

Travel time was long from where they lived in Shiloh, so they camped overnight in the cave at Big Spring. Stonewall wanted to sleep where his father used to sleep. When they reached the cave, they noticed that the front entrance had been nailed shut. Two large wooden planks were crisscrossed across the entrance to keep intruders out. They removed the planks and went inside. No one had visited the cave for a long time, so the stay was an adventurous one for the boys. Following a sleepless night, beset by the chill from the whistling wind, a battle with bats overhead, shadows, darkness, and strange noises, the boys were anxious to continue their journey at early sunrise. Stonewall remembered the place inside the cave where his father had received a vision. Before leaving to continue their journey, he checked it out carefully. There were no indications that the spirit of the White Buffalo had appeared, not a single sight or sound. Stonewall worried that his father's spirit had left him and was saddened by the thought of it. He worried that he might be on his own.

Stonewall had begun to be constantly plagued in his heart by the thought that he was not the fourth son. He had offered the entrustment to the fourth son, Matty, the rightful heir. Matty had settled his mind about the issue and had come to terms with the reasoning that the responsibility was not intended for him. He had released his desire to challenge Stonewall or to seek the care of the legacy. Matty had refused Stonewall's offer. His brother, Robert, the first son, had observed all of the problems that Stonewall had been through with the legacy, felt sorry for him and had also rejected the offer. He said that he had also settled in his mind that he was not the rightful son.

Robert had discussed the issue with Mother Ellen, long before the entrustment was bestowed upon Stonewall by his father. Minnie and his brother, Dave, had tried to convince Stonewall that an oath is more than a promise. Even promises are forever and that Stonewall was damaging the family image by not keeping his promise to perpetuate the legacy. Stonewall had fathered sixteen seedlings but nothing more was being done. He had put forth very little effort to monitor and model the values and traditions for the spirit characters handed down to him with the legacy.

Stonewall Releases the Jewels

Stonewall made sure that the deerskin pouch was tight around his neck and declared that this would be his final day to protect the jewels, as his worries would end once they reached the water. Like their father, the boys were avid fishermen. They only needed to be released to survey the area and test the water in order to select a good fishing spot. Perch, the size of one's hand, were running in schools of twenty to twenty-five. The hits were constant. The fish fought back like professional fighters who were well trained in survival skills. The boys had so much fun together that they established a competition to determine the fishing champion for the day based on the best catch of the day.

Stonewall sat quiet in his spot and attended to most of the hits on his line. He was waiting for a strong West Wind to arouse or agitate the currents in the water so that he could do what he had to do. He no longer had a passion or a desire to protect the jewels. All of the effort that he and Ida had put forth to spread the seedlings had not been acceptable to the Great Spirit. He remained in that spot for most of the day until Clyde called out from down stream that they were ready to leave. The boys wanted to leave early enough so that they could be on the other side of Big Spring before dusk and not have to spend another night of terror in the cave. They gathered their fishing gear and walked toward the wagon. Proctor noticed that his father was falling behind and called his slow pace to the attention of his brothers.

Stonewall was aware that he was being closely watched by his sons. He realized that he would not have an opportunity to stay close to the river's edge and release the jewels one by one into the water. Stonewall wanted the stones to drift away with the current and find their way back to the original place where his father had found them. Grayhorse had collected them from the creeks and rivers along the trail that ended at the mouth of the Cumberland. Stonewall knew that the time had come, so he lifted his right arm to throw the pouch into the water. Clyde, the sixth son, saw him and called out, "No, father, please don't release the jewels! Please give them to me, I'll take care of them!"

Proctor and Sully stood and watched in awe, they were amazed and could not believe what their father was doing.

Sully yelled, "I just can't believe that he would do such a thing!" Stonewall again lifted his arm and attempted again to throw the jewels into the water. This time, Clyde wrestled his father to the ground by tackling him around his ankles as the pouch eluded his grasp. Stonewall rolled over several times and broke away from Clyde. He hurled the pouch with the stones inside with all of the strength that he could muster. The pouch soared into the West Wind and was carried well out over the water and dropped into a swift current with a huge splash.

The boys watched to see if the pouch would rise to the top. Sully pointed it out as it surfaced one time and then floated with the current for a short distance and finally sank into the water. It surfaced again a short distance down stream and became wrapped around a large tree branch, anchored and riding against the current swiftly down stream. Neither of the boys could swim so they each tried to fish for the pouch with their fishing poles by pulling the branch closer to shore, but to no avail. They watched the pouch as it floated on its way, finally out of sight, destined toward the merging point with the Tennessee River.

Stonewall stood in a daze staring into the distance. Everyone boarded the wagon in silence. Clyde's voice was heard repeating the only spoken words, "Why, Father? Tell us why you just threw them all away. Don't they mean anything anymore? You threw them into the West Wind. Why?"

Trying to console Clyde, Sully responded, "We'll find them, Clyde. I know this place like I know the back of my hand. We'll find them down by the fork where the water parts and flows into the Tennessee. The Cumberland is muddy and we can't see it but the Tennessee is clear and blue. We'll find them Clyde, we will!"

Stonewall cracked the whip strongly and the horse team galloped along the way to Shiloh without a stop. When they reached the house, the boys were afraid to share what had happened to the jewels. No one told Ida and no one went through the kitchen where the family was gathered and family talk was always taken care of. Stonewall looked out the front window toward the west and dark storm clouds were gathering. With a quick flash of lightning, an image of Whispering Wind made its way through the tree branches. Recently, she always preceded the appearance of the spirit of the White Buffalo. Without a sound, the spirit of the White Buffalo appeared and vanished again just as quickly as it had appeared. This time, its

132

disappearance was not followed by a rainbow. There was complete silence. The spirit of Grayhorse was restless and not at peace.

Stonewall Seeks Approval to Relinquish the Jewels

Stonewall concluded that at his age he could no longer handle the stress that was constantly building up in him. He had already disposed of the jewels and now he needed to turn away from the Cherokee rituals and traditions and follow the morals and values of Mother Ellen. In order to do this, he needed to break his relationship with the Great Spirit and establish a relationship with the God of Mother Ellen. He had to seek the approval of the Great Spirit to relinquish his commitment to the family legacy.

Carefully, he packed away all of his Native American apparel and artifacts, placed them in a new burlap bag and buried them in a hole that he dug behind the barn. There was one item that he could not part with, his dreammaker. It had been passed to him by his father when Stonewall was just a young boy. It represented his dreams and the path finders that had directed his life. It had worked for his ancestors; so surely, it would work for him also.

For some time, Stonewall had not been consistent with his religious devotions to the Great Spirit. The prayers and chants that he learned from his father had begun to slip his mind. Ida had no interest in his Cherokee practices. She gave him very little encouragement to nurture this relationship with the Great Spirit. Stonewall made up his mind that if he did not hear from the spirit of the White Buffalo very soon, he would decide for himself which path he should follow. He rarely ate Cherokee food or went on animal hunts since these activities did not agree with Ida's culinary practices or choices. Stonewall was a farmer and raised almost everything that the family ate. They ate plenty of fish and they always had beef and lamb. At hog killing time (any month that contained the letter "R") fresh pork was plentiful. Smoked hams and shoulders hung in the smokehouse along with jowls, side pork and bacon. They made use of all of the hogs' organs. "Pluck and Plunder" stew was a culinary favorite (made from the hog's organs such as kidney, heart, sweetbread, and liver). Chitterlings (Kentucky oysters) were tedious to clean but they were a culinary and gourmet pleasure once they reached the table. Fresh homemade sausage was delightful and usually shared with the neighbors. Preparing the fresh pork was an art that was passed along from generation to generation, although some of these practices contradicted Native American practices.

Stonewall discussed his dilemma with Ida. Together they decided that he should take a three-day vision trip into the back woods of Quarry Town to see if he might be able to arouse the spirit of the White Buffalo. Stonewall wanted two of his sons to accompany him, just as he had done with his father, Grayhorse. It was not clear to Ida why he wanted the boys to go along or why he felt he even needed to pass the legacy to one of them when his real reason for the trip was to get rid of the legacy commitment. Stonewall was nurturing a double-pronged dagger in his heart. Even though he wanted to be released of his oath, he still wanted his sons to have the opportunity to receive their rightful portion to follow through with their responsibility to the family. Neither did Stonewall want any kind of evil omen to befall upon the Gray family because of the slothfulness of his commitment.

What about the future seedlings? He had hurled the jewels to the West Wind. It was he who had done this horrible act. Now who would oversee the future seedlings? He could feel the mighty forces of the West Wind in his life cycle, strong and unyielding.. Only the Great Spirit could save and direct his path.

Stonewall Confronts the Spirit of the White Buffalo

Before sunrise, Stonewall loaded the wagon for a three day camping trip at the North Cave in Quarry Town. Proctor and Sully packed their gear and went along with him. The boys carried all of their best fishing gear so that they could fish in the quarry pond at the North entrance. Stonewall wanted to visit a marker spot near the waterfall inside of the cave. It was a place where his father had experienced a vision and had received a powerful message from the spirit of the White Buffalo. He carried along his dreammaker and a water drum that his father had helped him carve for his crossover into manhood. At early morning, midmorning, noon, and early evening, Stonewall would leave the boys and pay his vows to the Great Spirit using his drum and dreammaker to accompany his prayers and chants. Two light and two dark periods passed and there was no response from the Great Spirit.

On the third day at midmorning, Stonewall's prayer chants were interrupted with a rush of white water cascading over the falls. A brisk whistling wind accompanied the rushing water in the image of a female riding

134

on the swift currents of the wind, ascending over and above the waterfall. A light as brilliant as the noonday sun followed the image, then the spirit of the White Buffalo appeared. Stonewall arose and stood steadily, facing the image, and waited for the spirit to speak first.

Stonewall then addressed the spirit and asked to be released from his assignment to protect the legacy and the jewels.

The spirit answered Stonewall, using his Native American name and carrying the intonation of Grayhorse's voice.

"Roaring Bull!" the spirit called out. "I have been searching for you. You have been away from my presence. I know of your stress and your worry. I also know of the conflicts that you have created. You dismantled the family legacy and now you are seeking to relinquish your vows. You have dishonored the dignity of the precious future seedlings by hurling the jewels to the West Wind. Now they sail hopelessly on a tempestuous wave, unprotected from the forces of nature, forces that will cause them to be separated and destroyed.

"You have broken the confidence and the covenant with your family. You have disconnected your relationship with me. I have protected the jewels; I have provided a watchful covering that hovers over each seedling. They will not be lost forever, no thanks to you. They are in my care! It is time for you to pass the legacy to a rightful heir but you are not worthy to anoint the blessing. When the rightful heir has been chosen, my spirit will return to cover his head and protect his heart. Remember that the succeeding heir is to be selected vertically and not horizontally. It is to fall upon one of the sons from the next generation, not a brother from the same generation as you have tried so hard to do. Remember that this weight is to be carried by the fourth son. Beginning with your first son with Ida, there will be a fourth son, called Sully, who will bear the weight of the fourth son. Be reminded that in the initial vision of Grayhorse, the seedlings are to generate through the lineage of a seedling called Sully. What will be your decision, Stonewall? Will you follow the guidance of the Great Spirit or will you follow the will of your own heart?"

Before Stonewall could give a response, with a flash, the spirit of the White Buffalo vanished with just as much drama as his appearance.

It was clear to Stonewall that he should began counting with his first son with Lucy, who was Harmon; then Proctor would be the fourth son, the selected heir. Knowing Ida's feelings about the Cherokee tradition and knowing that the legacy was to follow the lineage of Sully, he no longer had the strength or the courage to fight with Ida about the entrustment.

With no further wonder, he began the count with he and Ida's first son and the title of rightful heir fell on Sully.

Stonewall sat meditating quietly by the waterfall and thanking the Great Spirit for the visit. Time passed faster than he realized. Just as he prepared to leave the spirit reappeared and spoke to Stonewall again.

"I am cleansing the legacy of all of its evil pitfalls. You tarnished its meaning but I will polish it anew. I am giving the new heir an opportunity for a fresh start. It appears that your choice is the choice of the Great Spirit, the fourth son, between you and Ida. That seedling revealed will be called Sully. In order for him to remain loyal to his commitment, he must maintain a mutual relationship with the Great Spirit.

"Teach him the traditional ways of your father. Instruct him well. When he has mastered these traditions and concepts and received the anointment, you can then be released of your responsibilities. In the vernacular of his grandfather's heritage, he will be called Rising Sun, symbolizing the birth of a new beginning and a new day."

When the spirit left Stonewall, he was exhausted from the depth of the vision. Sully and Proctor had entered the cave about half way through the vision and had heard all that had been said about choosing the rightful heir. Sully was amazed and wondered if he was worthy and strong enough to carry the weight of this responsibility. He had carefully watched everything that had taken place with his father.

Stonewall spoke well and long to the boys about the vision. He spoke of what it represented, the spirit of Grayhorse, and the guidance of the Great Spirit. He explained the Cherokee rationale for having a totem spirit and the spirit of the White Buffalo and what it meant to their family. The boys were not certain that they understood everything that Stonewall had to say to them, but one thing was clear; they were not to discuss what they had heard or seen that day. They were not to talk about it with each other or their brothers—and certainly not with Ida. Stonewall did not want Ida to place a moratorium on what had to be done as he passed it along to his sons, nor the teachings or traditions of his father. He knew that one day soon, he would have to take the time to teach them the legacy.

When they left the cave, a beautiful rainbow encircled the pond at the North entrance. The boys noticed it first and then pointed it out to their father. All of the colors were brilliant and its concave position was perfect, touching the ground from point to point. The rainbow was indeed depicting a new day. Stonewall had observed a similar rainbow many times before when he had accompanied his father on their vision trips. He understood

136

that the spirit had delivered an important message, had given them a blessing, and was pleased with their response.

As they rode home, the boys watched for the rainbow which appeared to be following them to the front gate. But when they entered the gate, a black cloud arose overhead with a puff of air. It was the spirit of Whispering Wind. She had followed them home.

Double Vision for the Legacy

Stonewall was so anxious to pass the legacy that he lost little time training his sons in the Cherokee traditions. He spent much time with Proctor and Sully teaching them about the legacy and what their responsibilities would be if they received the entrustment. He had not shared with Sully that the Great Spirit had already assigned him the Native American name, Rising Sun. Proctor and Sully remained close to their father and were with him almost everywhere that he went. Proctor never had the courage to confront his father or Sully as to why he was being considered as a second choice but in his own mind, he knew that he could outwork and outwit Sully. It was his goal to become more dedicated to the legacy and to overshadow Sully as the most deserving son. Ida knew that this conflict would erupt and that this competitive spirit was surfacing inside Proctor so she discussed it with Stonewall. Stonewall pushed the thought aside in his mind and attributed Proctor's aggression to being older and a little more experienced than Sully at the time. Proctor worked especially hard on the spirit characters and family values. He became a strong spiritual mentor for the rest of the family to follow.

Sully was well aware of Proctor's plan and asked his father not to allow him to go along on any more vision trips, especially since the Great Spirit had selected him for the entrustment. Stonewall knew that this request would cause a disagreement with Ida so he continued to educate both boys with the same degree of training. It was obvious that Proctor was more dedicated and surpassed Sully in all areas of preparation. Sully approached his father again and asked to be released from the responsibility. Proctor grew very close to the family and became a favorite son. Sully's interest was directed toward his work and his own personal endeavors. Stonewall warned him of what would happen in his life if he rejected the will of the Great Spirit or if he pointed his life to move against the West Wind. He explained to Sully that one's life cycle is strongly directed by the

137

Four Winds and that to move against these currents might cause evil to befall one's family or his own life. Evils such as diseases, death, poverty, infidelity, or immoral omens could occur even within generations that follow. On a personal level, it could interrupt one's dreams or ability to move ahead in life, creating unsafe conditions surrounding one, and surely no one would wish to lay a path of evil omens to be tread upon by future seedlings! These principles were frightening to Sully, so he became determined to do what he had to do to fulfill his father's wishes.

Ida knew her sons well. She sensed Sully's hesitation and did all that she could to support him and to make him feel secure for the job that he had to do. Sully grew very close to his mother, Ida, his sister, Helen, and his brother Clyde. Before long, it was apparent that Sully was ready to go with his father on a serious trip to receive anointing from the Great Spirit for the entrustment for the family legacy. Proctor was very displeased with Stonewall's decision not to allow him to go along on the vision trip.

Sully and his father left the house well before sunrise and planned to reach Gilbertsville well before dusk. Proctor saddled his horse and followed along behind them staying well out of their sight. They traveled through Quarry Town, Eddyville, and Kuttawa. Then they crossed the Cumberland and stayed close to the banks of the Tennessee until they reached Gilbertsville. They followed the coast line until they reached a shallow spot near Grand River and parked their wagon. They had loaded a small canoe in the back of the wagon. They unloaded the canoe, placed it in the water and climbed aboard. Proctor hitched his horse to a nearby tree and walked closer to the water's edge so that he could have a better view of what was about to take place.

They had only been offshore for a short time when the spirit of the White Buffalo appeared on the waves of the water. The spirit appeared to propel itself above the water at about fifteen or twenty feet away. A voice called out to Sully, this time using his Native American name.

"Rising Sun, it is I. Listen to my words. Do not fear me, Rising Sun. I am here as your guiding spirit." Sully responded, "I am here, what is it that I am to hear?"

"You have been chosen to carry the legacy responsibility for your family. You have also been appointed as custodian of the precious jewels, protecting the future seedlings for your family. They are not in your vision but they are being continuously protected by my spirit. One day, they will be returned to you. Lean heavily upon the guidance of the Great Spirit, follow the will of your father, and you will be successful. My spirit is not at rest. My spirit will be at the ebb of the West Wind until I know that the family is connected, the legacy has been retrieved, and the jewels have been found and are safe. You are now an anointed blessing to your family, Rising Sun. Hear my words and do not move against the West Wind."

The spirit then vanished and a strong current arose and moved across the water, rocking the boat violently. It was the wind trail of Whispering Wind. When the wind settled, calmness came upon the water and the rocking ceased. In the distance, the voice of Grayhorse called out in repeated tones, "Rising Sun, Rising, Rising, Rising, Sun, Sun, Sun, Sun, Sun."

Sully was afraid and sat quietly in the boat without moving or speaking even to Stonewall. When their minds had cleared, Stonewall and Rising Sun rowed back to shore and loaded the canoe onto the wagon. Proctor stood soft footed in the leaves and continued to watch from afar. At one point father and son came very close to where Proctor was standing. He tightened his legs so that he would not make a single noise or rustle the twigs or leaves that were underfoot.

Proctor continued to follow them until they reached Eddyville, then he took a right turn for a shorter trip home. After this vision experience, Proctor was convinced that his chances to receive the entrustment had vanished but not his desire.

On the way home. Stonewall and Rising Sun stopped at the Gray farm for food and a little rest, and reached home well after nightfall. Rising Sun did not mention to his father that he was going to work hard to retrieve the jewels that had been tossed into the river. Since Clyde was such an avid fisherman, Sully had seriously discussed with him about taking the boat down to the Cumberland to see if the pouch had washed upon the shore somewhere along the way. After they had made several trips with no results, they both concluded that the jewels had likely sunk to the bottom of the river and would never be seen again. But in his heart, Rising Sun believed he had been given a promise by the spirit of the White Buffalo that one day they would be returned.

They reached the house, tired and weary. Rising Sun stopped by the kitchen for a cup of hot coffee and a slice of Ida's fresh apple cobbler. Proctor entered the kitchen by the sitting room stairs. Rising Sun greeted him and asked about their mother, Ida. Proctor stood very still and looked at him with fire in his eyes, bit his bottom lip, and answered not a word. Rising Sun caught the fire spirit ignited in his blood and realized that this act of commitment had dismantled their brotherhood.

"You know, Proctor," said Rising Sun, "one day we will have to talk."

"Oh, yes!" answered Proctor. "And one day, we may just have to fight it out of both our systems. Don't push me, Sully, or it could just happen today.

"You are not deserving," Proctor continued. "Filthy water settles in the bottom but it always rises to the top. And do you know what Sully? You are my brother but you are filthy water and one day the scum in you will rise to the top."

After this strong threat from Proctor, Rising Sun walked out of the kitchen and left Proctor standing near the stove waiting for a response. Ida heard their conversation as she listened from her bedroom door. She shook her head and walked away.

13

Tempest Fury

Severed Connections

Hattie packed her suitcase and went to bed early so she would not have to share her real feelings about leaving the place. Stonewall had told his sister, Belle, that he would arrive early to pick up Hattie so that he and Ida could be back home before nightfall. Hattie was pacing the floor and like always, she had rehearsed everything in her head that she wanted to say to her father about having to go. Hattie had no love in her heart for her stepmother, Ida. When she and Nina had lived with their mother, Lucy, they had watched Ida and Stonewall together. Hattie knew that Stonewall had always loved Ida more than her mother, Lucy, and Hattie blamed both of them for hastening her mother's death. Often when Lucy would sit by the window in her chair she would watch Ida and Stonewall together in the cypress grove. Hattie would get up from her reading corner in her mother's bedroom and move her mother away from the window.

When Stonewall married Ida, Hattie worried that her father would force them to live with him and Ida. Belle knew how Hattie felt about the issue and was sensitive to her passion for her mother. Belle had discussed the situation with her brother, but this time he had insisted that it was time for Hattie to come home so that she could bond with her other brothers and sisters. Hattie however had no interest in joining the rest of the family. She only wanted to remain with her Aunt Belle and be left alone. Since she had been living with Belle, she was much happier but she had lost respect and affection for her father, Stonewall. It seemed that recently whenever she and Stonewall were near each other they would belittle each other with hard harsh words and eventually part in anger. This time, there was to be no arguing. She already had a plan in her head. First she needed to have words with her stepmother, being sure Ida knew that Hattie considered her an upstart first cousin who had actually stole her mother's husband. As far as

Hattie was concerned, Stonewall would always be her blood daddy but he could never again be her father.

When Ida and Stonewall rode up in front of the house, Hattie walked out to the wagon and began to confront her father before he and Ida could disembark.

"Why did you bring her?" she asked. "I hate her; I hate every single hair on her head! She can never be my mother. You sent all of us away just so that you could be with her. You never really cared about me, Nina, and Harmon. You only wanted to be with Ida. I am not coming with you! You tortured my mother but I will not allow you to torture me. My mother's spirit rises up inside of me, Ida. I hate you, I hate your very being! Please let me stay here, please don't force me to go and live with her. I will never be happy in your house."

With those words, Belle had walked out to the wagon to join them. She reached out to Hattie with open arms. Hattie melted in her Aunt Belle's arms and cried hopelessly. Stonewall insisted that Hattie must go home with him and Ida. Ida sat quietly in the front seat of the wagon with no response.

Stonewall walked to the front porch and picked up Hattie's suitcase and a small knapsack of food that Belle had prepared for her to nibble on and placed them in the back of the wagon. Coached by Belle, Hattie reluctantly climbed into the back of the wagon, clinging tightly to Belle's arm. Stonewall all but picked her up and placed her in the back seat, ordering her to sit there without any further words. Belle placed a blanket over Hattie's knees to offset the chill. Stonewall gave the horses a roaring command and with a crack of the whip the horses took off with a thoroughbred pace. They rounded the corner with no one looking back or uttering a word. Belle could smell the dust as they rode away. She thought that after a few days maybe the emotional dust would settle and she would go to Stonewall and make one more attempt to persuade him to let Hattie return to live with her. Just maybe she would be able to make him understand that Hattie really wanted to be near her sister Nina. But for now Stonewall's head was set and once he set his head and put his foot down on an issue, then that was the way that it had to be.

Hattie sulked and wept in the back of the wagon. They had only gone a short distance before Hattie slid off the seat onto the floor of the wagon. She scooted her body over near the end-gate and began to fumble with the latch. Stonewall felt the weight shift in the wagon as she slid down to the floor but he did not say a word. Hattie noticed that Stonewall had left in such a hurry that he latched only one side of the end-gate. She sat facing the back so that she could fumble with the bolt on the right side as they rode along, which was the only bolt holding the latch in place. Hattie listened intently as Ida and Stonewall discussed how they would shuffle people around once they got home to make room for another girl to sleep. Meanwhile, Hattie continued to busy herself trying to open the end-gate. Finally, the holding bolt dislodged, the latch broke its hold and the end-gate fell down. It created a loud clanging noise and an opening that Hattie could slide through when the time was right.

Without making a commotion, Hattie grabbed her blanket and her knapsack and slid her body out the back of the wagon onto the ground. Due to the speed of the wagon, she fell with much force but landed on her feet with a perfect cat's landing. On the ground she began to roll until she reached the right side of the road.

Ida saw the dust and heard the scuffle. She cried out, "My goodness, Stonewall, she's running away! Stop the wagon! Hattie is running away!"

Stonewall commanded Hattie to stop where she was and pulled the wagon over to the side of the road. He rushed to the back of the wagon, yelling and calling out Hattie's name. "Hattie Gray! What the dickens do you think you are doing? Come back here, Hattie. It won't make a bit of difference where you settle, you are going with us."

Meanwhile, Hattie was running as fast as her feet would carry her. With marathon speed, she was weaving her way deeper into the thick of the woods, away from the beaten trail, away from Stonewall and Ida. Hattie knew from her childhood adventures if she stayed close to the Eddy Creek shoreline that she could find her way into Lyon County and be rescued.

Stonewall followed on foot as far as he was physically able with no sight or trace of Hattie. His shortness of breath would not allow him to go any further. He sat down on the cold ground in the shade of an oak tree to rest a minute before going back to Ida.

When he reached the wagon Ida was worried. She blamed herself for all that had taken place with Hattie, and she blamed her mother, Minerva, for poisoning the minds of Nina, Hattie and Harmon and causing them to turn against their father. Stonewall was afraid that he might never see Hattie again. She was so determined to not be near him. If only he had listened to his sister, Belle, and allowed Hattie to remain with her. Deep within his heart he had much passion and love for his children but—why couldn't they love him back?

The sun crept behind the western hills and nightfall was setting in.

Stonewall realized that not much could be done to locate Hattie before daylight. He drove home planning that he and the boys would return for an intense search at daybreak. Meanwhile, Hattie made use of the moonlight and details remembered about the area. She had no plans to go back to Belle's house in Caldwell County, where she knew that her uncles would search for her and return her to her father. She was certain that her father and her brothers would be in pursuit of her at sunrise. Hattie was hoping that they would only search along the Caldwell and Trigg County trails. She had set her sights toward Lyon County so that she could find her way to Calloway and McCracken Counties and then cross the river into Cape Gurada, Missouri.

Hattie sat on the damp ground near the creek to rest a bit. She opened her knapsack to find that Belle had made her two peanut butter and jelly sandwiches, with a cup of fresh cider, and a pear from the back yard pear tree. Hattie nibbled her way through half of one of the sandwiches and drank a sip or two of the cider. *Maybe*, she thought, *this will hold me until I can find my way out of this tangled maze. I need to get as far as possible before daybreak.* One thing she knew for certain, she would not turn back. She could never bear the thought of living with Ida.

The wind began to blow with a piercing bite and a chill so Hattie wrapped herself in her blanket and moved back a little further from the edge of the creek. Quicker than she realized, she had drifted off to sleep, protected only by the light of the moon, the fallen leaves, and the night critters that she always thought of as her personal friends.

Harmon Rejects Stonewall

When morning broke, Stonewall and all nine of the boys made their way to the place where Hattie had left the wagon. The boys were assigned to three teams with three people in each group. They brought along the family hunting dogs, Max, Pepper, Oreo, and their mother, Sugar. The teams were directed by Stonewall to completely search areas along the trails. West to Quarry Town, north to Cadiz and Ceruleum, and southwest toward Grand River, Eddyville, and Kuttawa. The dogs were also assigned a team to work with. Since the Southwest area was more spread out, two dogs were assigned to that team. Harmon pleaded with his father to allow him to team with Rising Sun and Clyde along the Lyon County trail. He thought that he knew some familiar places along the way where he and his sisters had gone with their father on camping and fishing trips.

As they journeyed deeper into the wooded terrain, Harmon and the dogs would often wander ahead away from Clyde and Rising Sun. Harmon would call out his sister's name into his cupped hands and then pause and listen for an echo or a response. After a few hours of intense searching, Clyde suggested that they whistle the dogs in and return to an agreed upon meeting place to join with the rest of the teams. This was so that they could check to see if any of the teams had made any progress with their search. They stopped along the creek shore for a break but Harmon continued to walk the shoreline and call out for his sister. He listened diligently as the water picked up his voice and carried it along the current, hoping it would send back an echo resounding off the hills from across the creek. He thought that Hattie might hear him, recognize his voice, and echo back his name as they had done many times when they played a childhood game. Rising Sun insisted that they really needed to return to meet the other teams. Harmon gave out one more call. This time, there was a response. It was not an echo but a very faint voice that called "Harmon! Harmon! Harmon!" instead of "Hattie! Hattie! Hattie!"

Harmon was excited and called out to Hattie at least three or four times more. Each time there was a response that seemed to grow weaker and weaker. Harmon called the dogs over and let them sniff Hattie's socks. They set out in front in search of the smell. Harmon and his brothers followed the dogs. The voice led them down stream along the creek shoreline. The dogs found Hattie wrapped in her blanket and covered under camouflaged leaves. She was exhausted, lying very still, hungry, and scared to death. Harmon ran straight to his sister and rocked her in his arms. Rising Sun gave her a drink of water from his canteen. Clyde lifted her head and attempted to feed her the rest of her peanut butter and jelly sandwich that she had left behind. He cut the pear into very small portions using a pocket knife and let her eat what little she could swallow.

Hattie slightly opened her eyes and recognized Harmon. She asked him, "Where is he, Harmon? I'm not going back."

"You have to," responded Harmon. "We will protect you. No one will harm you now. No one will take you away. You are my sister, Hattie, and I will always protect you."

Rising Sun and Clyde lifted her onto Harmon's horse and together they turned around to ride back to the meeting place.

As the dogs ran ahead, Stonewall saw them coming and rode out to

145

meet them. "Why, Hattie?" he asked, sadly. "Why did you run away from me?"

Hattie did not respond but Clyde spoke for her. "She is weak, Father," responded Clyde. "Give her a little time. She is cold, hungry, weak, and scared."

Harmon then spoke out to his father on Hattie's behalf. "Father, Hattie hates this place. She is scared to death. She will never really be loved or be at peace at this house. It will never become a home for her. Please, Father," pleaded Harmon. "Let her go back to Aunt Belle's, and I will go with her."

"No sir," ordered Stonewall. "Not on your life! It is time for all of us to be family and that's the way it's gonna be."

"We will never really be family, Father," replied Harmon. "Why would you torment us with false feelings? What happened to Hattie has also happened to Nina and me. We are all of the same blood twice and the feelings that you have for Hattie are the same feelings that you carry for me and Nina. It's no good. We are not in love with Ida, Father, you are. If you really love Hattie, Nina, and me, you will release us now and give us our freedom just as our mother gave you your freedom and released you to marry Ida. I am leaving, Father. Me and Hattie can make our way and we won't bother you ever again."

Harmon turned his horse around and he and Hattie rode away in haste. This time they went toward Quarry Town. They were going to their Aunt Belle's house to share their hurt and their story. Then they needed to go to their Uncle Matty's house to try to locate Nina, to chart a new path and create new beginnings far away from Trigg County and far away from Stonewall and Ida.

Stonewall was a man of hard decisions and his name epitomized his character well: hard, cold, and challenging. He loved his children, particularly, Harmon, his first son. Being rejected by his children, especially Harmon, broke his heart. Stonewall could no longer restrain his tears. He turned his back to his sons and wailed out loud as Harmon and Hattie rode away. Not only had he lost Hattie but now he had also lost Harmon. How long would it be before Nina would follow and he would lose her also?

Clyde and Rising Sun sat with their father and attempted to console him with kind words, as Matt and Proctor stood back and observed from afar. Proctor was thinking that maybe all of this emotional hurt was the result of Stonewall's selfishness and was a payback from the Great Spirit for the way that Stonewall had overlooked him, Proctor, for the entrustment of the family legacy. Maybe the hurt was reaching all the way back through two generations to the time when his grandfather, Grayhorse did the same thing for Stonewall.

Clyde asked his father the familiar question, "Why, father? Why are all of these things happening to our family? What have we done to deserve this?"

"It is not our fault, son," responded Stonewall. "None of these things are our fault. It is all because of the West Wind moving in our lives. We cannot escape the turbulence of the West Wind. It is the way that things have to be. This bitter West Wind will settle one day and when it does things will take a turn for the better and maybe a peaceful wind will blow in our direction and return all of us to each other. I just hope that I will live long enough to see the change. We all must keep our lives in favor with the Four Winds." He patted Clyde and Rising Sun on their shoulders. They saddled their horses and made their way back home.

Ida was standing at the front gate waiting for them when they arrived. She always kept a light burning in the sitting room until everyone was home. Clyde had made mention of that signal light when they drove up. "Mother must be still waiting up for us, the light is still burning."

Matt called out to his mother, "We found her. We found Hattie, Mama!"

"Where is Harmon?" she asked. "What happened to Harmon?"

Stonewall responded, "We found her, Ida, but this time we have lost her for good. This time both she and Harmon have left us. The turbulence from the wind won't leave us alone. This time it left no sign that Hattie or Harmon will ever return to us."

Stonewall stopped and sat on the top step of the front porch, untied his shoe laces, pulled off his shoes and socks, and started to walk towards the barn in his bare feet to put the horses away. Rising Sun met him half way, took the horses by their reins, and led them to their stalls. Stonewall turned and walked back to the house. He reached for a cup of hot coffee as he passed through the kitchen and moved on to the washroom to wash his face. Tears flowed down his cheeks as he wept in silence. He shook his head continuously and called his children's names out loud as he closed the door.

Death of Nina

When Harmon and Hattie went inside, Belle was sitting in a rocking chair by the window, starring into space with her arms folded and tears streaming down her cheeks. Belle reached for Hattie and Harmon with open arms. Before Harmon could begin to tell her about how they had found Hattie, Belle began to speak loudly.

"She's dead, children! Nina is dead. It wasn't anybody's fault. It was the horse. The horse was frightened by something on the ground. They think that it was a snake. She rose up and ran out of control and Nina couldn't stop her. Nina was a good rider but she lost control and fell off the horse. Tess ran right into the trunk of a tree and broke her neck. She had to be put to sleep.

"Your Uncle Arthur saw it all. He was riding behind Nina, trying to catch up with her but she rode so fast that he couldn't catch up with her. It happened so quick! Arthur put Nina on his horse and rode her to Dr. Hatten's office but he brought her into town riding face down. She had a crushed skull and the doctor said that she was already dead when Arthur caught up with her."

"Where was she going, Aunt Belle?" asked Hattie.

"She was trying to catch up with her father's wagon to tell him that the McGoodwins, your Uncle Matty's in-laws, had given their consent for you and Harmon to go to Chicago to live with them for a while. She was working as hard as she could to make sure that the two of you would not have to go live with Ida. She was so afraid that if you stayed around here your father would come for you and that neither of you would have a choice but to go and live with him."

"Does our father know about Nina?" asked Harmon.

"Dave and Arthur went to talk to him," Belle answered. "Mr. Morgan has her body at the funeral home."

"Is our father taking her back to Trigg County?" asked Hattie.

"He wanted to," Belle continued, "but Dave is trying to persuade him to allow us to keep her here."

"I won't go to Trigg County," responded Hattie.

"Neither will I," declared Harmon.

"Then we will keep her here," said Belle. "She is our Nina too, and three votes are more valid than one."

Early, the next morning, Belle left the house and walked down Main Street to Washington to Morgan's Funeral Home. Belle had no money or insurance with which to bury Nina and she wasn't sure about Stonewall. Feeling the way that he felt might mean that he would not be willing to contribute anything toward her burial expense. Harmon went along with Belle for support.

She rang the doorbell and told the lady at the desk that they had come to take care of the body of Nina Gray. Mr. Morgan told them that he would cremate her body for a cheaper amount than it would take for a traditional burial, so Belle and Harmon agreed to have her body cremated that afternoon. They were told that the urn of ashes would be delivered the following morning.

Since Belle had no money or insurance, Mr. Morgan made the same type of financial arrangements with her that he often made with poor families. He agreed to render his services on credit and Belle could follow a payment plan and pay him in installments with no money down. This was a payment plan that continues today by the Morgan Funeral Home for the needy families of Quarry Town.

Belle knew the Morgans as did most of the black families of Quarry Town. They trusted each other as good business practice.

Around midday, Arthur and Dave drove up in the wagon with Stonewall sitting in the back seat. Following close behind were Clyde and Rising Sun and their sisters, Helen and Mary Dee. The preacher from the new Shepherd Street Baptist Church came by and said prayers with the family.

Belle placed Nina's ashes in the middle of the mantel piece above the fire grate. She announced to Stonewall, "We are keeping her here, Stonewall, this is where she wanted to be and this is right where she is going to remain. Come by and visit her whenever you like but as long as I am alive, her ashes will remain right here."

Stonewall nodded his head to Belle's words. He thanked his sister and walked out the front door.

Harmon and Hattie refused to show their faces to their father. They slipped out the back way and crossed the path leading to the trail before he arrived. They made a promise to Belle that they would contact her as soon as they settled in Chicago to be with Matty's in-laws. Rising Sun helped his father climb into the wagon. He rode up front with Clyde. Helen and Mary Dee rode in the second seat, and Rising Sun climbed into the back and rode on the wagon floor. It was a quiet solemn ride for everyone. Stonewall was filled with grief now that he had lost his third child. A part of him had begun to die also.

Ida was waiting for them when they returned home but Stonewall walked right past her without saying a word. He refused to eat for several days. The family became concerned that his only intake was a few liquids. He stayed in his room staring into space and spoke only a few words whenever someone talked to him. Dr. Hatten's youngest son who had taken over his father's medical practice, came by the house to take a look at Stonewall. It was a longer distance than Dr. Hatten was used to making for a house call but he knew the family so well that he kept his promise to Clyde. The doctor diagnosed that Stonewall had a severe case of depression and a broken heart over the loss of his children. He recommended that they take him to Hopkinsville to see a doctor at the Western Kentucky Mental Hospital for some tests and treatment. The family hesitated to act on this recommendation because they were not comfortable with the thought that something was wrong with their father's mind. Stonewall increased his smoking habit and relied on his pipe more and more. This caused his problems with asthma and emphysema to worsen. His shortness of breath became serious. His body was so swollen with bodily fluids that he could barely wear his shoes. Dr. Hatten said that he had a bad case of dropsy, an aliment related to diabetes.

Once Rising Sun hid his pipe and Stonewall went into a fiery rage. Ida insisted that they return the pipe to him. Whenever he smoked, he would go into a stage of uncontrolled coughing and often had to be put to bed after inhaling a menthol powder. His eyes told the true story of what was happening to him. They were a real reflection of grief and illness. He missed Hattie, Nina and Harmon and he would carry this burden to his grave. He would forever regret how he lost them all at one time. They had been swept away from him by the West Wind. His life was well woven into the furious currents of this turbulent wind. The spirit of Grayhorse had left him and the Great Spirit had turned away.

Matty rode back to the house in Quarry Town in the funeral hearse because he needed to make one last trip to check on things before he left the place. Minnie had taken care of the rest of the funeral arrangements but he had promised Belle if he was the longest survivor that he would take care of Nina's ashes. He had left them on the mantel place during Belle's wake because he knew that Belle would want Nina to be there. Now that Belle had died, he was taking Nina's ashes home to remain at his place. He had talked to Stonewall about who would keep her ashes; Stonewall just stared into space and made no response. The rift between them had been settled some time ago and then Nina had found a comfortable home with her uncle

Matty, who had loved Nina as if she was his own daughter. Matty could not bear the thought of just sprinkling her ashes to the wind.

Matty unlocked the front door and went inside. There was a solemn silence unlike any that he could remember when Belle was alive. Her husband had passed away two years ago and even then, the silence was not this thick. Since he died, Minnie and her brothers had kept a close check on Belle and she had transferred all of her love and devotion to Stonewall's first three children. Matty walked through the house to make a final security check. He checked all of the windows and doors to make sure that they were properly locked. When he walked into the sitting room, he picked up the vase with Nina's ashes and slid them into a blue velvet pouch that Belle had made for them. He then placed them securely in a basket in the back of the wagon and headed home.

"Come on, Nina, girl," he called out when he rounded the corner. "We are going home and this time you will not have to worry about being taken away."

Stonewall Relinquishes the Legacy

Stonewall was struggling with an emotional battle over what to do about the family legacy. His health was rapidly failing and he had to do something soon before his brothers called a family caucus and appointed an heir without the guidance of the Great Spirit. Stonewall was bothered constantly by the fact that as a sixth son he had been entrusted with a responsibility that rightfully belonged to Matty. The West Wind had constantly plagued him and the totem spirit had continued to test him during his tenure. Stonewall had thrown the jewels into the river and now they had been washed away by the swift currents. He had turned his back on the morals and values of the Gray family and neglected the rituals and traditions of his Cherokee heritage. The only real commitment that he had perpetuated was to sow seedlings by fathering sixteen children.

Now, he had entrusted Rising Sun, a fifth son, with the legacy. He had made a commitment to mentor him until he could handle the responsibility. Rising Sun was older but Clyde was more mature and was emerging as the responsible family leader. Proctor, however, was carrying poison in his mind. He had grown bitter with Rising Sun and was harboring a hate just as Matty had done with Stonewall. Stonewall needed a message from his totem spirit, he wanted to hear from him. He wanted to make contact with the spirit of Grayhorse. He wanted his legacy watch to come to an end so that he could be released of his commitment.

Stonewall discussed his dilemma with Ida and requested that she summon the children to his bedroom for a family meeting. Ida did not share with the children the reason for the meeting but she simply ordered that each be present. Minnie and Will were also asked to be there. Minnie shared this request with Matty. Matty remembered how his father, Grayhorse, had called a similar family gathering and now Stonewall was following in his father's footsteps. With much haste, Matty made contact with Harmon in Chicago and insisted that he make arrangements to be present also. Matty rationalized this action because he did not want to see these sons squabbling over their father's decision to assign the blessing for the birthright as he and Stonewall had done.

After breakfast, Ida and all of the children went to Stonewall's bedroom for the meeting. Seated in his favorite chair, Stonewall called all of the children by name and had them answer to account for their presence. In his mind, he thought, Harmon, the first son, but he did not call his name out loud. At that moment, the doorknob on the bedroom door turned slowly.

The door swayed ajar with a ghostly squeak and a familiar voice called out, "Here, Father, I am present also." It was the voice of Harmon. Stonewall had an expression on his face that overcame the wrinkle on his forehead that had mounted from the grief and depression that he was carrying.

"Harmon, Harmon, my son, Harmon, it is you. How did you know to come?"

"In my heart, I have always known," responded Harmon.

"How is Hattie, my boy?" asked Stonewall. "Where is she?"

"Hattie is alright, but she is not here," responded Harmon. "How are you, Father?" he asked.

"My time is short and my spirit is wounded, but the wind is settling because you have returned," said Stonewall.

"Only for a short time," Harmon responded, "I will not stay long."

The sisters and brothers were excited about Harmon's return and welcomed him home with glad greetings. Ida gave him a warm hug and held his hand cupped in hers as Stonewall caught his breath and began to speak to them.

"Welcome home Harmon," Ida said to him. "This is your home too. Your bed is as you left it. Bring in your belongings and find your place like always."

Stonewall asked for assistance to be propped up in his chair as he spoke. "For some time now I have watched and waited for all of you to grow up. I was younger than the youngest of you when I took the oath to protect this legacy. The load was not mine to carry because I was a sixth son, and for generations, the load has been predestined to be carried by the fourth son. I tried with all of my strength to fulfill the commitment and I have failed. I have asked the Great Spirit to eradicate my oath. I was then commanded to watch over the legacy until Rising Sun was strong enough to carry the weight alone. Rising Sun has already received his anointing and now I am backing away. I am emotionally drained and I no longer am physically able to fight the battles. It is now all up to Rising Sun. Clyde, you are younger but you are mentally stronger. I am assigning you the responsibility to walk beside Rising Sun to support him and walk with him as he carries this load. My sister, Belle, has passed on and Minnie is growing old and tired. The Gray women need an image of dignity and the character of a strong woman to follow. Helen, you have no other choice but to be that woman. Mirror the character and dignity of your grandmother, Mother Ellen, and pass it on to the women of strength among the Gray women. See that these spirit characters remain the poise and character of the women of this family. The Gray women will respect you and want to follow your mentoring. Stay close to Clyde and to Rising Sun because you epitomize the true essence of Mother Ellen. Helen, you are to become the matrix aunt of the Gray family. Clyde, in keeping with our Cherokee heritage, you have no choice but to become the patriarch uncle. You will be loved and respected by the future seedlings that follow through the lineage of Sully, Rising Sun."

Stonewall Abandons Cherokee Traditions

As everyone left the room, Stonewall asked Walter Jack and Frank to assist him down the stairs. Slowly, he made his way to the barn, with Walter Jack and Frank following close behind him. He asked them to look inside for a shovel and a pitchfork. Stonewall pointed out a fresh pile of dirt behind the barn. Here he had buried his Native American clothes and his worship and ritual artifacts, most of which had belonged to his father. The boys helped him lift every item from the hole and placed them in a pile in the outdoor cooking pit. Stonewall sprinkled the pile with kerosene, lit a match and threw it on the pile and then stepped back to watch it catch fire.

153

He watched intently as it burned with a huge flame until nothing was left except charred remnants and ashes. When he turned to leave, Harmon had joined them and was standing close beside his father. Walter Jack and Frank were left to clean up the mess while Harmon walked his father to the back porch step.

Harmon sat on the step with his father and pleaded with him not to relinquish his total past, especially his Cherokee heritage, his worship and ritual practices.

Stonewall spoke softly to him, "I don't need any of these things any longer. The spirit of the White Buffalo has paid me a visit in a quiet vision. Only a few days ago, I saw its image and it spoke to me clearly. It was as real and as clear as any of the visions that I experienced when you used to accompany me and Rising Sun on vision trips. The time for my spirit journey is not far away. I want you to take me to the Gray farm so that we can carve petroglyphs together on the family petroglyph tree. We will carve a petroglyph for the passing of the legacy and one to mark my crossing over on my spirit journey."

Harmon, Rising Sun, and Clyde drove their father to the Gray farm early the next morning. Stonewall was so weak that he hardly had enough strength to sit up straight in the wagon. The boys let him sit most of the day in the front porch swing while they carved the petroglyphs. Sometimes, he would change his seat and sit in the padded rocking chair. Arthur and Otha sat most of the day with him. When the boys had finished the carving, Stonewall checked it to see that it met his approval. Before leaving for home, Stonewall visited the burial plots for his parents to pay respect to their spirits. He requested his water drum from Rising Sun, requested his children that remained with him as he chanted a crossing over chant. In a soft quiet voice, he chanted his final chant to the Great Spirit. The boys then helped him into the wagon and they made every effort to reach home before sundown.

When they returned, the boys immediately rushed their father upstairs. Helen brought him a bowl of warm soup and some fresh bread that she had just finished baking in the wood oven along with a hearty slice of his favorite freshly baked chess pie. Stonewall did not touch not one bite of any of the food. Ida tried to feed him with little results. She covered him with a warm blanket and he was soon fast asleep.

The next morning, the family noticed that Stonewall was sleeping later than usual. They thought that maybe he was just tired from all of the activity on the day before. Proctor and Frank went to his room and aroused him for his daily bath. They noticed that his strength seemed to have dissipated. They finished his bath and placed him in his favorite chair by the window. Here he had always enjoyed observing what was happening in that same cypress grove that he and Ida used to stroll in a few years earlier. Many times a heartbroken Lucy had watched them there. When Ida came in to check on him, she found him sitting with a bowed head. His eyes were set, and he had no pulse. He was no longer breathing. Stonewall had crossed over on his spirit journey and his responsibility to the family legacy had ended.

His sons washed his body and laid it out on a cooling board, covered it with a sheet, and placed it on the back porch where it was cooler, until the mortician could arrive to pick up the body. Since Morgan's Funeral Home was in Quarry Town, the family selected to use them just as they had for Nina and for Belle. Three days later, his wake was held at the Gray farm. The body was returned to the farm and the family and friends kept overnight watch until funeral time the next day. All of his personal belongings at home and at the farm were removed from inside the house. All mirrors were covered with a sheet to avoid ghostly reflections. Bed covers were taken off the bed and burned. The featherbed mattress was disinfected and left outside the house to air for three or four days. The funeral was held at Shepherd Street Baptist Church in Quarry Town. He was buried at McGoodwin cemetery just outside the city. Harmon walked with Ida in the procession and sat with her throughout the funeral. They were followed by Clyde, Rising Sun, Helen, and Cappatolia. Harmon was the first son and this was Stonewall's request. It was a cultural tradition for the family to line up for a funeral processional according to gender and lineage, a practice that continues to be followed today. No one complained about the order of the processional lineup. Everyone else just found their positions by gender and lineage and fell into place.

Ida's Welcome Return

Now that Will and Minnie had closed their place they were staying at Belle's house in Quarry Town. Five of their children were still at home and living with them: Carrie Lee, Johnnie Bee, Marshall, Queen Bee, and Robbie. The children had insisted that they move back to Quarry Town so that they would be closer to the rest of the Gray family. It was only a short time after Stonewall's death before Ida chose to do the same thing. Ida had bonded well with the Grays and most of them lived around Quarry Town. Moving to Quarry Town also offered a broader opportunity for her children to pursue their trades as entrepreneurs. Walter Jack was sought out as a self-trained interior decorator. He hung wall paper and did both exterior and interior decorating for the wealthiest families around the area. Clyde worked closely with his uncle Matty and was on his way to becoming a very skilled technician in automotive and electrical trades. Rising Sun worked as a contractor for the Farmer Contracting Company of the area. His work to help construct the Kentucky Dam over the Tennessee River in Gilbertsville, Kentucky and his work to help build all of the facilities at Camp Breckinridge in Morganfield, Kentucky became a lasting note of pride for the Gray family. Helen was a beautiful seamstress and made clothes to share with her siblings' offspring. Adeline was known as a skilled body piercer and almost anyone in Quarry Town who had their ears pierced had them done by Adeline. Cappatolia was a self trained beautician. She married young and moved to Indianapolis, Indiana, where she ran an ice-cream parlor for many years on Capital Avenue. Proctor followed his father's trade as a farmer at the Gray farm. Mary Dee, Lincoln, Matt, Harvey, Frank, and Harmon continued to live with Ida. Raising the children was a challenging task for Ida as a single parent. She needed and sought the assistance of their uncles for provision and rearing to help her.

Clyde and Rising Sun had searched for a suitable place for the family to live. Finally they moved into a small place located at the lower end of Donovan Street adjacent to Shepherd Street Baptist church. As soon as a vacancy occurred, the family moved to a larger place with indoor plumbing located at the upper end of Cave Street. They drove their wagon across town to the new place and quietly moved in all of their belongings while most of the neighbors were sleeping or were at church. Sunday was a day of rest to be respected and it was not the proper thing to do or even think of, moving on Sunday. Since moving involved labor, one would expect it to take place on a weekday.

When they opened the door and stepped inside, they were welcomed by the women of Quarry Town who let out a loud cheer. The women had cleaned the kitchen and brought over baskets of food that included fried chicken, potato salad, boiled corn, sliced tomatoes, and steamy fresh baked apple pie along with a beautifully baked pound cake. The Gray boys were champion eaters and it only took the wink of an eye for them to dig right into the food. It was such a warm, genuine gesture that Ida with her quiet

156

spirit, let tears flow down her cheeks like an open fountain. It took all the strength of her emotions to openly express her thanks to each of them.

Ida had been back in Quarry Town only a few months until she was stricken with a massive stroke that left her bedridden and completely paralyzed down her right side. The children took turns and tried to take care of her the very best that they could. Her devoted sister, Addie, still lived nearby and spent much time caring for her. Addie's husband, Horatio, came by often and helped to watch over the boys. So did Stonewall's brothers, Dave, Arthur, Otis, and Otha. Clyde had moved in with his uncle Matty. Referring to his sister Nina's ashes, he often stated that he and his sister Nina lived with their uncle Matty. Nina's ashes remained on the mantel place.

Currents of the West Wind were beginning to calm down. A new wave of serenity was in the air. Quarry Town was known for its sweet aroma of honeysuckles when they were in bloom, that sweetness was about to fill the air. Even the birds of Quarry Town were becoming intoxicated by the sweet aroma and the calmness. They were nesting and singing to announce new beginnings. The town gossip and busy rumors had ceased for a season. Family battles were being defused and people no longer seemed to be on edge. Rising Sun and Clyde still had to follow through with a mission. They had made a promise and they still had to locate the precious jewels as soon as the spring floods settled. They were convinced that the Great Spirit and the calmer winds would lead to the place where they would be found.

14

Calming the West Wind

Rising Sun Laments His Father

Day by day Rising Sun missed his father more and more. He remembered the vision trips that they used to go on together, the camping and fishing trips, and the family times when his father would talk to the family about their heritage, traditions, and legends. Stories of adventure, love, relationships, child's play, victories, successes, and conflicts were frequently retold until everyone comprehended the depths of every hidden meaning. The strength and rich history of the Gray family were built on these life lessons handed down from generation to generation. It was now Rising Sun's turn to make certain that these life lessons were passed along to their children. He wanted to be sure that his seedlings were fully exposed to their family history and understood the importance of the Gray legacy. No longer would Rising Sun misuse his energy by hanging his head remorsefully over the death of his father. His father had struggled with his commitment to the legacy but his spirit journey was one of dignity and honor.

Rising Sun wanted to begin this healing by strengthening the bond with his brothers, Matt, Harmon, and Proctor. He also wanted to take on the adventurous task of searching for the lost jewels that were sleeping somewhere in the swift currents of the Cumberland waters. Finally, he would work hard to become a good father to his future seedlings. He would passionately love them, provide for and protect them, and nurture them in what it meant to be a Gray seedling and what was expected in their character, labor, and intellectual endeavors.

Fishing for Jewels

Rising Sun had selected a spot near Eddyville at the bend of the river where he could be alone to meditate and think about the legacy oath. It was just beyond the spot where his father had released the jewels to the wind. It was a favorite fishing place for him and Clyde. He had asked Clyde several times to accompany him on a search for the jewels. On this trip, neither he nor Clyde dug earthworms or made fresh bait to attract the fish. They each took along their longest cane pole and their strongest fishing line to reach out into the deeper areas of the river. Neither Clyde nor Rising Sun could swim so they tied plenty of empty bottles around the lower sides of the boat to help stabilize its balance and increase the ability to float. They each took along an inner tube to use in case of emergency. They had a great fear of rocking the boat so they sat very still and straight facing each other in opposite directions. They rowed out to the middle of the river and dropped a homemade weighted anchor. They fished in an area half way around their selected spots in both directions for a set time and then moved further down stream in the direction of the triangle, which was an area where the Cumberland merged with the Tennessee and then finally met the Mississippi.

After toiling all day in search of the jewels with no success, the brothers grew hungry, tired and cold. They rowed their vessel back to shore and tied it to the same tree where they had found it. It had been left there by Ida's friend, James Crumbaugh from Kuttawa, for those who needed it to cross the river. This was a common neighborly act and a fulfillment of a family promise. The boat had been there for a few days in case the Grays needed to use it to search for the jewels. They checked the position of the sun and realized that they had overstayed their time and that nightfall had begun to set in. Because the boys did not swim, Ida had begun to worry and sent Lincoln and Harmon out to search for them. They met about half way home. They could see their house in the distance. Clyde pointed out the gleam from a light shining in the sitting room window. It was a family practice for their mother to always leave a light burning in the house until every family member had returned home. As they came closer to the house, the light shone brighter. Their hearts grew warmer just knowing that they were family and this little gesture of love from their mother meant so much to them.

Matt Steals from Ida

When they reached the yard, they heard loud angry voices coming from inside the house. No longer was the family upset because Clyde and Rising Sun had overstayed the sunset but they were angry because Matt had committed a dishonorable act for the family. Ida was paralyzed and could not turn herself. She always kept her money in a money handkerchief placed in between her featherbed and bed springs for safe keeping. While the boys were away and the girls were occupied in the kitchen, Matt had taken advantage of his mother's disability and committed a notorious act. He went in and turned his mother on her side and stole her money handkerchief. He left her lying on her side in an uncomfortable position and departed the house in haste. When the girls, Mary Dee and Adeline, went into the room, they knew right away what had taken place and just who was responsible. They turned their mother on her back and found her weeping silently, a fountain of tears streaming down her cheeks as with slurred speech, she attempted to explain what had taken place.

The Gray household was one of only a few households in the area that had a telephone. It was a queer looking black contraption with the features of a microphone embedded in a brown wooden box; It had a separate attachment for listening. It worked by cranking a handle to reach the operator, who would ask for a number and ring it for the caller. When the telephone rang, there was a ring code for the household. There was also a different ring code for one or more parties that shared the same line. If someone was using the telephone on the party line, you could listen in on their conversation and you also had to wait for them to complete their call before you could use the telephone on your line. This was referred to as a party line. Mary Dee had tried to make a call to Helen so that she could come over and settle the dispute but the telephone line was always busy.

Meanwhile, Adeline had walked over to Helen's house to get help and both girls were entering the front door when the boys arrived. Clyde tried to gather details about the incident from Mary Dee but in the midst of her fear and excitement, she began to stutter, her speech slowed, and she was able to explain only a very little. Adeline then poured out the entire story on the front porch. The commotion aroused the neighbors and it only took the flick of a moment for the entire story to spread to the far and near corners of Quarry Town. The incident became the talk of the town, peppered with the opinions of the neighbors. It was an embarrassing moment for the entire Gray family.

Helen and Clyde ordered everyone to settle down and quickly called a family meeting in the kitchen. They agreed that Matt had to leave the house. He was no longer welcome to stay there because of his treatment of their mother, and it became the duty of Rising Sun to inform him of the family decision. This was Rising Sun's first endeavor to fulfill the commitment of his oath to the family legacy. He wanted to confront Matt in a different manner but the role of his responsibility dictated an act of diplomacy by both principle and character. Rising Sun left the house in search of Matt, to retrieve his mother's money and to put the issue to rest. Helen went in to calm her mother and to straighten her bed covers. Meanwhile, Clyde made a vow to personally do what his father would do if anything similar to this act ever happened again.

Rising Sun Meets His Totem Spirit

Rising Sun realized that he could not handle these responsibilities alone. He needed the guidance of a totem spirit. He journeyed to his personal area of retreat in hopes that his father's spirit or a totem would visit him. He chanted his father's prayer chants and even made up a few rhythms of his own and danced before the Great Spirit with no results. He recalled that his grandfather, Grayhorse, always insisted that totem spirits respond best around fire and water, which was why he had selected this secluded place with a quiet little waterfall trickling down a hill and emptying into Beaver Creek. Beaver Creek was located just off the Marion/Fredonia Trail # 91. He left the house with a knapsack of food on a threefold mission that could no longer be delayed. He had to conquer first things first, a vision trip with his totem spirit. He had to locate Matt and settle this mess that was causing the family to be in such disarray. Finally, the disconnection with his brother, Proctor, had gone on long enough. He wanted to make amends with Proctor and heal the brokenness between them.

The distance to Fredonia was too far to walk. He set out around mid-morning for Beaver Creek, riding Ned. Since he had not eaten food, he began by building a camp fire and roasting three sausage links. The links were freshly made from a new batch of mixed pork left to season from the recent hog killing season. He strung the sausage on a clean green branch that he used as a kabob. The smell of the fresh wood mixed with the sweet hot savor from the sausage, and the fresh morning dew aroused an investigation of curious resident critters. Rising Sun had taken a few of Ida's biscuits as he passed through the kitchen on his way out. He ate enough to appease his appetite and then carefully extinguished the fire with water from the creek. In quiet meditation, he sat solemnly by the creek side, hoping to hear from the Great Spirit. There was no response. Rising Sun pledged to himself to remain in that solemn place until he made a contact and communicated with the Great Spirit.

Without a warning, Rising Sun was awakened from sleep by a moving popping sound. Quickly he sat up and noticed a swirling smoke plume emitting from the ashes of the camp fire. Without speaking a word, he arose and walked over to the smothering fire.

"Who are you? What in the Sam Hill do you want?" asked Rising Sun.

In the vocal intonation of Grayhorse, the voice spoke. The fire flickered and burst into a brilliant glow of yellow and red flames. "I am the spirit that has been assigned to guide you. I am your totem spirit."

The spirit appeared in the image of a medium-sized white bear.

"You are my totem spirit?" asked Rising Sun.

"I am that spirit," the spirit responded. "I am the spirit of the animal slaughtered by your grandfather when he conquered the animal for his crossover into manhood at only fifteen years old, a young boy. The spirit of the White Buffalo will not return to you."

The image then came closer with the whisk of the West Wind. "Listen carefully while I give you directions to follow. Go down to the creek and wash your face and your feet in four different areas of the water. You fear the water and you do not swim but do not be afraid, you will be protected. Hold your breath and cover your nose while you dip your face four times. Then pay your vows to the Great Spirit and leave the place in solitude. The jewels that you are searching for will return to you in four days. They are also being protected by the Great Spirit and the spirit of Grayhorse.

Rising Sun Confronts Matt

"Visit the waterfall inside the cave at Big Spring. Matt will already be there. Talk to him about being disbanded from the family. Give him directions to be followed to mend the brokenness with the family."

Then the totem spirit turned its back and suspended itself into the currents of the wind. The image was quickly lifted and dissipated into the clouds. Rising Sun gathered his belongings and whispered commands into Ned's ear. Ned gave a hearty neigh signaling that he understood, turned around, and headed toward Big Spring. As they approached the cave, Rising Sun could see from a distance that the wooden panel that had been placed across the front entrance had been removed. As he alit from his horse, a fat groundhog stood in a frozen pose as if to question his intrusion, followed by a raccoon. Rising Sun ignored them both. The raccoon seemingly had appointed himself as host or a security lookout for the young ones that scurried into the darkness. Rising Sun recalled his visit to the waterfall with his father. He was cautious of the slippery underfoot and the bats that clung overhead so he brought along a flash light to help light his way.

Rising Sun went directly to the waterfall chanting one of his father's prayer chants to the Great Spirit and waited for a vision. This time, he was expecting a visit from White Bear, his own totem spirit. It happened as if he had been followed by someone. In the ghostly silence, he heard footsteps echoing against the west wall of the cave. Rising Sun had never been on a vision trip alone and was uncomfortable about the thought that someone else was actually there. As he focused on the waterfall, he saw an elongated shadow appearing on the same west wall. Observing the movement of the shadow, he knew that it was his brother Matt. Matt walked with a limp in his right leg. His right leg had been amputated in his youth and he wore a peg leg (a wooden attachment with no foot but a round bottom covered with a rubber cap). The peg leg made a hard loud noise as he walked. Rising Sun was not sure of Matt's intentions so he arose to face him.

"So they sent you, did they?" questioned Matt. "Just what do you plan to do about it all?" he asked.

"The answer is not what I plan to do," answered Rising Sun. "What is important is what you plan to do about the money that you took from Mama. Matt, the whole family met and the answer points to only one direction. You are not to return to the house. You are no longer welcome to live there. Our sisters are fearful that your return will lead to more trouble. So just stay away. I gathered most of your belongings and brought them to you. I will meet you here tomorrow before noon and bring the rest of your belongings."

"I don't need to go back," said Matt. "It is not in my plans to ever go back there."

"So what about Mama's money?" asked Rising Sun.

"I no longer have it," responded Matt.

"How much do you have?" continued Rising Sun.

"Only a little," answered Matt.

"And how much is a little?" Rising Sun continued to dig for answers.

"Only fifty dollars," Matt answered angrily.

"You have to give it back, Matt, you have to and you have to do it right away. Go to the farm and talk to Uncle Dave. Ask him to let you borrow thirty-five dollars and tell him that you will pay his money back to him. Do you understand, Matt? You have to pay it back. Go there today and meet me here tomorrow at 11:00 A.M. and I will let you borrow the other twenty-five dollars. But guess what, Matt? You also have to pay me back. First Uncle Dave and then me. I do not want you to go back to the house so bring the money to me and I will return it for you."

Matt turned his back and started to walk away.

"Not yet," ordered Rising Sun. "Give me the fifty dollars now, place it right here in my hand. If you leave here with that money by tomorrow you will only have thirty-five dollars. Give it here Matt, right here in my hand."

Reluctantly, Matt reached in his pocket and threw the money on the ground. Rising Sun knew his brother well so he waited for Matt to walk away from him before he reached for the cash.

Rising Sun gave Matt enough time to walk back to the front entrance. He just didn't trust Matt because he was so unhappy with the arrangements. When Rising Sun reached the front entrance, Ned was waiting for his master. Matt leaped from behind an embedded rock and attempted to hit Rising Sun in the head with a blackjack that he picked up when he rushed away from the house. Thanks to Ned and the Great Spirit, Rising Sun saw Matt's shadow and fell to the ground. He quickly rolled over to the left side of the entrance to avert the blow.

Rising Sun got up and said to Matt, "You . . . I knew that you would choose the cowardly way!" Matt walked away without a word. Rising Sun called out to him, "When you meet me here tomorrow, don't bother to go inside, I will be right here at the front entrance. You are a two-faced coward!"

Minnie Saved the Legacy

Rising Sun rode back to Quarry Town to visit his Aunt Minnie and Uncle Will. Minnie met him at the door. "I have been waiting for you, I knew that you would be coming by here. Did you meet with Matt?" she asked.

"Yes," responded Rising Sun.

"Was he bitter? Did he have a fight with you? Will he be coming back?"

Rising Sun answered yes to the first two questions and no to the last one.

"Don't worry, Rising Sun," said Minnie. "I am going to help you with the legacy whenever you need me. I stood at my father, Grayhorse's, bedside when he dictated the legacy to your father, Stonewall. I know the depths and the importance of maintaining the legacy. I also know the struggle of keeping the oath. It goes far beyond just sowing seedlings. Seedlings have to be protected and nurtured into the legacy. The legacy was not openly entrusted to me and I did not openly take the oath. In the Cherokee tradition, it was passed to the male gender and it must continue that way, but my father spoke to me also. His eyes gave me his blessing to watch over our family and the legacy and it was confirmed in the spirit of Mother Ellen. So, in my heart, on that day, I too made a lifelong commitment. I took a silent solemn vow to my father's spirit to see that the legacy does not die. Trust me, Rising Sun, trust me. Until your death, I will not leave you. I will not let the legacy die. You carry the weight of the legacy load and I will lend you all of the support that you will need from the spirit of Grayhorse.

"Now you go, Rising Sun, go to your mother, her heart is bleeding as if it had been pierced with an arrow. It is the bleeding pain of a mother. Relieve her mind about Matt and let her know that he is still alive. She is a mother and in a mother's heart there is constant worry for her children. She is sick and nobody sick should have to be bothered with this kind of worry. So be on your way."

Rising Sun refilled his coffee cup, finished his sweetbread, gave his Aunt Minnie a warm hug, called out to Ned and rode home to be with his mother.

Rising Sun could not dismiss from his mind the prophecy that the lost jewels would be returned and that they were being protected. Even more, he could not release the feeling that the totem spirit had set a time limit of four days for their return. Clyde was determined to find the jewels. An inner spirit had spoken to Clyde and was guiding him back to the mouth of the Cumberland. The spring floods had come and gone and some of the areas of the river were almost down to the bare bottom. Clyde did not go fishing for fish that day, instead, he went fishing for jewels. He had fished in that spot for most of the morning when suddenly, he rose to his feet.

"My stars above!" he yelled out, "I don't believe this, I don't believe what I see."

Slowly floating down stream with a movement of certainty for its destination was a mass of tree branches. It seemed as if the branches had been broken from their roots by a violent wind. Tangled among the branches was an unusual branch in particular. It appeared to be the same branch that the deerskin pouch had wrapped around when it started its adventurous journey down the Cumberland. The sinew string had wrapped and tangled itself several times around the branch.

By now, Clyde was certain that it was the deerskin pouch that contained the precious jewels. Clyde reached for a longer pole and some stronger line. Several times he attempted to fish for the mass of branches and reel them over to him—or at least closer to the shore. He struggled with the large mass for hours, with no results. Every time that he was able to hang on to a portion of the mass, it would slip away.

Watching the mass closely so that it would not float out of his sight, he went over to the neighborly tree and untied the borrowed boat that the Crumbaughs had continued to leave in place. He checked inside the boat for an inner tube for his own safety and pushed the boat down to the water's edge, cautiously rowing the boat closer to the mass of branches. After a long struggle he was finally able to reel the mass over closer to the boat so that he could catch hold and pull it closer to him without tipping the boat over. Never losing sight of the fact that he could not swim, he was careful not to unbalance the boat. He tried with all of his might to reach the pouch but because of the way that it was tangled, he could not seem to get separated. Finally, he used his fishing knife and attempted to break or cut the branch that he needed from the mass. Fighting hard effort to remain seated in the boat, he now was slowly reaching his goal. He held on to the branch as tightly as he could, being careful not to let it drop into the water. Carefully, he placed it in the boat beside him and rowed himself back to the shore. Before disembarking the boat, he remembered his father and grandfather's way, reached for the pouch and paid his vows to the Great Spirit.

Once he was on solid ground, he opened the pouch, hoping that it had not been bothered by someone else or that the stones were not disturbed in any way. He prayed that they were all accounted for and in good shape. He lifted a good clean rag from his fishing box and emptied the jewels onto the rag that he had placed on the ground. He counted them more than once to be sure that they were all accounted for. There were three silver nuggets and twelve lustrous turquoise, a total of fifteen jewels. They had been protected by the Great Spirit and now they had been returned to the family to which they belonged. It was a testimony of faith. The Great Spirit had granted a victory.

166

Helen and Clyde Equalize the Fury

Now that Clyde had found the jewels, he wondered if he should even tell Rising Sun or his Aunt Minnie that he had recovered them. He wondered if they were now rightfully his. He wanted to ask Aunt Minnie if he could claim them now that he had found them or at least be in charge of them, but feared that she would tell Rising Sun. One morning shortly thereafter, Clyde became a little careless about his secret and emptied the jewels on a clean towel on the kitchen table. Little did he realize that his grandfather had originally found them in the shallow waters of the creeks and rivers and that being in the water would improve their luster.

Clyde had almost lost himself in the admiration of their beauty, when he looked up, and saw Rising Sun was standing over him at the kitchen table.

"What in the name of goodness do you think you are doing?" he asked. "Where did you get those and how long have you had them? You know good and well that they belong in my care. Weren't you even going to tell me that you had them? Clyde, you were stealing the jewels!"

Clyde made no attempt to answer any of Rising Sun's questions. Helen heard the anger in Rising Sun's voice and joined them immediately.

Clyde envisioned his role to the future seedlings to be that of a patriarch uncle and Helen viewed her role to be a matrix aunt. Clyde arose from his seat and began to speak to Rising Sun.

"Here, take these; they belong to the family but they are in your care. I fished them out of the river a few days ago. They are not mine to keep. I was waiting for an opportunity to return them to you. A time when we could be alone, your mind would be at peace, and you could receive them with dignity. There is no danger of any competition or confrontation between us or anyone who might envy your position. Take them Rising Sun and wear them around your neck as our father, Stonewall, and our grandfather, Grayhorse, always did. Now keep them protected and never again allow them to be taken out of your sight or away from your care. You are my brother and I will also seek to protect you, the legacy, and the seedlings, just as our father instructed me to do."

By then, everyone else in the house had come into the kitchen to join in the celebration. Rising Sun broke away from the group to share the good news with Ida. She reached for his hand and together they offered a prayer of thanksgiving. But for some strange reason, Rising Sun had a premonition that an evil notion was entering Clyde's mind to claim the jewels for himself.

Proctor's Suicide

Rising Sun had one more issue to settle in order to complete his mission of peace. He needed to search for his brother, Proctor; he was to stop at Big Spring along the way and collect his mother's money from Matt. Proctor and his family lived on a smaller farm just past the Gray farm on the Eddyville road. When he reached Big Spring, Matt was waiting for him near the front entrance just as they had planned. Rising Sun made a stop at the Gray farm to inform Dave and Robert that the battle between he and Matt had ended. He also wanted them to know that he was looking for Proctor in order to make a peace settlement with him. Rising Sun had come to realize that this had to be his mission because he was living under an oath made to the Great Spirit, to his father, and to his family. It was time for the battle to end, time for the bitterness and the hurt to heal. But more importantly, it was time for all sibling rivalry to cease, not only among he and his brothers but also never to enter into the minds of the seedlings in generations that would follow.

Proctor and his wife, Lillian, had birthed a dozen children. Meanwhile, Proctor had crept across the adjoining field and fathered two additional children with the neighbor, Sarah Maxie—Lillie and Shelly. This occasional adulterous journey to Sarah's house was only a short distance from Proctor's home. Fred Otha, Proctor's oldest son, was usually seen with his father wherever he went, except when Proctor made opportunities to be with Sarah.

Rising Sun was hurrying so that he could reach their house around supper time before Proctor left for a little night air. Recently, Proctor had developed the habit of leaving the house right after supper and usually did not return home until late. Rising Sun had no intention of discussing Proctor's behavior even though the family was aware and disagreed with how much his lifestyle was bothering his wife Lillian, and their children—as well as the spot of distrust that it had implanted against the family name. For now, Rising Sun's concern was to talk through their disagreement concerning the legacy and the jewels and come to some consensus to eradicate the bitterness that had continued to fester between them.

As Rising Sun rode along in the dusk of the evening, he noticed a bright red and orange glow in the western sky followed by a heavy dark plume of smoke. The smell of smoke began to fill the air, and Rising Sun could sense in his stomach that something terrible was happening at Proctor's farm. He hastened his ride in hopes that whatever it was, he would be able to help. When he reached the farm, the hysterical family was gathered in the back yard crying over what was taking place. Rising Sun could see that the fire was actually coming from a tractor parked in front of the barn. The tractor was completely engulfed in flames. He moved closer and observed that Proctor's body was actually sitting on the tractor. After supper, Proctor had walked out the back door with his Bible in his hand, drove the tractor out in front of the barn, drenched himself with a mixture of gasoline and kerosene, climbed upon the seat of the tractor, lit a match and set himself on fire while reading the Bible. He had taken his own life while reading the Bible, sitting on a tractor! The family was simply devastated.

According to family reports, nothing unusual, like an argument, or unkind words or actions had taken place before this horrible act happened. There had been no disharmony or hard feelings with anyone before the tractor exploded. The only visible warning that could be pinpointed that something might be bothering Proctor was his unusual withdrawal from the family. He did not want to carry on a conversation with anyone and he would not allow any of the boys to follow him around as they were so used to doing. He wanted to be alone. Nothing more has ever been revealed by the family regarding his death, and no one was ever able to determine why Proctor was so unhappy as to commit such a gruesome act.

The boys used every container that they could find to carry water to try to put the fire out. They even dug a trench between the fire and the house to keep the fire from spreading. They formed an assembly line that reached from the well to the fire to hasten the process. Neighbors from both up and down Eddyville Road came over with containers to try to help extinguish the fire. Drawing water from the well and then getting it over to the burning tractor was a slow, tedious task. Leroy, Proctor's second son, ran down the road to a neighbor farm to ask them to call the sheriff in Eddyville for help. Since the fire was burning from oil and gasoline, all efforts to try to put it out with water at some points seemed useless.

Rising Sun went over to the tractor and tried to help the boys lift his brother off the seat of the tractor, but Proctor's clothes were completely engulfed in flames. The hat that he was wearing fell off his head and his hair was completely burned right off his head. Proctor's flesh had softened and it was so difficult to catch hold of his arms to lift him onto the ground. The gas tank on the tractor exploded a second time and the flames spread. The fire was so hot that the rescuers could no longer even attempt to lift the body down. Finally, he tumbled onto the ground, burned to death, his face so badly charred that it was totally disfigured. The only thing that did not burn was the bible. Only the ends of the pages that Proctor had been reading were scorched around the edges.

Exhausted and sorrowfully wounded, Rising Sun sat on the ground beside his brother, weeping, with his head in his hands, rocking his body, and pleading with the Great Spirit for an answer. The smell of human flesh was sickening to his stomach, and the intermingled smell of gasoline and kerosone caused him to want to retch. He sat there in that position for more than an hour, weeping, rocking, and in prayer. Finally, the sheriff arrived, bringing with him a group of five volunteers from Eddyville. The fire was beginning to die down, but the odor from remnants and ashes from the fire along with Proctor's charred body and a stiffening smoke above was overwhelming not to mention the view of the premises. The children brought sheets from the house to cover their father's body, which they placed on a covered wooden plank to serve as a cooling board and removed it to the barn until a mortician could come to take care of his body. Rising Sun walked away in pain feeling that a part of him had died also.

Rising Sun could not comprehend his brother's death and consequently did not handle it well. He frequently wondered if his parents might have listened to an inner sense and recognized some degree of mental instability in Proctor. He wondered if even in his childhood maybe Proctor's intense quietness and desire to be alone was actually a warning signal of something more serious, like deep depression. Were his sudden bursts of anger and uncontrolled temper a concern that he needed attention? Maybe, just maybe, these acts of warning came into play when his father made a decision to pass the legacy entrustment to Rising Sun rather than to Proctor. He would never really know the answer but one thing he did know; parents in his time often did not expose difficult family issues and concerns to the eyes and ears of children.

Proctor's death never brought closure for peace to Rising Sun because he never had an opportunity to make peace with his brother, whose widow, Lillian, was left to raise the children alone. Today, she has reached the age of ninety years and resides in a nursing facility in Quarry Town.) Fred continues to carry a Gray persona in posture, character, and spirit. By family identity, he epitomizes the image of a typical Gray male, carrying the quietness of Mother Ellen and Mamaw Ida. He is a favorite cousin of the family for whom I never cease to search whenever I return to Quarry Town. Proctor's children, Lillie and Shelly were not raised in the Gray family but were reared by their mother Sarah in the Maxie family. Since becoming adults, they have sought to be connected with the Gray identity. Even today, the Proctor suicide is not a topic for family discussion, nor is the parentage of Shelly and Lillie. All of Proctor and Lillian's other children are deceased except Fred Otha and daughter Lillian.

One thing was real for Rising Sun—he knew that the time had come for him to make a change. He had no choice but to turn his back to the West Wind, which had only brought turbulent storms into his life. There had been storms of illness, death, family disconnections, battles of bitterness, pestilence, fire, and floods. He felt that the spirit of Grayhorse no longer followed his path and knew that his life cycle was no longer turning within the favor of the Great Spirit. He needed to think through the process. He had no other option. If he turned his back to the West Wind, then the East Wind would return or the North Wind would follow. His life cycle could rotate toward the North and the North Wind would be in control. Since he was destined to make a change, he left the farm and headed North, trying to escape the vengeance of the West Wind.

Voice of Cheyenne

The turbulent aftermath of the fearful West Wind that penetrated the life cycle of the Gray family spilled over into the childhood years for me and my brothers, James, "Rook" and Robert Lewis. We watched the remnants of family feuds waste away the strength of our family ties. We experienced the powerful hurt of separations from broken homes; the ravages of the disease of alcoholism and the neglect of nurturing family values and morals. These distracting forces set out to destroy the future seedlings, beginning with our generation. We had no path to follow but to try to reclaim and restructure the family legacy. A legacy of victories and success moving through the channels of education, such as academics, fine arts, athletics, and spiritual renewal. We set forth within our generation to propel the Grays to the top of the heap in whichever endeavor we became a part of. It was a task that had to be mastered in order for a new mission to take place.

Grandpa Stonewall died before my birth but my memories of Mamaw Gray (Ida) remain loyal and strong. I recall frequent visits to Mamaw

Gray's house, her quiet spirit and the stern demand from that little finger that stuck straight out in an uncontrolled manner and meant "behave yourself" whenever it pointed in my direction. The sweetness that came out of her heart whenever she would reach out to me as a child, beckoning me to come closer to her bedside, whispering in my eager ear, and sharing a pat on the head from her, helped to create a security cover for me during my childhood years. Some of the practices that she followed are now a part of my household, such as leaving a light burning until everyone in the household had returned home.

Never out of my heart are the childhood memories that I left in the family porch swing. Nothing can ever replace the excitement of the high rides that I always took in that swing, making it a first stop when I went to Ida's house. I would soar as high as my childhood energy would propel me until a voice of authority from a watchful aunt or uncle would demand that I descend before I experienced a broken neck. These were gestures of love from Mamaw Gray that not every Gray seedling had an opportunity to enjoy. Whenever I use her precious green depression glass iced tea pitcher that was passed on to me by Aunt Helen, I think of Mamaw Gray's love for all of us. That pitcher continues to be a connector to her inner spirit and all of her love and sweetness that passed on into my spirit.

During the writing of this document, I frequently felt her presence surrounding me and directing my movements. Like the spirits of Grayhorse and Mother Ellen, the spirit of Mamaw Gray is vibrant and strong and continues to dictate who I am and what I shall become.

I LOVED YOU MAMAW GRAY
YOU WERE AND WILL ALWAYS BE SPECIAL!
MAY YOUR SPIRIT REST!

—Cheyenne

PART III

North Wind
The Spirit of Grayhorse
A Brisk Bitter Wind—Legacy Lost

"Harvesting Wisdom"
Gift of Cheyenne

I

It dwells in the sphere of the firmament, ordained and created by God.
It is golden, unfaltering, and majestic, unfolding its worth in men's
    hearts.
He reveals the wisdom in wonders and the beauty of all the earth.
He speaks through the fury of lightning, and nature's new created birth.

II

He masters the mighty roar of the thunder, and the rhythm of
    earthquakes and winds:
Revealing the birth of creation where wisdom and new life begins.
It graces the strength of the universe; celestial beyond earth and sea;
Descending and treading new pathways, sprinkling its wealth around me.
So, go harvest the strength of true wisdom; at dusk, at evening, at dawn.
Never retreat from its power, know when you have conquered and won.

III

It visits the dark souls of mankind, at morning it showers its worth;
Sheltered in bright robes of sunlight; it waters and nurtures the earth.
It rides on the edges of storm clouds, confounding the path of the wind;
Draping all worried with rainbows, directing sad thoughts to an end.
So harvest its strength strong and powerful; capture it and pass it to a
    friend.

IV

It descends into the hearts of many, and journeys across vastly plains.
It brings messages of life and prophesies; igniting our lives with a flame.
It foretells the steps that we must follow, and turns us away from our
     past.
Go harvest its worth never ending; speak of its beauty foretold;
Harvest its worth at midday, and hide its strength in your soul.

V

Let it arise in the voices of children, playfully seeking a way;
Through their innocent souls and their humor, they release their fears of
     the day.
Take courage and harvest true wisdom, captured from children at play.
Harvest pure wisdom at sunrise, and let it take charge of your day.
There is never a reason for worry when wisdom is charting the way.

VI

Seek this enlightening power through children and elders, directly from
     God above.
Let it fall on the heads of the seekers, and penetrate every heart with
     love.
It is solid, golden, and steady; like iron, concrete, and steel.
Seek daily and harvest true wisdom, and never let go of its will.

—(The Wisdom of Grayhorse)

15

Hoisting Silver Seedlings

He stood at the door of the cave entrance remembering his past. He had to make a decision before the North Wind took hold of his life cycle completely, and pushed him in the opposite direction. He no longer had a reason to remain in Quarry Town except for his commitment to the family legacy. He wanted to move away from his mother, Ida, and the rest of the family. He was spending way too much time at Aunt Minnie and Uncle Will's house. His cousin, Robbie, was more beautiful now than when she was younger. He could hardly contain his heartfelt emotions whenever he was in her presence. Minnie and Will had birthed eighteen children and Robbie was their thirteenth child, their youngest daughter, and a double cousin to Rising Sun, Sully.

Grandfather Stonewall, Uncle Will, and Aunt Minnie, as well as the entire Gray family looked with respect upon double cousin relationships. The family had engraved the thought that a double cousin was as close kin as one could be other than being a brother or a sister. Both Will and Minnie were well aware of this untimely relationship that existed between their daughter and Rising Sun. Minnie had warned both of them that they had to maintain respect for the family values and refrain from fostering this relationship with such a close relative. Rising Sun denied the accusations, but he was having trouble staying away from Robbie. He was no longer able to control his feelings for her. He dreamed of her and longed to hold her in his arms, gently caress her, and lose his will to hers. Robbie was aware of Rising Sun's feelings and made no effort to back away. He had to talk to Minnie and Clyde concerning the legacy, then his plans were to gather his belongings and head North. Hopefully, he would not be tempted to look back or to return.

Clyde expected Rising Sun to come early and he had no intention of making things easy for him. Clyde wanted no rumors or scandals floating around Quarry Town to smear the family name. When Rising Sun reached the McGoodwin place, he and Clyde rushed toward each other as it had been some time since they were last together. After an exchange of warm brotherly greetings, they walked down the path to share Rising Sun's dilemma. Clyde confirmed his brotherly support for Rising Sun, but for the sake of the family image and the legacy, he encouraged Rising Sun to go away from Quarry Town. Maybe the rumors would cease if he only went a short distance, like Eddyville, Cadiz, or Ceruleum. Clyde promised to watch over the family and to take care of Mother Ida. He begged Rising Sun to leave the deerskin pouch with the precious jewels in his care and he promised to protect them. Rising Sun refused the offer. In no way was he going to part with the jewels again. These gems represented the future seedlings that were to come from his loins and no one, not even Clyde, would ever again have an opportunity to take this blessing from him.

When Rising Sun left Clyde, he went straight to his Aunt Minnie's house to discuss his commitment to the legacy. He was concerned about the oath that he had taken. Minnie was already watching over Rising Sun and keeping her eye on the legacy in his behalf. She had promised Rising Sun that she would always be there to back up his strength for the legacy. On the other hand, she was disappointed in Rising Sun's behavior and detested him having an affair with her daughter. Most certainly, she did not want Robbie to be with child by her double first cousin. It was not only a stain for the family but it also created a possibility that the child could be born with some physical or mental defects.

Minnie laid the family law down to Rising Sun and warned him that the family expected him to either break off the relationship or leave Quarry Town. If he could not be a Gray man and do this, then they would have no choice but to send Robbie away to the Gray farm to live with her Uncle Dave or to Kuttawa, in Lyon County, to live with her Uncle Harvey James. Robbie denied the entire affair with Rising Sun to her mother and father, but she mutually yielded to Rising Sun whenever they had an opportunity. Reluctantly, Rising Sun agreed to break off the relationship with Robbie, so that Aunt Minnie would not move forward with her warning. Minnie pointed out a safe place in the cellar where Rising Sun could leave the jewels. Again, he rejected her offer. He assured her that she had no further reason to fret about the safety of the jewels or about his involvement with Robbie. He was moving on, yet the yearning in his heart for Robbie caused his heart to stand still. He promised her that he would be out of town by the next sunrise.

Rising Sun had not saved enough money to purchase a car; he had not even learned to drive. He surely did not want to bother his Uncle Arthur to drive him anywhere. He had no notion to go out to the Gray farm to hitch a team of horses to a wagon and drive himself. He wasn't even sure if he would ever return to Quarry Town.

The Sullivan family had set up a wagon shuttle service with trips scheduled twice daily to Lyon and Trigg Counties. Rising Sun walked down to the livery stable on Market and Jefferson Streets to see if he could catch one of the shuttles. Old man Sullivan was just driving up to the stable entrance to unload passengers that were coming in from the Eddyville run. The next run was to Rocky Ridge, Cadiz, and Ceruleum. He told Rising Sun that it would be a thirty-minute wait for the next shuttle. This pleased Rising Sun. He stated that he had nothing but time on his hands and the wait would not bother him.

Rising Sun paid the seventy-five cents one-way fare, climbed aboard and seated himself on the back seat of the wagon. As they rode along, there was much conversation and small talk about the happenings in Quarry Town. Rising Sun listened carefully to hear if there was any mention about the relationship between he and Robbie. Not a word was said, but there were enough giggles and smiles from the two ladies on the front passenger seat to attract his attention. Rising Sun was good looking and easy on the eyes, with his curly locks, dusky sun-kissed hue, and slim features posted perfectly around his smooth round face. He carried a gentle smile and a constant playful wink of the eye, while at the same time, he was thinking only of Robbie. Rising Sun did not utter one word during the entire ride but he never let his mind slip away from the thought that he might not ever see Robbie again. As he watched the sun setting to set behind the western hills, he felt the chill from the North piercing his heart and signaling a new birth of loneliness—bitter, cruel, desolate, cold.

When the wagon rounded the "Y" junction at State Road 91 and the Cadiz turnoff, Rising Sun whistled and called out to the driver to stop the wagon. Without a word, he reached for his belongings, and slid down the backside of the wagon. He started the walk back to Quarry Town and never looked back, a distance of approximately five miles. When he reached the quarry, the workers were busy loading stones into piles from the heavy dump trucks. White powdery dust engulfed the entire area. It came from the mining of hewed stones inside the quarry and the loading outside. It seemed to be heavier than usual. Rising Sun picked up speed and rushed past the area so that he would not be completely covered with the white snowy mist as the workers were. When he reached the intersection of Main

179

and Washington Streets, he turned left at the dairy and followed the path along the way to Big Spring. He paused for a drink of fresh water from the spring and then entered the front entrance of Big Cave. Following his own shadow, he found his way to a familiar place near the waterfall where his grandfathers had always met their totems, the Spirit of the White Buffalo and White Bear.

Using left over branches from a previous campfire, he lit a small fire to take away some of the damp chill in the cave. Resting his head on a moss covered rock, Rising Sun closed his eyes and thought aloud, "Maybe tomorrow, but not today. My heart throbs for Robbie and I will not leave this way, I will at least say goodbye to her." Robbie and Rising Sun had selected this special spot inside the cave by the waterfall. They had come there several times before. Robbie trusted Rising Sun not to leave without saying goodbye to her. A spirit that moved inside of her led her to believe that he would go to their favorite place inside of the cave. She entered the cave by the North entrance. It was a longer path but she was comfortable that hardly anyone would see her if she used that entrance. She had told no one where she was going. Using a small, dim flashlight, she moved soft footed and cautiously, negotiating her way along the slippery path, following familiar white rocks that she had used before. Carefully, she sought the dimly lighted inside passageway that led to the falls. Awakened by the sound of quiet footsteps, a view of an elongated shadow appeared on the East wall. Rising Sun's heart beat faster. He knew that it had to be Robbie and that she had come to search for him.

Rising Sun arose with outstretched arms. He embraced Robbie and pledged his love to her. She found a safe place close to him and rested her head securely on his shoulder. In the dim flickering firelight, Robbie cuddled under his arms and waited for that special moment when she could lose her will to his. Rising Sun took a blanket from his travel bag and covered both of them. They huddled close by the fire and Rising Sun embraced her as they exchanged their vows and pledged to love each other forever. In her heart, Robbie carried a secret that she had never shared with anyone. Only her parents knew of the intense pain and discomfort that she suffered. She had carried this knowledge from early childhood years, but had not yet found the right time or the right way to share this secret with Rising Sun. Without complaining, she endured severe bodily pain.

The disease had weakened her muscles and she was not physically strong. Now that she was older, she was experiencing also a severe stiffness in her joints. Her illness had been diagnosed as a muscular disorder that was spreading through her bones. The family had kept silent about her illness and had made every effort to protect her and attend to her medical needs without public distraction. But now Robbie felt it was time to share this secret with Rising Sun. In spite of the pain that wracked her body from the long walk to the cave, tonight was the night for her to yield intimately to Rising Sun. As she shared her secret about the pain, he caressed her gently and the intrusive pain seemed to subside. Robbie focused on her love for Rising Sun and not on herself as she yielded her desire and her whole body to Rising Sun. For those special intimate moments, they knew each other and came together as one. She had confessed her most sacred secret to him and this night would make a new beginning for the troubled pair.

As sleep came upon Robbie, she snuggled close to him. A feeling inside called out a sense of new birth and she knew immediately that on that night she had conceived a child for Rising Sun. It would be a first seedling for a fulfillment of the legacy. He was to perpetuate the seedlings and this was his first seed. As daylight began to creep through the North entrance of the cave, Rising Sun and Robbie realized that they had spent their first night together. Robbie was not ashamed of what had taken place. She knew that Rising Sun was the keeper of the legacy and a part of that legacy was to reproduce and regenerate the Cherokee seedlings—and she had been a part of that process. She felt a special anointing to mother the first seedling for the legacy. Keeping these feelings inside, she also felt nervous because she knew that her mother and father would search for her if she did not come down for breakfast and daybreak had already arrived. Rising Sun was also afraid. He did not have the courage to walk her home and risk facing Aunt Minnie. Robbie assured him that she could handle the situation and would be fine. Still not sharing her feelings with Rising Sun about the seed that he had sown; she kissed him goodbye and left by the same entrance that she had used when she came.

Rising Sun sat looking into the dying fire. He stayed a few minutes longer before making his way to the livery stable in time to catch the morning wagon shuttle. When he saw the shuttle go by the dairy crossing, he knew that he had missed it by at least five minutes. Without hesitation, he went straight to his Uncle Arthur's house and asked him for a ride in his Model-T Ford to Ceruleum. Uncle Arthur asked many questions about why he was leaving Quarry Town, but he agreed to take him.

Uncle Arthur also offered unsolicited advice and opinions as they traveled together. Rising Sun held nothing back from Uncle Arthur, including his affair with Robbie and their overnight stay at Big Spring. Uncle Arthur's solemn response was "Well, I will be doggone, boy, couldn't you find nothing better to do?"

But befuddled with love, Rising Sun thought solely of the sweetness of Robbie, her innocent spirit, and how lovely she was. At this juncture, nothing else mattered; the cousin relationship no longer entered his mind.

When the wagon shuttle pulled up to the Ceruleum stop at the general store, two friendly gentlemen with wide smiles were waiting for them. They walked up to the driver with extended hands and announced that they were there to meet a passenger by the name of Rising Sun, whose aunt had sent word that he would be on the shuttle and that he was to stay at their house until he could "get on his feet." For two days now, they had hoped to meet Rising Sun to welcome him to their home and twice he had not been there. These friendly gentlemen were the Lander brothers, Thomas and Frank, who chuckled and laughed as they walked away as if they really did not expect him in the first place. With a disgusted smile, the driver informed them that Rising Sun had left the wagon at the "Y" junction on the day before, and this time, he was nowhere to be found when the shuttle left. The brothers again thanked the driver, shook their heads and boarded their own wagon for the return home.

The Lander family had been friends to Rising Sun's mother, Ida, and her brothers for many years and were being neighborly by allowing Rising Sun to stay with them until he had a place of his own. When Arthur reached the county line, he drove straight to the Lander house where both he and Rising Sun were welcomed as a part of the family. Before Arthur returned home, he cornered Rising Sun in the corner of the front yard and gave him a strict lecture about family respect and what was expected of him concerning his wild behavior. He challenged Rising Sun to uphold the family name and the Spirit of his great-grandfather, Grayhorse. Arthur made it very clear that the family had grown tired of covering for him and that they would no longer tolerate his wild wandering behavior. Rising Sun experienced an almost devout change of heart as he settled in with the Landers, avoided trouble and accepted a new life style.

It was a perfect, crisp, clear morning. The sun rose early and was already perched high up in the sky. Rising Sun arose early also and joined the Lander brothers with the outside chores in preparation for the annual hog-killing day, a neighborly event which the Lander family could host. Families from nearby areas would come together at one of their farms to slaughter, dress, and prepare the meat to be cured and put away for the season. Each family would then take its share of the sausage meat, which had to be ground and stuffed in clean white cloth or casing to be stored away. After the woman scrapped the skin, it was stored to be used to season vegetables or cooked for cracklings (pork rind skins). The cracklings were later used for delicious crackling cornbread.

Rising Sun's job was to help dip the hogs in the vet tub of boiling water, scrape the hair from the skin, and divide the meat into sections, making sure that each family had an equal part. He also had to make sure that enough meat was left along the backbone for tenderloin and pork chops. The loin sides were used for bacon while the ankle hocks were put away with the other seasoning meat. The prize section was the head, including the ears, nose and jowls, not to mention the tail.

Rising Sun emptied the stomach and chitterlings ("Kentucky Oysters") before passing them along to the ladies. The organs were also saved for a special dish known as pluck-and-plunders (heart, liver, etc.). Following hog-killing day, the annual chitterlings cook-out would follow and was shared by all of the participating families.

Rising Sun was vetting the hogs when he noticed Uncle Arthur's car drive up to the front gate. Without hesitation, Aunt Minnie, Uncle Will, and Robbie made their way around to the back yard unannounced.

Without even a hello, Aunt Minnie directed her words directly to Rising Sun. "Well you went and did it anyway, didn't you, Rising Sun? You just couldn't let well enough alone. I warned you and you made me a promise, but it looks like you left your load in Quarry Town before you went away. Don't you respect and understand the infinity of a promise?'

"What are you talking about?" asked Rising Sun.

"We are talking about Robbie," Uncle Will chimed in. "Do you have absolutely no respect at all for this family?"

"What is wrong, with you, Robbie?" Rising Sun questioned. "I don't know what you are talking about," he continued.

"I am talking about how you have ruined our daughter's life and taken dignity away from this family," scolded Minnie. "She is carrying your child!"

"Who told you that I am responsible?" demanded Rising Sun.

"Don't you question me, Rising Sun!" the angry woman went on, "Nobody had to tell me. Everybody in Quarry Town knows about you and Robbie. People saw both of you go into that cave. Everybody knows that you and Robbie slept together at Big Spring. Before then, she had never spent a night away from home. We took her to the doctor. She is three months with child. Just look at her. Her hips are round, her face is swollen but radiant, her stomach is protruding and enlarged, and everything that she eats makes her as sick as a dog. So don't you tell me that I don't know what I'm talking about. By the way, it's a boy, I can tell how she is carrying it, nice and high."

"Well, Rising Sun, what do you have to say about this?" asked Will.

"What did Robbie tell you?" asked Rising Sun.

"What do you say, Robbie?" asked both Will and Rising Sun at the same time.

Her pleading eyes filled with tears as Robbie answered, "I'm keeping my baby, Mama. There is no way that I am going to throw my baby away and there is no way that I am going to give my baby away."

"Well, what do you have to say, Rising Sun? Is she carrying your baby or not?" Minnie continued to question.

"Tell Mama, Rising Sun. Tell her the truth, Rising Sun," spoke Robbie. "If Robbie claims that it is my child, then it is," answered Rising Sun.

"That answer is not good enough," ordered Will. "Did you or did you not sleep with our daughter?"

"Yes," answered Rising Sun. "I claim this child as my blood, my first seedling. Aunt Minnie, this is the first seedling to fulfill the legacy of your father and my great-grandfather, Grayhorse. The legacy that you have protected for so long. It has been directed through my loins and lineage. It is a part of your blood, the blood of your father. Robbie is carrying my seed to a fulfillment for one of the silver nuggets that I carry next to my heart, the ones that you promised to help me protect. This child is a precious jewel. He will never be an outcast to the Gray lineage. He is my son, he is your grandson. He is our seedling, a descendant of Grayhorse, Stonewall, and me. And a descendant of Ida, Uncle Will, he also comes from your lineage; the lineage of the Hollowells, through the loins of your daughter Robbie. A first seedling, the first jewel.

"If it is a boy, we'll call him Robert after my father Stonewall's brother," spoke Rising Sun.

"Oh it will be a boy, all right," said Minnie. "He will be loved and protected according to the Gray legacy. He came from our child, Robbie. He is our family!"

"But what about you, Robbie? How are you?" asked Rising Sun.

"Robbie is sick," answered Minnie. "She has been sick this whole time and she is not getting better."

"I will love and protect you, Robbie," pledged Rising Sun. "Grayhorse's totem, the Spirit of the White Buffalo and the God of Mother Ellen will protect this seedling."

Rising Sun walked over to Robbie, held her by the shoulders, looked into her eyes, and said with tears streaming down his cheeks, "Thank you Robbie, thank you for a seedling son."

Robbie turned from him and ran back to the car, weeping heavily. Uncle Arthur was waiting in the car. Shortly, they were joined by Uncle Will and Aunt Minnie. Minnie then realized that she had just made a public announcement to the entire town about a private family matter.

As they drove away, Rising Sun retreated from the excitement of hog killing chores and ventured away from the crowd. He turned his back to the distractions, hung his head in his hands, and wept. First, there were tears of remorsefulness for the hurt that he had brought to Aunt Minnie and Uncle Will, for the pain and the struggle that Robbie was about to endure; and for the shadow of darkness that was being cast over his family and the family name. Then there were tears of joy and thanksgiving to the Spirit of Grayhorse for charting the direction of the legacy through his loins; for Robbie's yield to him and her willingness to carry his seed and her understanding of his love for her. And finally, for the gift of fulfillment to perpetuate the Cherokee lineage. He needed to talk to Robbie about the child, and they needed to select a Native American name (or wait for one to be assigned) so that the child could remain connected to the Spirit of Grayhorse and so that the ancestral heritage and traditions would continue. Rising Sun was convinced that Robbie would understand. But he was also concerned about possible rejection of the child by the people of Quarry Town and some of the members of both the Hollowell and the Gray families. If something fatal really did happen to Robbie, who would mother the child?

Rising Sun and Robbie's involvement did not go unnoticed by the Gray elders. The wise Gray uncles attacked the issue immediately with conviction and strong demands. They made certain that Rising Sun clearly understood their position on the matter and that any errors made by two nonthinking adults, were in no way to be handed down to an innocent child. The child would be nurtured and loved. There was to be no rejection, he was of Gray blood and that must be respected.

Even though continuously suffering from the severe pain that wracked her body, Robbie was able to carry the baby to full term. On April

4, 1928, she gave birth at home to a beautiful baby guided by the careful experienced hands of her mother, Minnie. The child was named Robert Lewis Gray, a namesake for Rising Sun's Uncle Robert. Not many days following the birth of the child, Robbie became very ill. Her body had continued to weaken and was so full of pain that she never gained enough strength to give much attention to her beautiful baby son. Aunt Minnie was so old and exhausted that she could not take on the responsibility of raising another child. Rising Sun's sisters, Helen and Mary Dee, spent much time helping to care for the child, so Myrtle Tinsley, a dear friend of the Gray family, volunteered to assist Minnie in caring for the child. Finally she asked Minnie if she would allow her to take the child to her home to care for him there, which would allow Minnie some relief so that she could take care of Robbie. Helen and Mary Dee continued to help look after the boy.

Only a short time thereafter, Robbie became critically ill and died from the illness that she was carrying in her body. Rising Sun was aware of these conditions but he did not return to Quarry Town to help care for either Robbie or the child. Robbie was buried in McGoodwin cemetery, off State road 139, just outside the city limits of Quarry Town. Myrtle became more and more attached to the child. She had now accepted him as her own son and the boy referred to her as Mama Myrt. Rising Sun remained in Trigg County, following a new life, with no intentions of returning to Quarry Town. Certainly, he was not prepared to take on the responsibilities of raising this young child. The infinity of a promise had passed him by. He had promised sincerely, to protect, nurture, and love his first seedling, but the child was nurtured and raised by Myrtle Tinsley and the Tinsley family, all of whom put their very best efforts to properly raise and provide for the child.

He grew up with the spiritual values and morals of the Tinsley family. It appeared as if Rising Sun had been caught up in the turbulent currents of the North Wind and could not find his way back to the anchor to which he had made a commitment; a commitment to love and care for his son. Little Robert was the spitting image of his father, Rising Sun; it was as if Rising Sun had burped and spit him out. The boy's tonality, physical stature, hue, physical features, even his curly hair and the way he walked epitomized his father and the male image of the Grays. Robert's relationship to the Hollowell family was identifiable by blood but their influence in his life in no way equalized the influence on his rearing as did that of the Tinsley's and the Grays.

Meanwhile, while Rising Sun appeared to have lost track of his commitment to the family legacy and his son was spinning his childhood years in Quarry Town, Rising Sun was focusing in a different direction. It was a direction established by the North Wind. Rising Sun had become involved with a lady in Ceruleum, Louise Dixon. He found a new beginning with Louise and five years following the birth of Robert Lewis, Louise gave birth to Rising Sun's second seedling. This son was born June 5, 1933, in Trigg County, Kentucky. They named him James Gordon "Rook" Gray. Later he picked up the name "Rook". Rook's mother died during his infancy and he was raised by his grandmother, Ledlie Dixon. Rising Sun was still not seeking to take on any responsibility to care for his second son, and he made little or no effort to care for the child. The grandmother who raised this second son continues to live in Ceruleum and is well over 100 years old.

Rising Sun made no attempt to share this new seedling with the Grays. The child was never presented to the Gray family, nor did Rising Sun ever bring him to Quarry Town. To the people of Trigg County, the boy was a Gray—but to the people of Quarry Town, Rising Sun already had one son, Robert Lewis. The two boys thus were denied the bonding and connection that they needed to share in their childhood and youth years to grow up as brothers. Rising Sun never discussed this second son; it was as if he did not exist. As far as the precious jewels were concerned, this son represented the second nugget of silver. Not long after Louise's death, Rising Sun again needed to strip away these responsibilities, so he made plans to leave Ceruleum just as he had left Quarry Town.

Now that Robert Lewis was anchored into a family, Rising Sun assumed that he could venture back to Quarry Town. He made arrangements to leave the Lander home, feeling that he would no longer be required to live under the threat of having to take care of his two sons. In Quarry Town and in Trigg County, if a man denied the fatherhood of a child or rejected the child, then without pressure, the child was simply cared for by the mother and / or her family and no support was sought from the father. Child support was not available or thought of; it simply was not an option. The child carried the father's name only if the father agreed, otherwise, the child carried the mother's last name and the father was released of any responsibility. This was a procedure that was common to the customs of the area. This is as it was for both Robert Lewis and James Gordon ("Rook") and Rising Sun went scott free.

Rising Sun then returned to Quarry Town and sought new pastures with a new family. Myrtle McCary Rice had recently divorced her husband, Samuel Rice and moved back home from Indianapolis, Indiana. This time she did not return to live on the farm with her father; instead, she moved her family into a new house at 525 Donnivan Street, located at the corners of Tyler and Donovan Streets. She lived less than two blocks away from Ida and her family. Myrtle McCary Rice was befriended by Myrtle Tinsley and Rising Sun's sister, Helen, who developed a sisterly friendship. They were much, much more than neighbors, they were family. They shared family concerns, successes, and failures. They also shared a true devotion and commitment for the children. Robert Lewis and Myrtle Rice's children grew up together as family. Not realizing that before long they would be considered brothers, Robert Lewis grew close to Myrtle's sons, John, Robert Lee, and Sylvester, also their sister Mary Helen. Robert Lewis and Robert Lee even shared the same birth year, 1928. Without much ado, Rising Sun moved in as a common-law husband and common-law stepfather to Myrtle's children. Robert Lewis was in that home so frequently that he began to bond with his father and soon they established a father-son relationship. Myrtle's children loved and respected Rising Sun as their father, they also accepted Robert Lewis as their brother.

In 1936, Myrtle and Rising Sun birthed a little girl, Rising Sun's first daughter, Roseline. Roseline lived only a few months. During early infancy, the little girl contacted a virus believed to have been caused from a tick bite carried by the family dog. The illness was diagnosed as spinal meningitis. It was a painful illness that damaged her spine and drew her neck back in a very uncomfortable position. She died from the illness and was buried with other members of the Gray family in the Tinsley cemetery outside of Quarry Town. On May 4, 1937, a second daughter was born, Shirley Mae. It was a difficult pregnancy for Myrtle. Shirley was born with complications. She weighed only four pounds and remained in an incubator for several weeks until her physical body weight and development reached a safe level. She was born with rickets (soft bones) and asthma. Because of her physical and medical struggles as an infant she was looked upon as a precious child. Myrtle carefully nurtured her as did the Grays, especially Helen, Clyde, and Mary Dee. Rising Sun loved Shirley and bonded even closer to Robert Lewis. Now he had three precious seedlings. It was a true fulfillment for the three silver nuggets that he carried next to his heart. Three precious silver nuggets: Robert Lewis, Shirley Mae, and James Gordon. Rising Sun was proud of his seedlings and showed them off to the people of Quarry Town whenever he had a chance. He liked to announce that Shirley and Robert were his shadows, following him wherever he would allow. This was not so for James Gordon (Rook), who was never around Quarry Town to go along with them.

The time had come for Rising Sun to communicate with the totem spirit of Grayhorse. He needed direction to steer him away from the North Wind. He could no longer take for granted the safety of his seedlings. Only the Spirit of Grayhorse and the strength of the Four Winds controlled the directions of his life cycle. To Robert Lewis and Robert Lee, Shirley was their baby sister and she was treated and referred to as such. Each of them watched over her and they were bonded into a loyal sibling relationship. Myrtle, as well, was accepted into the Gray family. Robert Lewis and Shirley spent much time at the house of their Grandmother Ida; whom they lovingly called Mamaw Gray. Shirley struggled with illnesses for most of her childhood years. She wore an evil smelling asafetida bag of herbs around her neck to help ward off other diseases. Shirley often felt embarrassed about the odor. After she became an adult, it was interesting for her to find out that most of her childhood friends also wore a bag and refused to tell anyone.

On April 28, 1945, Myrtle and Rising Sun birthed another son, Douglas McArthur Gray. Douglas lived to be only two years old. He contracted German measles which "went under" (never surfaced to the outer skin, did not break out on him). This caused his immediate death. According to the family elders and belief in the culture, measles that "go under" are a certain and instant cause of death. He died in Shirley's arms as she rocked him to sleep in her mother's big rocking chair. He was buried in Tinsley cemetery, next to his sister Roseline. The body was "waked" overnight at the house followed by a brief house funeral the following day. Rising Sun then purchased three additional grave sites in that family cemetery; one for Robert and Shirley and one for himself.

Rising Sun was a diligent hard worker. He worked as a contractor with the Farmer's Contracting Company. They completed projects, such as building the army barracks at Camp Breckinridge in Morganfield, Kentucky. One project he worked on that continues to bring pride to the Gray family is his laborious efforts to help build the locks at Gilbertsville Dam that spans the Tennessee River at Gilbertsville, Kentucky. The project was sponsored by the Tennessee Valley Authority (TVA). While working on these jobs, he took every opportunity to pass work skills along to his son, Robert and his stepsons. Whenever possible to do so, the boys would follow him to a job and work along beside him. He took up much time with the boys and passed quality training along to them from father to son.

These were years when devotion to his family was a priority to Rising Sun. But now the wind currents had changed and the North Wind had taken control of his life.

Rising Sun continued to carry in his mind a need to maintain a relationship with the Spirit of Grayhorse. He pondered over his responsibility to protect the legacy for the Gray family. Frequently, he sought a quiet place to polish and count the precious jewels. Now that the fulfillment had begun to take place, he needed to orientate his seedlings to the legacy. He needed clear directions as to how the legacy was to be passed to his seedlings and which one should receive it. Even though he and Myrtle had lost two seedlings in death, three seedlings still remained and he had to be true to the legacy. The silver nuggets represented these three seedlings that had been spared from the sting of death: Shirley, Robert and James. Two of these seedlings were in his care and time was fast approaching for the legacy to be passed. Rising Sun had to pause and offer thanks for this victory in the struggle.

He arose early the next morning and set out on foot in search of his brother, Clyde. He wanted to share this revelation about the seedlings with his brother. Clyde had arisen early also and was loading his fishing gear into Uncle Arthur's car. Rising Sun called out to him from the front gate. He shared his feelings with Clyde concerning his children; how precious they were and how their birth had fulfilled the legacy for the silver nuggets. He told Clyde that an unfamiliar spirit had visited him. It appeared as a wind cloud and traveled through the trees. It ejected a whistling sound like the wind and carried the voice of his grandfather, Grayhorse. The spirit had visited him on four different occasions, always among the trees. He called the spirit, Whispering Wind.

The mysterious spirit brought a message to Rising Sun as he was walking home in a heavy downpour of rain. The spirit was then encircled by a beautiful rainbow that reached from point to point. When it vanished, the Spirit of the White Buffalo leaped along in front of it. Rising Sun knew and could feel that his grandfather's spirit was following him. The spirit left a message with Rising Sun to assign his seedling Native American names so that their Cherokee heritage could be perpetuated and so that they could maintain an identity with the culture and a connection with the Spirit of Grayhorse. James Gordon would be known as Broken Arrow; Robert Lewis would be called Thundering Eagle, and Shirley Mae would be Cheyenne. The voice of the spirit also identified its name as Whispering Wind, a future seedling of James Gordon's, the second seed.

190

"Remember, Rising Sun," spoke the spirit. "As long as you carry the jewels and hold on to the legacy, you are not to forsake your Cherokee connections. You are identified in the cycle of the Four Winds as Rising Sun. Your seedlings must have a cycle identity also. Embedded in your name is your spirit, your mind, your ego, your character, your spoken words, your movements, your total identity; all that which is physical, emotional, spiritual, and real. Teach these spirit characters to your seedlings. Guard and protect your name and teach your seedlings to do the same. Protect your given name, Rising Sun. It means new beginnings. Protect also your birth name, Sully and your family name Gray. Your name labels you; there is much to gain from a good name. Teach your seedlings to carry their good name as precious cargo; protect it, respect it, wear it with courage and pride, and pass it on."

Clyde sanctioned everything that he and Rising Sun talked about and sent him on a return journey back to his seedlings to teach them not only about the legacy and the precious jewels; but also about who they were and what was expected of them. Rising Sun gave Clyde a brotherly embrace, talked about their good fishing days together, and journeyed on his way to locate his children. Rising Sun knew what step one needed to be. He needed to talk to Cheyenne and Thundering Eagle about their brother, Broken Arrow whom they had never met or even knew about. This would be the right thing to do; but Rising Sun was not ready to take that step. James Gordon would have to continue to be a phantom son for at least a while longer, a wait that lasted throughout their childhood years. Rising Sun just could not bring himself to bring that son into the Gray family cycle. In Trigg County, Broken Arrow was a Gray son but in Quarry Town, the only seedlings were Cheyenne and Thundering Eagle. This is how it was accepted in the Gray family and Rising Sun was not about to reverse that progress by explaining his wandering escapades in Trigg County.

With these thoughts, the strength of the North Wind was once again settling in the corners of Rising Sun's heart as a desolate, bitter, cold wind. He knew that turning his back and walking away was not the honorable thing to do; but the force of the mighty North Wind was liquidating his strength. Myrtle had birthed three children with Rising Sun and was living in common-law relationship with him; he needed to marry Myrtle. He also knew how important it was for him recognize Broken Arrow and bring him into the family lineage where he belonged. He needed to share some fatherly responsibility for the nurturing and rearing of all of his children, including Broken Arrow. Rising Sun was the only living parent for his two sons. Myrtle Tinsley needed his help in her struggle to voluntarily rear Thundering Eagle in a good home. Rising Sun shared none of the expense for the rearing of Thundering Eagle. But he shifted the responsibility for the rearing of his two sons to someone else. His actions had taken on the character of a cold, desolate, bitter North Wind.

16

Chastening the Legacy

Legacy Rekindled

Storm clouds were moving in from the Northwest. They had started to form well before sunrise. Rising Sun was awakened with the first clash of thunder and the bustling roaring wind. He arose and began to make his way to the north entrance of Big Spring Cave. He had marked a spot near Quarry Pond where brief intermittent downpours of rain frequently occurred, followed by a brilliant appearance of a covenant rainbow. Often streams of water could be seen draining from the darkened clouds. More than once, the Spirit of Grayhorse totem had been visible in that place and had carried a message for Rising Sun. On each occasion, he had observed a new spirit preceding the rainbow. The spirit always appeared among the branches with the voice of Grayhorse. Rising Sun always listened to the messenger and tried to obey its commands.

This morning, the clouds had an unusual appearance against the sunrise. He could foretell that this would be the day when he would have a meaningful experience with the totem spirit. Rising Sun sat quietly beneath the shelter of a grove of trees, facing Quarry Pond. He flinched at the clashing sound of heavy thunder and the quick flickering flashes of lightning. Quickly a downpour of heavy rain poured down his neck and the back of his shirt. The rain water ran off the tip of his nose. He buttoned his shirt to protect the pouch of precious jewels as they pressed against his body. He did not mind the wetness from the rain; it was as if he had received a response from the Great Spirit. Neither was he bothered by the waiting time for the approval of the Great Spirit. He was confident that the totem would appear and bring him a message.

After a few minutes, the clouds moved toward the East and the rain subsided. Out came a burst of welcome sun and a brisk whistling wind that aroused the leaves on the surrounding trees. The wind made its way among the branches of a sturdy oak tree that appeared to be a sisterly offspring to the oak tree at the Gray farm. It mirrored the petroglyph tree that housed the history for the Gray family. Perhaps the birds had transplanted a seed—or, more likely, the seed could have been carried by Whispering Wind. This time, the wind occurred three times, each time in a cycle of four brisk wind currents. The unusual cycle caught the attention of Rising Sun.

On the fourth cycle, Rising Sun spoke out to the wind, "What in the name of Grayhorse is the spirit message that you bring?"

Before a response could be given, the shape of the Whispering Wind transformed into the face of a friendly maiden.

"I, Whispering Wind," it replied. "I bring a message from the Spirit of Grayhorse regarding the protection of the precious jewels and the family legacy. The Spirit of Grayhorse is not resting, it is not at peace; it is not pleased. The spirit characters of the family legacy are broken and are being neglected. Family morale is being distorted and a disconnection has taken place among the lineage of the family. The Spirit of Grayhorse can never be at peace as long as there is brokenness and disconnection within the family. This brokenness must be healed. You were placed in charge of the legacy and given the care of the precious jewels. Rising Sun, you must re-affirm your commitment. You cannot turn away from the oath that is in your hands. Rising Sun, it is your responsibility to look toward the wind currents of peace. Connect with the compass points of discernment and seek new directions. Seek wisdom, peace, and understanding!"

Reaffirm the Cherokee Name

"Begin by preparing your seedlings to receive the passing of the leg-acy. The true seedlings will evolve from your loins. They are to come through the lineage of your first son, Thundering Eagle. Reassign their Cherokee names and teach them to wear their names as a legacy, a lasting identity, a connector with the Cherokee culture. They are to answer to the names of Thundering Eagle, Broken Arrow, and Cheyenne. Teach them to wear their names with a Cherokee spirit; a spirit that is proud and that has an identity that is eternal. Introduce them to the God of their ancestors; Je-hovah, the God of Ellen and the Great Spirit, the god of Grayhorse. Guide them as the keepers and the caretakers of the family history. Let them be armorial bearers for what is moral and right. Let them know that their lives are as nuggets of silver; pure, solid, of true quality and value. Teach them to walk close beside you and in the paths of their ancestors. When the time is right, pass them the legacy so that it can be continued and protected in their hearts by the Spirit of Grayhorse.

"Now go to the Great Spirit of your ancestors and speak to him about recommitment and reaffirming your oath to protect the legacy and the jewels and about your role as a responsible father."

With these words, the image quickly transformed back to the wind funnel and dissipated into the clouds. It was accompanied by a flash of lightning and a clash of thunder. The stern powerful tone of the messenger, accompanied by the strong moving action in nature startled Rising Sun. Then suddenly, the sun appeared, followed by a rainbow that touched the earth from point to point. Rising Sun then knew for certain that he was being directed by the Spirit of Grayhorse. He had began to feel secure. After such a dramatic moment he needed to catch his breath. He took a deep breath and with a sigh of relief closed his eyes and sat down underneath the oak tree and thanked both Jehovah and the Great Spirit. With a charge of this magnitude from the totem spirit, he needed to receive direction and protection from both Jehovah and the Great Spirit.

Assigning the Legacy to the Seedlings

Rising Sun realized that his seedlings were still young but, following directions from the Spirit of Grayhorse, he wanted to plant the seed for this responsibility while they were young. He wanted to guide and nurture them to bear this load even into their adulthood. As he thought about the character of the seedlings, the first son, Thundering Eagle, had a spirit to wander like his grandfathers, Grayhorse and Stonewall—and even like his own spirit. Thundering Eagle loved following his father and Uncle Clyde into the archives of nature to explore among the trees and around the water. He loved the practical skills of fishing and hunting but he loved even more to drift away on his own. Cheyenne had shown a spirit and a desire to wonder about the structure and order of things. She had been given a gift of music and creativity. She was quite verbal for her age and loved to create a play on words, reading and stories. She would lose herself in books and travel around the world. She followed closely in the shadows of her mother and her Aunt Helen. She was well mannered and well disciplined and was growing into the essence of her great grandmother Ellen. Imprints of Mother Ellen were already showing in her character spirits.

Rising Sun had no worry about passing the legacy and the jewels into the care of these two seedlings. They were bonded well enough as brother and sister to unite their spirits into one and keep the legacy alive. He was however, concerned about the role of Broken Arrow. Broken Arrow carried a quiet spirit and it was difficult to read into what he was thinking or how he felt about an issue. He was a loner with his siblings and had not bonded his spirit. Just what would his role be if he was not bonded with his siblings or with the Gray family? Would he be accepted by the other siblings to carry an equal role of the entrustment? Just when and how would Rising Sun reveal Broken Arrow as a legitimate son with a rightful place in the family lineage? This second son did carry a watchful eye and a heart of passion. These traits would be useful in carrying out the entrustment. At his age, would he now be ready to bond with Thundering Eagle and Cheyenne? Would he be accepted or rejected? It was a turbulent river to cross. Rising Sun pondered many days and finally decided that it must be done; but not now! What could it hurt to let sleeping dogs lie for a while longer? The time would present itself when the time was right.

There was no peace in the heart of Rising Sun. He finally decided to do what he knew had to be done; he sought wise wisdom of his watchful uncles, Arthur, Dave, Otha, and Otis. He conferred with each of them about how the legacy should be passed to his seedlings and what should happen to the jewels. Through two generations, the entrustment had been passed to the male gender and to only one son. According to the legacy, it was to be the fourth son. But Rising Sun did not have a fourth son. Cheyenne was a fourth child; but she was of the female gender and the legacy had never been bestowed to a female. He worried about passing the legacy to the first son when he had been instructed to pass it to the fourth son. He felt that one reason why the North Wind had taken over his life cycle was because he (a sixth son) had received the entrustment. Could this possibly have caused a bad omen to befall on him and his seedlings? The uncle agreed that the legacy had to pass through the loin of Rising Sun and since they knew nothing about the second son, their consensus was for him to pass it to the first son.

Rising Sun worried about the wandering spirit of Thundering Eagle. He wondered if he would grow up and settle down to take care of the legacy and the jewels. Since the second son had no bonding to the Gray family, Rising Sun did not see that it would be right to put him in charge of the legacy. He felt that his only option to fulfill the demands of the totem spirit would be to divide the responsibilities among the three seedlings. The uncles agreed with him. This was a different procedure and would break the traditional way of assigning the entrustment. Rising Sun was certain that this action would be questioned and maybe even criticized; but he had gleaned wisdom and support from his uncles. The family trusted wisdom and discernment so Rising Sun was assured that they would support him in meeting this challenge. On the other hand, he was following the guidance of the Spirit of Grayhorse.

After consistent meditation with the godheads, Rising Sun assigned Thundering Eagle the responsibility to sow seeds to perpetuate the reproduction of the seedlings in the culture. For Thundering Eagle, this would be a fun assignment, appeasing his pleasure to sow and wander. His right to fatherhood would increase, he would spread his seed and his seedlings would be blessed. His seedlings would be nurtured and yield a spirit of dignity, pride, stateliness, and joy. Being female, Cheyenne did not understand that her role was not to bear seedlings. This misinterpretation followed Cheyenne throughout her youthful years and into adulthood. She simply misunderstood her role, which included nurturing and protection of the seedlings and the precious jewels; but it was not to sow seeds. She was to care for and watch over the seedlings just as her Aunt Minnie and Aunt Helen had watched over Cheyenne and her father. The more Cheyenne thought about it all, the more confused she became about the assignment. Broken Arrow was known to have a watchful eye and a passionate heart. His assignment was to nurture a loving spirit with his siblings. He was to remain watchful for both of them and for any interference that might break their spirits and destroy the legacy. He was to use his strong sense of discernment to watch over his siblings.

Rising Sun took his children aside and carefully went over the purpose and duties for keeping the legacy. He explained the beginning of the legacy and how it came from the vision of their great grandfather, Grayhorse. He emphasized how it had been passed on for generations and now it was their turn to become the caretakers. The time was right to introduce the seedlings to their assignments. This all sounded so exciting to Thundering Eagle and to Cheyenne but it was much to complicated for them to thoroughly understand. It all but created a fear in their hearts as they talked about what was expected of them by the family.

Not many days later, Rising Sun took Cheyenne and Thundering Eagle on a vision trip inside Big Spring Cave. They followed the path that led to the waterfall, the place where Rising Sun and Robbie had conceived Thundering Eagle. In the shadows of a small flickering light from a dimly lit campfire, a soft gentle wind from the East blew pass them. The wind traveled toward the Northwest. When it settled, it was the image of Whispering Wind. She called out the seedlings by name. First, she called Thundering Eagle and then Cheyenne. They each responded to their names by saying, "Yes." Then she asked, "But where is Broken Arrow?"

Rising Sun did not respond.

Whispering Wind began to speak to the seedlings. "Thundering Eagle, the spirit has assigned you the duty to sow seedlings. Cheyenne, protect and nurture the jewels and the legacy. Stay close to Thundering Eagle, Cheyenne, provide an anchor for him to hold on to when his life cycle becomes turbulent. Perpetuate the spirit characters of the legacy, the family name, its morals and values. Thrive in the dignity and pride of your Mother Ellen.

"To Broken Arrow, Rising Sun, encourage him to carry a watchful eye for Cheyenne and for Thundering Eagle, siblings that he has not met; and share the passion that he carries in his heart."

The fire began to flicker until it went out and the spirit dissipated also, leaving them in darkness. Rising Sun knew how to find the cave exit, following a dimly lit pathway from the daylight that shone through the front entrance. He grasped the hands of the siblings and ordered them to hold on to each other as he led them out. Then they followed the hill downward along Plum Street and turned left onto Donnovan where they parted. Thundering Eagle ran ahead to his house just over the way on Cave Street. He wanted to share his vision experience with his Mama Myrt.

Cheyenne remained with her daddy as they walked on down Donnovan to her house. Rising Sun reached inside his shirt, pulled out the deerskin pouch, and tucked it tightly into Cheyenne's hand with his hand cupped solidly over hers. Not a word was said and Cheyenne met his eyes with a look of approval. She ran straight into the house to find her mother. Myrtle did not know about the legacy, the totem spirits, or the vision trips. She questioned Cheyenne about her experience and what this all meant. She was very concerned about the quality of the jewels and what they symbolized. She was concerned that Rising Sun had passed them to their child at such a young age. She talked to Cheyenne about what it would entail to keep them safe. She warned Cheyenne that she would have to discuss this responsibility with Rising Sun. Myrtle was not a Gray and she was not sure if she should even be in charge of the jewels; but she knew that someone would have to assist Cheyenne in providing this protection at such a young critical period in her life. Myrtle worried because she did not wish to do anything to bring an evil omen upon Cheyenne, Thundering Eagle, or the Gray family.

This action was so moving and exciting, yet it had created new beginnings for each of them. It was a transition that had to take place. Cheyenne had not really grasped the full meaning of the jewels and how they symbolized the birth of future seedlings for the Gray family. Myrtle took the jewels from her and placed them in an empty shoe box. She then placed the box on the floor in the back of her clothes closet inside a larger box filled with heavy quilts and blankets. It was the safest place in the house to keep things that needed to be protected, or that could not be permitted to just "walk away." Her plan was to leave them there until Helen came by and then she would pass them to her to keep for Cheyenne; at least until Cheyenne was old enough to understand her responsibilities to the assignment. Passing them to Helen would also keep them in the protective care of the Gray lineage. Neither the legacy nor the jewels were to be in the protective care of anyone whose lineage did not evolve from the Grayhorse bloodline. All of the children were very young but Rising Sun felt a commitment to his oath and no longer wished to be responsible, so this was his way of passing the entrustment and relieving himself of the protective care of the jewels and the legacy. After days of delay and pondering, Rising Sun finally made up his mind to go to Broken Arrow and talk to him about the legacy. This could not take place unless he also talked to him about his other seedlings. Rising Sun made a trip to Ceruleum to break the news. When Rising Sun was ready to return to Quarry Town, Broken Arrow was more confused than before he came. Now he knew about Thundering Eagle and about Cheyenne; but they did not know about him. Like Thundering Eagle, Broken Arrow loved to follow along with his father whenever he was allowed to do so; but Rising Sun still refused to allow the boy to follow with him to Quarry Town. The time had still not come for Rising Sun to share this phantom son with the Grays. Broken Arrow had a longing to meet and be near his brother and sister. Even more, he wanted to be included within the lineage of the Gray family. Rising Sun was not anxious to rush the time and he was not about to infuriate the family again with his escapades. So he remained silent with his children, his family, and friends concerning this second son. If the South Wind would blow in his direction, maybe he could find a way to meet this challenge; but his life cycle remained in the currents of the North Wind.

199

17

Treasured Cords, Broken

Coins in My Pocket

Cheyenne stood under the bedroom curtain waiting and watching for Rising Sun to return. Darkness had fallen and Myrtle had ordered her to come inside. She had waited on the front steps for most of the early evening. The sun had set, the wind had picked up a chill, and there was no one outside to watch her. To a four-year-old, her daddy's return was special and it seemed that the waiting hours grew longer with each passing day. When he was on time, she would hear his voice chatting with the neighbors before he came into sight. She would watch for his image to appear as a reflection in the big store window across the street from her house. Then she would leap off the front steps and run as fast as she could to meet him. Rising Sun would stand still, catch her in flight, lift her into the air, and they would walk back home, hand in hand. It was a childhood security ritual for Cheyenne to be able to place her small hand into his; his hand felt so big and strong. The next part of the ritual was for her to put her hand into his pocket and take out as many coins as her small hands would hold. When they reached the house, the coins would be deposited in a small worn calfskin coin purse that Rising Sun had given to her for their safe keeping. When the purse was filled, the coins were then deposited into a very strong papier maché piggy bank that was kept for her very own personal savings. Retrieving coins from her daddy's pocket was so special to Cheyenne. It was a ceremony that had taken place since before she reached two years old. It was only after Cheyenne had grown up and her daddy had gone away that her mother shared with her that Rising Sun was stopping by the neighborhood each day to pick up pocket change to put in his pocket just for Cheyenne. For Cheyenne, it was an unforgettable moment.

Waiting and watching underneath the bedroom curtain created a different reaction for Cheyenne. It was often dark when Rising Sun would arrive and Cheyenne was not allowed by her mother to even run out to meet him. She had to depend on someone else to inform her that he had reached the point for the store window reflection and that he was on his way home. On these days, Cheyenne always met him at the front door and waited for her sky ride inside. Ironically, these were also the days when Rising Sun appeared to be overly tired, irritated, rushed, and unfocused. He would respond as if his thoughts were elsewhere and that something else was more important. Cheyenne never retreated or gave up the opportunity to greet her daddy. She would wait for him to take his favorite seat in front of the fire grate, sit on his knee, and wait for he daily pony ride. Rising Sun never failed to remind her to glean his pockets for coins to fill her coin purse, a ritual that Rising Sun enjoyed as much as Cheyenne.

One day when Cheyenne was riding high on her daddy's knee, Rising Sun noticed that the piggy bank with her coins was leaning against the wall for support to stand up. It could not stand up on its own. Rising Sun lifted Cheyenne down from his knee and walked over to the corner to take a closer look. He picked up the piggy bank and observed that one of the pig's back legs had been cut off. The pig was resting against the wall with one leg stuck underneath its belly. When Rising Sun picked it up, the leg fell on the floor. All of Cheyenne's coins were missing. They had been stolen from inside of the pig. It was now a three-legged pig. One by one, Rising Sun questioned the other children about the slaughtering of the piggy bank. They each declared that they knew nothing about the intrusion.

When Myrtle heard about the incident, she was furious. She promised mass punishment to everyone in the house until the real thief confessed. If anyone was found to be hiding information about the thief, they also were promised a lashing. To Myrtle, a promise was a promise and every promise had infinity, and every child knew that to be so. Instant fear was then projected into each child. Mary Helen and Robert Lee were prompted by this warning to secretly tell their mother that they knew who the culprit was and pointed out their brother, Sylvester. They emptied their minds of every trace of information that they knew. Sylvester consistently denied his involvement or knowledge of the misbehavior. But the truth was, while Myrtle and Rising Sun were away from the house, Sylvester had taken a butcher knife from the kitchen drawer and cut off one of the back legs of the piggy bank. He then shook out all of the coins and placed them in a white sock, which he hid in the back of his underwear drawer.

Myrtle ordered Sylvester to empty the contents of the drawer. The coins inside of the sock fell out and scattered all over the floor. Sylvester was ordered to return the coins to Cheyenne. Robert Lee and Robert Lewis sat on the floor and counted the coins to see if they were all there. They counted $62.27; $3.10 was missing. Sylvester was then ordered to replace the coins but not without receiving that faithful promise, a lashing. Mary Helen and Robert Lee were scolded for not confessing sooner that they knew who had committed this terrible act. Myrtle made it very clear that this was the same as stealing; it mattered not that it happened at home. It was an immoral act that one did not want to grow up with and carry into adulthood nor into the community. Sylvester was placed on prolonged strict punishment, assigned extra house chores, and he wore plenty of "memorial strips" from the lashing that he received from Myrtle. When the next payday rolled around, Rising Sun came home with two large glass piggy banks; one for Sylvester and one for Cheyenne. Sylvester was taught to save a portion of all that he received, twenty-five cents from every dollar that he accumulated. Both pigs sat side by side on the mantelpiece where they could be seen and watched for the duration of Cheyenne's childhood years, but never again were they placed on the floor. They were even still there when each of them married.

Rising Sun grew older, his asthma and breathing problems grew more intense. His breathing rhythms were so irregular that he would sit up at night in a chair trying to catch his breath. The house was heated with coal and wood in an open grate fireplace and no one seemed to realize that the fumes and smoke often contributed to his attacks. Frequently, Cheyenne would wake up and hear him trying to catch his breath; she would then get up and sit with her daddy. She was bothered and worried over his deep coughing and wheezing and his struggles to catch his breath. Cheyenne would sit on the floor by his chair and watch over him protectively. She was too young to understand what was really happening or what to do for him to bring him some relief. Rising Sun would seek relief by inhaling fumes from a lighted can of menthol powder or an herbal mixture that he claimed would clear his nasal passage. These nighttime and pre-dawn encounters became more frequent as time moved on. Cheyenne heard her mother say that Dr. Hatten had diagnosed her daddy's condition as heart asthma and that he might stop breathing at any time during an attack and pass away. These words bothered Cheyenne so she watched him carefully. The condition was expected to worsen, as Rising Sun grew older.

It seemed that asthma conditions had now blazed their way through four generations of the Gray family and were now creating a path so that the affliction would likely filter down to future seedlings. It was an ailment that even Cheyenne was born with. She had experienced attacks of her own and wondered if someday her suffering would be as intense as her father's. She remembered inhaling the fumes from her daddy's menthol can and the odor that emanated from it; she also recalled how the strong odor had even opened her nasal passage as she sat next to him on the floor. The use of breathing inhalers was not an option at that time. No one in Quarry Town had even heard of such an apparatus. The asafetida bag that Cheyenne wore around her neck was supposed to help protect her from attacks of this kind. One thing was for certain; the garlic and menthol odor from the bag was so strong that her nasal passage was constantly kept open and pretty clear. Myrtle kept a watchful eye on Cheyenne as she wrestled with this childhood ailment. When Cheyenne approached her teen years, the attacks became less intense and eventually went away completely. The doctor stated that she had outgrown the ailment.

Dark Days

When Cheyenne entered elementary school, the ritual of waiting for her daddy had not ceased. The waiting time continued to be long and in some instances even seemed to spill over into the next day, and never reached closure. Rising Sun had picked up two habits that were affecting his relationship with Myrtle. First, he had begun to drink alcohol which he claimed gave him relief from his ailment. It was a nasty uncontrolled practice that was tearing his life apart. Second, he was building a relationship with new friends whose values and morals contradicted directly those of his own family. When he received his paycheck, he would stop after work and spend time with his new friends to participate in drunken house parties and social play with other women. Almost always, he would cash his paycheck before he reached home and would have wasted it on alcohol and pleasures for other women. This was always money that the family needed for household upkeep support. When he would stagger home, his demeanor would have turned into loud, belligerent outburst of abusive foul language and a push away intolerance for the children. He was usually too intoxicated to stand up and maintain his balance, so he staggered and fell around uncontrolled.

This behavior created an unhealthy atmosphere in the home that resulted in fear, insecurity, anger, disgust, and discomfort for the children. When they would see their father approaching the house, it was most likely that he and Myrtle would quickly be in disagreement and engage in verbal arguments. Sometimes even physical retaliations took place. The children were driven to quick quiet tears or withdrawal, and were often even forced to choose sides between their mother and their father, including Cheyenne.

Myrtle was a strong-willed woman as well as strong physically. When these disagreements turned into physical encounters, Myrtle usually won the battle. Following these escapades, Rising Sun often displayed bruises, knots, scratches, and blackened eyes as a cost that he paid for his foul tongue and his invitations to Myrtle to engage in physical confrontations, not to mention his waste of family resources. These encounters from alcoholic abuse soon led Myrtle to decree that no alcoholic beverages were allowed in the home by anyone, including Rising Sun and most certainly not by the children. Neither was the smoking of tobacco in any form allowed. Her decision had an impact on the four Rice children and Cheyenne. None of these five children ever indulged in either practice and all of them carried this moral into their adulthood. Rising Sun's dysfunctional involvement with alcohol had a personal impact on each child, especially the boys for whom Rising Sun was a father image.

Thundering Eagle loved his father and became very protective of his behavior. He followed Rising Sun as often as he was allowed. Cheyenne too, watched over her daddy as much as she could. Cheyenne could tell that sometimes her watchful tagging along bothered her mother but Cheyenne paid no attention to her mother's reactions and went along anyway, if her daddy agreed to it. Cheyenne did not understand that her mother's real concern was to keep her away from the influence of Rising Sun's new friends and alcoholism. Cheyenne was so bonded with her daddy that she sensed his erratic behavior as a turn away from her. She was saddened by the gulf that was widening between them. Rising Sun seemed to notice and began to try to reach out to Cheyenne but his efforts were inconsistent and unfocused. He continued to carry coins in his pocket for Cheyenne and she never stopped sitting with him when he had his asthma attacks. Cheyenne could not understand that the emotional changes that caused her father's erratic behavior were a result of his drunkenness. She thought that it was because of his illness and hoped that some day this would all change and her daddy would be better.

It was after sunset when Rising Sun staggered home intoxicated. He went into the backyard to chop wood for the fire grate. He picked up the ax, anchored it above his head and brought it downward to chop wood. He lost his balance and hit himself in the top of his head with the ax. He fell forward and blood gushed out of his head and ran all over him. Cheyenne was watching from the back porch. She screamed and ran for Myrtle, calling out, "Daddy, Daddy" at every breath. Blood was streaming down his face and neck; it covered the ground around him. He was bloodier than a pig for slaughter at hog-killing time. Myrtle and the boys ran to him with a pan of water and towels. Robert Lee remembered to bring a bottle of witch hazel to clean the wound. Even though Rising Sun was almost unconscious, Myrtle never forfeited the opportunity to give him a good tongue-lashing concerning his personal negligence and to verbally discipline him for his drunken encounters. She reminded him of what he could not do well even when he was sober, so how could he master any necessary life skills when he was totally drunk?

The next door neighbors called Dr. Hatten to come immediately to take care of Rising Sun. He cleaned and redressed the wound and cautioned the family to keep him awake so that he would not slip into an unconscious state. Cheyenne became a watchful little nurse maid for her father. She gave up her childhood play and stayed close to him. As Rising Sun's head began to heal and his headaches ceased, he returned to work—and also to the house parties with his friends, while Cheyenne returned to the front porch steps to wait for him.

One day, not long after Dr. Hatten released Rising Sun from his care, Cheyenne heard her father's voice as she waited for him on the steps. As Rising Sun got closer to the house she could hear his voice as he talked to the neighbors. When his reflection appeared in the store window, Cheyenne recognized his staggering steps, which had become a warning to Cheyenne that his return would not be a pleasant one. When he entered the house, Myrtle met him at the door and announced that he smelled like a pigpen. As she observed him, his pants were hanging low and soiled with feces.

Myrtle warned him not to take a seat anywhere. He was drunker than Cheyenne had ever seen him. Cheyenne began to weep and her mother ordered her to go into the kitchen and wait. Myrtle ripped the soiled clothes from her husband's body and tossed them in the open fire in the fire grate. She threw his shirt, pants, and underwear into the fire, declaring, "Rising Sun, you are an ugly mess and these clothes are too filthy to handle. Goodness knows, it's as if you have been swimming in this mess for weeks. Get into the bathroom and clean yourself."

She snatched a blanket from the bed and told him to cover himself. "Now get into the bathroom and wash!"

Rising Sun moved slowly into the bathroom as he had been told uttering foul language intended for Myrtle; but it was all spoken quietly, under his breath.

Cheyenne and the other children had reentered the bedroom by way of the kitchen. They stood quietly and watched the indoor bonfire unaware that not only did the clothes fuel the fire but so did all of the money that he was carrying in his pants pocket. He had stopped to cash his paycheck before coming home so all of the weekly household money burned right before their eyes. Myrtle was so upset with Rising Sun that she made no effort to retrieve the weekly payroll. All of the children cried out to their mother to let them try to get the money out of the fire.

"Stay away from the fire" she ordered. "We'll get by; my God will take care of us all."

Cheyenne simply wailed and clung to her daddy as he reentered the room, head bowed, silent, and fearful that Myrtle had not finished her outrage and wondering what she might say or do next. But Myrtle uttered not another word, except to order the children out of the room.

The next morning, the fire had smothered to ashes and coins from Rising Sun's pants pockets had fallen through the grate onto the hearth. John and Robert Lee scooped up the ashes to be thrown out so that they could restart the fire. They sifted out the coins and placed them in a pile at the side of the hearth and left them for Cheyenne.

Robert Lee called out, "Here, Cheyenne, these are for your piggy bank; but don't touch them until they are completely cooled so that you will not burn yourself."

"Okay," Cheyenne replied.

Some of the coins had turned dark from the hot fire. When Myrtle said that it would be all right for Cheyenne to take the coins, Cheyenne picked them up one by one and put them in her piggy bank, carefully counting them as she went along. A few currency bills with charred edges had also fallen through the grate along with the ashes. Myrtle said that the two boys could have them for themselves. The rest of the currency had become a part of the ashes to be thrown out.

It was a challenging week that followed. Bills that had to be paid were delayed and the food cupboard was thin. No one complained because no one wanted to be responsible for any more trouble or problems for the family to settle. The children were never informed of the true aftermath; but one thing they did know was that Rising Sun was invited to an unscheduled fishing trip with his brother, Clyde. Helen kept bringing over food dishes with the children's favorite pastries, and Uncles Dave and Otis made some frequent visits over to the house with watchful eyes.

Mystery Companion

It appeared unexpectedly, like the Spirit of Grayhorse. It changed its appearance as the house lights reflected against it, and it bore a reminder for a memory never to be forgotten. It had dwelled in the northeast corner of the bedroom, just above the head of the bed, near the ceiling; coming and going as it pleased. The room had been redecorated several times with both wallpaper and paint. It would disappear for a short time and then reappear. Each time that it resurfaced, one of the children would point it out to Myrtle. "Look, Mama, it's back!" they would say. She would then make an attempt to get rid of it but always to no avail. It was a grease spot, approximately the size of a medium sized grapefruit. It had been placed there by a country ham bone that hit the wall. Myrtle threw the country ham bone at Rising Sun on one of his drunken days. The scenario began with a verbal disagreement between Myrtle and Rising Sun. Rising Sun had used foul language and called Myrtle ugly names. Myrtle had hot boiling water on the kitchen stove and the bone was being prepared to drop in the pot to season some navy beans for dinner. Rising Sun was seated in the bedroom in front of the fire grate. As he raised his loud voice in invective Myrtle threw the bone with every ounce of strength in her arm. With a mighty force and perfect aim, the bone soared around the corner from the kitchen stove into the bedroom. Rising Sun was continuing his diatribe with outrage and was too drunk to duck. By the time he finished his speech, the bone struck him on his head and then ricocheted and hit the wall with such force that it made a dent in the wall. The bone also left its mark on the wall to accompany the dent, a large grease spot that never went away. Rising Sun fell onto the floor and before the boys could reach him to help him back into the chair a large knot, the size of a fifty-cent piece had begun to rise above his left eye.

As the bone soared overhead, the children saw it coming. Sylvester called out to the floor crew, "Everybody down!" With laughter, the children rolled around on the floor and ducked. Sylvester then said to Myrtle, "Oh no, Mama—we were going to eat that thing!" Not realizing the seriousness of the moment, the children all broke out into uncontrolled laughter. Cheyenne ran to her daddy and pleaded with him not to go away and to please be "okay."

Rising Sun tried to console Cheyenne by telling her not to worry. He then left the house and did not return for several days. Cheyenne sat on the front step and waited for Thundering Eagle and his Mama Myrt to come over to sit on the front porch for the evening. It was a family gesture that took place between them almost daily. When Cheyenne quietly shared with Thundering Eagle about what had happened to their daddy, so that the two Myrtles would not hear them getting involved in adult matters, they were both afraid that Rising Sun would not return.

When Rising Sun did return, he gathered his personal belongings, walked out the back door, down Donnovan Street, and took up residence with his friends in a house owned by a lady named Tootsie. When Rising Sun was around his new friends, he made no contact with his children. Not long after that, he wandered away from Quarry Town and no one claimed to know his whereabouts. Cheyenne and Thundering Eagle growing into their teen years, missed their Daddy and longed for his return. Thundering Eagle, nine years older than Cheyenne, decided that he would embark upon a mission and search for Rising Eagle. This mission extended into their youthful years, early adulthood, and for Cheyenne, even into her senior high years. It seemed that each time Thundering Eagle would locate his father or stay with him for a short time, like the Spirit of Grayhorse, Rising Sun would vanish again and the relationship would dissipate. During these years, the relationship with Broken Arrow was virtually nonexistent. So Cheyenne and Thundering Eagle were left alone to console each other. Now during times of reflection, it is sometimes revealed to Cheyenne that there had been occasions when Thundering Eagle knew about Rising Sun that he never shared with Cheyenne, such as, the existence of Broken Arrow.

No one in the family ever talked about where Rising Sun might be. He was "taunting" the family name. Uncle Clyde and Aunt Helen had by then evolved into the role of surrogate parents for Cheyenne and Thundering Eagle. They wanted to help nurture and love the children and see that they remained within the legacy of the Gray family. Myrtle Tinsley hovered over Thundering Eagle with much passion and protective care, emphasizing strong morals and spiritual values. Myrtle retained her sisterly relationship with the Grays, especially with Helen.

The North Wind had not only visited Rising Sun; but it had also darkened his days and taken total control of his life. He had lost contact with the god heads of Grayhorse, the god of his ancestors. He had debonded with his family, especially his siblings. He had rejected the advice of his wise uncles. His life cycle was spinning off the north point of the compass wheel. He was under the powerful control of the ugly North Wind. These episodes kept reminding Rising Sun that he was not the fourth son. Rising Sun wondered if this might be some evil omen. Could this be the reason for all of his troubles?

Death of Mamaw Gray (Ida)

The hearse had parked in front of the house to pick up the body. Funeral cars for the family had been lined up behind it for more than an hour. The family moved solemnly and slowly to board the cars for the processional ride to the church. Myrtle was waiting for Helen to stop by to pick up Cheyenne so that she could walk ahead to the church. Cheyenne was going over to her Mamaw Gray's house to be with the Gray family. When Helen called out, her name, Cheyenne ran from the front porch to join her Aunt Helen. Cheyenne called out to Myrtle, "She's here, Mama, I'm gone."

Myrtle came out to the front porch to greet Helen and then walked to the church. Cheyenne held on as tight as she could to her Aunt Helen's hand, which seemed to take away some of the fear that Cheyenne had wrestled with since she viewed her Mamaw Gray's body at the wake watch the evening before. Cheyenne was wearing a white ruffled dress that her Aunt Helen had made for her weeks before. They walked the block along Tyler Street and then called out for Thundering Eagle before they turned the corner to reach the house.

Thundering Eagle had been standing at the front door waiting for them to come by. He had been watching the family as they gathered, only four houses away. He unlocked the screen door and came out to meet them. Both of the children clung close to Helen and stayed close to her.

Uncle Clyde came over and checked Thundering Eagle's shirt collar and told him how nice he looked. "And you too, Sweetie," he said to Cheyenne, using the pet name that stuck with her for the rest of his life time.

Cheyenne and Thundering Eagle were aware of the family whispering and chatter, but only bits of it were clearly understood. *"He said that he would..." "Do you think so?" ... "Oh, he's coming...." "He had better be here...." And finally words from Clyde that let Cheyenne and Thundering Eagle know just who they were talking about.*

"He took the oath from the Spirit of Grayhorse." . . .

Helen responded, "What else can happen to this family, especially, if he keeps breaking his word?"

Instantly and with due speed, a car with Michigan license plates drove up on the opposite side of the street, driven by someone that they did not know. A handsome man got out on the passenger side of the car. Everyone on the porch and in the front yard sighed in awe. A voice from the yard called out, "It's him, he's here, I knew that he would come!"

Without a warning, again he had appeared like the Spirit of Grayhorse, from out of nowhere. He was so good-looking! He wore a perfect smile. His hair glistened in the sunlight. His complexion was radiant and he stood erect. With a soft voice, he spoke, "Okay, here I am. How is everybody?"

People gathered around him with warm glances, embraces, and greetings. However, he seemed not to have noticed the children in the porch swing.

Aunt Helen said to the children, "Look, children, look who is here! It's your daddy." Joyfully and with no restraint, both children downed from the swing nestled into his arms. He ran to meet them half way. Tears flowed down his cheeks as he embraced his two children. He was remorseful over the death of his mother, but he was also shedding tears of joy to be with his children.

Helen said to him, "Rising Sun, here they are, they are in your hands, now hold on tight and take good care of them!"

Rising Sun smiled and reached out his hand to both of them at the same time.

The undertaker proceeded to load the family into the funeral cars according to family lineage and gender, a cultural tradition. He called for the spouse and parents of the deceased; all of whom had preceded her in death. He then called for the sons and daughters according to lineage, with the male gender first. Next came the brothers and sisters, followed by uncles and aunts. Grandchildren were the last to be called. Following was general grouping which consisted of cousins and friends.

Rising Sun stood quietly with his children until his name was called and the undertaker pointed out which car he was to ride in. Rising Sun boarded the proper car, escorting his children. They rode quietly in the car with one child seated on each side of their father. There was complete silence in the car. Cheyenne was bothered by the silence because there was so much that she wanted to say to him. She especially wanted to tell him how much she had missed him and that she did not want him to go away again. In her heart, she wanted him to tell her that this time he would stay.

Broken Arrow was missing from this reunion. Rising Sun did not bring him along and none of the Grays seemed to even acknowledge his absence or to have been informed about him in any way. So, he did not attend the funeral and his name was not listed with the grandchildren. Neither did he ever attend any of the Gray functions or family gatherings. As he was never publicly mentioned in any of the Grays conversations, he remained Rising Sun's phantom son.

Following the funeral, Mamaw Gray's body was transferred to the Tinsley cemetery for interment. The children rode back to the Gray house with Rising Sun. He then put them in the back seat of the Michigan car and his unidentified friend drove them away where he bought them each a sandwich and ice cream and then proceeded to take them home. When he reached Thundering Eagle's House he sat for a few minutes and had a father to son chat with him before Thundering Eagle ran inside.

When he reached Cheyenne's house, she began to weep and did not want to get out of the car. She did not want him to leave her again. He coached her to wait for him on the step while he visited a friend; and told her that he would return shortly. Cheyenne got out of the car but constantly looked back and watched the car as they drove up Donnovan Street. They stopped at a beauty salon located at the corners of Donnovan and Calvert Street. A lady named Cardelia Grooms lived in an adjacent apartment to the salon. Rising Sun got out of the car and entered Cardelia's apartment and the driver drove away.

Cheyenne changed out of her funeral clothes into play clothes and returned to wait for her father on the front steps. She waited the rest of the afternoon until the sun was beginning to set for early evening. Finally, she saw the car approaching over the hill. She stood up and walked down to the big tree in the front yard. She knew that her father would stop because he had promised her that he would return and she was trusting in his word.

Before the car reached her yard, Cheyenne could see him seated in the back seat of the car with Cardelia, the owner of the beauty salon. When they passed Cheyenne's house, the driver blew the horn and her daddy waved, but the car did not stop. Never would Cheyenne have imagined that this would be the last time she would see Rising Sun or that the wave from father to daughter was a final goodbye. Cheyenne was so hurt. She wept for days, withdrew from the rest of the family, and began to lose herself in books. She learned that books could relieve her loneliness and longings and that she could travel around the world, learn about the cultures of other people, and the beauty of nature. She devoted even more time to her music skills and released her emotions on the keyboard. She was now carrying a hole in her heart for her daddy. A hole had been hewed into her heart by Cardelia.

Cheyenne was twenty-seven years old when Rising Sun returned, nineteen years later, she had been only eight years old when he went away. Myrtle had taught Cheyenne never to say or think evil thoughts about her father, so she transferred all of the hurt and hatred to his "friend" Cardelia instead. Cheyenne tried to be a loving daughter; but in her heart, she bitterly hated Cardelia and even through her adulthood she blamed Cardelia for taking her daddy away. Eventually, this bitterness that Cheyenne carried for Cardelia began to cross over to her daddy also; Cheyenne began to reject her father and to have very unpleasant thoughts about him. All of the positive childhood memories of her father turned into anger and bitterness. Thundering Eagle continued to search for Rising Sun and followed him to Detroit, Michigan where he found him living with Cardelia. Thundering Eagle stayed with them for a while and the three of them became family.

Rising Sun no longer had any interest in the family legacy and retained no commitment to protect the jewels or perpetuate the legacy. Cheyenne moved to Toledo, Ohio in 1965 and the saga reveals to her that while she was only 49 miles from Rising Sun and Thundering Eagle, she was not aware of where they were. Uncle Clyde knew of Cheyenne's feelings for her father so he did not upset her with stories of his whereabouts. At this point, Cheyenne was not interested in rebonding with him and without Uncle Clyde, there was no family connector for this to even take place. For Cheyenne, it was a treasured cord that had been broken, dismantled by the North Wind. For Cheyenne, the North Wind was epitomized by alcoholism, family brokenness, and the dreadful spirit and presence of Cardelia.

18

The Parting

The bitter wind was shifting towards the East and things were beginning to settle down for Thundering Eagle and Cheyenne. School days were happy days. Cheyenne was involved in most of the extra curricular activities. She loved wearing an imaginary character coat, pretending to be someone else. It helped her to emerge into a different world leaving behind many of the struggles that she had to contend with. She competed and won roles in the school plays and other drama productions; she led the choral groups, led the cheerleaders; was elected president of the national honor society; played on the volleyball team; and was elected valedictorian of her senior class. She was also crowned Miss Dotson High in her senior year. Her piano and vocal skills placed her in a special category for performance. She sang and played the piano and organ all around Quarry Town and later was recognized as a skilled piano teacher even before she enrolled in college.

These were glorious busy days for Cheyenne. Thundering Eagle and Robert Lee were both assigned the duty to look out for their baby Sis. They took their assignment seriously and protected her with diligent care and a watchful eye. Thundering Eagle's signals of approval for Cheyenne were usually indicated by two vertical nods of the head for a "yes" and three quick horizontal shakes for a definite "no." Either he or Robert Lee always accompanied their sister to most of the school events.

The Black children of Quarry Town attended Dotson School. Grades K-12 were housed in the same building. The school had been rebuilt and was now a two story brick building with a large surrounding yard. A creek ran through the middle of the school yard and another adjoining one ran along the back side. No one watched to see if the children stayed away from the creek, which was spanned by a bridge overpass. It was understood that everyone was to respect the border line. Seldom did anyone get into trouble about the creek.

The creek that ran along the back side of the school was filled with crawfish (crayfish). The older children always drifted back there during their lunch hour. The boys would catch the crawfish and chase the girls. It was a school ritual to be able to jump over the creek ditch without falling into the water. Both boys and girls rehearsed their skills until they perfected their jump. Almost everyone would save some of their one-hour lunch time to jump the ditch. Children who lived nearby were allowed to go home for lunch or they could bring their lunch and eat in the school cafeteria, where cafeteria lunches were prepared by the women of Quarry Town. These women knew every child by name as well as their families. A weekly favorite was homemade chili served with crackers and ice-cold milk.

Dotson School was named for a well-to-do respected black citizen, John Dotson, who was married to Mamaw Gray's cousin, Alvie Hollowell Dotson. Its mascot was a bearcat and its school colors were black and gold. The people of Quarry Town loved the school and supported all of its programs and activities. The after school activities actually enriched the social climate for the community, especially the athletic events, the annual prom, plays, spelling bees, sock hops, oratorical contest, and graduation ceremonies.

Charlotte's Pick

Black students from Cadiz (Trigg County), Marion and Fredonia, Kuttawa and Grand River and Eddyville (Lyon County), were bused to the school. The buses always arrived early so the students were usually there well before the teachers arrived, and school principal, James Polk Griffin, was always there to supervise the early arrivals. A regular practice was to have the students form a line on the front walkway and wait for the bell to ring to enter the building. Cheyenne always walked to school with Thundering Eagle. Robert Lee and Sylvester would go earlier to participate in athletic practice.

Thundering Eagle became involved with an oversized female bully named Charlotte Parker, whom everyone at the school referred to as "Big Flo." She stood very tall and weighed close to 350–400 pounds. She and her siblings rode the Lyon County bus to school. Two of her younger siblings had been fathered by Rising Sun's brother, Proctor and were cousins to the Grays. Charlotte would stand, watch, and wait for Thundering Eagle and Cheyenne to enter the school yard. Then she would make her way over to where they were standing in line. Thundering Eagle was handsome, soft-spoken, and pleasantly pleasing. The girls loved his smile and would smile back to him, giggle, and make eyes with him as he waited in line. This made Charlotte angry; she was determined to have Thundering Eagle for herself. She was also determined to take Cheyenne's completed homework every day or at least force Cheyenne to share it with her. Charlotte rarely completed or made any attempt to turn in her own homework assignments. She had failed several grades and was older than the most other students. Thundering Eagle would usually just stand and watch when she would confront Cheyenne and try to avoid a confrontation with the intimidating Charlotte. She would usually take Thundering Eagle by the hand and force him to walk around the building with her or go around to the side entrance to stand and talk with her. Her attitude for Thundering Eagle was "I'm gonna' make you love me."

Whenever possible, Thundering Eagle would hide himself in the line behind other people or try to dodge her by slipping out of sight away from her presence. Everyone at the school knew about this forced relationship. It became a regular free show in the morning and the children would gather to see what the next act would be like. But it was an embarrassing and very uncomfortable situation for Cheyenne and Thundering Eagle. Charlotte picked a fight with someone every day over her demands for their homework, her "come with me" requests, or some interference over her desired relationship with Thundering Eagle. Her language was loud, boisterous and foul, and her behavior was overly aggressive, harsh, and threatening.

The second free show was seeing Thundering Eagle's timid acceptance of Charlotte's demands. Thundering Eagle's true heart-throb was a sweet, young, pretty girl named Evelyn McCellan, and whenever Thundering Eagle could slip away from Charlotte, he would find his place with Evelyn.

Principal Griffin and all of the teachers knew about Charlotte's bullying behavior; but no one was moved to come outside and settle these encounters. Cheyenne's personal problem with "Big Flo" was that Cheyenne always set a high standard for the class to follow which was difficult for Charlotte to reach. Second, although Cheyenne weighed less than 100 pounds she had no fear when it came to arguing with "Big Flo." Cheyenne would always threaten her back in return, a real source of humor for the spectators, and Cheyenne was angry with Charlotte for badgering Thundering Eagle to be with her against his will.

Conquering Charlotte

One crisp, cool morning when Cheyenne and Thundering Eagle were waiting in line, Harry Woodridge, their cousin, came over to stand with them. Harry played basketball and had extra long legs. He was somewhat of a school hero because of his position on the basketball team. Charlotte stomped and wobbled over to where they were standing and demanded to see Cheyenne's homework so she could copy it. Cheyenne resisted her command. Charlotte repeated the command, to which Harry responded, "Oh no you won't, Charlotte, not today you won't! This is a new day and we are not giving you nothing this morning. Did you hear that, *nothing*!"

Charlotte walked closer to Harry with a threatening posture and asked him, "What do you have to do with it?"

Harry answered, "Not much, because you are going to have to whip us all this morning. I know that you are big and strong but can you handle that?"

With those words, Harry stuck his foot out as Charlotte walked toward him. Charlotte tripped over Harry's long legs and with a big bang and a bounce, without warning, she hit the ground, all 350–400 pounds of her. By then, a gathering of mostly Gray cousins had encircled the action. The spectating crowd that had gathered moved back with laughter and declared that something moved underneath the ground.

Charlotte had fallen on her back and could not pick herself up. Harry snatched Cheyenne by the hand and they both fell onto the ground, when they realized how close they were to the supine Charlotte, Harry called out to Cheyenne, "Roll over, Cheyenne, roll, roll over this way!" They both did just that.

Meanwhile, Charlotte's eyes were filled with fire, her voice amplified, and her hair stood straight up on the edge of her head. It appeared as if the devil's horns were protruding from her skull. Her tongue was filled with harsh, foul, threatening words for both Harry and Cheyenne. Charlotte had rolled over on one side and her siblings were working desperately to help her get on her feet. Harry, Cheyenne, and Thundering Eagle were each trembling in fear. Cheyenne knew not to cry, it would only fuel more power for Charlotte. Harry kept the threats and foot shuffles moving while Thundering Eagle stood trembling, biting his bottom lips with protruding eyes as big as half dollars; he was afraid to move, a pitiful sight. Principal Griffin watched it all take place from his office window; but he never came down to stop the fight. It was as if he really wanted someone else to intervene and take on this female bully and put these daily confrontations to rest.

Thundering Eagle yelled out to Cheyenne, "Now look what you did." Now you have us both in trouble." Cheyenne was surprised at his tone. As she turned to run away, she noticed her other two brothers, Sylvester and Robert Lee coming out of the school's side entrance as fast as their feet would carry them. They joined the rest of the encircled Gray clan.

Thundering Eagle said to Cheyenne, "Run, run Baby Sis, just run fast and I'll take care of it!"

Robert Lee called out to her, "Go home, Cheyenne, go home, now."

Cheyenne ran as fast as her legs would carry her. When she had almost reached home, she looked back to see what was taking place and to her surprise, there was Thundering Eagle running right along beside her. He passed Cheyenne and landed on the front porch before she reached the yard. She said to him, "You said that you would take care of it, well you took care of it all right. Just look where you are now." In total fear, he had run away as fast as he could and left Harry, Sylvester, and Robert Lee to settle it all.

Cheyenne's mother, Myrtle, heard them when they landed on the porch in uncontrolled laughter over the big bang of Charlotte's fall. They made so much commotion that Myrtle came out to see just what was taking place and why they had run back home from school. Myrtle was very upset over another encounter with Charlotte. She marched Cheyenne and Thundering Eagle right back to school and straight to Principal Griffin's office. The Gray cousins were still in their protective pack that included Sylvester and Robert Lee. Charlotte had quieted down and backed away because her protective siblings had gone to class and like all bullies, she was powerless alone.

Myrtle complained to the principal revealing all of the daily encounters that Cheyenne and Thundering Eagle had endured. She asked the principal why he had watched and made no effort to stop the feuds. Cheyenne and Thundering Eagle were allowed to tell their stories. Cheyenne did all of the talking for them, while Thundering Eagle sat quietly, while Charlotte denied every accusation; even the ones that Principal Griffin had watched from his window.

Charlotte threatened everyone in the office with her fiery eyes, clicking teeth, and shoulder gestures, including Principal Griffin. Myrtle angrily demanded that the principal put an immediate stop to the bullying or she was going to contact Police Chief Jones for protection. Chief Jones

217

was a black policeman assigned to the Black community of Quarry Town, a man well respected by the residents of the community. He would work with the school, Myrtle, and Charlotte's mother to end the controversy.

Myrtle then required Robert Lee and Sylvester to go to school later and walk to school with Cheyenne and Thundering Eagle. There were no more demands for Cheyenne's homework but Thundering Eagle was not so lucky. Charlotte was determined to have him for herself, even though he was not interested in her. When Cheyenne reached her high school years, Charlotte was still around and still being a school bully. Thundering Eagle continued to make periodic trips to the school to walk Cheyenne home just in case Charlotte's fury returned. All through her school years Charlotte continued to be a bully. Even today, she is identified by the people of Quarry Town as the town bully.

Thundering Eagle finished his high school years and left Quarry Town. He entered the military to serve his country. This departure marked the first separation for him and Cheyenne. He also left Evelyn behind this time without a pledge to return to her. Cheyenne received no correspondence from Thundering Eagle. Cheyenne completed her high school years at Dotson High in 1954. She graduated with honors, as valedictorian and her cousin, Lorita, graduated with her as salutatorian.

Cheyenne's childhood years, beginning at age eight, were devoted to developing her piano skills under the tutelage of Jack Blue, an accomplished blind pianist from Kuttawa. He nurtured her talents skillfully and offered her opportunities to play publicly all around Quarry Town. Following her high school years, Cheyenne worked two school terms in the music department at Dotson as an assistant to the music instructor, accompanying the choir and classes, while singing in most of the churches of the town. At Shepherd Street Church, she was given a position to train two church choirs (adult and youth), an opportunity that came to her at age fifteen, before she finished high school. She held the position of music director for the First District of the National Baptist Convention and taught classes in music theory, music conducting, and music in worship.

In 1957, Lena Hawkins, a teacher at Dotson and a graduate of Kentucky State University was impressed with Cheyenne's skills and offered to assist her in getting a scholarship to attend Kentucky State University in Frankfort, Kentucky. After the first semester, Cheyenne's academic average was good enough for her to get a state scholarship for minority children for the rest of her time at Kentucky State. Cheyenne remained on the Dean's list and was able to retain those scholarships. She also had a work assistantship to help with her financial demands at the University. Cheyenne worked diligently to maintain and meet her academic goals. Her fondest college memories are the experiences that she had with the college concert choir that allowed her to travel and represent the college. Cheyenne graduated from Kentucky State University in 1961 with a B.S. degree in Music Education and English. Following those years she worked diligently in post graduate work until she acquired three post graduate degrees; an M.A. degree from Bowling Green State University, a Specialist Degree and an Ed.D. degree from the University of Toledo in Curriculum and Administration. She did post graduate work at Austin Peay State University and Fisk University in Tennessee and Ohio State University in Columbus, Ohio. She began a teaching career in Hopkinsville, Kentucky at Attucks High School and completed thirty years of service with the public schools of Toledo, Ohio. During all of this time, there was no contact or word from Thundering Eagle. It was a parting with no return.

The Appearance of Broken Arrow

One day in Quarry Town Cheyenne was working with the worship music at Shepherd Street Church, when a young man entered and quietly took a seat in the rear. He did not appear to know anyone. The pastor, Rev. Lander, one of the Lander brothers with whom Rising Sun had lived in Ceruleum, noticed him as well. Rev. Lander was now married to Evelyn Wharton and they had a son named Cleveland Thomas, who everyone in Quarry Town referred to as Scratch. Scratch had become a close friend to Sylvester. Evelyn and Thomas were expecting their second child, Patricia. Because of the close brotherly relationship between Rising Sun and that family, the Landers had taken on a nurturing relationship for Cheyenne. Cheyenne was treated like their own daughter. They kept a watchful eye over both Cheyenne and Thundering Eagle. Patricia grew up like Cheyenne's little sister. Cheyenne taught Patricia to play the piano and Scratch was like a brother to Cheyenne. These family bondings have lasted not only through their childhood but even until today.

Meanwhile, the church visitor never opened his mouth to Cheyenne, but he watched her like a hawk all during the service. Cheyenne became uncomfortable at the way the stranger continued to stare at her. Following worship, the congregation went to the church basement for the usual fellowship, coffee and pie.

Rev. Lander called Cheyenne aside and asked her, "Do you know who that man is?"

Cheyenne responded, "No."

"Have you seen him before?" she was asked.

"No, sir," she responded.

"Well," continued Rev. Lander, "that man is your brother; That is your daddy's boy, and his name is James Gray."

"My brother?" Cheyenne asked in amazement.

"He answers to the name of Broken Arrow, they also call him Rook. He lives in Ceruleum. Would you like to meet him?"

Shyly, Cheyenne replied, "I guess so."

Leading the way, Rev. Lander and Cheyenne walked over to where the stranger was seated with a cup of coffee in his hand. Rev. Lander said to the man, "Hi, boy. I haven't seen you for a while."

Broken Arrow answered, "How are you doing, Rev. Lander?" calling him by name as if he was an old acquaintance. "It has been some time, I just thought I would come by today to see how everybody is getting along."

"Do you know who this is?" Rev. Lander asked.

"Oh sure, I know who she is. This is my sister, Cheyenne. I learned that she plays the piano here and that's another reason why I came by today."

"Is today your first time meeting her?" Rev. Lander asked.

"My first time," responded Broken Arrow. "Hi, girl, you played the piano good today."

"Hello, thanks," spoke Cheyenne, while backing away shyly behind Rev. Lander.

Rev. Lander said, "This is your brother, Cheyenne," and then to Broken Arrow, "This is your sister, Cheyenne."

Cheyenne dropped her head and smiled. She was surprised that Broken Arrow knew about her; for her father had never mentioned him to her.

"See you," Cheyenne said and walked away. Broken Arrow stood quietly and watched her as she left. From a distance, Cheyenne took a good look at him. He was definitely a Gray. He looked like her uncles, Frank and Proctor, and Proctor's sons, Fred Otha, LeRoy, and Proctor, Junior. Where had he been all of these years? Why had her daddy kept this son a dark secret from the rest of the family? How did he know about her? These were all questions that were going through Cheyenne's mind.

Cheyenne noticed that he was not driving a car when he left. Like the Spirit of Grayhorse, he just walked away and quickly vanished into the crowd. She did not have an opportunity to see which direction he followed when he went away. Cheyenne did not see him any more that day. When Cheyenne got home, she asked her mother if her daddy had a son named Broken Arrow who was her brother.

Myrtle responded, "I don't know nothing about that," and moved over to the kitchen sink to finish washing dishes.

Then, Cheyenne asked her Aunt Helen the same question because if any of the Grays knew him, it would surely be her Aunt Helen or her Uncle Clyde.

Aunt Helen's response was "Not to my knowledge, I don't know nothing about it, ask your daddy."

Daddy was not around to be asked so Cheyenne approached her Uncle Clyde with the same question. His response was, "Rising Sun never said nothing to me about another son, your daddy would know, ask him."

Finally Cheyenne mentioned it to Thundering Eagle. She asked him if he had ever met or heard of someone named Broken Arrow. "Did you know that we have a brother?" she asked.

Thundering Eagle turned his back and walked away. Somehow, Cheyenne felt that he knew but was not ready to discuss it with her. *But why didn't she know also? Why was it being kept such a big dark secret?*

This mysterious relationship bothered Cheyenne. She felt she was entitled to know more. Cheyenne was growing up and she had no desire to live the rest of her life in Quarry Town. She thought often of going away and of Broken Arrow, who even had a Native American name. How could this be if he was not a part of the legacy?

One night she dreamed that her daddy took her to meet Broken Arrow, but awoke to discover that it was only a dream. Why did he just vanish like that and not say more? When Cheyenne asked Rev. Lander to tell her more about her brother, he replied, "Maybe someday I will just do that—unless Rising Sun chooses to tell you first."

That day never came.

Not long after that church visit Cheyenne noticed that Broken Arrow had begun to come in and out of Quarry Town. He would drive a large truck from the quarry through the neighborhood where the black residents lived. He always drove up Donnovan Street to the Copeland house, turned around on Plum Street, made a circle and came back down Donnovan. He usually made two trips, one on his lunch hour and again at the end of his work day. He was always covered from head to toe with white dust from the quarry and resembled the little Pillsbury doughboy. He worked at the big stone quarry just beyond Big Spring. Cheyenne would watch the clock and sit on the front steps and wait for him to drive by. He would blow the horn and wave and she would wave back at him. Not once did he ever stop to talk to Cheyenne; but he would slow up in the truck, wave, and smile and Cheyenne would smile and wave back. He would then drive home to Ceruleum to be with his family.

Cheyenne was not then aware that he had seedling children or a wife. The saga reveals that he had five children and a wife named Clara. As the saga continues to unfold, Cheyenne has thought much about these children as seedlings to fulfill the legacy; but the Grayhorse legacy specifically states that the seedling fulfillment must come through the loins of Thundering Eagle, Rising Sun's first born.

Cheyenne never saw Broken Arrow with any of his children or his wife. Each time that she saw him he was alone. He would stand under the shelter at the Henry Restaurant, across the street from Cheyenne's house and stare at her as he had done in church on that first Sunday. He never visited any of the Grays, nor did he ever attend any of the Gray family gatherings. It was a quiet mysterious relationship. Cheyenne was now convinced that the man was her brother but neither of them had the courage to reach out to strengthen the bonding.

Rising Sun Returns for Evelyn

Thundering Eagle did return to Quarry Town. This time he returned for Evelyn fulfilling the infinity of a promise. Together they nurtured a quiet sweet courtship. Finally, an announcement came that a wedding was being planned and was to take place at the Presbyterian Church. Everyone in Quarry Town was expected to be there. On a quiet Saturday morning, the Grays, Hollowells, Tinsleys, McCellans, and a few friends gathered at the church located at the top of the Donnovan Street hill. Fred Otha and Evelyn's brother, John Elliott, stood with them. Cheyenne carried a small bouquet of flowers as did the bride. The short ceremony was performed by his Mama Myrt's brother, Jim Tinsley who pastored the church. The newlyweds left the church and went away for a short honeymoon; no one asked where they were going.

Cheyenne worried that like their daddy, he would not return. She did not want them to go away and not return as Rising Sun had done. After a couple of days they did return and took up residence not far from Cheyenne, on Seminary Street. Cheyenne loved Evelyn as her new sister. Unlike her older sister, Helen, she was quiet, soft-hearted and easy going.

Not long after their marriage, Evelyn became pregnant and subsequently a child, a son, was born. They named him John Elliott Gray, a namesake for Evelyn's brother, John Elliott. To Cheyenne and the people of Quarry Town, he was a precious seedling, born on July 24, 1955 and he was a perfect image of his father and his grandfather, Rising Sun. His physical features, vocal intonation, hair in curly locks, hue, and the rhythm in his footsteps perfectly mirrored the image of Thundering Eagle. He was the first seedling of fulfillment for the Grayhorse legacy directly from the loins of Thundering Eagle. A perfect first gem represented by the twelve turquoise stones that Cheyenne was holding on to. He was special to the Grays, McCellans, and Dotsons, and especially to Cheyenne. Right away he became known to everyone in Quarry Town as "Little John" although he could have just as easily been called "Little Sully." Everyone around him loved the child and carefully watched him grow.

The Parting

On a quiet evening, without a warning or a reason to be shared with those who loved him, Thundering Eagle picked up his hat, hastened his steps, and departed Quarry Town; leaving behind Evelyn, Mama Myrt, Cheyenne, and "Little John." There were many questions and rumors about where he went, why he decided to go, and if he would ever return. No one ever knew except he and maybe Evelyn. As for Cheyenne, the Grays, and of course the people of Quarry Town, these unanswered questions spun many rumors and untold speculations concerning his whereabouts. The departure marked a second separation of Cheyenne and her brother.

Already, Cheyenne missed her brother. Little John's Uncle, John Elliott drove a large delivery truck for the Dotson family business. Little John was often seen standing up in the front cab seat of the truck; riding along with John as he made deliveries. Mamaw Gray's cousin Alvie (John Dotson's wife) and her daughter, Berdie Lee, took Little John into their home permanently, when he was an infant and loved and raised him as their own son. This arrangement afforded for Little John a well nurtured life, sustenance for physical needs, spiritual training, and provisions for his education in later life. Little John was offered the very best that could be provided for any child.

The Dotsons had also taken in another Gray child, Helen Ann Gray, the oldest daughter of Rising Sun's brother, Ulysses. Evelyn's brother, John Elliott, continued to work for the Dotsons and was always around to see that he was cared for. For Cheyenne, Little John was a part of her blood, via her daddy, Rising Sun, and her brother, Thundering Eagle. He was so special and she loved him unconditionally. He was a little turquoise gem that had been protected for four generations by the Spirit of Grayhorse. Now, the time had come for Cheyenne to continue to watch over him. Even though her daddy and Thundering Eagle were gone, she would never be able to forget them as long as she looked into the eyes of Little John. He mirrored perfectly his grandfather; but he mirrored even more his father, Thundering Eagle. His curly locks, Gray intonation, quick steps, and combined hue of Mother Ellen and Grayhorse thrust him into perfect mold that epitomized the physical characteristics of a Grayhorse seedling.

In 1957, Thundering Eagle had still not returned. It was time for Cheyenne to take that initial onward and upward step in her life. The emptiness created in her heart by her brother had not gone away. Thundering Eagle had not written a letter or made a family contact with anyone in Quarry Town. Lena Hawkins, a Kentucky State University graduate, had joined the Dotson faculty. She was impressed with Cheyenne's talent, especially her musical skills. Lena talked to Myrtle about Cheyenne continuing her education at Kentucky State University in Frankfort, Kentucky. Lena was able to put Cheyenne in contact with the proper people at the university and it was through Lena's endeavors and recommendation that Cheyenne received a scholarship to attend the school. She also was assigned a work study position at the university infirmary that helped her to meet some of her financial obligations. Cheyenne maintained an honors average and remained on the Dean's academic honor roll. After the first semester, Cheyenne received an additional scholarship from the state (Assistance for Minority Students), that paid the balance of her tuition, including her books. She had to maintain a 3.0 average to keep this aid, but Cheyenne worked hard and had no difficulty meeting the requirements. She completed her studies for a B.S. degree in May, 1961 in the dual disciplines of Music Education and English. She completed her teacher training in the public schools of Louisville, Kentucky. But even before that, the university had recommended her for her first job in the Hopkinsville Independent School System, Attucks High School, in Hopkinsville, Kentucky.

Cheyenne's Wedding

Cheyenne announced to the people of Quarry Town about her teaching assignment in Hopkinsville and that she would not be living in Quarry Town. She also announced that she would be getting married in August to a college sweetheart, James Sebree, who was also from Hopkinsville. The wedding was set for August 6, 1961, before the school year began. The wedding was held at Shepherd Street Baptist Church in Quarry Town. It was the first church wedding for that congregation and the ceremony was conducted by Rev. Thomas Lander. It was a very dignified ceremony for the Gray and Hollowell families. The wedding attendees were mostly members of the Gray and Hollowell families; Fred Otha and his daughters, Little John as ring bearer, Ralph Hollowell, Cheyenne's brother Robert Lee, and his wife, Catherine, Patricia Lander and Cheyenne's college roommates, Doreen and Mary Lee. James brother, Owen was the best man. Little John was then five years old, and was dressed in a white satin short-legged suit that was perfect for the occasion. It was Cheyenne's special day but the effect that Little John left on the occasion left a lasting impression for new beginnings.

Rev. Lander and his wife Evelyn kept the bride at their home, checking and double checking to ensure that all things were in order. It was Rev. Lander's first church wedding and it was his brotherly friend's daughter, so everything had to be perfect. Cheyenne hoped and prayed that her father and Thundering Eagle would come; but neither one showed up; nor did Broken Arrow.

Passing the Jewels

Before the ceremony, Aunt Helen called Cheyenne aside along with her mother, Myrtle, to discuss the jewels and the family legacy. They gathered at Myrtle's kitchen table. Cheyenne knew when she noticed the deerskin pouch that this would be about the jewels. Helen went over the legacy with Cheyenne and explained every detail that Rising Sun had set in place for Cheyenne and Thundering Eagle to follow. Cheyenne thought that she understood her role to perpetuate the legacy. She was excited and happy to receive the pouch with the jewels. She understood the seedling symbolism and realized that it was Little John who represented the first seedling. The role of the silver seedlings were not clear to her. Helen could not clarify the role of the third nugget because Rising Sun had never discussed the second son with her. Helen directed Cheyenne to wait for the Spirit of Grayhorse to send her a revelation to clarify the role assignment. Helen told her that the revelation could occur in a vision or a dream and that she must be prepared to discern its meaning. Helen made it absolutely clear that it was Thundering Eagle's responsibility to sow the seedlings.

Even though Helen was definite about the assignment, Cheyenne left with a misinterpretation in her mind. She felt because she was female and because Thundering Eagle was no longer around that it was now her responsibility to see that every part of the legacy was fulfilled, including sowing seeds. Cheyenne was so certain about the role that she began to covet the position. She completely ignored the part of the legacy that stated that the legacy was anchored in the male gender and the fourth son. Cheyenne canceled out this portion of the legacy because there was no fourth son and she was the fourth child. This was an interpretation that had not been approved by the Spirit of Grayhorse. Helen shook her head in disbelief knowing that Cheyenne had planted all of these misconceptions in her mind and was determined to do it her own way. Cheyenne left rejoicing now that she thought that the assignment was all hers.

Rising Sun Returns to Cheyenne

While teaching in Hopkinsville, Cheyenne enrolled at Austin Peay University in Clarksville, Tennessee and later at Fisk University for post graduate work towards a masters degree. During the second year of her teaching career, 1962, Rising Sun decided to search for Cheyenne. Cheyenne's best friend and neighbor was Lula Quisenberry, Rev. Lander's sister. Cheyenne received a telephone call from Aunt Lula, informing her that her father, Rising Sun was at her house and was on his way to visit her. It had been nineteen years since Cheyenne had seen her father. She was overjoyed that he had returned; maybe this visit would help her to get rid of some of the hurt that she was carrying because he did not attend her wedding. He was a year late but to Cheyenne, it was better to be late than never.

Cheyenne quickly made things ready to receive him. Her husband, James, was also excited. He was finally going to meet his father-in-law. When the doorbell rang, Cheyenne opened the door. A spirit of evil arose in her countenance and in her heart. Cheyenne was filled with anger as he stood outside the door smiling at her. He was perfectly dressed in a royal blue suit; his hair had straightened out and lost its curl, but he was more handsome than Cheyenne had remembered. Cheyenne could only think of how she had missed him. She thought of how she had waited for him on the front steps that day and he never returned. She remembered how he had carried coins in his pockets for her. He had promised to come back for her and it had been a long, lonesome nineteen years of struggle for Cheyenne and Thundering Eagle. Cheyenne had grown up without him, finished high school, college, married, and started her career, all without his support. How could he possibly come to her now? She loved her daddy and had wanted him in her life. Now, what did he expect from her?

He spoke remorsefully to Cheyenne and asked for her forgiveness. He told her how sorry he was. Cheyenne wept bitterly but the pain did not go away. They had supper together and when he got up to leave, Cheyenne asked him not to return into her life. She opened the door for him to leave without saying goodbye. He stepped out the front door, remorsefully, looked back at her, and left. Was his heart broken, as hers was? Cheyenne never saw her father again.

In the late 1960s, a call came to Cheyenne that her father had died of a heart attack in Detroit, Michigan. His body was carried back to Quarry Town for the funeral and interment which were taken care of by Cardelia and Broken Arrow. He was buried with the Grays and Hollowells in Tinsley cemetery. No mention was made to Cheyenne concerning Thundering Eagle. Because of her adversarial relationship with Cardelia, Cheyenne declined to attend.

For the rest of these years, Cheyenne has maintained an unforgiving spirit for Cardelia. Through the release valve that came with writing this saga, Cheyenne has released much hurt and remorsefulness over the relationship with her father. She regrets that she was not able to accept her father's plea for forgiveness and rejected his love and his reaching out to her. She carries constantly a sharp pain in her heart and wishes that some day soon it will be removed from her before she takes her spirit journey and is placed in her tomb.

Just a few days ago, Cheyenne planted in her memory rose garden, a beautiful white rose for her father, giving him a rightful place in her memory along with her other loved ones who have passed on. If only she could have been strong enough to receive him maybe the hurt would not have been so deep. Maybe the tears would have flowed more gently and dried up sooner. Tears that she now sheds are no longer for his rejection of her but for her rejection of him. The bitterness for her father has now been erased but the emptiness remains and can never be filled. She missed the opportunity to tell him for the final time how much she loved him. It is a daily prayer of Cheyenne that maybe one day their spirits will meet and her contrite spirit of unforgiveness will be changed and erased by the God of Mother Ellen.

Unfortunately, Cheyenne's bitterness for Cardelia continues to linger. When Cardelia passed on a few years ago, Cheyenne felt no sorrow. When Cheyenne was told of her death, Cheyenne's response was, "She was never a stepmother to me. I had no relationship with her. I carry no regrets that she has passed on."

Family disconnections have been forceful in Cheyenne's life. She had no idea where her brother Thundering Eagle had drifted to. Rising Sun had taken his spirit journey as had her younger sister, Roseline, and her baby brother, Douglas. The wind had not blown gently in her direction. The relationship with Broken Arrow continued to depend on the currents of the North Wind. Aunt Helen had planted in her heart the idea that the Spirit of Grayhorse would not be at peace as long as there was brokenness in the family. Cheyenne had to turn her back to the North Wind and face a more peaceful wind current from the South. This shifting was the only option left to alter her life cycle. She had to focus her direction toward peace, forgiveness, and healing. Cheyenne was left with no other option. She had to take some course that would lead her to heal the brokenness. First, she had to make a connection with the Spirit of Grayhorse and seek wisdom and direction. Only the God of Mother Ellen could lead her to the right path.

19

Turquoise Gems Nestled in Aqua Stream

The Prayer of Cheyenne

Cheyenne had wrestled long enough with threatening clouds hovering over her. She understood that she needed to follow the instruction of her ancestors and rely on the God of Mother Ellen. Unlike her father, Cheyenne had never been on a vision trip before. She had no idea how these visits and visions with her father and grandfather's totem spirits could ever occur in her life, but she did believe and understand that true wisdom must be harvested. She knew the source from which it came: only from God through the teachings of her elders and the lessons of little children.

Cheyenne thought through the procedures that her ancestors had used for four generations when they sought direction for their lives and when they needed to communicate with the Great Spirit and the Spirit of Grayhorse. This very concept always startled Cheyenne. It created fear within her, a fear of the unknown. If the totem spirit of Grayhorse, the Spirit of the White Buffalo; or of Stonewall and Rising Sun, White Bear, should appear to her, how would she react? Would the totem appear in a vision or a dream? Would she be awake or asleep? Would it take place at her home or would she have to leave? Would her family understand or would they question the validity of the experience that was taking place in her life? Would the North Wind interfere? Cheyenne believed and trusted in the God of Mother Ellen and that is where she had to begin. She had to begin with a willingness and a mind to adhere to the directions coming from the voice of wisdom.

It was a clear day and Cheyenne had anchored her mind and her determination. Today was the day for her to take on the legacy responsibilities that her father and Thundering Eagle had left behind. She began her adventure with a vision journey that led her to a quiet favorite place—Maui, Hawaii, it was a place that she had visited many times before during her frequent escapades to the Hawaiian Islands, a continuous adventure that began in the mid 1960s. It was a beautiful and mystic spot at Haleakala Crate, an enormous dormant volcano, 10,000 feet high that has been inactive since 1790. Even though it is considered to be dormant, it is still expected to become active again at any time. The crater is one of the largest on earth, seven-and-one-half miles long, two-and-one-half-miles wide, and approximately 3,000 feet deep. Streams have eroded deep valleys into its flanks due to inactivity.

Each time that Cheyenne had stood on its rim, she was in awe. She would become mystified in the clouds that would reach down from the heavens and encircle her. There are cinder cones that were at least 700 feet high that reached through the clouds, forming musical pipes in a spectacular photographic work of artistry. Cheyenne made her way along the trail that led to Leleiwi Overlook where she hoped to see "The Specter of the Brocken," a phenomenon where a person's shadow can be projected onto the heavy cloud layers in the crater. Hawaii is known for its frequent spectacular rainbows and at Haleakala Crater they encircle the images in the clouds. The occurrence usually happens when the sun shines opposite the heavy clouds and mist at early evening, dawn, and midday.

To reach the spot, one has to travel by foot, bicycle, or horseback along the "Ohe'o" area beside the rain forest. There is a flowing stream that breaks away into 24 pools, of which 7 are identified as the sacred pools. These pools are a familiar tourist sight that breaks away into the beautiful aqua Pacific ocean. Quiet streams wind their way along the path and empty into Waimoku Falls. Cheyenne remembered from the wisdom of Grayhorse that these totem communications usually take place near water, since water is a good conductor of sound. She thought that if the Spirit of Grayhorse wished to communicate with her, then this would be the place. It was not Quarry Town, but it was like a second home to her and these special moments might lead her back to Quarry Town—this time with a vision that came from the God of Mother Ellen and the Spirit of Grayhorse.

When Cheyenne reached her place about half way up the summit she stood in silence to meditate in her usual way. She released her thoughts to free her mind, her spirit, her whole being and became one with the swelling forces of nature. She could feel the compelling strength of the mystic winds making way into her spirit, causing her to feel clean and serene. Cheyenne yielded every moment. She faced the East, opened her eyes, and lifted her voice in a solemn prayer to the God of Mother Ellen. As she prayed, the spirit continued to engulf her, while her shoulders felt damp and wet from the mist dropping from the encircling clouds.

"The Prayer of Cheyenne"

Oh God of Ellen, I beseech you to come into my spirit.
Bless me and release my life cycle from the North Wind.
To you, Oh God, the overseer of everything that is good;
The maker and keeper of the Universe;
The creator of the beautiful artistry of nature;
The conductor and director of the mighty Four Winds;
Come into my life and direct my path.

Ordain and prepare me for the journey that I must take.
Enlarge my spirit for the load that I am to carry.
Anchor me into your will and mold me into your way.
Enlighten my mind to understand the message that I am to deliver.
Cleanse me for the victories that I am to receive; and
Hasten me on to victory.

Protect the turquoise seedlings that are now placed in my care.
Ordain their spirits and the direction of their being.
Remove them from the forces of evil and temptations
that will easily beset them.
Direct the compass wheel of my life cycle;
and propel me into the chambers of
Peace, Forgiveness, and Goodwill.
In the name of the God of Ellen;
These petitions are lifted upward.
Amen!

—(The Voice of Cheyenne)

When Cheyenne finished her prayer, she walked closer to the rim of the summit and surveyed the vastness of the valley resting below on the crater floor. The heavy clouds continued to cover her like a dense fog. She slipped her arms into the sweater that she had remembered to bring along to ward off the chill. As she turned to walk away, her body was pushed and almost lifted by the powerful force of the brisk wind. When she reached the bottom, she looked back up at the summit. Appearing against the mystic clouds was an image of what appeared to be White Bear. It was embedded into the clouds and following their every move. Close behind was a profile of Grayhorse. These images startled Cheyenne. The wind then formed a spiraling dark cloud from the North that stopped directly in front of her. A rainbow appeared and encircled the protruding cinder cones that were extended beyond the clouds. Soon the wind cloud seemed to find its place on the summit, reaching down from point to point. Cheyenne loved rainbows, but this one was different. This time she knew that this special rainbow marked a sign of approval from the Spirit of Grayhorse and that even though she was female, now she could move forward with the legacy.

The journey downhill seemed longer and moving against the wind demanded more energy and strength than the upward climb. Cheyenne was no longer afraid. She had found her place and now she was ready to begin her journey. The forceful wind accompanying her was actually the appearance of Whispering Wind, the seedling messenger of Broken Arrow. Broken Arrow was keeping his commitment to the legacy. He was looking out for Cheyenne and Whispering Wind was his only source to stay in touch at such a distance from Quarry Town.

Cheyenne left knowing that she had to return to this place. As she walked along the path beside the rain forest, Whispering Wind stayed close to her. When they reached the waterfall, Whispering Wind dissipated. The sun was searching for its rightful place and burst through the clouds. A mongoose scurried across the path into a bed of lava rock, finding its way back to a familiar place of abode. Cheyenne looked up at Haleakala's overpowering and stately statue, thinking that it was all created by the God of Mother Ellen; and that she was nothing more than a tiny speck in the midst of this beautiful vast artistic creation.

Vision of White Bear

Cheyenne often thought about her experience on the summit. The slopes of Haleakala rested just outside of Cheyenne's bedroom window. Cheyenne could watch the slopes, search for a sunrise, rainbow, images in the clouds, or the mystic Whispering Wind; maybe even an image of the totem White Bear. The crater was quiet and there was no movement. Cheyenne would be leaving in a few days and she had to return to the summit. She did not want to leave that place without a visit from the Spirit of Grayhorse. This time, Cheyenne left early to reach the summit before sunrise. The temperature from the ocean floor to the apex had been known to drop as much as 30 degrees. She carried along a blanket wrapped around her shoulders for the cold. The arrival of the sun was especially meaningful. The Hawaiians believe that the sun has strong spiritual powers. A chanter is always there early to offer a chant to the sun (Hawaiian prayer / song of praise) before sunrise. The power from the sun is believed to help one get through the day. The wind was restless and more powerful than it was on the first trip. It communicated as if it was angry. The cold had already set in from overnight. It was almost uncomfortable.

As the sky turned orange and the sun began to rise above the ocean to find its rightful place, morning awoke to the brilliant glow, announcing a new day. The restless sound of Whispering Wind appeared, blowing against the stately cinder cones. The clouds were always present and this time they seemed to hang lower than before. Cheyenne was tired from the steep climb and sat on the ground facing the East. Accompanying the sound of Whispering Wind was her grandfather Stonewall's totem, White Bear. The clouds seemed to stand still and the images were suspended in front of Cheyenne. In the voice of Grayhorse, Cheyenne heard her name called out from the clouds. "Cheyenne!"

"Cheyenne, where are the precious jewels you are in charge of?"

"I left them in Quarry Town," Cheyenne responded. "They were passed to me by Aunt Helen and I left them protected with my belongings."

"You are not ever to part with them, Cheyenne! You are here and they are there. They have been left vulnerable and unprotected. They have been left open to evil forces. When you return to Quarry Town, you are to retrieve them immediately and always keep them close to you. Keep them close to your heart and never part from them. This is the same that you must do for the future seedlings. When space is allowed to exist between you and the jewels or your future seedlings, evil forces from the North Wind can blow in outside forces and foreign spirits that invade the space and create disconnections and brokenness between you. If that should happen to the jewels again, this time they will never ever be retrieved. If the future seedlings become influenced by false loves or unknown forces of evil, they may never be found.

"You are blessed, Cheyenne, this time the jewels are under the watchful eye of the Spirit of Grayhorse; but you have to retrieve them right away."

"How long am I to keep them?" asked Cheyenne.

"Until the births of the future seedlings are all fulfilled and they have gained enough strength to stand against the forces of the Four Winds; then

233

they are to be passed to the fourth son of Thundering Eagle. The fourth son will have been anointed at birth to receive the birthright of the legacy. He will grow up a different child and will seek a path that was paved by his ancestors and the God of Ellen. It is through this son that the legacy can be fulfilled."

"What about the spirit characters of the legacy?" asked Cheyenne.

"These spirit characters must continue to be nurtured and practiced, then pass them on to your offspring," the voice continued.

1. Carry the things that you love with you as you travel through life.
2. Chart pathways for lasting relationships with those whom you love.
3. Nurture and seek out those seedlings that are waiting in the corners of your life cycle.
4. Build connecting points for people and things that are broken in the lives of those that you love.
5. Seek to preserve the blood line of the Gray lineage.
6. Protect the jewels and cover them with your passion.
7. Seek wisdom from the Great Spirit and from the God of Ellen and pass it on to the next generation.

He then punctuated the message by saying to Cheyenne, "Be vigilant, Cheyenne, be patient, diligent, prudent, and peaceful. Follow the path of your forefathers and trust only those who are following in the same path. Do not trust or follow those who are charting their own pathways. Be certain that the path you follow has been charted by the higher one."

Immediately, the clouds lifted, the sky cleared, and the area brightened. The message was clear and the tone of the totem's voice was demanding. It was the voice of Grayhorse. A profile of Grayhorse's image directed Cheyenne along the downward path. She followed quickly, trying to step perfectly in the invisible footsteps that he was charting for her and that only she could see. She gave a sigh of relief and stopped near the waterfall to catch her breath. It was a beautiful portrait of natural beauty that only the Creator could get credit for. A burden lifted from Cheyenne's shoulders and she began to feel a new sense of freedom. No longer was she confused about the directions that she was to follow. It was her call and she was ready to take on the task. But Cheyenne needed one additional moment to release the tension inside of her.

She called out with in a strong voice, "Rising Sun, can you hear me?

Listen to me, Rising Sun! You should have taken me on a vision trip to show me the way. Why didn't you trust me? Didn't you know that I would try my hardest? I loved you, Rising Sun, and I am making a new commitment to you. I will carry this weight of the legacy entrustment and I will carry it well! And to you, Thundering Eagle, wherever you are . . . What in the name of goodness are you trying to do to me? Return, Thundering Eagle, you must return! Return to the sense of your duty! Return to the legacy! Return to carry your share of the weight. You too have a mission to fulfill for the legacy."

"I LOVE YOU THUNDERING EAGLE!"

Sowing Seedlings

Cheyenne returned to Quarry Town and waited for Thundering Eagle to answer her call; a time that did not come. The saga reveals that Thundering Eagle was sowing seedlings to fulfill his commitment to the legacy and was having much fun doing so. He was busy at his self-assigned enterprises and he had been busy since 1958. According to the saga, Thundering Eagle had found his Uncle Clyde and his Aunt Clara and was living with them in Toledo, Ohio. Aunt Clara Mae revealed that Thundering Eagle was ill when he came to live with them. No one knows what had caused his illness. Uncle Clyde took him into his home, carried him to a medical doctor for treatment, and nursed him back to health. When he regained his strength, he wandered away from them. It was later learned that he had bonded with a lady named Maggie and entered into a commitment with her. She and Thundering Eagle birthed eleven children together. For more than a decade, Thundering Eagle sowed seedlings. Little John and these eleven seedlings met the legacy fulfillment symbolized by the twelve pieces of turquoise that had been passionately nurtured for four generations. The children were born into the cycle of the four dimensions created by the Four Winds.

Cycle I— 1955 East Wind	Cycle II— 1958–1962 West Wind	Cycle III— 1965–1975 North Wind	Cycle IV— 1974 South Wind
John Elliott Gray (1st Son)	Robin Gray (1st Daughter)	Caroline Gray Linda Gray (4th Daughter)	Tycie Gray
	Manny Gray Ulysses Gray Anthony Gray (4th Son) Tammy Gray	Andre Gray Robert Gray Marquette Gray	

Now each seedling had to find its rightful place within the Gray lineage, after they were informed of the effects of the ancestral Cherokee heritage on their life cycle. They also had to be orientated about the strong currents of the Four Winds and how their lives would be affected, as the forceful currents and turbulent winds would dictate the direction of their life cycle. Thundering Eagle needed to do more than just spread seedlings. He also needed to nurture the seedlings in how to master and pass the tests of life and how to move against the powerful winds. The saga reveals that he followed the path of his father, Rising Sun, and wandered away from his family, leaving his seedlings with their mother when they were small children. He headed North, not to seek his fortune but to seek his father, Rising Sun.

Cheyenne moved to Toledo, Ohio in 1961 to work as a teacher in the Toledo Public Schools and earned three post graduate degrees. She worked for the school system for thirty years and then retired. She and her husband, James, taught over 3,000 children during their educational careers. These precious seedlings attended the Toledo Public Schools, some lived almost in Cheyenne's backyard, but not once did their paths ever cross nor did they ever meet or come to know each other. The saga kept its secret and they all grew up not knowing their Aunt Cheyenne. How could this be? Was this not a repeat of Rising Sun and the saga with Broken Arrow?

Thundering Eagle had fulfilled his mission and moved on. The seedlings had grown up virtually under the chin and elbow of their Aunt Cheyenne and yet she had missed all of their childhood years and opportunities to bring them into the Gray lineage and pass on to them the history of who they really are. It was a bitter hurt to taste to realize that she never knew that the seedlings existed. It was their Gray blood remained unidentified and unbonded to the Gray lineage.

These seedlings were the lost jewels of Grayhorse. They had began to create a legacy of their own. They were a lost legacy, and silently waiting to be found. Would the saga reveal its secret? How long before the truth could be told? Would Thundering Eagle return to Cheyenne and identify his seedlings?

Cheyenne continued to hold on to the symbolic seedlings represented by the precious jewels in the deerskin pouch; but who was holding on to the real seedlings? Cheyenne was afraid to let go and not follow through with her commitment. These seedlings were the blood of Grayhorse, Stonewall, Rising Sun, Thundering Eagle, and Cheyenne. They were being protected by the watchful Spirit of Grayhorse and the God of Mother Ellen. They were the lost jewels of the legacy but they were never lost from the Spirit of Grayhorse. It was time for a new carving on the petroglyph tree at the Gray farm.

To fulfill the legacy, the saga reveals that each seedling was assigned a Native American name to establish an identity with the ancestral Cherokee culture. The Cherokee concepts had already been factored into their life cycle; the concept of four, the Four winds, the fourth son relationship, Totem spirits, and ritual and ceremonial practices. Their Native American names were assigned as follows:

Cycle	Given Name	Native American Name
I	John Elliott Gray (1st Son)	Leaping Deer
II	Robin Gray (1st Daughter)	Moon Rae
	Manny Gray	Rising Star
	Ulysses Gray	Painted Pony
	Anthony Gray (4th Son)	Rising Eagle
	Tammy Gray	Echo Calls
III	Caroline Gray	Cherokee
	Linda Gray (4th Daughter)	Silver Cloud
	Andre Gray	Clear Water
	Robert Gray	Running Bear
	Marquette Gray	Prancing Bull
IV	Tycie Gray	Bright Shadow

The saga is clear that Thundering Eagle sowed seedlings and moved on. But how could he even dream of sowing and not nurturing? The Grays left a strong legacy for nurturing. If Cheyenne could have only reached him during those years, maybe things would have been different. Most certainly so for the seedlings. It was more than a fun adventure, it was a mission of life that carried a tremendous impact and left an enormous imprint

237

on the precious seedlings. It was really not about Thundering Eagle any-more, it was all about the seedlings.

Cheyenne Misread the Legacy

The message that Cheyenne received in her vision made no reference for her to sow seedlings. In her mind, she concluded that since Thundering Eagle had left that he had also reneged on his commitment and that she was the one to fulfill his assignment. Second, she had heard nothing from Thundering Eagle and she had yet to establish a strong relationship with Broken Arrow. Yet, she sensed that Broken Arrow was keeping his com-mitment to watch over her. She could feel this commitment through the growing relationship with the seedling messenger, Whispering Wind. Third, even though the role had never been bestowed to anyone of the fe-male gender, Cheyenne concluded that since she was the only female in Rising Sun's lineage, she was therefore the only link to fulfill the call for the seedlings to be reproduced through the loins of Rising Sun. She even attempted to rationalize how and why the seedlings should rightfully pass through her loins.

Cheyenne failed to recognize that decisions or changes in the proce-dure were not hers to make. The process had been firmly anchored for the legacy for four generations; the procedure was clear and the preceding heirs had followed it faithfully. The fulfillment to pass the legacy was a vertical process. It began with Grayhorse and was passed to his son, not his sibling. Then it passed to Stonewall and on to Sully or (Rising Sun); then to Robert Lewis or Thundering Eagle, and the next passing had to be to the fourth son of Thundering Eagle. The process of passing had to be carefully monitored as it was through the previous generations. But, being comfort-able with the conclusions that she had made, Cheyenne moved on with her life with no further concern that this blessing might not eventually fall on her.

Lost Seedling

In the autumn of 1964, Cheyenne was carrying her first child. The blessing that she had prayed and waited for had been answered. Her seed-ling role for the legacy could now be fulfilled. It was a difficult pregnancy for Cheyenne. She was constantly ill and suffered much pain and discomfort. Dr. Connors, the Hopkinsville physician, diagnosed that her complications were not due to pregnancy but to fibroid tumors. After several tests it was discovered that clusters of fibroid tumors were growing in Cheyenne's stomach and they were threatening the life of the unborn child. The doctors agreed to try to let her carry the child to full term and then remove the tumors. But as the fetus developed, the illness became more and more intense and the pregnancy more complicated.

A few days before time for the delivery, Cheyenne became very ill and was ordered to bed to try to save the child. The pregnancy reached full term but there was very little movement of the child and very weak vital signs. Cheyenne was rushed to the hospital for a spontaneous birth. The child infant girl was born with clusters of tumors wrapped around its neck from the fibroids which had choked the child to death. The birth was recorded and the child was given the name of Aprile Myrtell, after Cheyenne's mother Myrtle.

Cheyenne and James's marriage was only four years old when they lost their seedling. It created a period of testing for both Cheyenne and James. The North Wind would not allow them to rest from the emotional hurt. Cheyenne wept bitterly and constantly over the loss of her child. A stream of tears flowed inside of her for many days. She avoided being around women who were pregnant or who wanted to talk about their pregnancy and childbirth. Cheyenne could always deflect these discussions and conversations. Somehow she knew that she needed to seek healing for this bitterness. Although she thought of seeking counseling, she refused to discuss her problems with anyone except her sister-in-law, Catherine, and even that period of confidences lasted only a short period of time. The hurt was not only about her lost opportunity to fulfill the legacy but all about the lost of her seedling child. A fulfillment that was never meant to be.

In addition to the hurt, Cheyenne was still ill and was still in great pain from the tumors. Two months following the loss of the child, Cheyenne went to the hospital to have surgery to remove the tumors. The doctors counted a total of 40 tumors in the various clusters that ranged from the size of a nickel to a medium-sized grapefruit, all attached to a fibroid vine. Cheyenne had lost weight and was less than 100 pounds. Her physical recovery progressed perfectly but the emotional pain over the loss of her child continued to deepen.

239

The Hurt Returns

Cheyenne had began to wonder if she would be able to continue to pursue her role for the legacy. Of course, the responsibility was not totally hers to begin with. Rising Sun had assigned a shared responsibility for his children. Neither Cheyenne nor Thundering Eagle knew the challenging role for Broken Arrow, who was so secretive with Cheyenne and shared nothing about himself, his wife, or his children. Cheyenne felt a weight returning to her shoulders as she harbored these unhealthy feelings about her child and the broken bonds between the Rising Sun siblings. Her heart was wet with tears and her cheeks paved with paths of grief that would not cease. For over thirty-five years, her life has been symbolized as a part of her that was taken away and died, creating an emotional abyss that has never been filled. When the hurt becomes too piercing, Cheyenne will then create space and leave the conversation.

Cheyenne knew that she was not going to remain in Quarry Town or even close by in Hopkinsville. In 1965, she and her husband, moved to Toledo, Ohio. They had three other job offers but being near Uncle Clyde was a connector to the Gray family. She had no knowledge that Thundering Eagle was also in the area and the saga reveals that it was during these years that he was deeply involved in the third cycle of sowing his seedlings.

Cheyenne gave up on her commitment to the legacy and moved on with her life; but she continued to hold on to the precious jewels. She did not want an omen to befall either her or anyone in the family, for not keeping her oath. Many days she remembered that the Spirit of Grayhorse was not at peace because of the distance between herself and her siblings and the legacy fulfillment for these three silver nuggets.

Cheyenne knew that someday, somehow, and some way these jewels had to be passed to Thundering Eagle's fourth son. Was there a fourth son? What if Thundering Eagle sowed only females? Where was he, anyway? What if he had already experienced a vision?

Cheyenne began to feel from her inner spirit that somehow both brothers were watching her and actually knew more about her life than she realized. If not, then certainly the Spirit of Mother Ellen or Mamaw Gray was watching over her. The wind was shifting and she could feel it carrying a blessing from the God of Mother Ellen. Hopefully it would shift from the North to the East or the South for better times. According to her ancestors, when the current of the Four Winds shifted, the forces of control for Cheyenne's life cycle would also shift in the direction of the currents from the compass wheel. But for now, better times ahead were surfacing on the horizon. Cheyenne needed to wait for the wind and then refocus her directions in search of better times.

20

Bonding

For at least two decades, Cheyenne spent much time in the Hawaiian Islands and cleared her mind of any obsession with the legacy. In 1991, following her retirement, she began a new adventure as an author and wrote a book, *Pele's Tears,* on Hawaiian music and the life and culture of the Hawaiians, for which she researched the contributions of the Hawaiians to western music styles. The book was published in 1994. Cheyenne contacted Patricia Lander and together they planned a book signing for the Grays and Hollowells in Quarry Town.

First to arrive at the presentation were Broken Arrow who had returned from the quarry and moved his family to Quarry Town; and Fred Otha. Broken Arrow listened intently as Cheyenne spoke, and this event triggered a new relationship for Cheyenne and Broken Arrow. Cheyenne signed his book with a special message that included her address and telephone number. She asked him to contact her soon. Throughout the reception, he stood next to Cheyenne with a watchful eye, introducing her as his sister to those who did not know. After the event, Broken Arrow left with Fred Otha with his copy of *Pele's Tears* nestled tightly in his hand. This time he looked back at Cheyenne with a smile of approval.

When Cheyenne returned home, she received a telephone call from Broken Arrow, which was a sealer for a strong relationship and new beginnings. After that first call, he called Cheyenne once a week and she called him back. It was through these conversations that Cheyenne learned that Broken Arrow was not well. He was ill with diabetes and had been on dialysis for ten years. He had lost a leg to that illness. Cheyenne always remembered Broken Arrow; she wrote to him and stayed in contact. Broken Arrow spoke to her often about Thundering Eagle; but not once did he mention that he had helped Thundering Eagle in hard times, or that Thundering Eagle had brought his family to visit him. Broken Arrow was holding true to his commitment to the legacy. He was checking on both Cheyenne and Thundering Eagle. He was holding both of them in his heart.

The saga reveals that following the death of Rising Sun, Thundering Eagle continued to live in Michigan with Cardelia. Finally both moved back to the area of Quarry Town to live on a farm inherited from Cardelia's father. Cardelia misused her relationship with Thundering Eagle and began to treat him as a companion rather than a stepson. This arrangement grew into a mutual relationship and the people and voices of Quarry Town deemed it to be so. The rumor reached the Gray family and Cardelia carried the weight of blame for abusing the relationship with her stepson. There was much chatter and much rumor around Quarry Town concerning the matter.

One day, Broken Arrow called Cheyenne. He wanted to talk to her about this unusual relationship between Thundering Eagle and Cardelia. Not long after that, Broken Arrow's wife, Clara, called to tell Cheyenne that Broken Arrow had been diagnosed with cancer in three areas of his body and that he was very ill. This was followed by a call from Broken Arrow just to talk to Cheyenne. He had never asked Cheyenne for any favors; but this time he shared his yearning for a good fresh fish dinner. Cheyenne went that very day and sent him money to purchase enough fish not only for his dinner but also for his freezer. When he went for his next cancer treatment, Cheyenne asked Clara to stop at the fish house to purchase him some fish. Broken Arrow could not hold his peace. He rejoiced over the fresh fish dinner and expressed how happy he was to receive it especially since it came from Cheyenne. The final call came from Clara and Whispering Wind that he was refusing to eat, that the fish dinner had been his final full meal, and that the death process had set in and he had started his spirit journey. He lived only a few days more and died in the hospital in Paducah, fifty miles from Quarry Town.

Cheyenne packed her belongings and journeyed back to Quarry Town for Broken Arrow's funeral. The current members of the family were mostly strangers to Cheyenne, consisting mostly of his maternal relatives. Cheyenne was the only Gray represented at the funeral. Since they did not know Cheyenne, there was very little conversation exchanged. But the people of Quarry Town remembered Cheyenne and greeted her and welcomed her home. The next morning broke with a violent thunderstorm. Storm clouds and tornado warnings were all around. When the funeral ended fifteen miles had to be traveled for the interment. He was carried to a small unattended cemetery in Ceruleum, located in a desolate lonely church yard. The church was closed and no longer in use. The rain was blinding. Along the way, ponds had left their banks and spilled over on the roadway. Heavy thunder and threatening lightning took command overhead. The walk to the grave site was a rather short distance along a muddy path with ankle deep water from the rain. The family was seated outside under a tin roof shelter that amplified the sound of the rain.

When the minister finished his remarks, Cheyenne could only sit in sadness as she thought of another parting from her brother. The bonding between them had strengthened but now was rebroken Once again she was disconnected from both he and Thundering Eagle. Cheyenne was the last to leave the gravesite. Broken Arrow had been left sitting there forsaken in the pounding rain in a wet, desolate graveyard. It was a scene that continues to plague Cheyenne's memory whenever she thinks of her final days with Broken Arrow. But one pleasant memory remains; Broken Arrow loved Cheyenne and she loved him. Whenever they visited each other, or they talked by telephone, he never failed to tell Cheyenne how much he loved her and they never parted without Cheyenne sharing the same feelings with him. He would always begin their conversation by saying, "How are you doing, girl?" But his parting words were always; "I love you, girl, and there ain't gonna be no parting between me and you."

Cheyenne cherishes these words from Broken Arrow and in her heart, she carries a message for him. . . . "There ain't gonna be no parting for me and you."

Voice of Cheyenne

I am just a withered rose that grew between the rocks;
    Pressed down by the wind and the sun and
        Trampled by the wind.

I was caressed by the moonlight, and
    Watered by the morning dew.

I blossomed well at midday; while
        Struggling to survive.
    But Now I Am Free!

And only the God of Mother Ellen
    Could love a rose like me.

—(Cheyenne)

PART IV

South Wind

The Spirit of Grayhorse
Cheyenne Winds—Legacy Found

"Dream Builders"
Gift of Cheyenne

Follow your dreams to the rainbow's end;
There is a pot of gold where your dreams begin.
Plant them in your memory and watch them grow.
Sprinkle them with joy, compassion, and love;
Hold them fast and never let them go.

Gather them as seedlings and plant them in your mind.
Nurture them with knowledge, books, and wisdom;
Then carry them with you on your journeys far and wide.
Awaken them at the sunrise of each new beginning.
But hold them fast and never let them go.

Plant them in your memories, goals and ambitions;
Move them forward as you turn the corners of your life.
Bring them into reality while you are asleep.
Let them lead you to victory and winnings to keep.
Watch them soar and then lift you higher;
Shift forward in your thinking, your desires, and your vision.
So hold them fast, you can never let them go.

Celebrate now, as you conquer the task;
Carefully building them so that they will last.
Continue to build and mold new beginnings;
Fail not to create, study, and labor;
Be joyful and treasure clean laughter untold.
Take pride in your learning and never let go.

Hold on to your dreams with each fleeting moment;
Look up and follow, they dwell with the stars.
Lift up your head, focus your eyes, elevate your morals and enrich your
mind.
Choose things that are worthy, moral, spiritual, and wise.
Now your spirit will lead you to your new rainbow's end;
It's at the end of the rainbow where your new dreams begin.

SO

NEVER! EVER! NEVER, LET GO OF YOUR DREAMS!
—(Wisdom of Grayhorse)

21

The Mission of Whispering Wind (The Gathering)

Cheyenne arose early. Fresh peaches had fallen from the peach tree onto the ground and she was determined to beat the squirrels to them this year. It was a crisp September morning and Cheyenne wanted to bake peach cobblers and put the rest of the peaches in the freezer for winter. Last year, she lost at least half of her peaches because she waited too late to pick them. Just as Cheyenne started to pull the bruised fruit from the basket a brisk wind blew a dark spiraling cloud across the kitchen window before her very eyes and the telephone rang. Cheyenne hesitated to pick up the receiver, as she thought that it might be a talkative friend, and she did not have much time to spend on the telephone. But what about the sudden rush of wind and the mysterious cloud that had just moved across her window?

When Cheyenne picked up the telephone, a quiet, soft voice began to speak from the other end. "Well, hello Aunt Cheyenne, why haven't we heard from you? This is Juanita, Broken Arrow's daughter."

It was the familiar voice of Whispering Wind that Cheyenne had wanted to hear from, the totem spirit messenger for Cheyenne.

For three generations, the totem spirit of Whispering Wind had made vision appearances to the ancestors, especially to Cheyenne's father, Rising Sun, And now to Cheyenne. Cheyenne paused to remember when Whispering Wind had visited her on the summit in Maui at Haleakala Crater. The spirit had delivered her message to Cheyenne and then followed her down the hill to the waterfall. Each time that she had appeared, she had delivered a message to Cheyenne from the ancestors. Cheyenne no longer doubted the reality of Whispering Wind and was now certain that Whispering Wind was her totem spirit and that this time; she was bringing a message from the Spirit of Grayhorse and Cheyenne's brother, Broken Arrow.

The female voice said that her father's spirit had visited her and that she was on a mission for Broken Arrow. The message that she was to deliver would help to mend the brokenness and disconnection in the family and to reclaim the family legacy.

"But what about Thundering Eagle?" asked Cheyenne. "Thundering Eagle is in charge of the seedlings. And I hold responsibility for the spirit characters," pleaded Cheyenne.

Cheyenne did not wish to face the North Wind again by taking over Thundering Eagle's responsibility.

Whispering Wind reassured her that the message was sent by the Spirit of Grayhorse—and as unusual as it might seem to be, Cheyenne being female—this time the message was for her. The legacy was now being placed in her care.

"I am coming very soon for a visit," continued Whispering Wind. "I will follow the wind currents from the southeast. Look for my shadow against the clouds in the north in the early evening. I will appear following the next sunset in the dusk of early evening. I have contacted the first female seedling of Thundering Eagle. Her name is Moon Rae. I will spend time with you and with her."

"Wait! Stop!" ordered Cheyenne. "Who is Moon Rae? Thundering Eagle has only one seedling that I am aware of, his first and only son, Leaping Deer, who lives far from us. I know that he lives in the southwest, in Texas; but I do not know how to contact him."

"Thundering Eagle has been planting seeds," answered Whispering Wind. "He now has eleven other seedlings. He has fathered a total of twelve seedlings, including the first son. I have contact connection for each of them including the one in the southwest."

Cheyenne trusted the message that Whispering Wind brought. "Come, and come soon," she urged. "Stay as long as you wish and I will be watching and waiting for you."

When Cheyenne hung up the telephone, a heavy thunder roared and the dark spiraling cloud of Whispering Wind had vanished into the open sky. Cheyenne's heart began to beat rapidly and her knees and legs became very weak. She stopped to sit down at the kitchen table to catch her breath, thinking over the unusual morning.

Thundering Eagle had fathered twelve seedlings? How can this be? Where is he? Where has he been? These seedlings were born and reared in the same city where Cheyenne lived; but why didn't she know?

Where is Thundering Eagle? When was he here? When was he so near me? When and with whom did he sow so many seedlings?

His seedling mate had to be someone that Cheyenne had never met who had never attended a family gathering.

Cheyenne worked for the Toledo Public Schools for thirty years. All of these seedlings came through the Toledo Public School system. Neither she nor her husband had ever run into any students whose parental last name was Gray. Why hadn't their paths crossed during all of those precious years? Why was there so much secrecy? Why didn't the Gray family know about this missing link in the family lineage?

Here was a frightening thought. *What else was missing? What else was there for Cheyenne to know?*

How does one begin a family relationship with so many new seedlings who have reached adulthood without knowing anything about the love that has been lost for so many years?

Cheyenne continued to query herself. What are the first words to be said? What are the first feelings to be shared? Will there be a mutual acceptance between Cheyenne and the seedlings? Would they want to bond with her, or would they turn to rejection? Would they accept her as a part of their bloodline?

What about John, the first seedling? How much did he know about the other seedlings?

Cheyenne thought of John's awesome role in the new family structure and knew that he needed his Aunt Cheyenne to be near him especially during the trauma of this adjustment period.

"How would he handle the bonding with so many seedlings after forty years of believing that he was the only one? What would the other seedlings think about him and how would they handle the new bonding?

Cheyenne could only think of the struggle that had prevailed; and the wide gulf that had to be crossed between she and her brother, Broken Arrow, when they were forced to bond so late in their adult years. One thing was clear to Cheyenne: they each would have their own personal beginnings, moving within their own space at their own time. Some would have feelings that were warm, passionate, joyous, and loving while others would have feelings of anger, jealousy, fear, and bitterness. Each seedling had to answer to their own emotional call and discernment.

Cheyenne then thought of the fulfillment of the family legacy. Twelve seedlings equaled twelve turquoise jewels. This marked a second fulfillment for the symbolic jewels, while Cheyenne, Thundering Eagle, and Broken Arrow represented the fulfillment for the three pieces of silver. This now completed the fulfillment for the jewels. Meanwhile, Cheyenne

251

made things ready to receive her special and unusual guest and her new family. She was not certain how many seedlings she would meet, or even how many continued to live near by. Whispering Wind had given Moon Rae's married name to Cheyenne since she no longer answered to the name "Gray."

Cheyenne looked up Moon Rae's number in the telephone directory and decided to call her before Whispering Wind arrived. Cheyenne introduced herself as Aunt Cheyenne. Like Cheyenne, there was an air of apprehension and caution in Moon Rae's response. Cheyenne asked if Moon Rae had heard that she, Cheyenne, was her aunt. Moon Rae said she knew of her aunt and continued that she had seen Cheyenne singing with a local community choir.

Cheyenne could sense that Moon Rae's tone was becoming more apprehensive as the conversation progressed, and that they both were likely struggling with the same emotions. After some further discussion regarding the details of Whispering Wind's visit, they each hung up the telephone in silence, waiting for the moment and for the saga to unfold.

Whispering Wind made a second appearance to Cheyenne to finalize her mission and her stay. Unlike the first appearance, she appeared at early evening just after sunset while Cheyenne was outside her house gathering more fruit from the peach tree. Whispering Wind informed Cheyenne that she had indeed met all of the seedlings and in fact, knew them by name, as Thundering Eagle had brought them to Quarry Town and to Ceruleum during their childhood years, when Thundering Eagle and Moon Rae's father, Broken Arrow had exchanged family visits, so their offspring knew each other.

Moon Rae reported that Thundering Eagle was no longer a wandering son. He had returned to Kentucky with Cardelia. Following Cardelia's illness, he had rebounded with a schoolmate, Charlotte Parker, the female bully of Quarry Town. All three had ended up in a nursing home just outside Quarry Town. The seedlings had heard about Thundering Eagle's illness and confinement. They had pooled their resources for a visit to Quarry Town to see about him. The seedlings located the nursing home where their father was a resident, obtained legal permission to place him in their care, and brought him back to Ohio with them. Cheyenne then learned that Thundering Eagle had been stricken with Alzheimer's disease and probably would not know her or even be able to communicate with her if they met again.

This message brought much pain to Cheyenne. She sat on the ground and thought of their childhood years together. Thundering Eagle was returning to her once again; but how much of those experiences remained in his memory? Physically, he was returning but what about his spirit, his feelings, his emotions? Now he was a resident in a local nursing facility located—ironically—only a short distance from Cheyenne.

Thundering Eagle had left Cheyenne three times previously. First, when he went to serve his years in the military and Cheyenne left for college; second, when he left Quarry Town to sow more seedlings, and then when he went to live with their father. Now came the fourth parting and he was journeying through the stages and experiences of Alzheimers. In each instance, the Four Winds had dominated his life.

Cheyenne had just returned from burying her brother, Broken Arrow, less than six months before. Her maternal brother, Robert Lee, was ill with cancer and renal disease and was in her care. Now, she was also faced with the challenge of Thundering Eagle's illness, as well.

The North Wind had blown cold and bitter in her direction.

This one precept stayed with Cheyenne from the wisdom of her Aunt Helen. "The Four Winds always return and when they do, if the family is disconnected and not bonded, or not at peace, the wind currents always strengthen and blow stronger than before, leaving a mark never to be obliterated." A second taste of wisdom that she always reiterated to Cheyenne was that the Spirit of Grayhorse would not rest until the family is at peace. Each seedling has been born under the powerful force of one of the Four Winds. Cheyenne wondered if Thundering Eagle had alerted any of them to the effect that they held over their individual life cycles.

Cheyenne was curious to see which of the sons embodied the Spirit of Grayhorse, and which of the daughters captured the poise and dignity of Mother Ellen. She wanted to see which sons stood stately and tall like their grandfather and great-grandfathers, Grayhorse and Roaring Bull and their stately great uncles; which sons were shorter in stature and epitomized Rising Sun and the other Gray brothers; and which daughters mirrored the Gray women. Even more, she was anxious to see which seedling son would merit the honor of respect to receive the legacy entrustment for the family. There certainly was a first son; but to fulfill the legacy assignment, there must also be a fourth son with whom this weight of responsibility would be shared.

Was there also a fourth daughter? If so, did she carry the air of a matrix Aunt with a matrix spirit, such as Aunt Minnie, Aunt Helen, and Cheyenne herself? Now that Thundering Eagle was no longer able to make decisions for the legacy; and Broken Arrow was deceased, it was up to Cheyenne to assign the entrustment and make the anointment. Cheyenne had to be certain that the assignment was properly done and precisely followed as laid out four generations before by the Spirit of Grayhorse. If not, the fierce Four Winds would surely return. The seedlings would only be able to survive the force of the Four Winds if the birth lineage entrustment was properly assigned and followed. Family disconnections must be rejoined, dissensions must be healed. Peace must prevail. The cycle was evolving as the saga revealed and the fulfillment had begun.

Just as she had promised, Whispering Wind arrived at early evening. Spending her first night with Moon Rae, who had waited for her under a canopy of stars, watching the sky and waiting for her arrival. Whispering Wind had promised to appear in the northern sky following the wind currents of a southeast wind, and suddenly with a sudden burst of wind, Whispering Wind appeared. She followed Moon Rae across the sky heading north until they reached Moon Rae's front porch, then she dissipated into the clouds. When Moor Rae went inside the house, Juanita was waiting for her in the kitchen.

Early the next morning, Moon Rae went to her Aunt Cheyenne's house. Whispering Wind followed along above the trees as if she knew the way. When Moon Rae drove into Cheyenne's driveway, Cheyenne came out to greet her and asked about Whispering Wind. Moon Rae simply pointed overhead and said, "Up there."

Cheyenne smiled and they both went inside to find Juanita seated at the kitchen table. When they entered the room, Juanita spoke. "Aunt Cheyenne, this is Moon Rae."

"Yes, I know," answered Cheyenne. "And how are the both of you? Let me get you some fresh coffee."

Moon Rae and Juanita then shared with Cheyenne about the other seedlings, about whom Juanita did most of the talking.

Living in the city were five female seedlings. Living nearby in Michigan were two male seedlings, and living in Indiana were four male seedlings. The first seedling son was residing in Texas.

Juanita reached into a pocket and took out a piece of yellow paper on which was written addresses for each of the seedlings, including Leaping Deer. Cheyenne extended an invitation to take them out to lunch along with any of the other seedlings that wanted to go along. Juanita rode along in the car with Cheyenne and Moon Rae,. Silver Cloud joined the group later, but Bright Shadow was unable to come.

Cheyenne noticed that Juanita went through the motions but she really did not touch much of her food. Each seedling shared much about their family experiences and one thing that caught the passion of Cheyenne was that Silver Cloud was filled with hurt and emotional pain, tearfully speaking of her childhood years that she spent with her father, and the hurtful experiences that she then endured. Cheyenne knew that this was a very tender and fragile situation that needed to be handled with tact, care, and love. She needed to assure Silver Cloud that her Aunt Cheyenne could be trusted to give emotional support. Cheyenne did not wish to inflict any more pain or break the new relationship for any of the seedlings; she only wanted to portray a force of security and strength as she reached out to them.

From that day forward, Silver Cloud claimed a rightful and heartfelt place in Cheyenne's heart. As they grew closer, Cheyenne saw that Silver Cloud mirrored much of her own character and personality. Her physical appearance mirrored the Gray women. She nurtured a Gray tonality in her speech and vocal tone, while her temperament reflected Cheyenne. Immediately, Cheyenne knew that Silver Cloud could be the daughter she had never had. Cheyenne was elated to learn that both Bright Shadow and Silver Cloud lived only a few blocks from her front door.

When they were ready to leave, without warning, Juanita walked out the door ahead of the group. When they looked around for her, she was not to be found. Moon Rae pointed overhead and there she was as Whispering Wind, leading the way again, shrouded in her familiar swirling cloud.

Moon Rae spoke aloud, "I wish that she would stop doing that! It makes me nervous when she transforms herself into a cloud."

Just then, a voice spoke into the car and startled each of them. A gentle wind blew across the dashboard.

"Cheyenne, I am your totem spirit. I cannot harm you. I love you, Aunt Cheyenne, I am your spirit messenger from your brother, Broken Arrow. I am Juanita. Surely, you trust me. I am your totem spirit."

"Totem spirit?" Asked Silver Cloud. "Did she say spirit, Aunt Cheyenne? I don't want nothing to do with spirits. She frightens me. I don't want her to come again as a spirit."

"Tell us, Aunt Cheyenne, just what is a totem spirit? Where did all of this come from and who is Grayhorse?" asked Moon Rae.

Cheyenne then began to explain to them about Grayhorse and the Spirit of Grayhorse. Cheyenne also explained to them what a totem is in this new culture and what it meant for them. It was all so new to them to learn about the Cherokee culture. While Cheyenne had the opportunity, she began to talk to them about the forces of the Four Winds.

Whispering Wind made her way to Cheyenne's house and was waiting for them in the yard. Moon Rae and Silver Cloud got out of the car and walked cautiously close to their Aunt Cheyenne; but not very close to Juanita. As time passed, Moon Rae and Cheyenne made a concerted effort to grow close to each other. Moon Rae contacted Bright Shadow and Rising Eagle to meet at Cheyenne's for a warm and cordial Sunday dinner the following weekend. Both the seedlings and Cheyenne were anxious to bond with each other. They each found their own personal space in the bonding fellowship, while Whispering Wind stayed above the trees and watched from afar.

Following dinner, the new family made a trip to the nursing home to visit Thundering Eagle. Moon Rae and her spouse; Rising Eagle and his wife; Bright Shadow, Silver Cloud, Cheyenne and her husband James went along. Whispering Wind led the group from overhead, turning every corner perfectly to point the way. When they entered Thundering Eagle's room, Juanita was already there.

It had been fifty years since Cheyenne had seen her brother. Before they left the house, Cheyenne had slipped away privately to shed a few tears of joy. She was going to be reunited with her last living brother. She was so nervous and so afraid that Thundering Eagle would not recognize her after so many years and because of the illness that he was carrying. Cheyenne's heart beat rapidly; her knees were weak, and she experienced a shortness of breath as she entered the room. When Cheyenne walked into the room, she went over to her brother's chair, held his hands, and hugged him close. His eyes met hers in awe and Cheyenne wanted to believe and felt in her heart that he recognized her. He continued to watch Cheyenne although he never called her by name or referred to her as "Baby Sis", "Shirley", or "Cheyenne" as he had always done in the past. Cheyenne felt grieved and remorseful that she had not been around to assist Thundering Eagle when he went through all of these debilitating changes and really needed her in his life. In her heart, she could hear him calling out to her.

The seedlings were much more comfortable around their father than was Cheyenne. They showed him much love and affection. It was here that Cheyenne learned that Rising Eagle and Moon Rae had driven him home and that all of the other seedlings had also gone to Quarry Town to assist with the process. Thundering Eagle had stayed in Moon Rae's home when he first returned, and the seedlings' mother had been a "caretaker" for him while Moon Rae worked. His left leg had been amputated due to circulation problems. He was also suffering from heart and renal illness.

Thundering Eagle smiled a lot that day. Everyone stayed with him, taking pictures, until he began to show fatigue. Juanita was the first to leave. Cheyenne noticed that everyone left the room except Rising Eagle, who stayed behind for a private moment with his father and an offering of prayer. The Four Winds continued to blow and as the saga continues to unfold Cheyenne knows that Thundering Eagle recognizes her most of the time whenever she visits him. Cheyenne has accepted one true metaphor concerning his illness. It was passed on to her by his daughter, Bright Shadow; "His memory is like a light switch with a shortage in it. Sometimes the light comes right on when you pull the chain. At other times, you may have to jiggle the chain a little to get the light to come on. At yet other times, it may not come on at all. Sometimes when the light is on, it will blink on and off again. Such is Dad's memory and his visits in and out of reality."

One positive thing that Thundering Eagle and Cheyenne can share is that when he is nervous or afraid he loves to hum or sing, to calm himself inside. Being a music teacher, Cheyenne can usually pick up the tune in her ear and sing or hum along with him. He loves for her to do this and he laughs out loud when she reminds him that together they sang a wrong note. The tunes are familiar to Cheyenne because they are usually something that they learned in their youth that remains in their memory. Cheyenne has noticed that Thundering Eagle doesn't sing as much as he did when he first arrived at the nursing home. Seemingly, he would do this to calm himself inside. He has become more adjusted to the environment now and is more content.

A petroglyph moment that Cheyenne has treasured from the family gatherings with the seedlings is the passion and magnetic attraction that Rising Eagle, the fourth son, shared with Cheyenne. Cheyenne looked into his eyes a lot that day. She measured the depths and temperament of the beautiful clean smile that he displayed, symbolic of a special feeling that he was carrying in his heart for her. Instantly, Cheyenne read into his persona and personality that there was something different, spiritual, and special about this seedling son. As the female seedlings settled in the living room or made their way to assist with the meal, Rising Eagle remained in the kitchen, close to his Aunt Cheyenne. He shared with her that he was the seedling son who had always followed his father to church when Thundering Eagle would preach his sermons and follow along with the scripture

257

readings in his Bible. He also shared how hurt he was when his father left the family. He was a teenager, only fifteen years old. His father told him about his Aunt Cheyenne but he had no idea where she was or how to even begin to search for her.

Now that Cheyenne and Rising Eagle had found each other, they bonded immediately. It was apparent to the other seedlings that something real flowed from Cheyenne's heart to reach out to her nephew. From the very beginning Cheyenne realized that the bonding between them was real and different, and she understood that the spirit within this seedling had been touched by the ancestors, the Spirit of Grayhorse. Rising Eagle and Cheyenne pledged to each other to never let go of the bonding between them. They each made a concerted effort to nurture, strengthen, and seal that bonding.

At the close of the Christmas celebration, Rising Eagle went out to his car and returned with a gift for Cheyenne. Graciously, he placed it under the Christmas tree without saying a word. He then slowly turned to the family and announced, "I have something that I want to say."

With wonder and surprise, the family turned its attention to listen to what he had to say. As with teary eyes, he began to speak.

"I watched my father from the time when I was young, I followed him in my childhood and listened to him preach. I cannot run away from the Spirit any longer. This Spirit has been chasing me for many days. It has been within me for a long time and I have turned aside and failed to answer its call. I have discussed this with my wife and with my pastor. I am ready now to answer the call from the Spirit and go into the ministry to preach. I have been carrying this heavy weight and I know now that I want to preach. I am answering the call."

Cheyenne went to him and began to query him regarding his convictions about his calling.

"Did this calling come to you in a vision, a dream, the reading of the Word, your meditation, or a strange happening?" she asked.

"Some of all of these; it kept appearing to me at different times," he answered. "I have wrestled with this for a long time," he said.

Cheyenne then gave him words of encouragement and words of warning. She pledged to support him and walk with him as he embarked upon this new beginning. It was his first calling from the Spirit to redirect his life for this new adventure. There were hugs and tears of joy from the family.

This seedling had been imprinted and chosen from early childhood. The teasing and jolting that he had received from his siblings about being "different" were misinterpreted notions concerning his calling. He had been chosen and imprinted by his ancestors even before his birth and even as he grew up and did not understand what was taking place in his life. His childhood struggles and seasons of testing in his life cycle were preparing him with testimonies and experiences to bear the weight of his calling. Just as Aunt Minnie had been there for his grandfather and father, so would his Aunt Cheyenne be there for him. He had just made a personal commitment to the God of Mother Ellen and he was ready now to begin his adventurous journey.

Rising Eagle's field of ministry was to begin at God's Word Baptist Church in Detroit, Michigan, under the tutelage and monitoring of Pastor Miller. During the wait time, Rising Eagle studied hard and meditated consistently. Not long hence, he preached his trial sermon in February, 2003. He then enrolled in a school of theology in Detroit. To begin his studies in that field. It was another fulfillment for the legacy. The Spirit of Grayhorse was with the family and leading the way for Rising Eagle.

On Christmas morning when Cheyenne opened her gifts, she saved the one from Rising Eagle until last. When she opened the package, Cheyenne was overwhelmed because of the emotional weight that she was carrying in her heart for him. It was a lovely, soft, baby blue silk robe that had been chosen just for her. It gladdened Cheyenne's heart; her eyes filled with tears of joy. Cheyenne thanked Rising Eagle and his family for such a wonderful and meaningful gift. She said to his wife, "Thank you so much for the lovely gift! I am very grateful for your outpouring of love and kindness."

Rising Eagle's wife simply smiled at Cheyenne and responded, "No, Aunt Cheyenne, This gift was his choice. On the first day after Thanksgiving, he went shopping in all of the crowds and all of the hustle and bustle, the pushing and shoving for early Christmas shopping. He walked until he found the perfect gift that he was searching for just for you." Cheyenne's heart was glad, just thinking of the strong outpour of love that he had already showered on her. It was a season of joy for Cheyenne and it marked a new beginning in her life, which had become enriched and was changing now that she had found these precious seedlings. It was a mark for another petroglyph moment.

Rising Eagle was the fourth son and already he was proving that he was worthy to carry the weight of the entrustment. *Finally,* thought Cheyenne, *the precious jewels are going to fall into the hands of the proper son, an act that had been misassigned for three generations.*

Rising Eagle has remained close to his Aunt Cheyenne since that beginning. In spite of teasing and jolting from those near him, he has remained close and committed to his Aunt Cheyenne. He has kept the integrity of his word and his promise; a quality trait that measures the temperament of one's character. He stays close to Cheyenne and continues to check on her and his Uncle James. He shares consistent unconditional love with them, a birth son could not love them more. He has been accepted into their hearts and their home as a son.

Rising Eagle and Leaping Deer have now joined the lineage as the sons that their Aunt Cheyenne and Uncle James never had. These two seedlings have filled the hole in Cheyenne's heart that longed for blood relationships. It was created by the death of her parents and her maternal siblings, and her brother, Broken Arrow. The God of Mother Ellen never alerted Cheyenne as to just how He would heal the hole in her heart. Cheyenne had prayed so hard to Him to remove the emptiness from her life! It has now been filled with the endearment that these seedlings have planted in her heart.

Whispering Wind was last seen traveling across the rainbow sky at early evening. She was making her way back to Quarry Town. Her mission was now complete and she felt good about the mission that she had accomplished; not just for Cheyenne but for all of the other seedlings as well. Whispering Wind had intended to say goodbye to Cheyenne before she left but Cheyenne was preoccupied and Whispering Wind needed to catch the drift of the East Wind as it was passing by. Cheyenne waved at her and watched her showmanship. Whispering Wind flipped her cloud tail and quickly dissipated behind the clouds. Cheyenne chuckled underneath her breath and responded, "What a drama queen you are, Whispering Wind! Thanks for the performance."

Not many days following that gathering, a call came to Cheyenne from the second female seedling, Echo Calls, who did not attend the first gathering but wanted to meet Cheyenne. She spoiled Cheyenne by making frequent calls just to check to see how Cheyenne was getting along and to say hello. She always began by saying "I'm just doing what I do."

Cheyenne has nurtured a special bonding with Echo Calls because she works hard, seeks to be alone, and even on days she does not feel well, she has a genuine passion in her heart, and she loves her Aunt Cheyenne. Her quiet demeanor and love passion always seems to surface. Cheyenne feels that beyond Echo Calls calm, there is a free spirit and a depth of emotional pain that needs to be emptied. Echo Calls has shared some surface confidences with Cheyenne. In her own way, she supports her Aunt Cheyenne with kindness and respect. She has also allowed Cheyenne to reach back with tender love strokes for her. Not long after their first meeting, Echo Calls had to go into the hospital for surgery, and Cheyenne had an opportunity to be with her at that time. Cheyenne felt special and accepted by Echo Calls when she allowed her to be there at a needed time. She is soft spoken and candid in her speech while at the same time her love for Cheyenne is real and genuine.

It was a quiet, slow paced winter day and Cheyenne was excited about the family gathering. The new family had agreed to seal the bonding by worshipping together each fifth Sunday and then gathering at the home of one of them for a potluck dinner. It was Cheyenne's turn to host the gathering, and she shared with the seedlings what their lives would have been like thirty years earlier if they had known each other. The seedlings reflected back to their childhood years during the thirty-year period when they were aged 3–14: They sat close to Cheyenne and listened intently as she told them Christmas stories and sang Christmas songs. They hung Christmas ornaments on the tree, each ornament representing the seedling's personal connection to the Gray lineage. Cheyenne then gave them identical ornaments to hang on their tree when they returned home. A special ornament was hung on the tree to mark the return of Thundering Eagle and one for the rebonding of the Gray family. Cheyenne pledged to them that those precious ornaments would be hung on her Christmas tree each Christmas for as long as she lived. It was a Christmas prelude marking a new beginning and a petroglyph moment to be remembered.

At springtime, Cheyenne gave each seedling a rose bush to plant in his or her yard as a family connector. Some of the bushes lived and some died as determined by the nurturing that they received and in some instances, if they were even planted. Cheyenne had pondered over whether it was a sign from the Spirit of Grayhorse that the rose bushes that survived were planted by the hands of the fourth daughter and the fourth son, Silver Cloud and Rising Eagle. Cheyenne's connecting rose is a beautiful, American Beauty which has bloomed copiously and is currently in its fourth cycle. The opening of each bloom depicts a meaningful petroglyph moment. The fourth cycle had twelve blossoms, one for each of the precious seedlings. Its gift of beauty has been an episode for the saga that is worthy to be carved on the trunk of the old historic petrotglyph tree. That old stately tree on the Gray farm that harbors the history of the Gray family just outside the city limits of Quarry Town.

Meanwhile, two of the younger male seedlings from Indiana have nursed a longing to be a part of the new beginning. They were each born under the North Wind in the third cycle. The telephone rang at late evening. The voice on the other end sounded familiar. It was certainly a Gray. It was like the voice of Thundering Eagle. The voice introduced himself as an old friend. "Hello, Aunt Cheyenne," he said. "This is Prancing Bull, the youngest male seedling. I have been thinking about you and I wanted to meet you. I called to see how you are doing; and just to talk. We have a lot of things to talk about."

Cheyenne responded that she had heard about him through his sister, Silver Cloud. Cheyenne felt as if they had already bonded. Cheyenne assured him that she was saving a place in her heart just for him and that he was as precious to her as were all of the other seedlings. When the long conversation ended, Cheyenne felt close to Prancing Bull. In a few days, he sent her pictures of his family. She waited for his return to Ohio so that she could welcome him properly into her home, her arms, and her heart, just as she had done for each of the other seedlings.

Soon summer came and the family gathering was held in the neighborhood park nearby. Another male seedling from the third cycle appeared at the picnic with his family. He mirrored the physical features of Thundering Eagle, and he carried the tonality of his grandfather, Roaring Bull. His birth name was the namesake of his father, Robert. His Cherokee name was Running Bear. It was a clear sunny day in late June and the family engaged in outdoor competitions and culinary delights. Like Prancing Bull, he was anxious to meet his Aunt Cheyenne. Before he returned to Indiana, he came to visit Cheyenne and promised to nurture the bonding of their new beginning.

As in most families, there is usually one seedling who takes on the responsibility as keeper of the family history and maintains a scroll of contact for each family member. Without this gesture, Cheyenne knows her family would be lost. Cheyenne and Harvey, Jr., maintained the history and petroglyph records for their generation. It was now time to pass the torch to Bright Shadow. Even though she is the youngest seedling, she has already proven herself to be the most reliable family contact. She is diligent and can be trusted with this important phase of the saga, maintaining a catalog of family events, records of birth, marriage, death, victories, successes, failures, times of testing, and places of abode. She is already perceived by her elders and siblings as the proper person for contact in family matters. She has staked her place in the family lineage. Her contact with

262

her Aunt Cheyenne is genuine, respectful, and has remained constant. Since their initial bonding, Bright Shadow has never failed in her contact with Cheyenne.

Four seedlings have yet to find their place in bonding with the lineage and the extended Gray family. They remain bonded with their siblings but they each have yet to cross the emotional walls and barriers that mark their connection to the larger family. For reasons that are personal to them, the hurdles of family separation continues to foster this disconnection. Cheyenne has decided to allow them their own personal space, time, and opportunity for the moments of their choosing. From the voice of Cheyenne, it appears that her call to them has been one of open arms, heart, and home, just as it has been for all of the other seedlings. Cheyenne realizes often separations of this magnitude are fragile and can be easily broken even after they are bonded. Cheyenne is patiently waiting the return of the male seedlings from the West Wind, the second cycle, Painted Pony and Rising Star. She is also waiting for one female seedling, the third cycle, Cherokee and Clear Water. Cherokee has remained cordial in Cheyenne's presence. Meanwhile, eight seedlings have clearly connected with the Gray lineage and have genuinely accepted their Aunt Cheyenne and the rest of the Grays.

Reliving this saga has been an emotional time of testing for Cheyenne. It unfolded so suddenly without warning. There was so much truth and secrecy embedded into its content that it drained Cheyenne as she retold the story. With no apologies, and no warnings, Cheyenne's life, as well as the lives of the seedlings, has been completely changed. The emotional transitions that Cheyenne endured in the saga and its rebirth were unlike and unequal to any that had imprinted her life before. The mere size and number of people in the family was simply overwhelming. The love and passion showered upon Cheyenne by the seedlings has left her emotionally shattered. It was awesomely endearing and yet completely overpowering. In many instances, Cheyenne found herself lost in thought over whether or not all of this excitement and all of these changes were the result of a vision journey. Could she be dreaming, or was she really awake?

Cheyenne spent many hours meditating with the God of Mother Ellen. She searched many days for vision images from the Spirit of Grayhorse. Consistently, Cheyenne has been surrounded by the ancestral voices reminding her that "that which is real is also constant and will endure. That which is not real, but is only make believe, will fade away."

"Love is binding and is reciprocal when it comes from the heart.

When it does not come from the heart, it will break away and follow its own path. Unlike the boomerang, it will not return to its beginning, nor will it return its favors to those who released it and sent it forward."

Cheyenne maintains that love cannot be bought or hurried; neither can true relationships. For these reasons, Cheyenne does not wish to rush the bonding for those seedlings that are still searching to find their way back into the lineage. She is patiently watching those seedlings as they ponder and each of the other seedlings as they continue to grow into the relationship. Cheyenne is trying to make sure that each seedling settles into its rightful place in the family so that it can become productive and connected, and so that they can latch on to enough strength to hold on for a lifetime. She is careful not to forge unwanted love onto the seedlings, not even from her. It is an interesting and trying time of testing for Cheyenne.

Whichever of the Four Winds is dictating directions for the four pondering seedlings, Cheyenne has faith in her totem to initiate a perfect time for each of them to be connected. It has been willed by the totem Spirit of Grayhorse and it is by that Spirit that the saga evolves. Cheyenne understands that in due time, the Four Winds will blow full circle and every seedling will find its rightful place. It has happened for four generations and it is in the saga to happen again. If it is in the minds of some of the pondering seedlings that this delay evolves from a punishment from the Four Winds for the misjudgements or misdoings that have taken place with Rising Sun and Thundering Eagle, then the saga also confirms that that punishment has already been taken care of by the dictation of their life cycles that evolved from the Four Winds. Such punishment is not and can not ever be placed into the hands of sibling seedlings.

22

Symmetrical Winds: First and Fourth Cycle Seedlings

The birth of the first son, Leaping Deer and the youngest seedling, Bright Shadow, were almost symmetrical. The seedlings of Thundering Eagle were born in four cycles. These births equalized a complete cycle of the forceful Four Winds. Leaping Deer's birth took place in the first cycle, under the East Wind, during the midterm of the 1950s. The East Wind currents were gentle and warm. They culminated a successful and victorious life cycle. Two decades later, twenty two years in the midterm of the 1970s Bright Shadow was born. Her birth came under the cycle of the South Wind. The South Wind currents blew peace and good will into her life cycle. Asymmetrical factors also had an influence on their lives, such as age (a difference of twenty-two years), gender, demographics, social and economic changes, and far more, the fact that they were reared in different homes by different maternal parents. The siblings also practiced different morals and social values. In spite of these differences, the symmetrical factors in their lives produced a stronger influence on their life cycles.

Each of these seedlings was the only seedling in their birth cycle of the Four Winds. Leaping Deer was born in cycle one as the first born child, a son. Bright Shadow was the only seedling born in the fourth cycle and was the youngest seedling. A time lapse of more than two decades between their ages accounted for some of the differences in their responses and reactions to some of the common issues that confronted them. Both of them were just little babies when Thundering Eagle left them behind. Leaping Deer was two years old and Bright Shadow was barely three years old. Neither of them were exposed to the childhood experience of growing up with a father. Because they were single seedlings, the emotional pain that they bore seemed to have drawn them closer than that which they might have shared with the other seedlings. This essence of time and the demographics of their individual dwelling places may have flavored a difference in their reactions to the trauma. The depths of that burning desire to seek their blood lineage created another parallel that reached farther than just being symmetrical.

From early childhood years, neither of the seedlings knew their father or had any paternal-to-child connections except via the experiences of others. They each knew of Thundering Eagle only from a distance; but never close up. Bright Shadow learned of him by tapping into the experiences and conversations of the other siblings. Leaping Deer did not have this opportunity, so he modeled his mother's brother, John Elliot and other children in the home that Birdie and Granny Alva had also taken in to raise as their own children.

Both Bright Shadow and Leaping Deer were brought up with strong spiritual values. They each developed a strong functional relationship with Jehovah, the God of Mother Ellen. Leaping Deer's academic endeavors led him through Tennessee State University (Nashville, Tennessee), with a degree in Biology. He then progressed to master a high level of technical skills for computer technology through his occupational experiences with Hewlitt Packard (HP). Bright Shadow paralleled Leaping Deer with a strong yearning to master her academic endeavors in Criminal Justice. She has worked consistently and has also to complete her academic work in that field. She also has a mastery of computer skills. A point of asymmetrical parallels is Leaping Deer's pursuit of educational opportunities that were in place and waiting for him to take hold and soar. For Bright Shadow, these opportunities were not waiting in place for her. Instead, she has had to create makeshift opportunities in order to pursue her educational dreams. This she has done and has found to be rewarding in her field of endeavor. Soon she will be ready to soar as well. These periods of testing became symmetrical for each seedling as they sought their way through the maze of educational advancement.

More symmetrical was the path that each seedling had to follow in order to endure the pain of misjudgment and wrongdoing inflicted upon their lives by their father's absence from the home. Separated by the mighty force of time between their births, the fact that they never knew that each other existed was a hard pill to swallow. They never met each other face to face until 2004. The very fact of their existence, twenty-two years apart, reflects the truth of the saga. A living truth that confirms that time does repeat itself and that the cycle of the mighty Four Winds will always return.

Thundering Eagle left an imprint upon each of these seedlings, through age two, and then he departed from their lives. Leaping Deer's early childhood response must have been, "Why did he vanish from my life? Where did he go?" The reactions of Bright Shadow must have been, "Who is this person? I never knew this man! Will he ever return?" Each response was indicative of a broken and disconnected relationship. It signaled no connection with the paternal parent, one that they each wanted so badly and so much to share.

During most of their lives, they had given up believing their father would return. A meaningful symmetrical divergence did take place when Thundering Eagle did return on the currents of the North Wind. For Bright Shadow, it was as if she was rebonding with a stranger. She was trying so hard to recapture the feelings and emotions that reality never did exist. She was attempting to erase the loneliness that had festered and the grief of living without a father for over twenty five years. Now she had transferred all of this pain to the back of her mind with unrecycled memories.

For Leaping Deer, it was a time to rid himself of the bitterness that he had carried for his father's rejection. It was a feeling that had overshadowed the right for Thundering Eagle to even be referred to as "Father" or "Dad." Cheyenne was able to reach Leaping Deer. She asked him to make a step forward toward forgiveness and reconnection with his father before his father closed his eyes to take his spirit journey. Cheyenne never wanted Leaping Deer to experience the pain that she had endured when she rejected her father, Rising Sun. In the summer of 2004, Leaping Deer took that step; it was a giant leap forward. He drove across the country with his family from Houston, Texas to Ohio to visit Cheyenne, meet his siblings, and to reunite with his father.

The father and son reunion was filled with emotion. When Leaping Deer walked up to his father and said, "Hi, Dad," Thundering Eagle was filled with emotion and astonished that he was there. Their eyes met. Thundering Eagle's eyes filled with tears that flowed down his cheeks. His body shook nervously. He held on tight to Leaping Deer and did not want to let him go. Leaping Deer embraced his father tenderly and said to him, "I used to call you Robert, now I call you Dad." He told his father how much he loved him. Thundering Eagle could not speak back to him but he listened intently with his eyes. As Leaping Deer stood before his father his physical features mirrored Thundering Eagle's in a perfect image. Thundering Eagle rested his head gently into the bosom of his son and the room lit up with joy and was filled with emotion. The nursing staff put their work on hold and came down to the room door to witness the joyous reunion of father and son. It was a petroglyph moment that all of us were caught up in. Cheyenne was nervous and a bit afraid that Thundering Eagle would not recognize his son. Not so; instantly, he knew his first son. Both Cheyenne and Leaping Deer were convinced that he understood what took place—every moment, every emotion, and every detail. It was hard for Leaping Deer to take; but it happened and everyone was certain that the Spirit of Grayhorse was at rest. It was a rewarding day for Leaping Deer, Thundering Eagle, and Cheyenne.

Cheyenne had promised Leaping Deer that she would stay close to him and be right beside him as he released the pain and reconnected with his dad. Leaping Deer said to his Aunt Cheyenne, "Aunt Cheyenne, this is so hard, it is so hard."

Cheyenne embraced him and told him that the weight in his heart would be much lighter now that he had taken that step. Cheyenne left with Leaping Deer and his wife, Regina, assured that through the Spirit of Grayhorse, the bitterness had ended and that Leaping Deer and his father were now reconnected and free to love each other.

Two days later, Leaping Deer returned to the home with his family. He wanted his daughters to visit with their grandfather. Thundering Eagle was having a good day that day. He was happy that the children were there. They referred to him as "granddaddy." The older girls remembered him from a visit in Quarry Town. Thundering Eagle laughed and smiled a lot when the girls gave him hugs. Leaping Deer shared a photograph that was taken when he was eight years old. Thundering Eagle laughed and held on to it tightly. It was as if his mind reflected back to the past for a brief moment. We constantly referred to Leaping Deer as Little John, to keep Thundering Eagle remembering the past. Leaping Deer returned to Houston relieved that he had made the long journey but missing his new family. One thing was for certain, not one moment of this journey was spent in vain.

The symmetry was now evolving between Thundering Eagle and the two seedlings. Bright Shadow works with her father as a champion daughter. She checks on his condition, picks up his laundry, and tries to rebond with him on each visit. She has begun to bridge the gap from stranger to friend to father. When Thundering Eagle left home, Bright Shadow was so young that she only knew her five older sibling seedlings of the second cycle, the cycle of the West Wind. The younger sibling seedlings of the third cycle were living in Kentucky with their father. Bright Shadow was left at home with her mother and developed a sibling relationship with her two nephews, Jermaine and Jamel, rather than with her own brothers, Prancing Bull, Running Bear, and Clear Water.

Bright Shadow's early memories revert back to her childhood years that were spent in North Toledo. She reflects on domestic issues that took place in her home life and recalls that by the time she reached the sixth grade, the family had moved several times. In some instances transitions were made to accommodate the growing size of the family while at other times it was to lighten the demands of domestic concerns. By the time she reached her junior high school years, grade seven, Bright Shadow asked to live with her older maternal brother in the South area of the city so that she could attend a different school. Bright Shadow was allowed to leave home to live with this sibling.

Bright Shadow's maternal grandmother died when she was in the ninth grade. She recalls that at the funeral she was seated in the rear of the church with the other grandchildren. A stranger entered the church and seated himself next to her. During the ceremony, he placed his arm around her shoulder and began to speak into her ear words of comfort as she wept over the death of her grandmother.

In her words, "He continued to bug me. He continued to refer to me as his baby."

She asked her sisters, "Who is this man?"

They responded, "He is your father. This is our dad."

"What?" answered Bright Shadow in amazement. A strange feeling came over her. "I did not recall ever seeing him before," she continued; "but I was glad that he was there. During my senior year, my brother, Rising Star, drove him home. This time I knew him and I was glad to see him.

"At age twenty-five, I worked at an office in the downtown area. I tried to call my father almost every day. Most of the time, I could not reach him. Instead, I would reach the lady that he lived with, Charlotte Parker, Big Flo, a childhood heart throb. I always felt that Charlotte never passed my messages on to him. I even sent him pictures of my children, but I did not receive a response."

Bright Shadow was now feeling rejected all over again. At times, when she was able to reach her father, his response was always reversed, depending on whether or not Charlotte was near by listening to the conversation.

"I never failed to ask him when he would be coming home," Bright Shadow said. He would reply, "It won't be long now, soon, very soon. I love you." But if Charlotte was around, he would respond in a hostile tone,

"Why are you calling? I don't know when I will be back, I'm not coming back to that place."

Bright Shadow was torn apart by these reversed responses and transformed his words to mean that maybe her father really did not want to return home to be with them. Her feelings of rejection grew deeper. He always sounded as if he feared Charlotte and did not want her to know that he was communicating with his seedlings. Bright Shadow had no desire to see or visit Charlotte. At this stage of the saga, Thundering Eagle, Cardelia, and Charlotte were all residing together in Paducah, Kentucky.

Bright Shadow's feelings for her father had now turned from rejection to fear, anger, and stages of bitterness that were fostering disappointment and disconnections. As the saga evolved, Bright Shadow's feelings for her father became symmetrical to those that were harbored by Leaping Deer. Their seedling paths had paralleled once again as their life cycles were being directed by symmetrical winds from the East and the South. Somehow, it seemed that these wind currents had merged into one, a new Southeast Wind with warm moist currents that would eventually bring peace, unity, and reconnections to the family legacy.

Bright Shadow and Leaping Deer were now aware that each other existed. They had started to bond with each other by communicating on the telephone and longed to meet each other face to face. Bright Shadow wondered what her older brother was really like. Did they actually mirror each other's lives, as the saga said? In her heart, she thought of him often while he was becoming her personal hero. He had already paved pathways where she wanted to go. He had soared as an eagle in flight. Bright Shadow knew that once they met, she would glean strength from beneath his strong powerful wings.

When Leaping Deer made the journey to Ohio, it was truly a petroglyph moment to be remembered. He was able to meet his siblings face to face, including Bright Shadow. It was also a petroglyph moment when he stood face to face and shoulder to shoulder with his brother, Rising Eagle. They were able to embrace each other as brothers for the first time. They too had bonded by telephone but it was so much more important to be able to share these feelings face to face.

Cheyenne had already spoken with both seedlings about bonding together as true brothers. She wanted them to be concerned about each other and to love and look after each other from the birthing of each new day until the sundown of their life's end, even to the point of sharing each other's pain. Both seedlings promised Cheyenne a commitment to that end, and to nurture their mutual passion in that way. It warmed Cheyenne's heart to see them come together as the first and fourth sons. It was a fulfillment for the family legacy, ordained and anointed by the Spirit of Grayhorse.

Bright Shadow has spent much time in confidence with her brother, Rising Eagle. She has trusted and respected his integrity, identified his fraternal passion for her, and relied on his wisdom. For Bright Shadow, she has always felt the vibrating spirit that Rising Eagle carries. She also felt that these two seedling brothers were moving under the guidance of the Spirit of Grayhorse and the wisdom of the God of Mother Ellen. Bright Shadow has often wondered if these two brothers were really aware of just how much she admired, loved, and trusted them. Did they have any idea just how proud she was of both of them? Did they realize how happy she was to be their little sister? It was all another miracle for the Gray family; a miracle blessed by the Spirit of Grayhorse.

23

Shifting Chinook Winds: Second Cycle Seedlings

The second set of Thundering Eagle's seedlings were born on the shifting wind currents of the Chinook West Wind. These wind currents surfaced from the compass wheel of the Four Winds. As the western Chinook winds often blew a warm dry breeze down the eastern Rocky Mountain slopes, they also frequently shifted to warm moist winds along the Oregon and Washington State coastline, bringing an unexpected shift in the wind and weather patterns of the west. So it was with the life cycle changes of these seedlings who were born under the forces of the West Wind in the second cycle. Controlling forces in their lives spun off the powerful wind currents that frequently appeared under the disguise of peaceful winds. Emotional turbulence took hold in their lives during their peaceful mid-term years. By the time they had reached their latter teen years, strong and stormy turbulence from these winds had already thrust them into early adult life situations that they were not physically, emotionally, or mentally prepared to deal with at such a young age. These early maturational wind shifts created emotional pressures that, in some instances, led them to seek relief through feelings of fear, anger, bitterness, and loneliness and resulted in instances of withdrawal and rebellion.

The birth years of these seedlings took place three years after the birth of the first son, who was born under the East Wind. Two female and three male seedlings were born under this cycle. They were Moon Rae, Rising Star, Painted Pony, Rising Eagle, and Echo Calls. In addition to Rising Eagle being blessed with the lineage status of the fourth son, he was also the fourth child. Building on the concept of four in the Cherokee culture, this was a meaningful and blessed position to be in for the calling of the family legacy as dictated by the Spirit of Grayhorse. It was a position in the family lineage that had been ordered, protected, respected, and used as a passageway for the legacy entrustment for more than four generations.

This saga of family history acknowledges the pain and turmoil that domestic separations inflict upon a family; but it acknowledges more, the painful inflections that are imprinted into the emotional stability of the seedlings. These five older seedlings had each reached their teen years when their father left home. In addition to the changes brought about within the family, they were also forced to cope with the social and economic changes of the late 1970s. As young teens, each of them was forced to seek their own paths to adjust to a new way of life; the emotional pain of losing a parent. The pain for these seedlings had a more lasting affect on their emotional and social adjustments than it did for those seedlings who were born in the first and fourth cycles under the East and South Winds.

First these seedlings had shared childhood years with their father. Positive or not, the father had imprinted each of them. They had connected and bonded into a father/child relationship. For some of the seedlings, it was a bonding that could not be broken. For others, it was a bonding that was now broken and might never be reconnected. When Thundering Eagle turned and walked away, leaving these seedlings behind, it was as if half of themselves had been taken away; never to be mended, healed, replaced, or returned. Each of the seedlings has mirrored traits from their father. It is as if Thundering Eagle worked to mold and imprint them into his personal image. His speech patterns and vocal intonation, the rhythm in his step, his hair texture, his bright eyes, his body gestures, his temperament, his body responses and reactions (the way that they turn their head or bite their lips when they are reacting or responding to a call or a situation) to anger, fear, happiness, or a surprise were all mirrored and passed along to his seedlings.

Cheyenne's concern is that in light of all of these similarities, Thundering Eagle still did not do enough to pass along or expose these seedlings to the spirit characters that serve as the lineage connecting points for the Gray family. Hence, in most instances, they omitted and missed the ancestral bonding, family relationships, and inclusiveness within the Gray family. They were not exposed to the social morals and family values that had strengthened the Gray family. They were not acquainted with the Gray family relatives, missed the Gray family gatherings and celebrations, and did not glean wisdom from the Gray elders.

Because the patriarch Uncle, Clyde lived near these seedlings, and because Thundering Eagle was so close to Uncle Clyde, the seedlings did become acquainted with Uncle Clyde and his wife, Clara Mae. When they visited Kentucky, they visited Mamma Myrtle 'Myrt', their paternal grandmother (who had raised Thundering Eagle). Thundering Eagle was well aware of his commitment to the family oath and traditions; yet he removed himself from these fatherly responsibilities with the exception of just sowing seedlings. Thundering Eagle held a moral responsibility to introduce his seedlings to who they really were. He should have enlightened them about the accomplishments that had come through the Gray family. More importantly, he did not enlighten them about the moral and social values that were accepted as standards in the heritage and traditions of the Gray family. Instead, each seedling was left to chart its own path to be followed for a meaningful and successful life. Thundering Eagle gave them no knowledge of the course that their life cycles might be altered to follow because of the shifting and/or strong force of their birth winds. He was not just running away; he was also turning away from his own blood, his seedlings, and his responsibilities as a father. He gave up his commitment to the family legacy and the family expectations that he would stand up and be tall as a Gray man. As a results of these misdoings, his seedlings were then forced to alter their choices for successful life journeys and season them with a life style influenced by their maternal parent. In spite of these deplorable paternal influences ,most of these seedlings are able to proclaim a strong relationship with the God of Mother Ellen; strong spiritual values; respect for their elders, the zeal to toil and labor, strong work ethics, a desire to have intact families, and to never cease to dream and enjoy laughter.

Each of these seedlings has now struggled with periods of testing and has met with life situations that taught them how to grasp an opportunity in life and mold it to work to their advantage. This saga evolved in truth and it cannot unfold in peace without revealing the realities and the real truth of the saga. These seedlings are very tightly and securely bonded with each other. They live separate and independent life styles; but they will quickly rally together in support of each other when there is a family crisis or a need to do so. This has proven to be a very important, positive, and strong family trait. This kind of response is what has provided positive reinforcement and has sustained them during their life struggles. However, one trait that continues to surface strongly among them is the syndrome that frequently leads them to become dependent upon each other. Watchfully, Cheyenne is hoping that in each of their lives, each seedling will be prepared to stand alone, strong, and tall, to think independently, and move gracefully through their individual situations without depending on the approval or moral support of each other. Some of the seedlings are striving desperately to move forward to reach that end. Others sometimes appear to be comfortably nestled in that level of dependency.

Cheyenne seeks constantly to encourage them to never accede silently to the pressures of life, pressures which may be sometimes propelled from within the family. She enlightens the seedlings with these words . . . "Seek to maintain a peaceful relationship with the God of Mother Ellen. Cover these emotional pressures and stress with meditation and outward relief. It is during these times when you must draw upon the strengthening power source from your soul and the intellect of your mind. Seek consistently the wisdom of your elders. Never seek to deny your culture or your family history. It is the strength within that history that keeps you sane, refreshes and reiterates your heritage and traditions. It renews you with emotional and mental healing and projects you into new beginnings. It sends you searching for realistic pathways that you are to follow. It is that sphere within you that captures your dreams. Remember, a person who does not dream has no place that he can go, no path that he can follow. He loses his beginnings, he is lost on his present pathway and may never find his way. So never, ever, cease to dream!"

For Cheyenne, this has become a particular concern for the seedlings of the male gender. The ancestral culture that has molded the Gray culture is a dominating one for the male gender. It is a blended culture of Cherokee, African American, and Caucasian practices. In both the Cherokee and the African traditions, a strong concept of the family and its social practices are reserved for the male gender to take the lead as the dominant family influence. In both the Cherokee and the African cultures, when the paternal parent is absent, it is the brother of the mother, the strong uncle, who must take over the rearing of the children and control of the family. In the Cherokee culture, this is a particularly strong role for the fourth son. If the uncles are absent from the family blood line, the responsibility is then passed along to the matrix aunt, the fourth aunt. This is also the path that the Gray family has followed as handed down through the dominant role of the great, great, grandfather, Grayhorse, the prevailing procedure in the Gray family for more than four generations.

These seedlings of Thundering Eagle were not enlightened to the concept and importance of lineage nor the passing of the family legacy. Cheyenne can never cease to remember the agony that she went through when the legacy was misinterpreted in her favor. She moved forward with responsibilities for the legacy when it was not her gender assignment to do so. The North Wind blew long and hard into her life because of this mistake, this misinterpreted leadership role. Never again would Cheyenne want the force of these winds to return to the seedlings for such a selfish and mismindful act. For the seedlings, the dictates for the legacy and its procedures to be followed have been handed down by the Spirit of Grayhorse.

In words of the Gray elders, "a Gray man is a Gray man and he is to stand tall and move in front of his family." Not to do so was looked upon by the elders as a sign of weakness in manhood and in spirit, marking an act of neglect and responsibility. Fortunately, the fourth son is a member of this cycle of the West Wind. This virtue of dominance in independence is of particular concern to Cheyenne. The passing of the family legacy and the protection of the precious jewels has already been clearly defined and ordered by the Spirit of Grayhorse. It is to be passed to the male gender, the fourth son of Thundering Eagle through the loins of Rising Sun. Cheyenne is carefully supporting this seedling in preparation for the role as he seeks to move closer to grasping the process of stabilized decision making, and as he grows stronger in his spiritual relationships with his new ministry.

Echo Calls demonstrates the following of a different seedling, even though she was born under the same wind cycle. With her quiet demeanor, she seeks to follow her own calling. Kindled within her emotions is a burning fire spirit. She has structured a protective wall of silence and frequently does not share the intervals of internal stress, or physical ailments that she so often endures. Rarely, does she allow anyone to approach or break through that wall. Her personal social struggles have carried her through rivers of testing that have served to strengthen her determination to survive, become a productive person, and a good and caring provider and parent for her children. Her strong inner strength has conditioned her to become an independent thinker, a hard diligent worker, a proud caring parent, and a seedling that is well bonded and securely connected with her siblings. Echo Calls has demonstrated a reaching devotion to her Aunt Cheyenne and has expressed a close bonding to the second sibling son, Rising Star.

Even though Echo Calls sometimes cloisters herself behind that protective wall, she continues to allow her Aunt Cheyenne to reach beyond that wall to touch the tenderness of her heart and to love her. She shows outward respect and devotion to her Aunt Cheyenne and to her elders. These love gestures are special for Echo Calls because in her quiet spirit, it is very clear when she chooses to be left in her silence when she retreats and prefers to be left alone within her own space. Cheyenne has been able

276

to reach inward to Echo Calls in spite of these emotional barriers. It is clear to Cheyenne that much of the internal silence, the quiet anger, the fire spirit, and the withdrawal are somehow related and rooted in the pain that was inflicted upon her by the absence and turning away of Thundering Eagle during her teen years. A common demonstration for all of the seedlings of the West Wind is that each of them left home and charted their own paths to follow in adulthood before they reached the age of twenty-one years old.

It is not clear to Cheyenne, nor does the saga clarify the reason for these early exits from the home. One factor that is clear is that leaving home and charting their own pathways for their life journeys during these teen years left imprinted effects of storms, pain, and struggles on their life cycles. First, they were forced to be adults and take on adult responsibilities and life styles when they were only young teens. They were thrust into the problems of establishing homes, beginning their families and rearing their own children when they were quite young. They were required to seek remunerative employment and to deal with adult problems and issues without the experience or problem solving skills to resolve these adult matters.

Second, the saga confirms that they were forced to step ahead of the socialization process and the development of maturational skills that takes place during the teen years. It was as if the turbulent West Wind was in control of charting the course for their lives to follow.

In addition to these teen hurdles, they were each nursing pain that refused to go away. Their father, someone that they each loved, had vanished. The emotional stain that was left on each seedling has surfaced differently. Feelings of loneliness and rejection abide within each of them while feelings of anger, fear, bitterness, lost love, displaced passion, and grief have found a place of abode within them. It is clear that for some of them, these negative feelings have been replaced with forgiveness, remorsefulness, passion, and love for their father—but it is also clear that for other seedlings, feelings of anger, fear, and bitterness continue to find a place of abode within them.

It is obvious that, Moon Rae and Rising Eagle truly love their father and have each found a place of forgiveness for him in their hearts. They demonstrate the depths of this transition when they visit him and as they care for him as he battles with Alzheimer's disease, renal and other physical ailments. It is also clear that Echo Calls strong feelings of pain continue to throb within her emotions. She has kept these feelings private, yet, in her countenance, her eyes and through her deep-seated silence, the hurt continues to emanate from within her.

Moon Rae has been granted guardianship for the care of her father. She has been strongly supported in these efforts by Rising Eagle, Silver Cloud, Bright Shadow, and her Aunt Cheyenne.

Rising Eagle visits his father for extended time periods. When either he or Moon Rae visit him, they try to express their love and passion for him. It is as if both of them are continuously seeking to regain the time that was relinquished, and to recover that portion of their childhood and teen years that was taken from them when they parted. It all has been left in the currents of the shifting Chinook winds.

Each seedling was born with a dream; a dream to be followed. To have begun their adult life during their teen years meant that building their dreams either became a lost goal or their dreams were placed on hold in hopes that the opportunity to pursue them would resurface later in life. This is always a possibility as long as one does not lose sight of his dreams. The danger rests in the fact that dreams are fragile and when they are misdirected or placed on hold, they may never again resurface. Second chance opportunities are not promised. Interest and priorities shift and dream nurturing may no longer fit into the format of one's career or life goals. This may sometimes be due to a change of interest or attitudes that originally embraced the initial goal. It may seem that chasing the dream is just too difficult and the dream chaser will just retreat and decide, "what's the use."

Regretfully, these attitudes are reminders to Cheyenne of trying years for the seedlings when she was not in their lives during those difficult periods of testing. Cheyenne now feels that if she could have embraced these seedlings in the early years of their childhood, she would have tucked them in her heart, held them hand to hand, and maybe, just maybe, their lives would have been different also. She would have helped them to travel, as she did; touched every continent. They too would have reached their academic goals in life, following their careers and earning advanced degrees.

One seedling in this cycle did just that. Rising Eagle also began meanderingly and then altered his life course to follow an alternative pathway. Cheyenne reminisces over the thought that if she had found Rising Eagle sitting on that step weeping the day that his father went away, she would have petitioned his mother to allow her to take him as her own son. Now that he is past forty, the thought has not been relinquished from Cheyenne's heart to follow through with those adoption procedures.

If Cheyenne had found Echo Calls in her internal silence when she was fighting demons in her youthful years, she would have embraced her and taken her under her wings as her own daughter and worked to assist her in redirecting her goals. Cheyenne is still concerned that it is not too late for the seedlings to follow their dreams or to even change careers. She wants them to continue to build dreams that will propel them farther into the sphere of success and new beginnings. Cheyenne addresses them with a voice of passion and a heartfelt desire to watch them soar in life. She wants them to soar as high as they can fly.

The voice of Cheyenne calls out to them. "Every time that an individual fails to reach his goals, or to develop his/her abilities, the entire generation that follows is weakened. The strength to move forward and to be productive now rests upon the shoulders of these seedlings. It is your time to give back to society some of what you have taken away. You must rebuild and replace that which has been given to you.

"You are the fourth generation of Grayhorse and Mother Ellen, it is time for the world to hear from you. It is time to glean from the yield and fruit of your labor. You have reached the prime of your productive years. Your minds are programmed to do well and to be productive. Your spirits are youthful and yearning to be released. It is time to expand your intellect, to seek knowledge, and to glean from the wisdom of your elders. You are still harboring much talent that is ripe for harvest and waiting to be developed.

"Every time a Gray seedling misses his goal in life, he releases his dreams and it weakens the entire Gray lineage. Every member of the Gray lineage holds a responsibility to be socially productive and to perpetuate the heritage and traditions of the Gray family. This yearning to excel must then be passed on to your offspring. Flood and surround their minds with books and teach them to be avid readers so that their minds will expand with knowledge and that which is good and will enlighten the mind. Teach them the values and the legacy of the Gray family so that it will not fade away. Seek wisdom and go after your dreams. They are at the end of the rainbow. Your dreams will not come to you, you must go after them.

"To succeed in life, you can never lock out the strength of hope and wisdom as you seek. That in itself will direct you to your rainbows," continues Cheyenne. "Each time that you seek to climb the ladder of success, never cease to remember that the prayers and struggles of your ancestors have become your stepping stones. Life is not about where you are now or where you have been; but it is all about where you are going and what your eyes are focused upon. When you continue to look ahead and to walk proudly, the shifting West Winds can then be transformed to become peaceful winds, and they will then lift you to greater heights along your journey."

24

Dueling Winds: Third Cycle Seedlings

Beginning with the late 1960's through the midterm of the 1970s Thundering Eagle's third set of seedlings was born. These seedlings were born under the influence of the cold, dark, desolate North Wind. Like the seedlings of the second cycle, these third cycle seedlings consisted of two females and three males. Their names were Cherokee, Silver Cloud, Clear Water, Running Bear, and Prancing Bull. As in most families, these five young seedlings looked up to their older sibling seedlings with much admiration. These older seedlings became their mentors and role models, to whom they looked for guidance. These young seedlings were in childhood years when Thundering Eagle left the home. Some of them were young children and were just mastering their maturational skills. They were far from being old enough to chart their own life pathways. Their only alternative was to depend solely on their older siblings and their maternal parent. Silver Cloud was approximately nine or ten years old when this trauma took place and the three male seedlings were younger than she. At the very most, their ages were somewhere between five to nine years old when their father went away.

Like the older seedlings, their childhood years were also imprinted by their father. At this young age, their strong feelings or their father's rejection simply translated into feelings like, "He doesn't like me," "He doesn't love me," or "What did I do to cause him to go away?"

The strongest feeling for all of these changes was one of self blame. "I am responsible for my father leaving the family." "If I had behaved differently, maybe he would not have gone away." Again, these feelings of self blame were transferred into feelings of sadness, fear, loneliness, and rejection. Like the older siblings, they missed their daddy and there were many details regarding the separation that they did not understand and even now they are unable to communicate. They were not only missing their daddy; but their entire lives and the world around them suddenly changed. They bled inside and felt as if a part of them had been taken away. It was the same kind of grief that one might experience with the death of a loved one, such as, a spouse, child, or parent.

As the years rolled around, time seemed to stand still while the seedlings continued to search and hope for their father's return. They were searching for the lost love of their father. When diplomacy no longer seemed to work and all else failed, Thundering Eagle made a move to work out an agreement with the seedlings mother to take the five younger seedlings of the third cycle, (numbers 6–11), with him excluding Bright Shadow who was only a baby. This arrangement included all of the seedlings of the third cycle, North Wind. He took them to Paducah, Kentucky to live with him and Charlotte Parker, fifty miles west of Quarry Town. This agreement created another round of trauma in the young lives of the seedlings. What Thundering Eagle actually did was to remove them from the only stability and security covering that they knew, their maternal parent, and place them in an environment that became insecure, abusive, disruptive, and unloving.

According to the saga, the maternal parent signed an agreement that—according to her interpretation—was fraudulent with unclear language and understated intent. It was her understanding that the children were going for a short visit. She did not understand that they were being taken from her by some legal force that provided no provisions for the children to be returned to her care. She was being locked out of their lives and they were being taken so far away from her and the other siblings.

While the children were with their father, they experienced episodes of verbal abuse, harsh threats, and excruciating discipline from Charlotte Parker. Thundering Eagle never listened to the cries of the seedlings. He responded only to the shattering demands from Charlotte. Silver Cloud carries the inner spirit of her Aunt Cheyenne and would often speak up, talk back, or resist the harsh treatment and demands. Because of her aggressive reactions, she frequently stayed in trouble with her father and the other seedlings.

A concern for Cheyenne is where was the compassion in Thundering Eagle's heart for his seedlings? Why didn't he sense the abuse of his children when they began to withdraw and demonstrate emotional traumas of fear and anger? Why didn't he intervene and stop the hurt and release the pain? He was their father, their only blood relative in that house. The seedlings trusted him to protect them. He was to have been in control. He was the backbone. It was a spirit character from the Gray heritage for him to stand up in support of his children. He was losing his children, right before his very eyes.

The painful stories that these seedlings shared within the saga concerning their experiences in that home are emotionally moving and bring one to tears. The bullying demeanor that Charlotte held over Thundering Eagle was one that was continued from their youthful years together. Charlotte used it as a weapon of control not only for Thundering Eagle; but also for the seedlings. The children simply were in terror of her verbal commands, her threats of discipline, her demanding calls to action, her temperament, and her arrogant behavioral responses. These rude characteristics drove the seedlings into stages of withdrawal and rebellion. Even though the seedlings consistently tried to reach their father by sharing these painful experiences with him, he too simply feared Charlotte's frequent outburst of anger and fiery outrage and would do whatever he had to do to avoid a confrontation with her.

During these years, the ancestral elders and most of the Gray family that had resided in or near Quarry Town were deceased or they had moved away, including Cheyenne. A few distant relatives, such as, cousins or in-laws remained in the area. Broken Arrow and his family lived in Ceruleum, Kentucky. Whenever Thundering Eagle would return, he would visit Broken Arrow and his family in Ceruleum. As young children, the seedlings were introduced to their uncle Broken Arrow and his family. Nothing was passed along to the seedlings concerning the family history, its heritage, traditions, victories, successes, or failures. Like the seedlings of the second cycle, these seedlings missed the opportunity to learn about who they really were, or to be introduced to or enlightened about the Gray lineage. The seedlings attended the McCracken County Public schools while they lived in Paducah. Their presence in that family was tolerated but not inclusive to the bonding or the household. The seedlings missed their maternal parent and the other seedlings. Their tears flowed constantly.

Even now, as an adult, Running Bear continues to nurse the hurt that he carries in his heart. He queried his Aunt Cheyenne with questions like, "Why did these things have to take place in our lives?" "Why did all of these things have to happen to us?"

He asked bitterly, "Why does Charlotte Parker have to be a part of our lives?" "Why?" "Why does this have to be?" Following her consoling outreach to her younger siblings, Silver Cloud quickly responded, "We don't know, Running Bear, we just don't know. We just have to put all of those things behind us and move on with our lives."

At the same time, the voice in her eyes and the countenance in her face and posture reflected the same emotional pain that Running Bear was carrying. Cheyenne had no answer for him except to say, "Running Bear, we cannot always control our life cycle nor the outside forces that come into our world. We cannot always have complete control of our destiny, especially when the Four Winds are in control of our life cycles. Sometimes life is cruel; and the dictates of life knock us to the ground; but we must always have the strength to get up and start over, never looking back on our failures and always, moving ahead and not giving up on our dreams. Sometimes life is hard, it evolves that way and whatever is to be, will be.

"Running Bear, do not allow your pain to overtake you and keep you looking back." All of these cruel bitter years were nestled in the North Wind.

Running Bear and Silver Cloud then recalled days when they were disciplined by being placed in a room with the door latched. These acts of discipline were generally administered for trivial acts of responses and reactions to demands by Charlotte. Running Bear would call out through the key hole, "I love you!" with no response from the other side of the door. Not a word of "I love you," would echo back, not even from Thundering Eagle or from the step-mother. The children knew that their wailing cries of "I love you" fell upon the ears of their father. Thundering Eagle was only thinking of himself and displayed no compassion for his seedlings.

At age thirty, Prancing Bull continues to display feelings of nervous energy and internal unrest. He is emotionally fragile and will quickly become tearful, causing streams of tears to flow. It only takes a mustard seed of fear and testing to cause him to become tearfully drawn into an emotional outburst. It is as if a carry over of childhood trauma continues to abide within his emotions and seeks to be released through unlatched passageways of tears. His smile, eyes, and countenance often speak of his emotional unrest, yet he is so compassionate and has much love to give. He always approaches his Aunt Cheyenne with open arms, outwardly sharing his love for her. He is also thirsting to receive much love in return. Like Rising Eagle, he carries an unselfish spirit with his love and each of them seek genuine love in return. Cheyenne has continued to remind Prancing Bull that she is reserving a place in her heart for him. Cheyenne just feels and knows that each of these seedlings are trying continually to search for the love that was lost in their childhood. It is a missing link that their Aunt Cheyenne is diligently working to help them recover.

Silver Cloud is also stricken with painful memories of her past. Like

Running Bear, she simply does not understand and is bothered by the thought of the "wait time." She does not understand why it all had to evolve as it did and why all of the pain had to be. It is not clear to her why her father could not have stopped the pain and why he made no effort to do so. Why did it take so long to resolve the issue and bring them some relief? Why did it seemingly take forever for someone to come for them, to take them away, to reclaim them as family, and to return them to their rightful place?

Finally, the wait time did resolve when the maternal parent and some of the older sibling seedlings came to reclaim them and brought them back to Ohio. They were being released from that emotional prison. Thundering Eagle made a legal claim to the authorities and tried to insist that his children were being kidnapped. He became outraged about the seedlings being taken from him and returned to their maternal parent. He proclaimed that his children were being taken away from him without his consent when he had a legal right to keep them with him.

The mother stood firm and declared, "These are my children and they are not being kidnapped. I am taking them with me." Although this was a deep trauma for the seedlings, it was also a victorious day! They are still wearing emotional scars from these painful experiences.

When the seedlings returned home, sibling separation continued. Each seedling was faced with a period of readjustment with the rest of the family, their maternal parent, and the other siblings. Their return enlarged the family structure and domestic adjustments had to be made. Cherokee and Clear Water took up residence with an older maternal sister, while Silver Cloud moved in with Moon Rae. The younger male seedlings, Prancing Bull and Running Deer, remained at home as did Bright Shadow. Sibling rivalry then set in over who was the true baby of the family and deserved to be treated as such. They competed for the affection of their mother while they sorted out the solution to the problem of which one actually deserved the most love. Bright Shadow did not understand and refused to accept that the love of the maternal parent had to be shared among them all. Consistently, Bright Shadow and Prancing Bull had sibling squabbles over this lineage identity.

When the seedlings returned home, Bright Shadow did not remember them because she had been so young when they went away. Her reaction was, "Who are these people?" She only knew the older seedlings from the second cycle. Because of the age difference between Bright Shadow and the older seedlings, she bonded with her nephews, Jermaine and Jamel, connecting with them as if they were her blood brothers. When these younger seedlings returned home, Bright Shadow had no interest in breaking the bonding with her nephews and replacing it with bonding with her brothers. She fought an emotional battle so that she would not have to do so.

The seedlings shared stories and experiences about their father with each other that Bright Shadow could not relate to because she did not remember him. They learned that they had a patriarch uncle, Clyde, their grandfather, Rising Sun's brother, who lived near by. They began to visit him and his wife, Clara Mae on a regular basis. Not once were they informed that they also had an Aunt Cheyenne, their father's sister, who also lived less than a block away from their Uncle Clyde. As time progressed, Clear Water wanted to return to live with his father. He went back to Paducah, Kentucky and resided with Thundering Eagle for a while. When he left Kentucky, he took up residence in Michigan.

So the turning of the tide and the bitter cold wind was harsh and unkind for the life cycle of some of the seedlings, but some of them also were able to lighten the loads that they carry. Silver Cloud, Running Bear, and Prancing Bull have received their Aunt Cheyenne into their lives. They have also accepted the return of their father and the weight of illness that he carries. They have each begun to put the past behind them in order to overcome the emotional hurdles that they have had to negotiate along their life journeys. Through the voice of Cheyenne, a message rings loud and clear, to all of the seedlings of every cycle. "Listen clearly now, young seedlings, to a message that was sent on the wind directing the dream path that you are to following in order to reach your rainbow's end. . . ."

Build your hopes and your tomorrows; let them season all of your
    dreams.
Use the stepping stones that were laid yesterday and today; and seek
    higher grounds as you soar.

Season your conversations with good words and with knowledge.
Erase malice, envy, and strife from your past.

Think quality thoughts and forgive those who harm you; offer love and
    good deeds in their lives.

Set your sights on new beginnings. Push forward, no matter how hard.
With each failure get up and start over; Keep your eyes focused ahead.
Do not carry the baggage of yesterday's failures; Only carry the victories
    and success
That you have won.

Remain Strong! And Always Remember!

It's the essence of Ida and Mother Ellen;
The Spirit of Grayhorse and Roaring Bull;

    The passion of Rising Sun;
    The care of Thundering Eagle; and
The love and devotion of Cheyenne that will
Lead you to your dream path's end.

From the strength, wisdom, and spirit of these ancestors, you have been
    lifted.
Now you are destined to reach your rainbow's end.

So,

Never! Ever! Cease to follow your dreams!

Epilogue: Legacy Dawn Begins
(Gift of Cheyenne)

The new dawning of the family legacy appears as the saga ends. The sage began as the story evolved, resetting the stage and reliving the experiences that took place for the Gray family over four generations ago. It had its beginning in the dreams and visions of the Gray ancestors. Being in charge of the legacy, it is now Cheyenne's responsibility to pass the entrustment to the proper and deserving seedling. Cheyenne has taken careful steps not to make a mistake in assigning the entrustment. Once again, she has found her way back to Maui, Hawaii to revisit the summit of Haleakala Crater. Here she has sought and found directions to guide her in administering her role to protect the legacy. Now, she is seeking directions for the fulfillment of her final commitment for the oath that she has taken.

This time she is making her journey in autumn. During this season, the chill in the mountain air is much cooler and the ocean tradewinds are stronger. She is hoping that the Spirit of Grayhorse will meet her there and confirm which of the seedling sons is to receive the entrustment blessing. Haleakala is known as "The House of the Sun." Being on the mount of the crater at early sunrise holds special meaning for the Hawaiians and for Cheyenne. It depicts the dawning of a new day and announces a new beginning. It is a first appearance of morning light. These beginnings parallel what is needed to reinstate the family into the hearts and souls and minds of these new Gray seedlings.

Cheyenne joined a group of anxious tourists who were seeking a new adventure and were making their way up the challenging climb at early dawn. Like Cheyenne, they were anxious to reach the top of the mount before sunrise. As they climbed, they carefully watched the eastern sky with great expectation. The air was chilled and it actually was much colder than Cheyenne had anticipated. Having experienced this climb once before, Cheyenne was more prepared for the sudden drop in temperature. She wrapped a light blanket around her shoulders that she had brought along in her backpack. Just before the sun peeked above the horizon, a cluster of clouds moved overhead and dropped suddenly to embrace those who were waiting for the sunrise. Cheyenne could feel the dampness in her clothes as she waited for the sun to warm the area and kiss the silver dew away that was resting on the leaves of the trees. This brilliant appearance of the sunrise signaled and welcomed a new day, never seen before, marking a new beginning.

People then began to search for silhouettes nestled against the clouds. Cheyenne searched for a silhouette of the White Buffalo, totem spirit for Grayhorse, or White Bear, totem spirit for Roaring Bull. Neither of these totems made an appearance and Cheyenne was beginning to feel somewhat disappointed. Could it be that the Spirit of Grayhorse was no longer with her? Did it not follow her spirit for such a long distance? Maybe she was too far away from its usual place of abode? Should she have made a stronger effort to recapture its spirit at one of the familiar places where it frequently appeared?

Prayerfully, Cheyenne thought, *I do not wish to move ahead of my time and place again. Is this not the correct time to pass the legacy?* The sun then moved quickly to find its rightful place for the new morning. First there was a Tahitian sky of brilliant colors of orange, red, yellow, and a sprinkle of violet. The artistic blend of colors created a pictorial scene that only the Creator could paint. This colorful painting was then followed by a sudden burst of light that cut its path through the dampening clouds as if to announce, "I am in control of this bright new morning." A statement and a voice on the wind resounded. It was a sound that only the Great Spirit, that Jehovah could make. He was in complete control of such a lovely morning.

Cheyenne followed the other tourist to the bottom of the crater. By then, the wind was pushing at her back and the journey downhill was much faster than the climb to the summit. Quietly, she counted the ocean waves as they rushed in to shore. Standing above her in the overhead sky was that familiar spiral cloud with the voice of Grayhorse. It was Cheyenne's totem, Whispering Wind. Cheyenne had been watching for the totem Spirit of Grayhorse or Roaring Bull when she should have been searching for her own personal totem spirit. The cloud stopped over the ocean, directing the sets of waves as they washed in to shore. The waves approached the rocky shore in sets of two and four, making a huge splash with each majestic force. It appeared that there was an orchestrated change in the sets of wave patterns from three to five to now two to four. The cloud stood firmly over the first wave of the set of two and then dissipated. It then reappeared and stood over the fourth wave of the second set and dissipated again. The wind cloud continued to appear and disappear following this sequence through four cycles for each set of waves. Cheyenne was now certain that this really was her totem, Whispering Wind.

The totem was confirming the numbers one and four. The totem also remained through the four wave cycles confirming its relationship to the Four Winds. Cheyenne had no doubt in her mind that this was a message from the Spirit of Grayhorse. When Cheyenne reached the waterfall, the cloud appeared in front of her with a simple message. "Listen, Cheyenne, listen to your totem spirit, the first and fourth seedling sons; the fourth and first seedling sons."

The message was repeated four times. The fact that the voice reversed the numbers one and four each time that it was announced, said to Cheyenne that the entrustment should be bestowed upon both the first and fourth sons and the responsibilities should be equally divided, including the keeping of the precious jewels. There was then a heavy clap of thunder followed by a sudden downpour of rain. Then a burst of sunlight followed by a brilliant traditional Hawaiian rainbow that hovered overhead and arched around Cheyenne's shoulders. The rainbow touched the earth from point to point forming a perfect semicircle that had never before been seen.

Cheyenne was not afraid. It was very clear to her that the Spirit of Grayhorse had given his approval, had selected its choice, and confirmed the appointment of two seedling sons. Cheyenne was excited and now ready to begin her task. She knew that she would return home very soon and then the anointment could take place. The directions were now clear and Cheyenne was comfortable with what she had to do.

The time had arrived for a new dawning. The time for the legacy to be passed into the safe keeping of the first and fourth sons of Thundering Eagle was now. It was now time for the spirit characters of the legacy to be reinstated and restored. The family morals and social standards must be practiced and passed on, first to the present generation of seedlings and then to the offspring of the next generation. These values had to be protected in order for the status of the Gray family to be reinstated. This is the only way that the family heritage and traditions can be kept alive. The precious jewels that had been protected for more than four generations were symbolic of the birth of these precious seedlings. Now that this symbolic act has been fulfilled, it is now time to pass these precious jewels into the hands of their caretakers. Once these jewels are equally divided between these two seedling sons, they are to remain in their possession until the dawning of their spirit journeys or until they are no longer physically or

291

mentally capable of maintaining protection of the jewels. If one of these seedlings should precede the other on his spirit journey, then the jewels and legacy in his procession are to be passed on to the other surviving seedling. The passing of the legacy and the jewels to the next caretaker should take place at the midterm dawning of their sunset years.

For four generations, the legacy and the jewels have been protected by the descendants of Grayhorse via the loins of Rising Son. They were carried in a deerskin pouch and kept next to their hearts. They were protected from the forces of the Four Winds, the turbulent storms of nature, and the selfish, grasping hands of greed, the will of others outside of the Gray bloodline.

When the time comes to pass the legacy and the jewels to the recipients of the future generation, the first and fourth sons must step forward to anoint the next caretakers of the entrustment. Neither the legacy nor the jewels are to ever be passed on without confirmation from the Spirit of Grayhorse and without seeking wisdom from the God of Mother Ellen. They must be passed vertically and never horizontally father to son not brother to brother. If there is no fourth son, then they are to be passed to the fourth daughter. If there is also no fourth daughter, then they are to be passed to the fourth child. They are not to be shared with or passed on to any recipient who does not have a direct connection into the blood line of the Gray lineage.

The jewels and the legacy are never to be passed without being blessed or anointed. They are to be offered up to the God of Mother Ellen for protection. The present fourth and first sons are to receive the same anointing for the entrustment as that which Grayhorse placed upon the head of Roaring Bull when he received the entrustment, and also to Rising Sun. The fourth daughter is to receive the position of the matrix aunt. This is a role which she is to continue to fulfill until she embarks upon her spirit journey. It must then be passed to the fourth daughter of the fourth or first sons. If there is no fourth son or daughter, it is then to be passed to the fourth child of the first or fourth sons. It is the responsibility of the matrix aunt to support the mission assignments of the first and fourth sons, to promote the fulfillment of the legacy, and the observation of the spirit characters. It is the responsibility of all three, the matrix aunt, the first son, and the fourth son, to not only uphold the fulfillment of the spirit characters; but to promote the entire legacy and its mission, including the heritage, traditions, and culture of the Gray family. The fourth and first sons then become the patriarch uncles for the children of the next generation to follow. They are to function as a role model for the children to and a stronghold of trust and integrity; setting an example for the young seedlings to grasp and hold on to.

Each of these seedling sons that have been selected have already established patterns of strong values and moral life styles that are indicative of a dedicated patriarch uncle. With their seedling siblings, they are trusted for their integrity, respected for their worth, loved and hailed by their family. They have each crossed the initial milestone as strong protectors of the Gray name and good family providers. They have demonstrated a working faith relationship with the God of Mother Ellen.

Following a public presentation of the sage, the chosen seedlings are to receive their anointment and entrustment blessing for the care of the legacy and the jewels. The jewels will then be passed to each son. The assignment of the matrix aunt will be passed to the fourth daughter. Cheyenne will mentor her until she is confident enough to function independently. With these acts, the rebirth of the legacy will have begun. *The saga must not die*! It must go through the rebirthing process and be reborn. This is the fervent prayer and determination of Cheyenne. How else will the heritage, history, and traditions of the Gray family be reinstated and continued?

THE SAGA NOW ENDS AS THE SAGA BEGAN.
"AUNT CHEYENNE"